Rose of
Ruby Street

By the same author
Lizzie of Langley Street

Carol Rivers, whose family comes from the Isle of
Dogs, East London, now lives in Dorset. *Rose of Ruby
Street* is her second novel.

Visit www.carolrivers.com

Carol Rivers

Rose of Ruby Street

SIMON &
SCHUSTER

London · New York · Sydney · Toronto

A VIACOM COMPANY

First published in Great Britain by Simon & Schuster, 2005
A Viacom company

1 3 5 7 9 10 8 6 4 2

Simon & Schuster UK Ltd
Africa House
64–78 Kingsway
London WC2B 6AH

www.simonsays.co.uk

Simon & Schuster Australia
Sydney

A CIP catalogue record for this book is
available from the British Library

ISBN 0 7432 5942 4
EAN 9780743259422

Printed and bound in Great Britain by
Mackays of Chatham plc

For my family

Acknowledgements

My sincerest thanks go to my agent, Dorothy Lumley, for her help and encouragement and to Kate Lyall Grant and all the team at Simon & Schuster, for giving me a chance.

Chapter One

Rose Weaver held her breath as she took in the scene before her. It was a once in a lifetime moment and she intended to savour every second. A room barely big enough to squeeze a dining table and couch into it now held at least twenty people. The focus of attention was the television in the corner, surrounded by a halo of red, white and blue bunting and handmade paper chains.

Rose sat on the moquette couch at the back of the room. Rows of wooden chairs, footstools and pouffes were spread out in front of her and every seat was taken. The heavy curtains were drawn together, shutting in the dark and cigarette smoke, lending a theatrical air to the proceedings.

Rose felt as though the whole country was waiting. Her heart started to beat a tattoo inside her chest as she listened to Sylvia Peters' soft, cut glass accent flowing from the miracle invention of television. The women perched on the edge of their chairs and even the men, for once, didn't look bored. The children snuggled between legs, feet and knees, and stared at the flickering screen.

The day had finally arrived, Tuesday 2nd June, 1953. Queen Elizabeth II's Coronation.

'Your other half coming?'

Rose turned to find Olga Parker sitting on the couch beside her. Olga was their host and owner of the new television.

'Oh yes, he'll be here.'

'Let's hope before nightfall.'

'He'll show up. He always does.'

All the same, Rose wished Eddie would make an exception from his normal behaviour and turn up on time. Olga was pleasant enough and so was her husband, Leslie, who was a clerk in the city, although no one ever saw much of him. They were different somehow. The childless couple never seemed hard-up, not like the rest of Ruby Street.

A pair of shrewd eyes studied her. 'That's a nice dress.'

'Thanks.' The dress was as old as the hills, the little pale flowers fading over the years. But Rose liked the tiny waist and full skirt and the way Eddie could fit his two hands round her middle.

'Your hair could do with some attention, though.'

Self-consciously Rose drew her hand through the heavy brown locks that fell across her face. The same chestnut brown as her eyes, her thick and lustrous mane tumbled naturally to her shoulders.

'Doesn't Eddie ever treat you to a hair do?'

Rose almost laughed at the thought of the hairdresser. Eddie provided her with enough housekeeping to cover a family of four's expenses, but there wasn't much left over. He always maintained that one day their boat would come in and Rose believed him. She could only guess it had a long way to sail.

'I like doing my own hair,' Rose shrugged. 'The hairdresser always wants to cut it.'

'Every woman needs a little luxury now and then,' Olga said, smoothing down her elegant two piece suit. 'Your husband should spoil you once in a while.'

'He does,' Rose said too quickly. 'Eddie's very thoughtful like that.'

Olga's voice lowered. 'I'm not picking holes, Rose. I mean, your Eddie is a good man.'

'I know that.'

'How is business?'

'Fine.' Rose feigned knowledge. The truth was she didn't know the ins and outs of Eddie's trading business and didn't want to know. Olga didn't realize it, but the television was a sore subject. She'd rowed with Eddie over selling it to the Parkers, pleading with him not to get involved with them as friendly as they appeared to be. The Parkers had only moved into Ruby Street two years ago; no one really knew anything about them.

'The telly's an exception to me rule,' Eddie had promised her last week. 'And anyway, what was I to do? Leslie Parker asked me straight out for it.'

'I still don't like the idea,' she'd persisted, but Eddie wouldn't listen. 'Where's the harm in it?' he'd asked innocently. 'After all, it's only a telly.'

'Yes, and everyone will want one when the news leaks out. But people round here can't afford new televisions.

You'll make enemies that way.'

'Oh, come on, Rose,' he'd laughed, trying to cuddle her.

'Eddie, I mean it. You promised me you'd never sell to our neighbours. I want us to keep on the right side of everyone.' Not that she didn't trust her husband but she'd learned to distance herself from his business deals. And Eddie was happy enough to oblige, it seemed. Until last week.

'Yeah, I know,' he'd agreed, cuddling her all the more and rubbing his jaw against her cheek. 'But this is the one and only time, sweetheart. And I'll tell Olga to keep stum. No one will ever know.'

Rose had hesitated just for a moment.

'Come on then, give us a kiss.'

And like it or not, she'd lost the argument over the television.

Rose, like most of the women born and bred in the East End, prided herself on having a nose for trouble. Probably, she had once remarked to Eddie, because she'd been married to it for the last eight years. She loved her husband, but she'd been very annoyed when Leslie Parker had persuaded him to break the golden rule.

'It is a good model, don't you think?' Olga's voice brought Rose back with a jump. 'Leslie bought it for me as a surprise.'

Rose looked round. Had anyone heard? She tried to draw Olga's attention back to the pictures flashing up on the screen. 'Look, there's the coach coming out of Buckingham Palace.'

'Struth! A moving mountain of gold!' Cissy Hall gasped. 'Poor bleeding horses'll get a hernia.'

'Just one of them big knobs on the roof would do me,' Fanny Grover wheezed lustily.

'Yeah, we know that,' Cissy shouted lewdly. 'But what about the gold?'

The room went into uproar, but the diversion didn't last long. When the noise and vulgar comments had died down, Olga went over to the television.

'Quiet, everyone!' She clapped her hands and achieved silence, placing her hand self-importantly on the top of the bakelite box. Rose could see the smirks, but Olga seemed oblivious. Most of the women in the room were all hard-working cockneys and to them Olga could have been from another planet. She was childless, of Polish extraction and because Leslie had a good job, she didn't need to work. Her husband seemed rather cold and aloof and didn't mix socially, appearing to work long hours in the city.

A rueful smile touched Rose's lips as she thought of Eddie. He worked long hours too, but personal warmth wasn't lacking in the Weaver household. Eight years of marriage had provided her with the best years of her life. Eddie was a passionate, romantic man, who rarely hid his emotions and they had learned early in their marriage that her worrying and his business didn't mix. The compromise they'd made had worked a treat. Rose didn't ask any questions and Eddie kept his promise not to trade amongst their friends and neighbours.

Since many of the East End women had boozers for husbands she regarded herself as lucky she wasn't one of them. As far as she was concerned, Eddie was one in a million.

Rose wondered where her two daughters had got to. Five-year-old Marlene and seven-year-old Donnie had promised to be over as soon as they were dressed. They wanted to show off the red and blue gingham dresses Rose had made for Coronation Day. But time was getting on. The crowning started at eleven.

As the oohs and ahs filled the room, the camera panned inside the coach. The audience gasped. 'Ain't she pretty!' Fanny exclaimed breathlessly.

'Even you would be pretty if you had millions sitting on yer titfer,' Fred Dixon laughed raucously.

'We should be respectful.' Olga drew herself up. 'She's your new Queen.'

'And yours,' Fred retaliated. 'That's if you count yourself as British.'

'As British as you, Mr Dixon.' Olga tightened her lips. Rose knew that Olga's sore point was her Polish nationality. She'd fled Poland in the war and even though she'd done wonders with her accent, she was still a foreigner to the women of the Isle of Dogs.

'Look at all them people. Just like ants,' Cissy gasped, shaking her head. 'They've been queuing all night, so I heard on the wireless. Some of the mad buggers even slept rough.'

Fanny agreed. 'I ain't never seen the Mall so full, not even when the King died.'

'And it's raining too.'

'Always is, in England.'

'No, it ain't. It was lovely last week.'

Rose chuckled as the arguing continued, mostly good-natured banter, but her attention was soon riveted as the gold encrusted coach, pulled by the team of magnificent white horses, wove ceremoniously through the streets of London.

Rose was in a world of her own. This was the closest she would ever be to a royal princess. Quietly adjusting her position on the couch, she could see the smallest details right down to the way the Princess' dark hair fell softly round her beautiful face. Had this young woman any worries at all, Rose wondered? Despite all her wealth, was she afraid of becoming a queen?

'Hello, Mum.' A pair of lips brushed Rose's cheek. Her daughter was standing there.

'Donnie! I was beginning to get worried.'

'I was doing meself up. Look.' She held out the skirt of her blue and white check gingham dress, all Rose's handiwork. 'I put on my best white socks too.'

'You look smashing, pet.'

'And look at me!' Marlene was wearing a red and white gingham identical to her sister's except for the colour, a vivid cherry selected by Marlene herself. Rose had been reluctant to buy the material; she would have preferred a green check to complement Marlene's bright auburn hair. But today both her daughters with their beautiful big brown eyes and smiling faces could have worn sackcloth, Rose thought ruefully, and would have done it justice. She was so proud of them.

'You both look lovely.'

'I couldn't find me—' Marlene began but Cissy turned round and glared.

'Look, the coach is on its way,' Rose whispered, grasping their little arms and bringing them towards her.

'I can't see nothing,' Marlene strained to see through the heads in front.

'Well, sit on my knee.'

'I still can't see.'

'Shush!' This time a cross voice trumpeted, 'If you girls want to wee you know where the lav is.'

'I don't want to wee,' shouted Marlene indignantly. 'I said I can't—'

'Crawl round to the front,' Rose interrupted quickly as Marlene slid off her lap. 'Don't disturb anyone and don't talk when you're there.'

'Do I have to go too?' Donnie held back.

'Yes, you'd better, love.' Rose gave her hand a squeeze. 'Keep an eye on her.'

Donnie followed obediently, holding her clean frock out of harm's way. Rose thought her girls were good enough to eat. How she and Eddie had ever managed to make such lovely productions, she'd never know. They never stopped being proud of their family and even though Eddie was a bad timekeeper, he never failed to attend their Friday night session of Snakes and Ladders, the highlight of their week.

The coach drew up to Victoria Embankment. Rose wondered what had happened to keep Eddie so busy that on the one day of the year that was so special, he would miss the best part of the celebrations. Just a few jobs to do, he'd insisted, a few Coronation souvenirs to trade to the right people ahead of the ceremony.

'Listen to all that cheering!' Cissy sat back in her chair with a heavy sigh. 'Old Berkeley Smith can't get a word in edgeways.'

'It ain't Berkeley Smith,' Fanny contested, folding her arms across her chest. 'It's Chester Wilmot. Said so in the *Radio Times*.'

'Since when do you read the *Radio Times*?'

'Well, how would I know, if I hadn't read it?' Cissy snapped and Len Silverman threw up his arms in disgust.

'It is both Berkeley Smith and Chester Wilmot,' the old man informed them patiently. 'Now, can we please listen in peace?'

'Oiy, you! Watch your tongue, my lad.' Cissy wagged a nicotine stained finger in the air. Len Silverman was about to respond when Olga's high pitched voice echoed round the room. 'Quiet, please! We can't hear what's going on.'

'Then turn the sound up!'

'I can't. It's on full volume.'

'Bloody lot of good that is then,' Fanny spluttered. 'Thought it was supposed to be new.'

'It is,' Olga said indignantly. 'It's the latest model.'

'Probably on tick,' another troublemaker whispered loud enough for their host to hear. 'Or second-hand.'

'My husband doesn't agree with hire purchase,' Olga declared and looked meaningfully at Rose. 'The television came from somebody very reliable. Very reliable indeed. Didn't it Rose?'

Rose was speechless. Eddie had said he'd told Olga to

keep the details under her hat. But it was clear Olga had no intention of keeping anything to herself; it would be much more interesting to drop a bombshell and she'd found just the right moment to drop it.

'Eddie sold it to Leslie,' Olga said looking straight at Rose. 'It was a bargain, too.'

Olga's clear, clipped pronunciation brought the room to a standstill. Every eye in the room swivelled to gaze at Rose. The fact that the crowd crescendo on television was at fever pitch as the golden coach rolled past the high, covered stands opposite the specially built annexe to Westminster Abbey, was lost on the assembled throng.

Rose had lived on the Isle of Dogs all her life. She knew what her friends and neighbours were thinking. What could be more newsworthy than the fact Eddie Weaver had sold a brand new television to a resident of the Street at a knock-down price. *And* kept it quiet.

Fred Dixon nearly choked on his Woodbine. Dora Lovell, the street mouse, cried, 'Oh my God, did you hear that?' Cissy's grey frizzy hair trembled round her plump face. Fanny's toothless bottom jaw sucked noisily.

Rose knew every eye was on her. The images of the coach, cheering crowds and soldiers, statesmen and dignitaries, the Queen Mother and Princess Margaret in their big hats and silk dresses, were ignored. The audience was hypnotized, waiting for the next revelation.

It came from the least expected area, the door. Rose's heart lurched as Eddie strolled jauntily in. 'Blimey,' he said softly, 'I thought it was Coronation Day, not someone's funeral.'

Even though Rose was annoyed with him it was a relief to see his smiling face. He looked as if he didn't have a care in the world. His thick, black hair was brushed back over his head and his white shirt gleamed below a striped tie. Rose had spent all last night pressing his suit with a damp cloth and now it hung smartly from his tall, lean frame

He grinned at Olga. 'Not a cup of Jenny Lee going, is there?'

Silence.

The only noise was from the television where the cameras were inside the Abbey and Richard Dimbleby was giving the commentary. Rose knew this was the moment the nation was waiting for. But not one head in the room turned to see the view recorded from the camera set high in the Abbey's Triforium. Every eye was on her husband.

'Of course, Eddie,' Olga said, breaking the silence at last. 'Or we have beer.'

'Now you're talking. A nice glass of Christmas cheer would set me up fine.'

When their host had gone, Eddie looked cheerfully round. 'Good, is it? Missed much, have I?'

'Not as much as we have,' someone muttered.

'Well, better late than never.' Rose knew that Eddie had chosen to ignore the sarcasm, giving her a wink as he came to sit beside her. She felt as though she had just fallen into a deep well and landed on a feather bed at the bottom. She didn't have any broken bones, but she'd left her stomach behind.

'Hello, my lovely,' he whispered, snaking an arm round her waist.

She kept her voice low. 'Where have you been?'

'Rushing to get here of course.'

'Well, you didn't rush quick enough.'

'Yes, I did. She ain't crowned yet, is she?'

'And that's exactly what I'd like to do to you, Eddie Weaver!'

He looked all innocence. 'Now what have I done?'

'Olga told them about the television. That you sold it to Leslie.'

Her husband shrugged. 'Well, no one's walking out in disgust, are they?'

'You said she was going to keep it under her hat.'

'You ain't half got a good memory,' he teased.

'Eddie, this isn't funny.'

'She must have forgotten.' He tried to take her hand but she pulled it back. 'Anyway, what does it matter?'

Rose glared at him. 'It matters to me.'

'Well, it shouldn't,' he returned, his smile fading. 'I'm the only one who should matter to you. Me and the dustbin lids. Talking of which, where are they?'

'Up the front,' Rose replied tersely.

Eddie sighed. 'Well, this is a nice welcome, I must say. All I've done is try to make a few bob and this is the thanks I get. Charming.'

Rose didn't want to admit it, but she realized there might be a grain of truth in what Eddie said. There usually was, if she took the time to dig deep enough to find it. He always told her she worried too much about what people thought. Perhaps she did.

She glanced at him sideways. He was staring at her

with those lovely misty grey eyes and even though she
was angry, she was melting inside. She couldn't be angry
with him for long, but when they got home, she'd have
a few choice words to say.

'Miss me?' He nudged her knee.

'No.'

'Go on. You did.'

'Keep your voice down. They're in the Abbey.'

'She ain't as beautiful as you,' he whispered, blowing
on her hair.

'Eddie. Shush.'

'She's not, you know.'

Rose found herself smiling as his fingers tickled her
side. His strong, hard thigh moved up against hers. He
was certainly one in a million, her Eddie.

'Dad?'

Rose and Eddie both jumped guiltily. 'Hello, Toots.'
Eddie held out his arms to his youngest daughter. 'Come
and sit on me knee.'

'Can we have one of them?' Marlene pointed to the
television.

'What, a custard and jelly?'

Marlene giggled. 'No you silly, a telly!'

'That's what I said. A custard and jelly.' Marlene and
Eddie went into smothered hysterics.

'Don't you Weavers ever stop gassing?' Cissy yelled
over her shoulder. 'Have a bit of respect, will you? She's
getting bloody crowned!'

Eddie grinned. 'Sorry, love. Just taking a deep breath
that's all.'

'Yeah, a bloody loud one an' all.'

Rose smiled. It didn't take long for normality to resume when Eddie was around.

''Bye, Dad,' Marlene whispered, all smiles and laughing brown eyes as she slid off her father's lap.

''Bye Toots.' Eddie patted her bottom as she went.

Rose felt his strong shoulder pressed against hers. She looked sideways and saw him smiling at her. He gave her such a wonderful feeling inside and she couldn't resist him when he blew her a kiss. Once again they shook with suppressed laughter and only stopped when Olga appeared.

'I hope it's cold enough, Eddie.'

'I ain't fussy, gel, thanks.'

Olga stared down at them. A chill went through Rose's bones and she didn't let out a breath until Olga walked away.

The mantel clock chimed eleven and Rose gazed at the small square picture that was transporting them into another world. Eddie's hand folded over hers as the commentator's smooth commentary described a world hitherto unknown to the public. A fairytale land where Rose felt what it was like to be a queen.

Multinational guests had been assembling at the Abbey since early morning. The whole of the British Royal Family, the Maids of Honour and the Ladies of the Bedchamber had arrived.

The royal procession set the stage for the main event and the magnificent splendour sparkled and glittered in front of them. Everyone moved an inch forward to get a better view of the fourteen-inch screen. It seemed of no consequence that the screen was small, the universe inside it was huge. Rose felt the power and presence of majesty flow out and light up their lives so different now to the dark days of the wartime years. The deprivation and fear of those times had passed and reconstruction of the East End had started to lift people's spirits. The Coronation heralded a new era full of hope and prosperity.

Princess Elizabeth moved towards the High Altar. Every ear in the room now listened intently to the description the commentator gave, describing the six Maids of Honour, each wearing white satin embroidered with pearl blossoms and trails of small golden leaves. Carefully they supported the six-yard long robe of state made of crimson velvet and edged with ermine and gold lace, which was attached to the Princess' young shoulders.

'Ain't she brave, Eddie?' Rose whispered hoarsely.

'Who wouldn't be with all them sparklers? Enough to sink a battleship.'

'She's only two years older than me.'

'Blimey. She's done well for herself.'

'She must be terrified with all them people watching.'

Eddie was silent as his fingers squeezed hers.

Rose sighed. 'She's got two kids like me, a husband and a home like me, yet . . .'

'You're my princess, love.'

Rose gazed into her husband's face and what she saw there captured her heart. He was so handsome with his dark good looks and warm, open smile. She had loved him for as long as she could remember. They'd grown up together in the poverty ridden streets of the East End and she knew she would go on loving him till the day she died.

'And you're my prince. Even though I'm gonna kill you when we get back home.'

'I can't wait,' her husband grinned.

Rose smiled as she turned back to watch the crowning. A big lump filled her throat when the six royal maids began to disrobe the Princess and remove her jewellery, a process that continued throughout the ceremony according to ancient custom. Her abiding memory of the service would be the new Queen's pale and beautiful face as the cry of '*Vivat Regina*!' went up.

As she replied 'I am willing,' to the Archbishop's query, 'Madam, is Your Majesty willing to take the oath?' Rose thought she saw a tear glisten in the royal eye.

Her own eyes were moist. So too, she realized was everyone else's. The world was transfixed.

Rose thought how every head seemed to bow as the Archbishop of Canterbury lowered the heavy, glinting crown studded with precious jewels on the new sovereign's head. As if each person was sharing some of the reputed seven pound weight.

Elizabeth looked so fragile, her neck so slim and delicate. But she bore the crown with pride and elegance and everyone breathed a sigh of relief when it remained in place. Never before had Rose experienced such a feeling of loyalty or respect for her country. The ceremony had made it clear to her just who she was. A citizen of the British Empire. And this was her Queen.

Eddie nudged her. He was handing her a big, neatly ironed white handkerchief. Rose took it gratefully to dab her eyes.

'Bet she couldn't half do with a cuppa.'

Rose sighed. 'You never take anything seriously.'

'I do. You, my beloved.'

'Yes, well, and so you should.'

'When does it all finish?'

'What, you're not going out again, are you?' Rose demanded suspiciously. Trust Eddie to bring her back to earth with a bump.

'No. Well yes, but just for an hour. I'll be back for the old Moriarty.'

'Oh, Eddie!'

He silenced her with a big, warm kiss full on the mouth. Luckily no one noticed as the musical fanfare filled every square inch of the Abbey. Everyone in the room jumped to their feet laughing and clapping.

'I won't be long, love. Promise.'

'You always say that.' She knew his promise to return for the street party was only to keep her happy and she would be lucky to see him again until much later tonight.

'Don't I keep me promises?'

'Not always. You broke one last week. Selling that television to the Parkers.'

Eddie looked crestfallen. 'I did it for us, sweetheart. Look what a lovely morning you've had. You'd have been at home with your ear glued to the gram if Olga hadn't sported out.'

17

'Don't try to talk your way out of it, Eddie, it's me you're talking to, your wife.'

He pulled her close again. 'Go on, say something nice for a change, I dare you.'

She gave in a little then. Eddie was right. It had been a lovely morning. And all because of the telly and Olga's hospitality.

'We're gonna dance the night away,' Eddie promised her. 'I'm gonna swing you round the street until you beg me to stop. Then after the kids are in bed we can—'

'Eddie!'

He grinned. 'All right. All right.'

'You'd better go while I'm in a good mood.' Rose's beautiful dark brown eyes sparkled.

'See you in a cock linnet, then.' He gave her another kiss and disappeared.

Eddie Weaver, why do I fall for your patter every time? She sighed softly as the National Anthem prompted a short pause for solemnity. Then everyone let loose to Elgar's 'Pomp and Circumstance'.

The great royal procession travelled jubilantly back to Buckingham Palace cheered on by thousands of well wishers. Rose wanted to treasure every moment of the historic day. Suddenly there was a close-up. Inside the coach, a little white handbag lay on the seat. It seemed a tiny, vulnerable human idiosyncrasy, not of the Queen, but the young girl left behind.

It wouldn't be an easy road to travel, Rose thought. *But it will be a lot easier than yours* another little voice cried in her head. *She's rich and you're poor. Money will*

18

make a difference. It always did. But as the girls came back to sit with her, Rose decided money wouldn't buy happiness or add to the love of her family. She was just reminding herself how lucky she was when there was a noise in the street. Rose thought it was probably the men erecting the tarpaulin over the benches. It was still raining and everyone wanted to eat, drink and be merry in the dry.

'Blimey, is that the coppers?' someone screeched.

'Yeah, what do they want up 'ere on Coronation Day?'

'Half a crown to go away I suppose,' Rose heard Cissy cry.

'Struth, there's a rumpus!'

Everyone rushed to the window. ''Ere, Rose, it's your Eddie! He's taking a right hiding.'

The two girls wriggled from her arms and ran to join the others. Rose heard Donnie scream, 'Daddy!'

In that moment, Rose knew her life had changed forever.

Chapter Two

Rose rushed into the street. The men had stopped pulling the waterproof covering over the benches. 'What's happened?' Rose ran over but a big policeman blocked her path.

'And who might you be?'

'I'm Mrs Weaver. Where's my husband?'

'His wife, eh?' The policeman wiped the dirt from his face with the palm of his hand and replaced his helmet. He was out of breath and his uniform was all crooked. Another policeman was limping towards the police car. He, too, was replacing his helmet.

'Your husband is what happened, that's what.'

Rose pointed to the car. 'Is he in there? I want to speak to him.' She tried to go round but he blocked her way.

'You'll have to speak to the guv'nor first. He's inside.'

Rose turned to follow the policeman's nod. The door of her house was open and a stranger was standing in the hall. 'What's he doing in my house?' She didn't wait to hear the answer. Her heart was pounding as she rushed in and confronted the man. 'Who are you?'

He looked her up and down. 'My name is Inspector

Williams.' He was dressed in a raincoat and wore a trilby hat pulled over his forehead. 'We have a warrant to search the premises.' He flourished a piece of paper in her face.

'What are you looking for?' Rose stared at him.

'We've reason to believe there may be stolen goods here.'

'Stolen goods!' She laughed in astonishment. 'That's ridiculous. There's nothing under this roof that would interest you. All our stuff's been in the family for years.'

'Well, then, you won't mind us looking.'

'I do mind,' Rose said indignantly. 'Wouldn't you if someone went in your home without permission? And what about my husband? Why's he in that car?'

Just then a uniformed officer trod heavily down the stairs and disappeared into the front room. As Rose was about to follow, there were screams outside. Her heart turned over. It was Marlene.

'Let my Daddy go,' she was screaming as Rose ran out. The policeman by the car was trying to dodge the tips of her black patent shoes.

'That child's a menace,' he complained as Rose swept Marlene into her arms.

'Not half as much of a menace as you lot,' Rose cried angrily.

'What's happening, Mum?' Donnie arrived beside them. Her small chin was wobbling.

'It's all right, pet. Come here.' She hugged them tightly as the man in the raincoat walked towards them.

'You do realise your husband attacked two of my officers?'

21

Rose looked up at him. 'What do you mean, attacked? Eddie wouldn't hurt a fly!'

'He prevented us from our search by using physical violence.'

'Well, I still don't believe you,' Rose declared, trying to see into the car. 'I want to speak to him.'

A surly smile crept across the policeman's hard mouth. 'I'm afraid that's not possible.'

The whole neighbourhood had now gathered round and Rose decided this was her one chance of speaking to Eddie. If the inspector refused again he would have to do so in public. 'Just give me a few minutes,' she pleaded in a voice that everyone could hear. 'It's about the kids.'

There was a look in his eyes that she didn't like, but finally he nodded. 'Two minutes,' he growled.

Rose flung herself at the open window of the car. Eddie sat inside, squashed between two policemen. His nose was bleeding and his hair was all over the place.

'Oh Eddie, what's happened to you?'

He tried to lean forward. 'They just barged their way in the house and sent me flying.'

'What do they want? Why are they taking you away?'

'They keep harping on about a Whitechapel job. But I ain't got a clue what they're talking about.'

'Did they hurt you?'

He gave her a shaky smile. 'No, don't worry about me, I'm all right. Take care of yourself and the kids. I'll be back just as soon as I sort it all out.'

'Oh, Eddie!'

The window went up and she was pulled back. She felt like screaming at the inspector to leave them alone.

'Look Mummy, they're taking Mrs Parker's telly away.' Marlene pointed across the road. Two policemen carried the television from Olga's house and packed it into a van.

What connection had the television to Eddie's arrest? Rose wondered in panic. 'Where are you taking my husband?' she demanded as the inspector climbed into the passenger seat.

'To Bow Street to help with our enquiries,' he answered gruffly as the driver started the car.

'How long will that take? How will I know what's going on?' she yelled as the car began to move away.

'Try phoning,' he threw over his shoulder as the window went up and the car sped off followed in hot pursuit by the van. Rose stood in the road, watching them disappear.

'Where's Daddy going?' Donnie's face was white.

She swallowed. 'To the police station, pet, to help the policemen with their enquiries.'

'Why?'

Before she had time to reply Olga came hurrying towards them. 'Do you realise your husband sold us stolen property?' she shouted all red in the face.

Rose bent down to the girls. She didn't want them to hear any more unpleasantness. 'Go inside and wait for me.' She gave their shoulders a gentle push, then turned to Olga. 'What did you just say?'

'That television was stolen. The police have taken it away and I don't suppose we shall see it again.'

'Who told you that?'

'The policemen of course.'

'Well, there must have been some mistake—' Rose began but Olga shouted over her.

'Yes, the mistake was in trusting your husband.'

'Leave it out, Olga. Eddie is an honest man. He wouldn't do anything dodgy.'

'Oh no? I was questioned like a common criminal. As if they thought I had something to do with stealing it.'

'Well, I'm sorry for all that,' Rose apologized, wishing hard that she hadn't lost that argument with Eddie over the telly and wishing even harder she could turn back the clock.

'We've been swindled and all you can do is stand there and say you're sorry!' Olga screamed as they stood in the middle of the road.

'Eddie wouldn't touch anything that was stolen.' Rose knew she wasting her breath.

'They might have thought we were involved if we hadn't got a receipt!'

'Well, if you've got a receipt, doesn't that prove Eddie wasn't out to cheat you?' Rose felt as though she was sinking in quicksand.

'It proves your husband sold us a stolen television!'

Rose lifted her chin. 'I'm sorry for the trouble of course, but you're judging Eddie before you know all the facts.'

Olga laughed coldly. 'There is only one fact. We have just lost fifty honestly earned pounds. We might as well have thrown it down the drain.'

Rose nearly choked as she heard the price the Parkers had paid for the television. Fifty pounds was a small fortune in Rose's books.

Just then Len Silverman appeared. 'Leave the child alone,' he said quietly to Olga. 'She is upset.'

Olga turned on him fiercely. 'And so am I, old man!'

'It's all right, Len. I can fight me own battles,' Rose said shakily, taking his arm.

'You haven't heard the last of this.' Olga lifted her shoulders and marched off. Rose could almost see the steam coming out of her ears.

'I'm truly sorry, Rose,' the widower apologized as he pushed his fingers through his thin grey hair. 'It is me who is the cause of your trouble. One of the policemen asked if I knew of anyone owning a new television. He said they were prepared to search in every house so I had better speak up.' His thick grey eyebrows knitted together. 'I did so, unfortunately. I hope you are not angry with me.'

Rose was aware that the retired jeweller kept his home as a shrine to his dead wife, Lena. He hated any intrusion into his life. Since her death ten years ago, the word was he hadn't moved a stick of furniture. All her clothes and belongings were still in the wardrobe. 'Forget it, Len. Olga would have told them if you hadn't,' Rose said kindly.

'Is there anything I can do to help?'

'No, thanks all the same.' Only a miracle could help now, Rose thought as she hurried back home. Upstairs the girls were sitting on Donnie's bed looking lost and alone. Rose hugged them hard. 'Don't worry, Daddy will be all right.'

'What's he done wrong?'

'Nothing. The police have made a mistake.'

Donnie shuddered. 'Everyone was looking at us funny, like we'd done something wrong.'

'Well, you haven't and neither has Daddy.' They had no reason to be ashamed. Whatever the police thought, Rose knew her husband wasn't guilty of any crime. He worked hard for his living, even though she didn't like the idea of him dealing in pubs and cafes, anywhere in fact, he could turn a profit. He never cheated anyone and was always the first to offer help if someone was in trouble. There was no way Eddie would deliberately take something that didn't belong to him.

'Those policemen were horrible.' Donnie's brown eyes filled with tears. 'They hurt Daddy.'

'But he fought them back.' Marlene wiped the dirty tears from her cheek with the back of her hand. 'I saw from Mrs Parker's window. I tried to kick one of them too.'

Rose took the little hand and gave it a squeeze. 'You were sticking up for Daddy I know, but you mustn't kick people.'

'They came in our house without asking.'

'Well, they did have a search warrant.'

'What's that?'

'A piece of paper that says you can search someone's house.' She pulled them along. 'Let's go in and see if they've left the house tidy.'

What had the police expected to find, Rose wondered as they all filed in looking this way and that, first in the front room and then in the kitchen. The front room was her pride and joy with the green moquette couch standing in front of the window and the big shiny radiogram sitting against the far wall. On the mantel was Rogue's Gallery, photos in brown wooden frames of all the family dating back to her grandparents. On the wall above was a large round bevelled edge mirror that had always been part of the house for as long as she could remember. There were a few rust spots that had begun to creep over its surface, but if you didn't look too close, it looked as good as new. To soften the austerity of the room she had made her own flowery cushions and a thick hearthrug sat cosily in front of the black leaded Victorian fireplace. A large brass coal scuttle and companion tongs rested on the ornate brass hearth surround and a framed needlework tapestry her mother had made hid the emptiness of the grate behind. It was slightly askew and some soot had come down on the shiny green tiles. Whoever had been searching up the chimney had found nothing but cobwebs!

Other than this, the room seemed to be as it was although a few pieces of china looked out of place on the shelves above the radiogram. Rose replaced them asking herself why the police would want to search their modest little home. God knew they had very few possessions and what they did have had been in the family for years.

Then she thought of the one item of value in the whole house. Not of material importance but certainly of sentimental value. She ran upstairs. Her mother's necklace was kept in the bottom drawer of the dressing table. The slender row of imitation pearls meant the world to her. She pulled out the drawer and saw Eddie's socks in a muddle. It was her practice to turn each pair into a ball after washing and lay them side by side. Her hands went shakily to a navy blue pair, well worn and long ago rejected by Eddie.

'Are you looking for Nana's necklace, Mummy?' Donnie asked as she came to stand beside her mother.

'Yes, darling.' Rose shook out the socks and a dainty row of pearls slithered out. 'They're still here,' she sighed in relief as she pressed their comforting shape between her fingers. Whenever Rose held them she felt close to her mother.

'The wardrobe door's open.' Donnie pushed her head inside.

'Probably thought we had a television hidden there,' Rose grumbled as she returned the pearls to the socks.

'They pulled everything out of the toy box,' Donnie said haughtily. 'Marlene's tidying them up.'

Rose smiled. 'What a waste of time, searching a lot of old teddy bears!' They laughed as, hand in hand, they went to help Marlene.

What was going to happen to Eddie? Rose wondered as they arranged the toys back in the box. He wasn't a criminal. They didn't have a lot of money to flash round. One week she had barely enough to make ends meet, the next she managed to buy a few extras. She never quite knew how much Eddie would bring home and, since he wouldn't agree to her working, one wage was all that ever came into the house.

Rose looked around her daughters' bedroom. You certainly couldn't call a wardrobe, chest of drawers and two single beds, luxuries. All the furniture had belonged to her parents who had been killed in an air raid in 1942. They had been sitting in a cinema when the siren went off and failed to reach shelter in time.

Ruby Street was one of the many island roads that had suffered badly in the bombing. Piles of smoking rubble had mounted daily as the aerial barrage intensified and buildings were flattened. Many of the two up two down Victorian houses that characterized the East End were blown away overnight. Even after eight years, there were still big gaps in the roads and it was only the children who appreciated the debris as they built camps and dug for treasure amongst the dusty remains.

Rose was well aware that she and the rest of the forgotten island, as it was sometimes called, had to be patient. The authorities were faced with an enormous task. Even though low-rise flats and maisonettes had been built to compensate for the destruction, prefabs abounded. But it was the islanders' tough attitude to adversity that Rose admired so much. She was proud to be part of the community. Even the factories and wharves along the river's edge were becoming busier again and the ruined Island Baths had now been successfully rebuilt thanks to local support. In defiance of poverty the women cleaned and polished their front steps even more thoroughly than they ever had before.

A soft summer breeze drifted under the sash window and Rose drifted back to the present as the brass band began to tune up. She drew her fingers through her untidy hair. 'Well, that wasn't too bad, was it?' she said brightly.

'Are we still going to the party?' Donnie asked.

'Course we are,' Rose said cheerfully, although secretly she didn't feel in party mood, but she also knew that there was nothing more she could do to help Eddie tonight.

'Oh, it's you, Neet.' Rose answered the tap on the back door.

The caller was Anita Mendoza, her next door neighbour and Rose smiled trying to hide her blues as Anita entered, dropping her bags and flopping into a chair. 'Just finished work. Got soaked too. This bloody weather.'

'Pity you had to work on Coronation Day.'

'Had to look after Mrs H's blooming kids, didn't I? I've got two of me own and there I am, bawling me head off at someone else's little herberts. Talk about the middle classes. They had a blooming great champagne do and wanted the kids out of the way. Those two little sods are a nightmare. Still, she made it worth me while and I couldn't refuse.'

Anita worked as a daily for a wealthy West End family and received very good pay. Rose had often wondered about getting a similar job herself but Eddie was old fashioned enough to believe a woman's place was in the home.

Anita blew out a puff of air. Well built, with short, straight fair hair and soft blue eyes, her friend gazed solemnly at her. 'So, you'd better tell me what happened to Eddie today.'

Rose lifted her soft brows. 'How did you know?'

'Saw Cissie and Fanny but you know what they're like for exaggerating.'

'Well, for once they probably haven't,' Rose said quietly. 'In fact I don't know where to start.'

'You were over at Olga's,' Anita prompted making herself comfortable. 'You all turned up to watch the Coronation on her telly . . .'

Rose sat down. 'Well, it was all lovely at first and the coach had just got to Victoria Embankment when Olga broadcast that it was Eddie who sold them the telly. I didn't know where to put me face. As I told you, Eddie promised she was keeping it under her hat.'

'What did he say?'

'Who, Eddie?' Rose shrugged. 'He wasn't there.'

Anita smirked. 'Surprise, surprise.'

Rose frowned at her friend. 'Oh, he's not that bad, Neet.'

'As long as you don't blink, no.' Anita's eyebrows lifted. 'You gotta admit it Rose, your old man is faster than a streak of greased lightning.'

Rose had long accepted Eddie's restless and unpredictable nature so that she almost didn't notice now. 'What else did they say outside?' she asked quietly.

Anita hesitated. 'The word is Olga's telly was stolen and Old Bill carted Eddie off to the nick.'

Rose closed her eyes. 'It's true. I warned him not to get involved with the Parkers. I knew it was bad luck from the moment he mentioned it last week. We had such a row. It's our golden rule not to sell round here and yet he still went and did it.'

31

'So what did Mrs High and Mighty Parker have to say about all this?'

'She said the police questioned her as if she was a common criminal. She was furious.'

Anita groaned. 'I'm really sorry I wasn't here,' Anita muttered. 'I'd have given the coppers a piece of me mind.'

Rose believed Anita would have done just that. They'd been friends for a long time and knew each other very well. Since before the war the Nortons had lived next door to Rose's parents, but Anita had moved to Stepney and into her in-laws' house when she'd married Benny Mendoza. Benny's father Luis, was from Argentina and had sailed to England as a young merchant seaman. On one of his visits he had met Benny's mother Mary, after which Luis had never returned to Argentina.

It was when Benny and Anita and their two sons had returned to Ruby Street in order to care for Anita's widowed mother that Anita and Rose had grown close. Sadly Mrs Norton died and the house had passed into Anita and Benny's hands.

'Try not to worry,' Anita said gently. She looked at her wristwatch. 'Look, I hate to leave you like this. But I have to go over to Stepney. Benny's mum is keeping an eye on the boys for me. Are you still going to the party tonight?'

'Yes,' Rose nodded. 'The girls need cheering up after today. Marlene even tried to kick one of the policemen because she saw her father do it.'

'They must have got rough with him, then.'

'His nose was bleeding and his hair was all over the place.'

'Look . . .' Anita scraped back her short hair with the palm of her hand, 'if I know Eddie he'll be home in no time, getting round you as usual and claiming it was all just a storm in a teacup and you'll have spent all this time worrying for nothing.'

Rose smiled. 'I hope so.'

'Now I'd better be going. There's no buses, so I'll have to bike it over.'

'Where's Benny today?'

'Up in the Lake District somewhere. He's on a three-dayer, delivering metal locks for sheds to farmers.'

They walked along the hall and heard the girls giggling upstairs. 'They seem none the worse for wear,' Anita pointed out.

'I hope not. They've been so excited about the party. I even made them special red, white and blue dresses.'

'Well, enjoy it for their sakes.'

Rose nodded. 'I'll try.'

Anita smiled. 'See you later, then. I'll get away from me mother-in-law's as soon as I can and give you some moral support.' She stepped out into the busy street and waved goodbye.

Rose surveyed the colourful scene. All the school benches and tables were lined in the middle of the road. The children were eating and drinking as the women rushed up with refills for their empty plates. Flags were tied from window to window and everyone was laughing and having a good time. Rose knew she must join in and be merry for she was certain the Weavers were not the only ones in the area to gain the attention

33

of the police and she very much doubted if they would be the last.

The rain had finally stopped.

Under the crudely painted crowns and Union Jacks strung across the gutters, the bunting hung like bowers of blossom. Festooned lampposts became street maypoles and the tarpaulins had been rolled way. Plates of cakes, sandwiches, jellies, custards, pies, sausages and even jugs of flowers were spread like a medieval feast over the tables. Rose was happy to see the small weekly donation she had made to the celebrations had resulted in this. With meat and sugar rationing still in force the party was nothing short of a miracle.

'Where are we going to sit?' Marlene asked as they pushed their way through the crowd.

'Over there.' Rose pulled the girls toward a vacant bench but they were just beaten to it by some boys. They ended up standing outside Olga's house and Rose felt uncomfortable there, but there wasn't any room to move. She didn't know what she'd do if Olga started another scene.

Suddenly the brass band struck up. The conductor spoke through a loudhailer explaining they would play a medley of tunes. 'Buttons and Bows' first, then 'Riders in the Sky'. This announcement received more good-natured heckling than it did applause. Undaunted, the band let rip.

'Rose!' It was Len Silverman. He pointed to his own seat. 'This is for you.'

Rose knew he regretted having told the police about the television, but she didn't blame him. She understood the reasons why he kept himself to himself. He'd loved his wife dearly and if he chose to keep her memory alive by preserving the house as it was on the day she died, well then, good luck to him.

'Thanks, Len.'

'No hard feelings, I hope, my dear?'

'None,' she assured him.

'I'll squeeze the girls in over there.' He pointed to a bench. A little black boy and two tiny girls sat on it, stuffing cake.

Donnie gripped her hand. 'I want to stay with you, Mum.'

'What about you, Marlene?' Len held out a shaky hand. It was deformed with arthritis, but Marlene took it, looking up at him with a beaming smile. Rose knew the children trusted and liked him. Len often sat outside his front door in the sunshine when the weather was good. The elderly Jew would give them boiled sweets in paper wrappers as special treats.

'I like the look of them jellies,' Marlene said eagerly.

'Then you shall have one.' With Marlene's little fingers wrapped in his, the old man led her slowly to the table.

'Hello, Rose.' It was Mabel Dixon and her husband Fred. He wore a newspaper hat in the shape of a boat. Mabel, as small and plump as her husband was tall and lean, waved a Union Flag. Dora Lovell joined them, a red scarf covering her thin hair. She had a big, red white and blue crêpe paper flower pinned to her baggy jumper.

'Hello,' Dora said timidly.

Rose summoned a smile. 'You all look festive.'

Fred laughed. 'Yeah, don't they? Like blooming Christmas trees.'

'You want to take a look at yourself,' Mabel said crisply, frowning up at her husband's head.

'I was just listening to the news on me wireless,' Dora interrupted quietly. 'They said the Royal Family all waved from the balcony when they got back to the Palace. Apparently little Prince Charles and his sister, Anne, looked lovely. The Duke of Edinburgh and the Queen Mother was there too, all smiling and waving to everyone.'

'Yes, but the wireless is nothing like the television,' Mabel argued, glancing at Rose. 'You can't beat actually seeing things.'

'I dunno about that,' her husband frowned. 'Personally, I prefer me wireless. Don't go along with all these new fangled contraptions.'

Mabel cast him a withering look. 'That's the first I knew of it, Fred Dixon. You're always quick enough to park yourself right in front of our Susan's telly.'

Rose stood up. 'You'll have to excuse us. I'm gonna get the kids something to eat.'

She could feel their eyes in her back as she walked away. Was it going to be like this all evening, hints rife? When she met Fanny and Cissy, who sat on wooden chairs outside their front doors, she decided to get the first word in.

'Enjoying it, are you?' she asked brightly.

'Oh yeah,' Cissy and Fanny nodded. 'We were just talking about you. About the rollicking the police gave your 'ubbie.'

'The band's good.' Rose was determined not to let Cissy and Fanny get to her as they were experts at winding you up.

'Yeah. Poor bloke. He didn't deserve to be bashed like that.'

Rose looked away. 'The kids are having a really good time.'

'But how are you feeling, gel? You must be dead worried.'

'All right, thanks.' She pulled Donnie with her, deciding it was time for action. 'We're going over there now. There's a couple of spaces.'

But they hadn't gone far when Olga Parker appeared. 'I want to talk to you, Rose Weaver.'

'What about?'

'The television, of course.'

'Not that again.'

'We want our money back,' Olga shouted over the music. 'Leslie said he wouldn't touch the television with a bargepole now even if the police returned it. In the circumstances this has been a very distressing experience.'

Rose could hardly believe that two years ago when the Parkers had moved to Ruby Street she had felt sorry for them as newcomers and had been the first to invite them in for a chat. 'You could give Eddie the benefit of the doubt,' Rose said knowing that Olga had no intention of doing so.

'Why should we? It was hard earned money we parted with. Now, are you going to return the fifty pounds?'

'You have to speak to Eddie when he comes home.'

'And when will that be?' Olga arched a thin pencilled eyebrow. Rose thought that if looks could kill she'd be dead right now. 'After what he did to those policemen I don't think you'll be seeing your husband again for a while.'

'What do you mean?'

'Assault is a very serious offence, in case you didn't know.' Without another word she strode away.

'Eddie didn't assault anyone,' Rose called after her but Olga didn't look back.

'And she didn't even see the fight,' a voice chimed in behind Rose. Cissy and Fanny had been standing there listening. 'She was too busy bossing everyone about to notice what was going on.'

'Yeah. Stuck up cow.'

'Eddie's an honest man and he wouldn't deliberately hurt someone,' Rose said shakily.

They both nodded fiercely. 'We know that, love. But do the police?'

Rose looked down at Donnie. The sad and bewildered expression in her daughter's eyes hurt Rose deeply. 'Come on, pet,' Rose said softly, knowing without Eddie's presence beside them tonight would be a half-hearted celebration.

They sat down at the table and began to help themselves to the food and drink. The shouting, laughing and talking went on around them, but Rose couldn't help seeing the odd glance or two thrown her way when they thought she wasn't looking. Did her friends and neighbours believe Eddie was a thief and were too kind to hurt her feelings by telling her? The Pipers from number eighty-two, Mike Price and Heather who lived at thirty-six, Sharon and Derek Green from forty-two and the Patels at the top of the street, all attempting to act as though nothing had happened. Did they know something about Eddie that she didn't?

'Mum, have a sausage roll.' Donnie lifted a big plate. 'They're lovely.'

Rose took it and swallowed even though it tasted to her like rubber. She wanted to look as though she was enjoying herself, even if she had to force it down her throat. Donnie was such a thoughtful, sensitive child and so pretty too. Long black hair like Eddie's mane and brown eyes that were always soft and kind. Rose felt a terrible ache in her heart for what they had undergone today.

The evening wore on and the drinking got serious. Children crawled into laps or sat on the steps and yawned whilst the tables were pushed back and dancing started.

Rose recalled what Eddie had whispered to her before they took him away. He was going to dance her off her feet tonight. As the music, dancing and laughter filled the night air, Rose wondered what was happening to him. The miss of him was so strong it was almost a physical pain. Just then she spotted Donnie and Marlene who were playing with the Piper kids swinging on a rope tied round the lamppost. They wouldn't notice if she went in for a while.

Minutes later she was sitting in the kitchen, gazing into space. Everything reminded her of Eddie. The chair he sat on, the mirror he shaved in, the cup he drank from. Her mind flew back to last year when she'd painted the walls in light green distemper and Eddie had bought her a tall cupboard with glass doors at the top and two drawers beneath. There was a drop down flap to chop the bread and vegetables on. Opposite was the old coal cupboard transformed to a walk in larder with a meat safe and outside there was still the shed they called the washhouse. In winter she provided the girls with china pots so they wouldn't have to traipse outside to use the toilet. Rose's secret wish was to have a bathroom but she knew it was a dream. Number forty-six Ruby Street was her little world and she loved it.

Suddenly the words of Prime Minister Winston Churchill went through her mind as he rallied the people of the British Isles in 1941. *With the help of God, of which we must all feel daily conscious, we shall continue steadfast in faith and duty till our task is done . . .*

His courageous speech had won the hearts of every British citizen and given them hope as Hitler cast his terrifying shadow across Europe. Rose remembered how the nation had fought back so bravely and, squaring her shoulders firmly, she took comfort from the words in her own darkest hour.

Chapter Three

Rose looked round and saw two sets of big brown eyes watching her.

'We wondered where you was, Mum.'

Rose beamed her girls a smile. She didn't want them to see she was unhappy. 'I just came in for a cup of tea.'

'The kettle ain't on.'

'No, I was just going to fill it.' She lifted the kettle and took it to the sink. 'Did you have a good time at the party?'

'Yes. But everyone's getting drunk now.'

Rose laughed. 'That's what parties are for.'

'We saw Auntie Anita. She said she'll be in soon.'

'She must have got back early.' Rose sat down on the chair. 'Marlene, are you all right?'

'No. I feel sick.'

'No wonder,' Donnie said, frowning at her sister. 'I told you you'd get a tummy ache if you kept on stuffing yourself.'

'Come and sit on me lap.' Marlene crawled into Rose's lap.

'She ain't gonna be sick is she?'

'No, she's just tired.' Rose stroked Marlene's dirty forehead. 'Now Donnie, set the cups and saucers on the table. There's a tin of condensed milk in the larder.'

Rose glanced at the wall clock. 'Half past nine. We've missed the Queen's speech. Still, we might hear it later.'

'Can I stay up and listen?' Donnie's eyes widened. 'As a special treat.'

Rose smiled softly. 'Well, why not? It is Coronation Day. Now, I'm going to put Marle to bed. Just turn down the gas when the kettle whistles.'

Upstairs, Rose undressed Marlene's skinny little body, postponing a good wash. Her daughter was asleep the minute her head touched the pillow. Rose went to her own bedroom and looked out of the window. Donnie was right, there was singing, dancing and general mayhem. The night was going to be a long one.

Rose sat on the big double bed and looked at the two pillows. Eddie's head wouldn't be resting there tonight. His warm, loving body wouldn't be wrapped round hers. What had the police expected to find in this room? She studied the double wardrobe, chest of drawers, dressing table and treadle sewing machine. If they had searched under the heavy horsehair mattress on the iron bedstead all they would have found were Eddie's trousers. There were only six inches remaining to the floor. What could be squeezed under there?

'Mum?' Donnie peered round the door. 'Auntie Anita's here. She's making the tea. Is Marle asleep?'

'Yes, out like a light.'

'Sally Piper's called for me. Can we sit on the doorstep?'

'If you like. Do you want some supper?'

'No. I don't want to get sick like Marle.'

Rose smiled wistfully. Donnie took her role as the oldest child very seriously. She overdid it a bit sometimes and Marlene resented her bossing. Rose was happy that Sally had called and Marlene was absent for once.

'We might play hop-scotch,' Donnie said as an after-thought.

'All right. But don't go anywhere near the debris.' Rose had forbidden the girls to play on the piles of bricks and rubble in Ruby Street. She didn't want them treading on any nails or broken glass.

'Hello, love,' Anita welcomed as Rose entered the kitchen. 'I've added an extra spoon for a strong brew,' she said as she pulled on the tea cozy. 'I still can't get used to the fact that tea rationing ended last year and we can make a decent pot now.'

'Yes, out of habit I'm still a bit on the stingy side too,' Rose agreed with a wistful smile as she pulled out a chair. 'To think we can have unlimited cuppas for the first time in thirteen years.' She nodded to the sugar bowl. 'And in another four months sugar followed by meat next year.'

'Benny likes his Sunday roast,' Anita nodded. 'But in the week I stick to stew or mince. It'll be nice to have a choice whenever the fancy takes me.'

Rose nodded slowly. 'What's it like out there?'

'Pandemonium. I'm surprised we managed to stay on our bikes what with all the celebrating. There'll be a few sore heads tomorrow. Last piss-up we had like this was VE day, remember?'

'Don't I just.' Rose sipped the strong tea. 'We were married the month after, in June. You'd just moved back in with your mum then.'

Anita sank down on the other chair. 'That's right. Dad had died and Benny and me came back from me mother-in-law's to look after Mum. Didn't think me poor old girl'd be popping her clogs so soon after Dad.'

Rose nodded, her mind going back to Mr and Mrs Norton next door. They had survived the war, only to have Mr Norton suffer a heart attack at the end of it. Mrs Norton had never recovered. The only good thing was that Anita and her family had moved back from Stepney and brought the house to life again.

Anita smiled reflectively. 'I was ten when you came along. I remember it as if it was yesterday. The midwife turned up at breakfast. And by dinner time you was here. Your dad came into our house looking for all the world as though he'd won the pools. Rose, that's what we're going to call her, he said. 'Cos your cheeks was like roses from the moment you was born.'

'I don't know where time has gone.'

'Bloody quickly is the answer to that.'

'I'm twenty-five this year. Em's thirty-one.'

Anita laughed. 'I feel blooming geriatric when I look at you. All that lovely brown hair and big brown eyes. And a figure I'd give me right arm for. Eddie's a lucky bloke. What the hell has he got himself into, that's what I'd like to know.'

'Wouldn't we all,' Rose agreed quietly.

'He don't help himself, that's the trouble,' Anita

continued relentlessly. 'Why doesn't he buy a shop or run a proper market stall?'

'You need a licence for the market. And we can't afford a shop.'

'Why don't he get a licence?'

'They're usually handed down in the family. Either that or they cost a fortune.'

Anita softened her tone as she looked at Rose. 'No word, then?'

'No. Tomorrow I'm going to ask the Wrights if I can use their phone. I know they were waiting for one to be installed.'

Anita leaned back. 'Tell me again what happened.'

Rose obliged starting from when they were watching the television in Olga's house to the part where she found the police inside her house and Eddie sitting in the back of the police car. 'He said something about a job in Whitechapel,' Rose ended breathlessly. 'I don't know what that meant, either.'

Anita looked furious. 'They had no bloody right, the bastards!'

'They had a search warrant.'

'Is that why Eddie got clobbered?'

Rose frowned. 'I didn't have time to ask him.'

'Did you read this here search warrant?'

'What was the point? They were already inside.'

'I'd have kicked them all out again,' Anita growled. She was seething, her lips tightly compressed.

Rose finished her tea waiting to drop the next bomb-shell. 'Olga Parker wants her money back.'

'Do me a favour!' Anita exploded, her eyes bulging. 'Does she think you're made of money?'

Rose shook her head. 'I wish I'd had time to speak to Eddie without the inspector listening.'

'Do you think someone put the finger on him?'

'Why would they do that?'

'I dunno. Has he got any enemies?'

'None that I know of. But then, I'm beginning to think I don't know very much.'

Anita paused. 'A search warrant ain't no ordinary piece of paper, love. That copper must have thought he'd find something here. He didn't plan on walking away with egg on his face, did he?'

Rose stared into her friend's eyes. 'Do you know something I don't, Neet?'

''Course not.'

'Would you tell me if you did?'

'Yes, you know I would. It's just that—'

'You think he stole that telly, don't you?' Rose wavered. 'Why don't you just come right out with it?'

'Rose, sit down. 'Course I don't think Eddie nicked the telly.'

Rose walked out of the kitchen. Even her best friend thought Eddie was guilty and didn't have the courage to say. In the front room she sat on the couch. The lights from the party outside reflected in the room and the music and laughter echoed in the street. The nation was celebrating.

A hand touched her shoulder. 'Rose, don't get the sulks, love.'

'I'm not sulking. Eddie would never have stolen a television. Never.'

'I shouldn't have said all that about enemies. I know Eddie is straight.'

'So you don't think he's a thief?' she asked again.

'No. But I'm furious with the bugger for putting you through this.'

Rose drew her hands down her neck and sank against the cushions. 'That inspector said they wanted him to help with their enquiries. But what does that mean?'

Anita squeezed her hand. 'When you ring the police tomorrow, it'll be a different story. I reckon they're just keeping him in for a night. Just to prove a point. They don't want no one ballsing up their day.'

'You think he'll be home, then?'

''Course I do.'

'I'll turn on the gram.' Rose felt more cheerful. 'We might hear some of the Queen's speech.' She looked out of the window as she went. Donnie and Sally were dancing in the street. 'The kids are enjoying themselves,' she smiled softly.

'You bet,' Anita laughed. 'My boys have disappeared too.'

'Where are they?'

Anita grinned. 'Chatting up the Travers sisters. Necking somewhere I expect.'

'They're very pretty those two.' Rose bent to turn the knobs on the big walnut case. The 1940s radiogram had been her father's and he'd polished the case lovingly all through the war, cursing the bombers for the dust that fell down from the ceiling. Although it once played the heavy His Master's Voice records, the turntable had long ago refused to operate. But the radiogram was in good working order and had a faultless tone.

'At fourteen, Heather is a year younger than Alan,' Anita continued in a worried tone. 'Iris is thirteen, also a year younger than David. And both of them with tits.' She rolled her eyes. 'Talk about well developed.'

'They start early these days.'

'You're telling me. I sent them over to me mother-in-law's today so I wasn't going to have them hanging round street corners waiting for an opportunity to blot their copybooks. And I've told them to be back home tonight by ten-thirty sharp. They didn't like it but they'll just have to lump it.'

Rose tuned in to the Home Service. 'Listen!'

Anita sat forward. 'Is that her?'

'Yes, our new queen.'

The noise of the party outside seemed to fade as the eloquent voice coming from Buckingham Palace entered the front room of number forty-six Ruby Street. Rose felt lifted from her worries into that fairyland that had enchanted her so briefly before Eddie had been taken away.

'. . . *As this day draws to its close, I know that my abiding memory of it will be, not only the solemnity and beauty of the ceremony, but the inspiration of your loyalty and affection. I thank you all from a full heart. God bless you all . . .*'

'And you, love,' Anita said quietly.

'Yes.' Rose swallowed. 'God bless.'

The National Anthem played and the two women rose, their hands linked. When it was over, they hugged. Rose thanked God for her friends and for what she had been given in her life when so many millions were starving and had miserable, unhappy existences.

Tomorrow she wasn't going to shed one tear of self-pity. With a bit of luck the Wrights who owned the corner shop would let her use their new phone and she could find out when Eddie was coming home.

Mrs Wright was cleaning the shop step when Rose arrived. Her turban bobbed up and down and her muscular forearms went this way and that, the dirty lather rolling over the pavement.

'Joan?'

The shopkeeper sat back on her heels. 'Oh, it's you, love.'

Rose pulled her cardigan round her. 'Do you have a telephone yet?' she asked quickly.

'Yes. It came last week. Our eldest son, Gerry, works for the telephone company and pulled some strings. Do you know, half of London is waiting for a telephone and some of the people have been waiting not months, but years. It's a bloody scandal if you ask me. My Charlie thinks it's the old supply and demand ploy, where they get everyone wanting something so badly they'll pay a fortune to—' She stopped as she saw the expression on Rose's face. 'Not anything wrong love, is there?'

'I've got a favour to ask.'

'What is it?'

'Could I use your telephone? I wouldn't ask normally but it is an emergency.'

'Not the kids, is it?'

'No, Eddie. Didn't you hear the news?'

'No. We've been over at Gerry's. What's up?'

'It's a long story. Eddie was taken to Bow Street police station yesterday and I've got to find out what's happened to him.'

'Oh, you'd better come in, dear.' Joan climbed to her feet with difficulty. She was a big woman and her stockings were always wrinkled at the ankles. Joan and Charlie Wright were in their sixties and talked endlessly of their retirement. Wright's Grocery Store was one of the few corner shops that hadn't been flattened by a bomb or shuttered up after the war. All round it there was debris and boarding erected to keep out the children. She threw her scrubbing brush into the bucket with a splash and Rose followed her in the shop.

It was dark and gloomy inside, with the blinds pulled down on both windows. The bread was always under a plastic cover, as were all the perishables that got stowed in the cabinet under the counter.

'We ain't got anything fresh today,' Joan said as she closed the door behind them and the bell tinkled. 'People will take a week to get over yesterday. Come along to the back room when the phone is.'

The storeroom was filled with boxes and crates all piled on top of one another. A strong smell of rancid cheese, pickles, bacon and old vegetables hung in the air. The big wooden table in the middle was filled with newspapers and brown bags, beside which lay a scruffy accounts book and a big black telephone.

'Gerry said we was really lucky to get the phone,' Joan told her proudly. 'Apparently ten thousand of them are going to be installed this year in London alone and we're one of the first. Now sit yourself down and find out what's happened to that husband of yours.'

Rose perched on the edge of the hard seat by the table. 'How much do I owe you?' She opened her bag.

'It's on the house. I've known your family long enough to know you wouldn't ask a favour if you didn't need it.'

Rose smiled gratefully. 'How do I find the number?'

'Just ask the operator. It ain't half funny hearing a voice on the other end. But you'll be all right. They're very helpful. Now I'll leave you to it and finish me step.'

Rose summoned up courage. She didn't want bad news; she needed to hear that Eddie had been mistaken for someone else or the television wasn't stolen. When she had to repeat herself to the operator her voice became as shaky as her fingers. After a series of loud clicks she was eventually put through. 'I'm Mrs Rose Weaver from number forty-six Ruby Street and I'd like to know what's happening to my husband,' she said clearly. 'His name is Eddie Weaver and he's helping Inspector Williams with some enquiries.'

There was a long pause before the man spoke again. 'What was the name again?'

'Eddie Weaver.'

She could hear strange noises on the other end as she waited. Finally the news came.

'Edward John Weaver has been formally charged. His hearing is at central London magistrates' court tomorrow morning, nine sharp.'

Rose gasped. 'What's he been charged with?'

'Obstructing police in the line of duty, assault and handling stolen goods.'

'But that's ridiculous!' Rose exclaimed trying to take in what she'd been told. 'He was only trying to defend himself. And he didn't steal anything.'

'Then he hasn't got anything to worry about, has he?' The policeman's unhelpful attitude was like a brick wall.

'What happens now?' Rose asked in bewilderment. 'Will they let him come home?'

'Depends if he gets bail,' was the impatient reply.

'What does bail mean?' Rose asked, only ever having heard the term once or twice before and not really understanding what it meant.

'Bail is money guaranteed to a court to make sure the person who has been charged with a crime returns for the next hearing – or trial.'

'Trial?' Rose felt her blood run cold.

'I've no idea what will happen to your husband,' the voice continued. 'You'll have to ask his solicitor.'

'But we haven't got a solicitor. We couldn't afford one,' Rose protested in a hoarse voice.

'Everyone is entitled to a defence, no matter what your status,' the policeman said shortly as if he were talking to a child. 'Now, if that's all, I wish you good day.' And before she could think of another question a long burring sound rang in her ear.

'Joan, I think they've cut me off,' she said to the shopkeeper who had just come in.

'Yes, I'm afraid so,' Joan nodded as she took the phone and listened. 'Did you get the information you wanted?'

'I . . . I think so.'

'What exactly did Eddie do?' Joan asked curiously.

'Nothing really, that's just it. There's been some kind of mistake.'

'Is he coming home?'

'I don't know.'

'Didn't you ask?'

'Yes, but it's not easy to take it all in over the phone. I'd better get back to the girls,' Rose evaded, fearing more questions that she couldn't answer. 'Thanks, Joan.'

'Anytime. And if you want some groceries, we'll put them on the slate. Just till you know how you stand.'

Rose walked back over the rubbish of the night before, the strewn bunting and the food and paper still lying in the road. A few women were cleaning their windows and brushing the dirt from the doorsteps. At eight-thirty in the morning they were the only ones up. The men and the kids were treating Wednesday as a holiday.

Out in the fresh air, Rose went over in her mind what the policeman had said, wondering how could she get to central London whilst the girls were at home? Would Eddie get bail? And how much money did that involve? She would have to wait until tomorrow to find out the answer to that. Rose could hear the girls as she opened the front door. 'I'm back!' she called, hoping they didn't

53

ask dozens of questions all at once. And more to the point, what answers could she give them?

They came tumbling down the stairs still wearing their nightgowns. 'We washed, look!' They held out their hands and lifted their chins. Faces, necks and fingers were spotlessly clean.

'Very good, both of you,' she smiled, hoping for some sort of inspiration in the next few minutes.

'When's Daddy coming home?' Marlene was the first to ask.

'Soon.' She couldn't say otherwise.

'But when?'

'I don't know exactly, pet. The policemen still want Daddy to help them with their enquiries.'

'Can we go and see him?'

'No, we'll just have to be a little patient and wait for him to come home.'

'But we miss him.' Marlene was almost in tears.

'Yes, so do I. But it's no use getting upset. Daddy wouldn't want that. He'd tell us to do just like we always do and look after each other while he's away.' Rose recalled Eddie's last words to her before the police car had driven off and her spirits lifted a little. 'Now, what shall we have for breakfast?'

'Soldiers,' Marlene replied at once. 'But I don't want me egg all drippy.'

Rose smiled and patted her bottom. 'Off you go and get dressed, then. I'll be in the kitchen.'

But Donnie hesitated. 'Is Daddy really coming home?'

Rose hugged her little girl. ''Course he is, love. We

just have to be patient. Now, do you want soldiers, too?'

Donnie nodded but went slowly up the stairs, her small shoulders sagging. Dragging the kids through such an ordeal was unforgivable, Rose thought unhappily. She wanted all the good things in life for her family. She was suddenly so angry with that Inspector Williams she could have cheerfully strangled him. But by the time she got to the kitchen, the anger had disappeared and her heart was aching for her husband and the feel of his strong arms around her again.

The sunlight crept through the kitchen window as Rose finished her letter. As she had been writing to Em she had come to the conclusion that if she hadn't given in on her rule not to sell to the street Eddie would be at home right now. But she'd let him have his own way and Eddie being Eddie, he'd needed no encouragement to sell that bloody television.

Rose was just licking the stamp when the back door opened. Anita's face was red from riding her bike. 'Crikey, I'm done in.' She sank down on a chair and pushed her damp fringe from her eyes.

'You work too hard.' Rose lit the gas.

'Tell me about it. But we're trying to save for a holiday at Butlin's and there's no way we could if I didn't char. Cleaning's good money even if it is back breaking sometimes. And Mrs H has got a lovely house. It's nice surroundings. So I count me chickens really.' She frowned at Rose. 'Heard anything from Eddie?'

'I phoned the police station. He's been charged with obstructing the police in the line of duty, assault and handling stolen goods.'

'You're joking!'

'He's up before central London magistrates' court tomorrow at nine.'

Anita swallowed. 'Are you going?'

'I don't see how I can, not with the girls.'

'If I wasn't at work I'd have them for you.'

Rose shook her head slowly. 'I don't suppose they'd let me speak to Eddie anyway. The policeman wasn't very helpful, he just said Eddie might get bail until the next hearing. He even said the word trial. Oh, Neet, I can't begin to imagine what that would involve.'

'Trial?' Anita repeated in a confused voice. 'I don't understand.'

'Nor do I,' Rose shrugged gloomily. 'I was told that Eddie will have a solicitor though. The policeman said everyone gets one of those, rich or poor.'

'What else did he say?'

'Nothing. Before I could ask any more I got cut off and I didn't want to ring again because Joan was asking questions.'

'So there's a chance he might get this bail, then?'

Rose nodded. 'A chance yes, and it's one I'm banking on. I don't want to think of him not walking through that door tomorrow.'

'Did Eddie have any money on him?'

'I don't know. It depends what business he'd done.'

Anita was silent again. Then, resting her arms on the

table, she looked at Rose. 'You know, you can always borrow the Butlin's money if you need it.'

'Oh, Anita, I don't know what to say.'

'Well, it's there if you want. The best part of thirty quid.'

Rose swallowed on the lump in her throat. Anita was so generous. Joan Wright had been kind too. And Len Silverman. But when people were nice it was even worse than when they weren't.

'I hope it won't be necessary to ask,' Rose said quietly, wondering if she would find herself in such a position tomorrow.

'Enough said, love. You know you can.'

'I've just written to Em to tell her what's happened,' Rose said as they sat there thinking.

'It'll be a bloody shock for her, I can tell you that.'

'I know. But perhaps Arthur can help.'

'Her hubbie? What makes you think that?'

'He works in Eastbourne Town Hall. Em says he's very high up in his job. I just thought he might know something about legal procedures.'

'Yes, I remember him,' Anita said with narrowed eyes. 'From when they lived here with you before they moved to Eastbourne. Personally I couldn't see what your sister saw in him. Sorry if I'm speaking out of turn again.'

'He's all right really.'

'He never said so much as a hello to us in all the time they lived here.' Anita sniffed.

'Oh, he didn't mean any harm,' Rose shrugged. 'Arthur isn't very talkative.'

'He's bloody mute if you ask me.' Anita glanced at Rose quickly. 'They haven't come to visit you much since they moved to Eastbourne, have they?'

'No. It's a long way.' Rose knew it wasn't because of the distance they didn't visit. It was because of the two men's dislike for one another. Eddie was chalk to Arthur's cheese. Luckily the four of them hadn't been forced to share the house for very long, just a few months, as she and Eddie had married in the June and Em and Arthur moved to Eastbourne in the December. But it was long enough.

'Maybe they'll come down and visit soon.'

'Yes, I hope so.' Rose missed her sister. They were very close after their parents had been killed in the early part of the war. Em had been twenty and Rose almost fifteen. The authorities had tried to evacuate Rose, but she'd found a job at Horton's munitions factory where her sister worked.

'How old is their boy now?'

'Will is ten. Eleven in September, I think.'

'They ain't got no other kids, then?'

Rose shook her head. She was always a bit touchy where the subject of her sister's marriage was concerned. There was something she didn't quite understand about their relationship herself. Fourteen years separated Em and Arthur; it was a big age gap.

'Anyway,' Anita continued, searching her bag for her cigarettes and not finding any. Rose knew she had given up smoking but still went through the motions. 'What will you do tomorrow?'

'I'm hoping that Eddie will walk in the door and we can sort all this out.'

Anita passed no comment. 'Have you told the girls?'

'No. Only that he'll be home.'

'Well, that's being positive.'

'What else should I be? Eddie's innocent.'

Anita heaved herself up, drinking her tea as she stood. 'I gotta go, girl. Benny's back tonight.'

'Thanks for looking in.'

After her friend had gone Rose sat down in the front room. The two girls were over at Sally's house until six. It was only five. How would she fill the hours till tomorrow? The minutes were weighing heavily. She didn't know anything about legal procedures; would Eddie want her there tomorrow? But what could she do? Besides, it was impossible to attend court with two little girls.

Rose found herself gazing at the big walnut radiogram sitting squarely against the wall. How her father had loved that old relic. But the veneer still looked quality even though it was the devil itself to shift and too cumbersome to move unless she leaned her back against it and wriggled it across the floor. She smiled. She remembered when Eddie had once prized up the loose floorboards beneath to hide a few trinkets. His hidy hole he called it . . .

On sudden impulse, Rose stood up and went over. She leaned her back against the cabinet and pushed. Perhaps a little housework would distract her mind. But finally, after a lot of pushing and shoving, she gazed down at perfectly clean floorboards. A moment later she lifted one of the boards. In the recess below there was a shoebox.

Carefully, she slid back the lid. Rose gasped aloud, unable to believe her eyes. A bundle of notes was tied up with string. Swimming at the bottom of the box was a sea of loose change: pennies, halfpennies, shillings, three-penny bits, farthings, shiny half crowns. With trembling fingers she untied the string. Even more carefully, she separated the notes.

Over five hundred pounds in total.

Chapter Four

Rose woke with a start next morning.

Was the shoebox a dream? Slowly the events of yesterday filtered back and she knew the money was real. Five hundred pounds – surely sufficient for Eddie's bail! What was happening to him at this moment? Was he in court? And should she be in attendance? But there was Marlene and Donnie to consider.

She dressed quickly and went to look at the radiogram. It was still standing over the loose floorboards, of course. When had Eddie hidden the money, she wondered curiously? Rose turned the knob as though she might receive an answer from the machine itself. But the announcer's voice was miserable. America was testing a nuclear bomb five hundred times more powerful than the one that had destroyed Hiroshima. She switched the gram off again quickly.

Rose turned her thoughts to breakfast. As the girls were off school this week, she had bought extra eggs as a treat. How many eggs would five hundred pounds buy she wondered ridiculously? The rent was a hundred and twenty pounds for a whole year, gas and coal was less than fifteen; her thoughts were revolving so fast she didn't hear Marlene behind her.

'Mummy, when's Daddy coming home?'

'I told you, soon. Now are you ready for breakfast?'

'I don't want any.'

'Look, I've made soldiers.'

'Don't want them.' Her daughter ran up the stairs. Rose called again and both girls came down looking subdued. When the gloomy breakfast was over, they went out to play. Rose accepted there was no way she could have gone to the hearing this morning.

She watched the girls through the window. She never worried where they were. If they went to someone's house or backyard, they always told her first. Sometimes they dressed up and did little shows. Rose loved that. Marlene was a natural actress and always took the lead. Donnie, as usual, operated from the wings.

Rose sighed softly and went in the yard. Beside the washhouse there was a patch of worn grass that never needed mowing. It saw too much activity to grow. A deep hole was beside it where the air raid shelter had been. The corrugated iron roof was now the fence that divided them from the Mendozas. On the opposite side the house was boarded up, virtually derelict.

Rose looked across the corrugated iron fence hoping to see Anita. All was quiet. The Mendozas were out.

There and then Rose made up her mind. If Eddie wasn't home by this afternoon she would go to a public call box. She didn't want to bother Joan again. There was a box up Poplar by a small park. Whilst she used it the girls could play on the swings.

'Why aren't you eating dinner?' Donnie asked as they sat at the kitchen table at one o'clock.

'I ate while I was cooking.' Rose trailed the thick gravy over the stew on their plates. She was too disappointed to eat. Eddie hadn't shown up.

'What are we doing this afternoon?'

'We're walking to Poplar.'

'I don't like long walks.' Marlene pushed her spoon away.

'Walking is good for you. It'll be nice to see somewhere different.'

'What are we going to do in Poplar?'

'I'm telephoning about Daddy.'

Both girls looked up. 'Can't we use Mrs Wright's telephone?' Donnie asked.

'Once was enough to ask a favour.' Rose looked sternly at their plates. 'Now, finish your dinners before they go cold.'

They ate in silence, which Rose knew was a bad sign. Dinner times were always noisy and fun. After she'd washed up and the girls had scrubbed their hands in the big white sink in the kitchen, Rose went upstairs and changed. She put on a cotton dress and cardigan and brushed her long brown hair, then pinned it into a roll behind her head. By two o'clock they were ready. Rose couldn't wait to get there.

★

They passed The Lock and Key at the top of a short uphill road and, as the children skipped ahead, eager to play in the park, Rose wondered if Eddie was the topic of conversation in the public bar. A frequent user of the pub, he was known to most of the regulars. The market traders congregated there, as did the scrap metal dealers who were enjoying, as Eddie put it, 'the life of riley'. After the war scrap had become a lucrative business as the metal was melted down and sold for good money to the building trade. Rose loved the sight of the brightly painted pub. During the war so many pubs, churches and schools had been blown apart or damaged and many of the grimy, smoke-covered houses they passed were uninhabited.

Rose recalled the war years with mixed emotions. The sudden death of her parents had been devastating, but Rose had found herself a job and put to use the typing and bookkeeping she'd done at school. Although she hadn't been a very fast typist at first, by the time she left Horton's she was.

Rose watched Marlene and Donnie as they skipped under the plane trees. Once they had been plentiful on the streets, now they looked grey and sparse even though it was summer. Perhaps they remembered the war too when the bombs had fallen and left craters where a profusion of lovely tall trees had once grown.

Further on they came to more terraced houses. These backed on to the docks where the cranes, boats and bridges were all in working order again. The island was experiencing a new lease of life. It was wonderful to see the barges and ships move effortlessly down river. She never tired of watching the sun rise or set at night, knowing that just over the rooftops the Thames was changing into a wild ribbon of orange.

Rose loved every square inch of the island. It was a survivor, just as she was. Even the smell of the dustbins that stood by the doors as the kids played round them was familiar. All the children looked happy. Rose knew that most of them had been given, officially or not, the rest of the week off.

'Where's this park?' Marlene was dragging her heels. 'Me feet are tired.'

Rose ruffled her red hair. 'They weren't tired just now when you chased that cat.'

'I only wanted to stroke it.'

'More like pull its tail,' Donnie grinned. 'Just like you do with Sooty across the road.'

'I never!' Marlene was bright red.

'You do. You make it hiss.'

'It's always hissing.'

'Yes, because you always pull its tail.'

Rose pointed across the road. 'Look, there's the park.' She looked for the bright red telephone box. It was on the other side of the road.

'Can we play on the swings?'

'Yes, but stay together.'

'Are you going to speak to Daddy?'

'I hope so.'

Once they were occupied, Rose made her way to the telephone box. She pulled open the heavy cast iron door.

Inside it smelt of cigarettes and beer. Placing her pennies on the shelf, she lifted the heavy bakelite handset, reading aloud the numbers she'd written on a piece of paper when she'd used Joan's telephone.

'I'm Rose Weaver,' she said when she heard the deep voice of the policeman. 'My husband, Eddie Weaver, was due to appear at central London magistrates' court today at nine o'clock. I'd like to know what happened.'

After a long silence, the man said, 'Hold on.'

Just as before, there was a series of clicks. Rose wondered when her money would run out. She wished she'd brought some more of the coins from the bottom of the shoe box. She had only ever used a public telephone to call Em before and that was not very often. Dialling and pushing the money in was a frantic business.

The voice returned. 'Edward John Weaver was remanded in custody this morning. Bail was refused.'

Her mouth fell open. 'But why? I was told he would get bail!' Rose couldn't believe it.

'The police opposed bail. All I can tell you is he was remanded in custody until a later date.'

'But . . . but when can I see him?' she managed to ask as she sagged against the glass panes.

'That's not up to me.'

'Who is it up to, then?'

'The prison will send you a visiting order.'

Rose gasped. 'What prison?'

'You'll be notified in due course.'

She couldn't take it all in. Eddie was in prison. They

weren't going to let him come home. Suddenly the pips went and the line went dead again.

'Did you speak to Daddy?' Donnie was breathless as she ran over from the swings.

'No, to someone else.'

'A policeman?'

'Yes.'

'Is Daddy coming home?' Marlene joined them.

'I don't know when exactly.' Both girls stared at her, waiting for more. Rose couldn't tell them their daddy was in prison. 'He sends you his love.'

'How do you know that? Did the policeman say?'

Rose nodded. 'Do you want to play on the swings a bit longer?'

'I need a push.' Marlene wiped her dirty fingers across her face.

Rose didn't want the girls to know how worried she was. Luckily they forgot to question her as they enjoyed their rides on the swings and played with some other little girls.

When they were occupied she sat down on the park bench. Eddie was in prison. What prison? And when would they send her a visiting order? She had never been inside a prison before. She recalled a family, the Dobsons, who had lived at the end of the street but had now moved away. The father and three sons were in constant trouble. She had pitied Elaine Dobson who had tried to live a decent life despite the frequent incarceration of her husband and sons.

Had she looked down on that woman, indeed on anyone who suffered in the same way, she asked herself? Well, she herself was now in that same situation and like Elaine Dobson she had to face the street. It was up to her to show everyone the Weavers were still a close family.

On Friday morning, Anita called round. 'Sorry I couldn't get in yesterday. Me father-in-law had one of his turns and we was out till late.'

Rose was washing up at the sink. She hadn't stopped thinking about Eddie. She hadn't slept and had no appetite. 'Is your father-in-law all right?' she asked vacantly.

'As right as he'll ever be. It's his heart, you see. One of those thirsty ones. Needs a lot of filling up.' Anita rolled her eyes. 'Benny maintains it's the Argentine blood. More like the bottle, I say. Anyway, enough about us,' she finally looked at Rose. 'Well, where's Eddie?'

Rose dried her hands on the towel. 'Let's go in the front room.' The girls were playing in the street as usual and Rose sat on the couch, looking at them out of the window. 'Eddie's in prison.'

Anita gasped as she sat beside her. 'What!'

'He was remanded in custody. The police wouldn't agree to bail.'

Anita looked confused 'But he ain't murdered anyone. What right have they to keep him in?'

'I'd like the answer to that meself.'

Anita snorted. 'How bloody ridiculous! You know what I think? Them coppers wanted a result when they searched your house. They must have thought that

68

something was hidden here to have gone to all the trouble. I don't like to think it, but maybe someone's trying to fit Eddie up.'

Rose's chin wobbled. 'You think someone would do that?'

'It's not out of the question, is it? A business rival, or some mean sod spilling beans to the coppers and putting the finger on Eddie – well, it would account for a lot of what happened, wouldn't it?'

'Yes, but it seems so far-fetched.'

'So does what's happened over the last few days and I ain't talking about the Coronation.'

Rose let out a long and shaky sigh. 'Who would hate Eddie that much?'

Anita patted her arm. 'Now, I'm only throwing around a few ideas here,' she said as she saw Rose's worried expression. 'When can you see him?'

'I have to wait till I hear from the prison.'

'How long will that be?'

'I don't know. And I couldn't just go knocking on a prison door, I suppose, even if I knew which one it is.' Rose stared at the radiogram. Should she confide in Anita about the shoe box? It was weighing heavily on her mind.

'Have you heard from Em yet?' Anita asked.

'No. I only posted me letter yesterday.'

'I don't mean to keep on, but how are you going to manage? I mean, do you have any money put by?'

Rose bit her lip. 'I've got more than I thought.' She paused. 'Neet, there's something I want to get off me chest. I've got to share it with someone or I'll bust.'

'Blimey.' Anita lowered her cup into the saucer with a clatter. 'Not more bad news?'

'No . . . not really.'

'You've got me guessing, girl.'

'I found some money.' Rose paused.

'Yeah? How much?'

Rose went pink. 'Five hundred pounds.'

Anita sat in silence, but not for long. 'Five hundred quid! Are you certain?'

'Positive.'

'Where did you find it, for God's sake?'

'There.' Rose nodded to the radiogram. Both women stared at the big, highly polished walnut case.

'Under that old thing?'

'Yes.'

'And you didn't know it was there when the police searched?'

Rose closed her eyes at the thought. 'Thank God I didn't. All I was worried about was Mum's pearl necklace wrapped up in Eddie's socks. It wasn't until I sat down on Wednesday night and found meself staring at the radiogram that the thought crossed my mind about Eddie's hidy hole. He used it for a few bits and pieces, but that was ages ago. I was gonna dust under the gram to keep me mind occupied, but when I pushed it back, the boards were spotless. 'Course, I had to have a look then, didn't I?'

'Blimey, if that was Benny's hiding place I'd be down it the moment he walked out the door. Amazing the coppers didn't find it though,' Anita murmured, shaking her head in disbelief. 'Your old man is a dark horse.'

That was exactly what Rose had been thinking. She'd known Eddie since they were kids. He was just a few months older than her and they'd attended the same school. Raised in a large family by foster parents he'd never had much of a home life, but his quick wit and broad sense of cockney humour had endeared him to his friends, especially Rose. She was well aware of his keen eye for a business proposition but during their marriage her reluctance to enquire into his affairs, their compromise as she thought of it, had broken all boundaries. It was as if she'd been afraid to ask for fear of what she might hear in return.

'Five hundred smackers will see you all right whilst Eddie's out of action.'

'Yes, but I wish I knew where it came from.'

'Only Eddie can enlighten you on that score,' Anita remarked dryly.

'It's a large amount of money.'

Anita nodded, calculating swiftly. 'Five hundred quid ain't chicken feed and that's the truth. It could feed you, pay your rent and settle all your bills for a year and still leave you plenty left over.'

Rose looked up. 'Some of it must be the Parkers'.'

Anita scowled. 'You and your conscience, Rose Weaver. You gotta put your family first now.'

'I don't want people to think Eddie swindled them. By rights fifty pounds is theirs.'

'You're not thinking of giving the money back?' Anita sucked in a sharp breath.

Rose chewed on her lip. 'There would still be plenty left.'

Anita sighed and lifted her hands. 'Well, I don't know what Eddie would say about that. And anyway, won't questions be asked as to where you got the money to give to them?'

Rose shrugged. 'I'll just say that after giving the matter some thought and as a gesture of goodwill, I'm returning the money they gave to Eddie.'

They lapsed into silence, staring at the radiogram under which was hidden Eddie's treasure. After a while Anita glanced at the wooden clock on the mantel. 'I gotta go. Will you be all right?'

Rose nodded. 'Are you cycling today?'

'No, bussing it. Me back's playing up.'

'You should rest more.'

Anita laughed coarsely. 'Yeah, in me dreams. But I'm off tomorrow. We'll have a nice long chat on the way to market. You are still coming, aren't you?'

Rose shrugged. 'I suppose so.' They always walked to Cox Street market on Saturday mornings to buy cheap veg and meat for the week.

'I'll take that as a yes.'

At the front door Rose leaned forward and kissed her friend on the cheek.

Anita looked surprised. 'What's that for?'

'For listening to me.'

Her friend smiled. 'You've done the same for me often enough.'

'We're lucky to have you and Benny as friends.'

Anita shook her head. 'Do you remember when we first moved back to Ruby Street after our Dad died? Everyone gave us a wide berth, 'cos they classed Benny as black. And it wasn't until Eddie took my old man to The Lock and warned everyone they'd have to answer to him if they didn't drink with Benny, that things changed. Your Eddie had the courage of his convictions. We won't forget that in a hurry.'

Eddie's generous nature was why Rose loved her husband so much. He treated everyone the same. He was first to approach the Indian family who moved into the Dobsons' house two years ago, when he'd marched down there one Saturday morning, knocked on the door and took Mr Patel's hand. He didn't care about colour or creed. As long as a person returned the time of day, Eddie was happy. Just like the Parkers. Eddie hadn't cared they were the odd couple. Rose knew he'd felt sorry for them too, just as she had.

Rose waved goodbye. Her gaze went to Marlene and Donnie playing marbles in the street. She was filled with a love for her family that went deeper than anything she had ever known before. Despite all their troubles, she believed in her husband's innocence; he was an honest man and somehow she would prove it.

Chapter Five

Anita called round on Saturday morning. 'Did you buy yesterday's *Evening Gazette*?' she demanded immediately.

'No.'

'Then you'd better see this.' She produced a folded single sheet of newspaper and handed it over. 'I've had it in my purse to show you.'

Rose read the two short lines. 'Oh, Neet!'

'Well, it ain't very much. Just what the charges were and that Eddie's been remanded in custody. Not exactly headlines, love. Luckily they're still banging on about the Coronation.'

'Do you think everyone round here read it?' Rose asked dejectedly.

'Everyone knew anyway.' Anita replaced the cutting in her shopping bag before Rose could agonize again. 'I thought it was best to show you and get it over with. Now, come on, don't look so glum, it ain't the end of the world. In fact it was a blessing Eddie's trouble arose at this time 'cos no one's bothered about the small fry. All they want to see is the Queen and the Royal Family, dressed up to the nines.'

But Rose turned and walked to the kitchen. 'I know what that poor Elaine Dobson felt like now. No wonder she kept herself to herself.'

'Yes, poor cow, she had a lot on her plate,' Anita agreed. 'But you're not in the same league as the Dobsons. They were a rough lot.'

'Even so my sympathies are with her.'

Anita caught her arm. 'Listen, your situation is different altogether and you want to remember that. Now fetch your coat and we'll go up the market.' She frowned at Rose's apron and slippers. 'Blimey girl, you look like Mrs Mop.'

Rose shook her arm free. 'You walk on, Neet. We'll catch up.'

'No you won't,' Anita guessed. 'You'll stay in and mope all day.'

'Hurry up, Mum!' Alan called from the open front door. He was the older of Anita's two sons and at fifteen looked smart in his white cotton poplin shirt, slim jim tie and dark trousers. He had combed up a quiff of dark hair and plastered it with Brylcreem. Fourteen-year-old David looked round his brother's shoulder and gave Rose a cheeky smile. He was an inch or two shorter than Alan but in looks both were a replica of Benny.

Donnie and Marlene came tumbling down the stairs. They paused to stare at the boys then ran to Rose. 'David and Alan are coming with us,' Donnie whispered excitedly. Rose knew she had a crush on David.

'You girls all ready?' Anita asked and they nodded, looking back shyly towards the front door.

'It seems I'm outnumbered,' Rose said resignedly. 'I'll get me bag.'

Five minutes later they were on their way. 'Life has to go on,' Anita was lecturing her as they went. It was a dry, fine morning and the two girls were laughing and giggling as they walked ahead with the boys.

'I know. I'm just feeling a bit sorry for meself,' Rose admitted.

'Your Eddie wouldn't want you upset. Put it out of your head for now, Rose.'

Rose wanted to make the effort. It was a lovely morning and she didn't intend to be a misery. 'Your Alan is shooting up,' she said, looking at the two solid frames of the young teenagers striding out in front.

'He's costing us a fortune in trousers. Our Dave has always worn his brother's but soon he'll want his own.'

Rose wondered how long it would be before Donnie asked for new clothes. Girls were more advanced than boys. In a couple of years she wouldn't appreciate Rose's hand sewn garments.

'They look very smart.'

'We had a real row over clothes the other day. Alan only favours these horrible new trousers called drainpipes. I told him if he thinks I'm buying that rubbish for him he's got another think coming. He'll be wearing those 'orrible crêpe-soled shoes and gaudy ankle socks next. Or one of them long coats with the velvet collars that you see around nowadays.'

Rose nodded. 'Don't they call themselves Teddy Boys

after King Edward VII, I think it was, who started the fashion?'

'Yeah and what an idiot he must have looked.'

Rose smiled. 'Oh, I can't see Alan as one of them.'

'Give him half a chance and he'd be standing on the corner combing that damn quiff until it fell off his bloody head.'

'Boys will be boys.'

'Tell me about it.'

The market stalls came into sight and Rose gave Donnie and Marlene a few pennies. They ran off and the two boys turned to their mother. 'We'll see you later then,' Alan said, grinning at two pretty girls who gave them the eye as they passed.

'Make sure you do.' Anita folded her arms across her chest and threw her sons a frown as they disappeared after the girls. 'I don't trust either of them further than I could throw them. The last thing I need is some young piece with a bun in the oven.'

Rose looked shocked. 'Alan wouldn't!'

Anita sniffed loudly. 'Don't you believe it. They're randy little sods at their ages. I've told Alan to tie a knot in it till he knows how to use it properly.'

'Oh, your poor Alan.'

Anita saw the funny side. 'I remember what his father was like. Benny couldn't keep it in his trousers from the moment we met. Gawd knows how I had the nerve to walk up the aisle in white.'

'Yes, but you did.'

'Just about.' She looked at Rose. 'What about you?'

'I wore white on me wedding day in 1945. It was summer and very hot. The war was almost over and we were still alive. Our service was a quiet one with just a few friends and neighbours. Your mum and dad came. You was living with your in-laws in Stepney, remember? You couldn't come to the service because one of your boys was down with the measles.'

'Oh yeah,' Anita nodded. 'That was David. After which Alan caught it. We had to keep out of circulation for a while.'

Rose smiled reflectively. 'Em was bridesmaid and Arthur gave me away. Me and Eddie were only seventeen. Donnie was born the following year.'

Anita grinned. 'You and Eddie made up for lost time, then.'

'Well, we were mates at school but we never went out or anything.'

'Didn't you fancy him?'

'I never thought about it.'

'So when did you?'

Rose smiled. 'After he got back from Normandy. He lied about his age to get into the army. He was only sixteen but said he was seventeen. They needed recruits for the second front and sent him across on D Day. A bullet went through his shoulder as he tried to leave the landing craft.'

'Blimey love, I ain't heard him talk about that.'

'No, he doesn't much. He still can't lift his arm above his head.'

'It must have hurt.'

'He don't remember much. He was fished out of the water by a mate. He thought he was going to drown.'

'But they brought him back in one piece?'

Rose nodded. 'I went to see him in hospital. The bullet chipped a bone. He was out of the action for six months and in a lot of pain. When he returned to his unit the war was almost over. Our forces were closing in on Berlin. He wrote to ask me if I'd marry him when he got home.'

'And you said yes.'

'I knew I loved him and I'd nearly lost him.'

Anita sighed. 'Well, that's really romantic.'

'What about you?'

'Benny was away in the merchant navy. I didn't get back from Stepney much to see Mum and Dad. I still feel guilty about it now. But what with the doodlebugs and V2s you took your life in your hands if you only went up the street. Benny never had a scratch on him at the end of the war. He's a lucky sod.'

'We were all lucky,' Rose commented quietly.

'Where did Em meet Arthur?' Anita asked after a while.

'He worked at the town hall in Poplar. The births, marriages and deaths department. He was exempt from the services because of his job. Em met him in the February of '42. She'd gone to get Mum and Dad's death certificate and he was very helpful. He asked her out and they got married at Christmas.'

'Was she up the spout?'

'No. 'Course not.'

'Don't tell me she fell for Arthur's good looks and outstanding personality, 'cos I won't believe you.'

Rose hesitated. 'Well, she was still getting over Mum and Dad being killed. We were alone in the house. I suppose he was there at the right time, a shoulder to lean on.'

They strolled slowly through the crowded market and stood by the fruit and veg stall. 'So what about you and Eddie? Was it a mad, passionate romance?'

Rose grinned. 'To tell you the truth, Eddie was a bit shy. Though you'd never believe it now, would you? He never tried anything on. Not till just after he was discharged from hospital.'

'What happened then?'

'He had to report back and we went out for a couple of drinks before he left. When we got home the sirens went. We was a bit merry and a bit sad. We went down the Anderson and listened to the bombs coming close. I thought at least if we went we'd go together. Eddie cuddled me and then fell over. I thought we'd been hit.' Rose laughed softly. 'There he was, lying flat on the floor.'

'Well, obviously he wasn't dead?'

'No. He'd just had too much to drink. The only time I've ever seen him like that. You know he's not a drinker.'

'So what did you do?'

'I got the torch and made sure he was in one piece.'

Anita eyed her carefully. 'So you had a good look, did you?'

Rose nodded. 'Yes, I said I did.'

'No, I mean, did you have a *good* look?'

The two women burst into laughter. Rose didn't know if she was laughing because she was happy or sad. Either way it didn't seem to matter.

'It's good to have a laugh,' Anita said, wiping the tears from her eyes.

'Yeah.' Rose sighed reflectively. 'Poor Eddie.'

Anita spluttered again. 'I can't get the picture out of me mind of Eddie flat out and you looking down his trousers.'

'I didn't look down his trousers!'

'I know, but I've got a good imagination.'

Suddenly two little girls appeared before them. Donnie stood with a toffee apple in her hand. Marlene was already half way through hers.

'Where did you get the toffee apples?' Rose asked.

'Mr Silverman bought them for us. Said not to dirty our frocks.'

'That was nice of him. Did you say thank you?'

Both girls nodded. 'We saw Mr Parker too but he ignored us.'

'Mr Parker – Olga's hubbie?' Anita was swift to enquire.

'Yes. He was up that little lane there, by the toilets.'

'You're sure it was him?'

'He was talking to a lady. She had one of them shiny coats on. Look, there she is now.'

Rose followed Marlene's grubby finger. 'Not *that* lady?'

Both girls nodded.

Rose met Anita's stare, then looked back at her

daughters. 'Do you want to have a bit longer to look round?'

'Yes, please!' both girls shouted.

'All right then. Off you go.'

Rose watched them skip away then glanced at Anita.

'Are you thinking what I'm thinking?' Anita asked at once.

'No.'

'Yes you are.'

'Well, I'm not going to say it.'

Anita smirked. 'Well I will then. Leslie Parker ain't out to buy any veg, at least not the eating variety.'

Rose frowned. 'He might be doing the shopping.'

'Blimey, what's up with your eyesight?' Anita teased. 'Didn't you see that bit of skirt he was chatting up? He wasn't talking to her about the price of spuds, was he?'

'It's easy to draw the wrong conclusion.'

'All right then. Maybe she's a Salvationist in disguise. Chucked in her bonnet for a bra.'

Rose sighed. 'Olga don't know the half.'

'The Parkers are square pegs in Ruby Street. Gawd knows why they moved here.'

'It's a mystery,' Rose agreed. 'I wouldn't want to be in Olga's shoes. They don't have kids to worry about and she always wears nice clothes, but I feel lucky in comparison.'

Anita nodded. 'Ain't that the truth.'

'I just wish Eddie had never sold them that rotten television.'

'Oh don't let's get on that subject again,' Anita

interrupted giving her arm a shake. 'Come on, I'll buy you a fried egg roll at Alf's.'

Despite her friend's abruptness, Rose knew Anita was salt of the earth and doing everything in her power to cheer her up. 'But you're saving for Butlin's and every penny counts. And anyway, I'm not hungry.'

''Course you are. This is on our Benny. He gave me two and six for grub and another five bob for a new bra and stockings. Black ones with seams.'

Rose grinned. 'You and your stockings.'

'It's his hot Argentine roots, he says.'

'I'll bet.' Rose knew Anita and Benny enjoyed themselves when they got the chance. Just like she and Eddie did.

'Well, it's better than having your old man fall asleep on the couch every day.' Anita nudged Rose's arm and winked. They began to walk across to Alf's, an old van with a hole cut in the side. The counter was laden with vinegar bottles, salt and pepper pots and the aroma of fried onions, sausages and bacon oozed from the stove at the back.

Rose remembered how Eddie was addicted to Alf's bacon sandwiches. Once in a while he'd bring them all to market and treat them to whatever snack they wanted. The memory of his smiling face and twinkling eyes as he handed out the grub made her miss him all the more. But she mustn't get miserable again, not when her friend was trying to cheer her up.

And there were always some worse off. Olga Parker for instance.

'What do the girls want?' Anita asked as Alf smacked a greasy tray of sausages on the counter then forked two sizzling bangers into a bap. Rose licked her lips disregarding his dirty fingernails and filthy apron.

'They'll share one between them,' Rose said gratefully. 'My shout next time. I'm gonna raid the shoe box and treat us all.'

Anita giggled. 'I'll look forward to that, girl. Gawd bless that bloody shoe box.'

Rose discovered Eddie's whereabouts and what a visiting order was the following Wednesday. She had just taken the kids to school and found the envelope waiting for her on the mat. She sat down at the kitchen table to tear it open and read the short letter from Eddie. He said he was in Brixton prison and asked her to visit in a week's time. She had to bring the permit with her. But what upset her the most was that it didn't sound like Eddie. Though it was his big, broad handwriting, the few lines seemed so formal.

Rose had thought she couldn't cry any more. But the letter was a body blow that she was unprepared for. For an hour she sat at the kitchen table, just reading the two pieces of paper over and over again. Then, as if they had been waiting to erupt, huge big sobs climbed up her chest.

After a strong cup of tea she felt better and began to think along more practical lines, for instance, planning her journey to Brixton. The best route would be through the foot tunnel from Island Gardens to Greenwich and then take a bus on the other side of the river. She would visit whilst the kids were at school.

Rose got out her blue Basildon Bond notepad, a present from Em last Christmas, and wrote to Eddie saying they all loved and missed him and confirming she would be there without fail the following Wednesday.

The letter went in the post immediately. When she got home she put on her apron and started the chores. Her mind was full of next Wednesday's visit. She wanted to see Eddie so much. What would he look like behind bars? Could they touch each other? How much time would they be allowed?

At half past three Rose put her duster away. It was time to collect the children. At least she could tell them she'd had a letter from their father. Then it dawned on her: he was in prison not on holiday at the seaside. By the time Rose arrived at St Mary's, she was in more of a muddle than ever. Should she tell them where Eddie was? The answer came quickly.

Donnie and Marlene ran towards the school gates. 'Mummy, Mummy!'

'What's wrong? What's happened?' Dirty tears had dried on Marlene's cheeks.

'I got bashed,' Marlene whined.

Rose was horrified. 'Who bashed you?'

'Michael Curtis.'

Donnie's voice quavered. 'Miss Keene wants to see you.'

'What, *now*?'

'Yes.'

Rose got out her hanky and wiped Marlene's face. 'Are you cross with me?' Marlene mumbled, sniffing back her tears.

'No, why should I be cross with you?'

'I ain't done nothing. It was Michael Curtis what said it.'

'Said what?'

'That Daddy's in prison.' Donnie stared into Rose's eyes. 'And he's not ever coming out.'

'And he's got big chains and a ball on his leg,' Marlene added loudly.

'Rubbish!' Rose put her arms round her girls. 'It's all right, I'm here now. Come along and I'll talk to your teacher.'

It was a long walk across the playground. She looked into the other women's faces. What were they thinking? What had been said behind her back?

'I'm sorry about Marlene.' Vivien Keene addressed Rose as she stood in the first year's classroom of St Mary's Primary. The prefab section of the school didn't have much allure but Rose had always liked Miss Keene, a slight, mousey-haired young woman with a genuine interest in her pupils.

'What happened?' Rose asked coolly.

Miss Keene turned to the girls. 'Go and sit on the bench in the corridor, please. I won't keep Mummy long.' When they had gone she looked Rose in the eye. 'Marlene hit a boy today because of something he said in the playground. Unfortunately, he retaliated.'

'I know what he said but where did he get it from?' Rose asked angrily.

Miss Keene paused and Rose knew she was choosing her words carefully. 'There have been comments from the parents, Mrs Weaver, which resulted from the piece in the newspaper. I can only surmise Michael overheard and then embellished.'

'It's so unfair,' Rose burst out. 'Why couldn't they say it to my face?'

'I understand but—'

'And you teachers . . . what were you doing when this was going on? You should have been there to stop it.'

Vivien Keene smiled sadly. 'In an ideal world, yes, we should be able to prevent our pupils from being bullied or hurt. But it's always the vulnerable – the children – who suffer. All we can do as teachers is try our best, which often is not good enough, as in Marlene's case, when a child spoke such cruel words and in all probability, didn't understand the meaning of them himself.'

Rose was only concerned with her girls. 'What if it happens again?' she asked helplessly. 'What then?'

'I'll do everything in my power to see it doesn't.'

But that wasn't enough, Rose realized. Miss Keene couldn't be everywhere at once. And it only needed a few words. 'Well, you can tell everyone this: the children's father is in prison, but he isn't guilty of stealing or any other crime.'

Miss Keene frowned. 'Are Donnie and Marlene aware of all the facts?'

'No,' she had to admit.

'My advice is to tell them all you know,' Miss Keene said gently. 'Then they won't be so hurt by what the

87

other children might say. In my experience it's the lesser of two evils.'

'It's a bit late now,' Rose answered abruptly. 'The harm's been done. I don't feel like sending them to school again.'

'It will be harder if you keep them away,' the young woman warned in a cool tone. 'You would always be worried about letting them out of your sight. At least at school there is routine. And most families, you know, have problems of one sort or another. Some children come from very difficult backgrounds. Michael, for instance, is from a family of nine, has no father and his mother is often absent, leaving the grandparents to cope. Your girls are fortunate. They will get through this, I am sure.'

Rose swallowed hard, not trusting herself to speak. Emotion was welling up inside her. It didn't help to be told they were lucky in comparison to others. She turned and walked out of the classroom. Donnie and Marlene jumped off the bench and ran towards her. She couldn't wrap them in cotton wool, but from now on she was going to make certain no one hurt them again.

When they got home, she decided, she would tell them everything. Then there could be no more shocks in store.

'I miss Daddy.' Donnie was snuggled on her pillow, her big brown eyes staring up at Rose.

Rose was sitting on the end of her bed. She had followed their teacher's advice and told them everything she knew, stressing that Eddie was innocent of any crime. 'I know, pet. So do I.'

'It's because he hit that policeman,' Marlene said as she sucked her thumb, her red hair spread over her pillow like a bright red cobweb.

'Well, it was all a misunderstanding.'

'And he hasn't got a ball and chain round his leg?'

'No, that's only in comics.'

'Can we go to see him?' Donnie's lips trembled.

'Not yet, sweetheart. Mummy has to go first.'

'When?'

'Next Wednesday.'

'Is it a long way away?'

'Not far.'

'What if anyone says nasty things about Daddy again? What do we tell them?'

'To mind their own business,' Rose replied firmly.

'Mummy?' Donnie was finally looking sleepy. Rose got up and tucked the sheet over her. 'Does Daddy still love us?'

'He loves you more than ever. And he's very proud of you. You can write him a letter tomorrow after school,' Rose murmured as she bent to kiss them. 'And I'll take it with me when I go next Wednesday.'

'Me spelling ain't that good,' Marlene yawned.

'It doesn't matter.'

'Me painting's better.'

'Well, you can paint him a picture then. Now, off you go to sleep, my darlings.'

By the time she switched off the light, they were both

far away, dreaming, she hoped, of fairytale castles and princes and princesses. She didn't want her girls to grow up. She wanted them to have a long childhood, full of innocence and happiness. But would that be possible now?

For the next couple of days Rose waited at the school gate after the girls went in. She wanted the other children and their parents to see her there. Even when a teacher came out and blew the whistle she didn't leave the railings, but waited until the last child disappeared inside and all the parents had gone.

Most of the mothers returned her smile or said hello. But she knew what they were thinking. They had read that piece in the newspaper and had marked Eddie down as guilty.

Only Sally Piper's mum, Jane, spoke more than a few words. 'I was sorry to hear about Marlene. Sally told me,' she said as they walked back to Ruby Street. 'Is she all right?'

'Not too bad,' Rose nodded as Jane tried to control her two toddlers. 'It was over the bit in the paper about Eddie. It was the parents' fault, not the little boy's who didn't really understand what he was saying.'

'Kids catch on pretty quick,' Jane said ruefully as she battled with arms and legs all wriggling in the pram. 'I'm sure it'll all blow over.'

'I hope so,' Rose wondered how Jane kept so calm with her multiplying family.

'Try not to worry,' Jane said as she struggled to push her second youngest back on the seat attached to the bassinet. 'You won't be the first to encounter ignorance and definitely not the last. Time spent worrying is time lost, love.'

'Yes, I'm sure.' It was nice talking to Jane who, despite frequently being in a tearing rush, always had time for a few words at the school gates. Their daughters were good friends and had been since they'd started school at St Mary's two-and-a-half years ago.

'See you later,' Jane grinned as she left and Rose told herself that if all her neighbours reacted to the news of Eddie's imprisonment like Jane, she would consider herself lucky.

When Friday evening came Rose waited outside the playground and was relieved to see happy faces coming towards her. 'Had a good day?' she asked hopefully.

'Yes.'

Marlene, slightly red faced, said eagerly, 'Can we play snakes and ladders tonight?' Friday was a special night. Usually Rose allowed them to wait up for Eddie, as they didn't have school in the morning. But it wouldn't happen this evening, Rose thought, then remembered Miss Keene's words about routine being good for children. It also appeared the situation had improved in school too as Jane Piper had insightfully suggested it would.

'We'll have a little party,' she said joyfully. 'I'll make a cake too.'

'I hope I don't go down that big fat snake in the middle,' Marlene wailed. 'He's got a mouth as big as Blackwall tunnel.'

'Just like you,' Donnie giggled.

'I ain't got a big mouth.'

'Now you two, don't start.'

Rose smiled as they skipped in front of her. For the first time since Eddie had been away, she felt a flash of normality in her life.

Rose made her first major decision in Eddie's absence. She was going to return the Parkers' money and clear Eddie's name on that score. That night, after snakes and ladders when the girls were tucked up in bed and fast asleep, she removed fifty pounds from the shoebox.

It was late when Rose knocked but Olga opened her door at once. 'What do you want?' she demanded in surprise.

'I've got something for you.'

'What?'

'Here's what you asked for.' Rose drew the money from her pocket.

Olga stared, her eyes wide with shock. 'Where did you get that?'

'Do you want it or not?'

'Fifty pounds?' Olga took the money and counted each note.

'Is your husband there?' Rose wanted him to witness the transaction.

'He's not at home.'

'Well, I've got no option, then, but to leave you to tell him the money has been fully repaid.'

Olga looked up suspiciously. 'Where did you get this?'

'It's the money you gave to Eddie for the television, of course.'

But Olga was in no mood for forgiveness. 'It was still an embarrassment,' she said acidly.

Rose bit her tongue with difficulty. 'For which I have already apologized.'

'Your husband should never have sold it to us.'

'If you hadn't gone on at him, he wouldn't. Eddie said Leslie asked about the telly. Anyway, I'm not here to argue and I don't bear any grudges,' she said quietly. 'And I hope you won't.'

Olga sniffed loudly. 'No, I suppose not,' she conceded.

'Goodnight, then.' Rose turned and walked away hoping to be called back. But she wasn't. The door closed sharply behind her. Although Rose had derived satisfaction from settling the debt she knew that in a strange way she had alienated her neighbour even more. What was it like, she wondered, to be a foreigner living in another country? It couldn't be easy and since the Polish had suffered badly in the war, perhaps there were things in Olga's past that made her unhappy too.

I should have been friendlier, Rose worried that night as she got into bed. She had wanted to impress on the Parkers and her neighbours that Eddie was no thief. Well, she'd done that all right. But what had it achieved? A clear conscience, yes. But Olga still bore ill will. Rose slid down between the sheets, sadly aware of the cold space beside her. At least she could tell Eddie she'd returned the money and people would know then he hadn't intentionally deceived the Parkers.

The following morning brought another surprise. Rose had just got up and was brushing her hair, wondering what she was going to give the girls for breakfast, when she heard the letterbox go. Marlene was down the stairs first. 'We've got a letter,' she shouted up and Rose hurried down.

'I'll open it in the kitchen. Get dressed now.'

'I ain't brushed me teeth.'

'You can brush them in a minute.'

Rose sat at the table. It would be wonderful to hear words of support, something she could always rely on with Em. Her sister might even suggest they visit Eastbourne for a holiday. Not that she could afford to travel, but it would be nice to be asked.

Rose opened the sheets of thin, lined blue notepaper. As she read, her jaw dropped. She couldn't believe what Em had written.

Just then Donnie appeared. 'What's the matter, Mummy?'

Rose blinked. 'It's Auntie Em. She . . . she—'

Donnie sat down on the other chair. 'She what, Mum?'

Rose looked at her daughter. 'Uncle Arthur's dead. They've just had his funeral.'

'So Auntie Em and Will are a bit like us, then? All on their own,' Donnie questioned with childlike innocence.

Rose nodded, aware that her sister Em, at only thirty-one years of age, was now a widow. Her brother-in-law Arthur, a man who had always boasted good health, was dead and buried.

Chapter Six

Anita's eyes were wide. 'I can't believe it.'

'Nor can I.' Rose slid her sister's letter back in the envelope. 'Arthur always boasted he'd live to a hundred.'

Anita raised an eyebrow. 'Just shows you don't know what's round the corner.'

'What will Em do now, I wonder?'

'Poor cow.' Anita frowned. 'Funny she didn't invite you to the funeral.'

Rose nodded. 'I know.'

'When are you writing back?'

'Tonight, when the girls are in bed.' It was Sunday morning and the two women were talking over the fence. The sun had disappeared and there was a faint mist creeping over the houses. To call the year a wet one so far was an understatement, but now there was a gentle mellowness that heralded the long-anticipated summer.

Rose loved the light evenings when the girls could play out until late knowing the exercise would guarantee a good night's sleep for all concerned. On occasions she would take them down to Island Gardens with a flask of tea, a bottle of lemonade and a bag of sweets. Here they would play for hours and run around the small park as though it were the never-ending countryside. With the noise of the boats on the river and the factory hooters there wasn't much peace. But the kids didn't mind and nor did she as she sat on the bench and decided what to buy for tea. Eddie liked his steak and kidney pie winter and summer alike, followed by roly poly pudding and custard, a unanimous vote as afters.

Rose pushed Em's letter in her pocket and brought out another one. 'I had this from Eddie.'

Anita whistled through her teeth. 'At last.'

'I was beginning to wonder if I'd ever hear from him again.'

'What's this?' Anita held up the slip of paper.

'A visiting order for next Wednesday, two o'clock. Trouble is I'm worried about getting back in time to meet the girls.'

'I'll tell the boys to fetch them and bring them home,' Anita volunteered. 'I'll be back from work meself at five and give them tea.'

'Will David and Alan mind?'

''Course they won't.'

'If you're sure, then.'

Anita narrowed her eyes, leaning forward a little. 'What's the matter? And don't say nothing, 'cos I can tell there is.'

Rose knew she couldn't hide much from her friend. 'A little boy told Marlene her dad was in prison with a ball and chain round his ankle. Marlene walloped him. And he walloped her back.'

'Oh, blimey.' Anita gave a soft sigh.

'Kids can be so cruel.'

'Just say the word and Alan and David will sort out the mouthy little blighters.'

'I hope it won't come to that,' Rose added quickly.

'Don't worry, my lads can be very diplomatic when called for. They've had a good deal of practice watching us get me father-in-law out of trouble. Falling over in a stupor in the middle of the street is the norm for him when he's on a bender. Lucky Benny and the boys are big lads and can take his weight, managing to make it look like he's just dodgy on his pins.'

'Why does your mother-in-law put up with it?'

'She doesn't. She waits till he sobers up, then lets him have it.' Anita tilted her head. 'So what did you do about this little sod bashing Marlene?'

'The girls' teacher, Miss Keene, asked to see me. She said there's been talk after the newspaper piece.' Rose paused. 'She advised me to tell the girls everything and so I did.'

Anita nodded slowly. 'She's right, you know.'

'And I've let my presence be known at the school gates.' Rose pursed her lips firmly. 'If anyone's got anything to say they can say it to me.'

Anita couldn't hide her smile. 'That's the spirit, love.'

In the deepening warmth of the summer's day they spoke a few minutes longer until Rose turned and looked at the house. 'Better get the dinner on the table,' she smiled and Anita nodded.

'Yeah, me too. See you Wednesday, then. And don't worry about the girls. Alan and David will look after them. Oh, and when you write to Em, tell her I'm sorry about Arthur. Or, I'm sorry for her.'

'I will.'

The front door was open and Rose went in. Donnie and Marlene were sitting on the doorstep, two little backs leaning together. 'Time for dinner,' she told them as they jumped up.

'Smells like stew.' Marlene rubbed her tummy appreciatively.

'Yes. Now wash your hands and I'll dish up.'

'Can I help?' Donnie loved cooking, in fact any household duty that Rose allowed her to perform.

'You can stir the gravy.'

'Do I have to lay the table?' Marlene asked reluctantly.

'Yes. That's your job.'

'Can I have another job instead?'

'Why?'

'Knives and forks are boring.'

'But important,' Donnie reminded her sister, glancing at Rose. 'Or else we'd have to eat with our fingers.'

Rose smiled. Donnie knew how to handle her sister even if Marlene thought she was the boss. As Rose prepared dinner she thought about what she would write to Em. It was strange how her sister hadn't asked them to the funeral. But Rose assured herself it was probably because Em didn't want to worry her after receiving the letter about Eddie.

It was Wednesday morning, visiting day. Rose had taken the girls to school and was trying to decide what to wear.

She tried on the dress she wore on Coronation Day but it was too full of memories and she hung it back in the wardrobe. Next, she chose her dark blue suit, all hand made from a Simplicity pattern. Her mother, a seamstress for a big Jewish tailor's, had taught Rose all the tricks of the sewing trade. All her clothes and the girls' were either made or repaired on the old Singer treadle sewing machine in the bedroom. But today nothing seemed appropriate. What should she wear to a prison?

June had begun cold and wet and little lakes had formed in greasy pools on the badly worn roads and blocked gutters. And though it had become warm for a while it was now cool again, with a sky that veered between bruised and misty blue. The spells of heavy rain came without warning and the thundery outbreaks, such as the one yesterday, had drenched the clothes that hung miserably from Rose's washing line. If she was to arrive at the prison looking half decent, she would need a mac if not an umbrella.

Eventually she settled upon the mac and a plain, dark green dress that she had bought from the market some years ago. Although the repairs were extensive the material was pure cotton and the full skirt with white trimmed pockets and cap sleeves, was fashionable.

Footwear posed no problem. She only had one pair; light brown court shoes that Em had given her years ago. They might be years old, but they fitted and looked smart. Rose knew her long legs looked best in nylons, but she had none without ladders. Eddie, like Benny, preferred the seamed variety and had expressed disappointment during the war when the girls, because of rationing, had drawn lines down the backs of their legs to substitute for the real thing.

Finally she was ready. Rose checked her purse. She had used some of the loose change from the shoe box for the bus fare. If she walked through the foot tunnel under the river, she could catch a bus to Deptford, then one to Peckham.

Rose set out under a clear blue sky. She walked briskly, inhaling the sickly sweet peanut aroma of the British Oil and Cake Mills wharves. Here the cattle cake was processed and packed and loaded into the barges, their blackened hulls low in the water. She loved smelling the river. The docks had not been this busy since before the war.

The park still boasted a few green trees, their tops obscuring the tall white funnels of McDougall's Mill. Mudchute banks were bronzed with the sun, the dusty earth dry where everyone tried to grow a vegetable or two. Scruffy and bedraggled, the island basked in the heat like a barnacled old whale.

It was such a lovely day.

How could Eddie be in prison?

Why, oh, why had she let him sell that television to the Parkers?

The journey took much longer than expected. The buses were either late or crowded and her heels had developed blisters from all the walking she'd done.

The prison in Jebb Avenue was hidden behind tall grey

stone walls that reminded Rose of a castle without a moat. Along with the other visitors, Rose entered through a big wooden door and was confronted with uniformed guards. They carried keys, chains, locks and had unsmiling faces.

'Wait here,' she was told as the prison officer took the permit. Rose stood in line behind the other women, some of them with young children and babies. They all had an air of defeat about them, as though they had been waiting in the same queue for years.

Rose kept her gaze ahead. The conversation mostly consisted of four-letter words. She tried not to inhale the odour of soiled nappies and cheap perfume.

Finally they were led into a courtyard. The main prison doors were unlocked and locked behind them, shutting them well away from the living world. Here in the claustrophobic atmosphere there was an absence of colour, light and fresh air. The visitor's room smelt of tobacco as it reeked from the old, peeling walls. Combined with the disinfectant and the odour of unwashed clothing, the stench was stomach churning.

Some women were already seated at the small tables, talking to inmates. Rose sat on an empty chair and held her breath, trying not to feel faint. She drew her tongue over her lips and dabbed a handkerchief on her forehead.

She waited, heart pounding as more prisoners filed into the room. Their eyes searched the crowd anxiously. Women reached across the tables trying to take their men's hands. The children were restless and clambered everywhere making an unbearable noise.

Where was Eddie? Rose craned her neck to look for him. Why hadn't he appeared?

Then suddenly he stepped through the door, his gaze going over the gathering of wives, mothers and children filling up every inch of the room. Rose sat up, smiling at him, her heart pounding inside her chest. As he walked towards her, she saw him pull back his shoulders and beam that wide and wonderful smile at her. It diminished the shock of the rough grey uniform that covered his tall, slim body. As he sat down she saw the collar of the jacket was frayed and his shirt was crumpled and a wave of panic swept over her. Eddie was a smart dresser and would never be caught dead in such clothes. But his lovely dark hair, which was always immaculate was still combed neatly over his head, the rich thickness tapering down his neck making her want to reach out and stroke it.

'Eddie . . . Eddie . . .' was all she could say, reaching for his hands.

He grasped them tightly. 'You got here then,' he said as his continuing smile lit up every lonely corner inside her.

'It took me longer than I thought. I should have started earlier.'

'It doesn't matter. You're here now. It's good to see you, sweetheart.'

She couldn't speak. They held hands across the table and looked at each other with tears in their eyes. Rose knew she had to be strong.

'I don't know where to start,' she whispered breathlessly.

He laughed softly. 'That's unusual for you.' He still had his sense of humour. 'How are you and the girls? Tell me everything.'

'We're all right. We miss you.'

'And don't I bloody miss you!' He didn't speak for a moment, then it all came out in a rush. 'That custard and jelly was kosher, honest.'

'Yes, but where did you get it?'

'I bought it off a bloke called Syd who was drinking at the pub. He said he had some stuff in his van and I went out to have a look. All he wanted for the telly was twenty quid 'cos he needed the cash quick. So I got him down to ten and asked Ted, the landlord, if I could keep the telly in his lock-up out the back. Well, the following night, when I was walking home from the rub-a-dub I saw Leslie Parker. Talking we were, about this and that, and I happened to mention the telly. He said he'd buy it for Olga to keep her sweet. And that was that.'

'No it wasn't,' Rose said in a hurt tone. 'I tried to persuade you not to get involved.'

'I know. And I regret I didn't listen. It just seemed too good to pass up. That telly was a big mistake.'

A fifty pound mistake she was about to add but didn't as he looked at her with contrite eyes. 'I couldn't get to the magistrates' court,' she said regretfully. 'The girls were home from school.'

'I didn't expect you to be there,' he said with a sudden urgency. 'I got meself into this mess and I'll get meself out. Not that I'll get much help from that copper Williams who objected to bail because, he said, of the seriousness of the assault charge. But it wasn't assault, at least not on my part. I'd just gone back to the house after leaving you at Olga's and there was a dirty great thump on the door. When I opened it, they were all over me like a rash.'

'Did you tell the magistrate that?'

'No, this was just a hearing. You have to wait until you go before a proper judge and jury and then you can speak your piece. Meanwhile, me solicitor is trying for holy nail again.'

'Does he think he can get you bail this time?' Rose asked hopefully.

'Yeah, while I'm waiting for me case to come up.'

'When will that be?'

'Dunno. There's a bloke in here called Christie. The one that killed all them women? They expect his trial to last weeks, even months. It's messed up a lot of dates. Me solicitor is on the case.'

'How much does a solicitor cost?'

'If you ain't got no money, they can't get blood out of a stone, can they? And you've got to have legal representation, so they give you one. I told him I was innocent and I intend to speak me mind before the old Barnaby Rudge.'

She looked at him and imagined having him close against her, nuzzling his face into her neck as he loved to do and telling her silly but lovely things that made her feel a beautiful and wanted woman. She couldn't wait until they were reunited again and she promised herself she would buy something new to wear on his release. Then the thought of money brought her back to reality.

'Eddie, I understand about the telly,' she hesitated, 'but well, one night I looked under the gram—'

He leaned forward suddenly, giving a little shake of his head. 'Sh, Rose!' She watched his eyes swivel as a prison officer walked past. They waited until he was gone and he breathed out slowly. 'They've got ears like magnets round here.'

Rose glanced discreetly around, her eyes coming back to rest on his face. 'I found *it*,' she whispered, her gaze full of meaning.

He gave her a slow nod. 'Well I never. What made you look there?'

Rose shrugged. 'I was gonna dust underneath and suddenly remembered what you used it for years ago. I can tell you, I had a shock.'

He gave a funny little smile. 'What the eyes don't see the heart don't grieve over, don't they say?'

'But what if the police had found the floorboards?'

'My point entirely,' he agreed. 'I didn't want you implicated. You could look the coppers in the eye with a clear conscience.'

'What do you mean clear conscience?' Rose asked in dismay.

'Just a figure of speech love. The money's all legit.'

'But where did it come from?'

He drew back a little as though shocked she should ask such a question. 'Where do you think? Me business of course.'

'But five hundred pounds—'

'Sh! Keep your voice down,' he warned, glancing

round again. 'Sweetheart, trading ain't like the old days when you could barter and swap your stuff to make a few bob, now everyone wants cash up front.'

Rose hesitated. 'Like you asked Leslie Parker for fifty pounds?'

He shrugged casually at her intended sarcasm. 'Yeah, well, he got his money's worth. Do you know that some of them new fangled models go for as much as a ton?'

'But the telly was stolen, Eddie!'

He rolled his eyes. 'How was I to know that? The deal was done in good faith.'

Rose sighed. 'Oh, Eddie, you always come up with an answer.'

He reached over to tilt her chin. 'What's the matter, Rose sweetheart, don't you trust me?'

She melted, as usual. 'Of course I do, but so much has happened lately. And with you being in here—'

'What matters is you,' he cut her short as his fingers dropped away. 'A monkey will see you over till I'm back on me feet. And there'll be enough for me bail, too.'

Rose thought how hard it was going to be to tell him about giving Olga her money back now.

Eddie glanced at the big clock on the wall. 'The bugger is, time's almost up.'

'There must be something I can do to help,' she said as she searched his face. 'Can't you remember anything more about Syd?'

Eddie thought for a moment. 'Only that he works the markets. Watches and stuff is his line, but he never had a stall. Nothing regular like. Sells out of his Peter Pan.'

'Weren't you suspicious when he told you that?'

'Why should I be? Look at me, I don't have a stall, do I?'

Rose was tempted to point out that not having a legitimate place of work was what had caused all the trouble in the first place. 'What did he look like?' she asked instead.

'Well . . .' Eddie screwed up his eyes thoughtfully. 'My height. Older than me, forties I'd say. Long camel overcoat and titfer. Yeah, and a fistful of rings, whopping great knuckle-dusters and a massive bottle of Scotch on his wrist.'

'What make was the van?'

'Humber was it, or Morris? Darkish, could be brown – or blue. Or dark grey. To be honest, I didn't take much notice. I was keen to do the business.' Before she could ask another question, he leaned forward. 'Have the coppers been worrying you?'

She shook her head. 'No one's come round.'

'Was it in the papers?'

'Only the *Evening Gazette,* but it was just two lines,' Rose dismissed as she didn't want to reveal the trouble at school and add to his worries. 'No one was interested in anything except the Coronation.' Before he could ask more she said quickly, 'I miss you, Eddie.'

He swallowed. 'Me too.'

'Look at these.' Rose took Marlene's drawing and Donnie's note from her pocket and spread them on the table. 'They took ages doing them. Don't Marlene draw well and look at Donnie's lovely handwriting.'

He looked at them, pain and pride written over his face. 'Tell them,' he said hoarsely, 'I love them to bits and I'll stick 'em up in me cell. Well, you'd better tell them I've got me own room.' He grinned.

But she couldn't laugh. 'Oh Eddie. You shouldn't be here, locked up like this.'

'My feelings exactly,' he joked.

'I want to put my arms round you and cuddle you.'

'Now that's an offer I can't refuse.'

'I've been counting the hours till today. Your letter was so short. I was worried about you.'

'You know me, love, I can't think of what to say. 'Sides, they censor everything so watch what you write and don't ever mention the bees and honey.' He tapped the side of his nose and Rose knew he was referring to the five hundred pounds.

'When will I see you again?'

'I'll send you a permit in the post, but don't bring the girls.'

'Don't you want to see them?'

He reached for her hands. ''Course I do, but not like this. It's degrading. I don't want them here, as much as I long to see them. And anyway, it won't be long before I'm out.'

'I hope so.' Rose's eyes were filled with deep longing. 'I'll come when you send for me,' she assured him.

A loud buzzer sounded. 'That's it,' he sighed heavily.

'Oh Eddie, don't go!'

'I have to, sweetheart.' He quickly bent to press his lips against hers, all the pain of parting written in his eyes. She yearned to hold on to him but he stood up and walked away, his tall body clad in the unfamiliar grey prison garb. All the women and children filed out, eager to return to freedom.

Eddie disappeared through the door and she remained alone, knowing that she wouldn't be properly alive again until they were reunited.

'Mummy, did you see Daddy?'

'Yes.'

'Is he coming home?'

'He sends you his love and sends a cuddle. Like this.' She wrapped her daughters in her arms and kissed the tops of their heads, hoping they wouldn't ask again if he was coming home. She was lucky. They didn't.

'Did he like me picture?' Marlene asked.

'And my letter?' Donnie cried as she sat beside her sister at Rose's feet.

'Yes. He's going to stick them up on the wall.' Rose drew in a deep breath, relieved to be home. Or at least, almost home. They were sitting in Anita's front room; Alan and David on the couch and Benny in the chair by the fire. Anita had gone out to the kitchen to prepare supper.

'Auntie Anita made us a cake. A chocolate one. It was lovely.'

'I hope you said thank you.'

Marlene nodded. 'We had seconds too.'

'Go and see if you can help Auntie Anita in the kitchen.'

The girls ran off and Rose, seated on one of the wooden dining chairs, looked at Benny and the boys. 'Thank you for looking after them.'

'How's Eddie doing?' Benny asked looking at her solemnly with his dark, almost black eyes. His wiry black hair was beginning to recede, but he was still a handsome man.

'He's trying to get bail until his case comes up.'

'So he might be home soon?'

'I hope so.'

'It's a long way over by bus. I would have taken you in me lorry if I'd been local.'

She smiled. Benny was kind, but she couldn't impose. Today had been an education. Her heels were still smarting where she had worn no stockings and the shoes had rubbed holes in her skin. The buses had been slow or full up, forcing her to change several times. She had arrived late in spite of starting off before midday. All in all, it was an uncomfortable experience but she would go through it all again for Eddie.

'I wouldn't want to bother you, Benny.'

'It ain't no bother if I'm working this way.'

'What's the prison like, Auntie Rose?' David asked.

Rose glanced at Benny. Did he want his sons involved in knowing about such things? But they were all looking at her and she felt obliged to answer.

'Prison is not nice at all,' she said quickly. 'It's the last place on earth anyone would want to be.'

'What did Eddie say about the television?' Benny wanted to know.

'He said he bought it from a man called Syd at The Lock and Key and had no idea it was stolen.'

'But if that's the case,' Benny pointed out, 'the police should trace this Syd.'

'Yes, but the law has been very unhelpful. It was Inspector Williams who opposed bail.'

Benny shook his head slowly. 'I don't know anyone called Syd at The Lock. I'll ask Ted when I go up next.'

Rose sighed. 'If this Syd was selling stolen stuff he wouldn't want to be seen there again, would he?'

'No, but you never know.'

'We made sure the girls was all right, Auntie Rose.' Alan stood up and combed back his hair, causing his father to grimace.

Rose smiled. 'That's nice of you, Alan.'

'We're going out, now, Dad.'

'Where to?'

'Down the park.'

'Be in before dark.'

'But it's almost dark now.'

Benny stood up, his strong, broad-shouldered body filling the room. 'No it ain't. You've got an hour. And if you're not home before ten, watch your backs, because I'll be standing right behind you. With me belt.'

The two boys went out and Benny rolled his dark eyes. Rose smiled. 'I'm sure they can be trusted.'

'Well, I ain't about to take the chance.' He gave her a grin. 'Don't forget. I'll take you to Brixton next time, Rose. Just give me a few days notice. Eddie's been a good mate to me.'

'That's nice of you, Benny.'

Rose was left alone, listening to the sounds of the Mendoza household. Benny was off for a quick pint, the boys to chat up their girls. Anita came in with a tray, Donnie and Marlene following.

'Thank the Lord, we've got a bit of peace at last. Girls, give your mum a plate. Rose, help yourself to a sandwich.' Anita set the tray down on the table.

Rose grinned. 'This looks lovely.'

'Bet you haven't eaten all day.'

Rose hadn't had the stomach for food lately. In fact she'd been feeling very queasy, no doubt the result of all the shocks. But as she swallowed the soft white bread and tasty cheese, the food tasted like manna.

As they ate the two girls excitedly told her how David and Alan had escorted them home and entertained them with stories about the Travers sisters.

'More than I blooming get to know,' Anita scowled, winking at Rose.

'You girls can go out and play for half an hour if you want,' Rose offered and glanced at Anita.

'Thanks, Mum.' They jumped to their feet. 'Thank you for the nice tea, Auntie Neet.'

'Don't go far,' Rose warned as they bolted.

Anita grinned as she moved to sit next to Rose. 'Right, now you can tell me all about it.'

Rose relayed all the events of the afternoon now that the girls were out of earshot. As she talked, relaxing at last from the tension of the day, she felt so grateful to her neighbours.

What would she do without friends like these?

Chapter Seven

On Friday morning Rose went to buy bread at the corner shop. Charlie was serving, his lean frame bent over as he rummaged in the boxes behind the counter. Cissy and Fanny were in front of her but turned as the doorbell tinkled.

'Hello there, love.'

Rose nodded. She hoped she wasn't going to be drawn into conversation. But before anyone could speak there was a shout from the storeroom.

'For Gawd's sake, get a move on, Charlie.' Joan's command caused her husband to pass the bottom of his apron across his forehead. 'We've had a delivery and it needs to be brought in out of the rain.'

''Ang on a minute love, I'm trying to find them matches.' He lifted the wooden boxes that were stacked in front of the shelves and sighed. 'Where are those blessed things?'

'You need yer specs.' Cissy was watching the situation closely.

'No he don't,' Fanny disagreed as usual. 'Look, there they are.'

'Them's the lav rolls. Them soft ones that don't scratch your bum.'

'What a waste of money too,' Fanny sniffed. 'You can't do better than newspaper.'

'You gotta move with the times,' Cissy argued as the grocer unearthed more boxes. 'And at my age you like a bit of comfort.'

'Which you pay for,' Fanny noted, tugging the collar of her old tweed coat up to her ears. 'Don't make sense to me. Your arse is as hard as nails by now. You could wipe it with glass and you wouldn't feel a thing.'

'How would you know what me bum is like?' demanded Cissy coarsely. 'It ain't you that wipes it.'

'Who wants the matches?' Joan entered the shop breathlessly, carrying a brown paper bag.

'Me.' Cissy smiled broadly. 'Have you found where they were hid?'

'They weren't hidden.' Joan frowned at her husband who was now kneeling on the floor. 'They were in the storeroom where they always are.'

'In a nice safe place,' Fanny echoed.

'Which I didn't know about,' Charlie complained as he hoisted himself to his feet with difficulty.

'Yes you did.' His wife tipped the bag on the counter and the boxes of Swan Vestas toppled out. 'I've told you a dozen times where I keep them.'

'Yeah, but he's got a lot of things on his mind, ain't you Charlie?' Cissy threw a sly glance at Joan. 'I mean, shifting all this heavy stuff around and everything, he's on the go all day long I shouldn't wonder.'

'So am I, Mrs Hall, so am I,' Joan said sharply. 'I ain't sitting out the back with me feet up you know.'

'O' course love,' Fanny nodded, grabbing the matches and shovelling them in her pocket. 'I dunno how you do it.'

'It ain't easy.' Joan was watching where the matches went. 'And there's all the accounts to do as well.'

'You work too bloody hard,' Fanny commiserated, throwing a glance at Charlie. 'Why don't you get someone in to help?'

'She's got me, that's why,' Charlie growled.

'You ain't no spring chicken,' Cissy observed. 'You'll do yer back in lifting heavy.'

Rose was only half listening to the conversation. Her mind was still on the prison visit. The smell of the visiting room hadn't gone from her nose.

'That's three and six for you Mrs Grover and three and eight pence for you, Mrs Hall, including the matches,' Joan calculated, bundling their shopping into the straw baskets on the counter. She glanced at Rose apologetically. 'Won't be a mo, love.'

'That's all right.'

Cissy and Fanny struggled with their purses. 'Bung it on the slate, Joan. We'll settle up Friday.'

'There's already five bob outstanding,' Joan pointed out as they snapped closed the edges of their frayed shopping baskets.

'Don't we always pay up?'

Joan didn't reply and Charlie shuffled off.

As Cissy turned to leave she looked at Rose. 'We saw

the bit about your old man in the newspaper. What nick's he in?'

Rose was on the verge of giving the nosy parker short shrift, but in a way she was relieved that Eddie's name had finally been mentioned. 'Brixton,' she said and saw the look of delight spread across Cissy's face.

'I knew someone whose cousin was there,' the old woman crowed, tugging at Fanny's sleeve. 'It ain't no place to wind up either. It's like a whopping big dungeon inside and out, ain't it?'

With a growing sense of dread, Rose was forced to acknowledge just how accurate Cissy was and for a few seconds more she attempted to listen politely as her elderly neighbour regaled them with the gruesome details. But eventually Rose had to ignore the tirade and turned quickly to Joan. 'I'd like a small loaf, please.'

But Cissy was not done. 'Is 'e up before the beak soon? How long do you think he'll get?'

'Was that telly really stolen?'

'What you gonna do if 'e goes down for a long stretch?'

Then Fanny said her piece. 'Them girls of yours'll suffer. Poor little blighters. You hear of some kids who don't know their own fathers when they've done their time.'

Cissy nodded fiercely. 'Miss all their growing up some blokes do and then parents wonder why their kids go off the rails these days.'

Joan, with eyebrows raised, gave Rose a wink. 'Anything else love?'

Rose stared at the walls and shelves, the piles of tatty boxes behind the counter and the plastic container where the perishables were kept. She felt hot and dizzy, her mind becoming a blank. Despite her earlier resolution to put on a brave face, Cissy and Fanny had done more than enough damage to her equilibrium.

She swallowed. 'I . . . er, want . . . some potatoes, please.'

'Charlie!' yelled Joan. 'Bring in the spuds!'

Rose listened for the bell to go behind her. She was feeling very dizzy. Everything seemed to be on the move, including her legs, which had gone weak at the knees.

'Are you all right, love?'

She didn't know if she was or not. The next thing she knew everything went black. She didn't know how long she was out, but when she opened her eyes she was sitting on a sack of potatoes. 'Drink this slowly, gel.' It was Charlie, holding a cup to her mouth.

She sipped the cold water. 'What happened?'

'You fainted, ducks, and no wonder with them trouble-makers squawking like two constipated parrots. I've sent 'em on their way.' The elderly man hovered over her. 'How do you feel?'

'Better, thanks.'

'Charlie, wave this newspaper in her face.' Joan put her arm around her shoulders and eased her forward. 'Take it easy, ducks.'

'I don't know what came over me.'

Joan grabbed the paper from her husband. 'Wave it like a fan you silly sod, not a bloody bargepole.'

117

'I'm alright,' Rose smiled weakly.

'It was that daft pair,' Charlie accused again, nodding to the door. 'They're bloody menaces.'

'Don't take what they say to heart,' Joan advised gently. 'You'll get one or two round here who need a lesson in manners. But in the main, folk have good hearts in this neighbourhood.'

Rose nodded. 'Yes, I'm sure.'

'They catch you unawares, that's the trouble,' Joan murmured in a kindly fashion. 'I remember feeling just the same when our Dave ran off with that Mrs Watkins from Manington Road. Charlie and me had to harden up a bit with all the gossip going on.'

Rose looked up at the smooth round face staring down at her. 'That must have been awful.'

'It was five years ago now but seems like yesterday. And all the rotten things they said about Dave when he'd gone, still stabbing him in the back even though he wasn't around to defend himself. But as I say, the majority of people are kind souls round here and knew he was a good boy at heart, but for a while he could have been a mass murderer for what the few said about him.' Joan's eyes watered. 'You still blame yourself, you know, even if your kid is twenty-five and old enough to know better, like our Dave was. But he fell in love with a married woman and that was that.' Joan heaved another sigh. 'So you see, young lady, you must look to the future and leave the past behind.'

Rose stood up shakily. 'Yes, I'm trying.'

Charlie kept his hand under her arm. 'Do you want me to walk you home?'

'No, I'll manage, thanks.'

Joan handed her the loaf and a few potatoes heaped in a bag. 'They're on the house, love.'

Rose protested, but Charlie opened the door. 'Give them kids something nice to eat for dinner.'

When she got home she was sweating and still felt very peculiar. She placed the potatoes and bread in the larder and sat in the front room, hauling in breath.

Everyone knew about Eddie now, since they'd all read the *Evening Gazette* and gossip was inevitable. Rose didn't want to blame Eddie, especially as he had seen the error of his ways. As Joan had said, the past is over and done with, the future is what counts. But Rose had to admit to herself she still felt annoyed and, to an extent, deceived. Was her reaction because of the money? He had maintained she'd never wanted to know about his business affairs and he had a point. But there could have been a dreadful catastrophe if the police had lifted those floorboards. If Eddie had been falsely accused of assault what would they have dreamed up over the five hundred pounds?

Later, she peeled the potatoes ready for dinner, then dusted. Afterwards she had a step to polish. And polish it she would.

She had just applied a coat of Red Cardinal to the front step when a pair of brown shoes appeared beside it. They were shiny and well heeled and she looked up slowly, noting the carefully pressed trousers of the smart dark suit. The clean-shaven face above was unfamiliar to Rose. She climbed to her feet.

He smiled. 'My name is Bobby Morton. I wondered if you would like to read one of these?' He held out a sheet of paper.

'What is it?'

'The fact is I've taken a shop in Amethyst Way and thought I'd come round and introduce myself.'

'So you're not a tally man, then?'

He took a few moments for this to sink in, then laughed. 'Do I look like one?'

'You can never tell these days.'

He smiled pleasantly. 'All I want to do is talk about my shop and put the word out that I've opened.'

'Is it the one that was boarded up?'

He nodded. 'Yes, you know it?'

'I take the kids to the newsagents sometimes to buy sweets.'

'Well, I hope you'll stop by on your next visit and have a look round.'

Rose glanced suspiciously at the pile of papers in his hand. 'What are you selling?'

'I'm an electrician and starting off in a small way by doing repairs. But I hope to stock things soon like vacuum cleaners, washing machines and televisions. The big stores like Gamages are selling them like hot cakes. Especially televisions which have really caught on now.'

Rose thrust the leaflet back. 'I don't want any, thank you – especially a television!'

'Well, take the leaflet. It won't bite.'

'No,' Rose refused emphatically. 'I'm not interested.'

'But why?' The young man frowned. 'Did you know

that it's possible to buy a television on hire purchase these days? After the initial deposit of ten pounds, the weekly repayments are only one and six pence. And for all the enjoyment the family would reap, you'd consider the purchase well worthwhile.'

'Look, I don't want to be rude,' Rose said coolly, 'but the answer's no.'

'And I thought you looked the friendly sort,' he sighed dismally.

'Well, you thought wrong. And as I have two young children and a house to run, I'm very busy—'

'Yes, I can see that, and I'm sorry to intrude,' he apologized in a sincere tone. 'But you see, I really believe in everyone having a bite of the apple, not just a privileged few. A woman shoulders the lion's share of household chores. Washing, ironing, cleaning and sweeping. It's about time, don't you think, she had assistance?' He fanned the paper gently in the air. 'Just read one of these in your spare time.'

'I haven't got any,' Rose said grudgingly, though she admired him for his persistence. In a vague way he reminded her of Eddie. He was nothing like him to look at, as blond as Eddie was dark with deep-set blue eyes that held none of Eddie's natural humour, but he was trying hard to sell against impossible odds.

To her surprise he nodded fiercely. 'You couldn't have said a truer word. Time is of the essence for busy housewives.'

She had to smile. 'Don't you ever give up?'

'Not when I think I can help.'

121

'You haven't helped me so far,' she replied with a straight face. 'You've just stopped me polishing my step.'

He looked down, then moved back. 'Ah, yes the step. Well, Mrs—?'

'Weaver,' Rose provided letting go of the door and placing her hands on her hips. 'Now you're going to tell me you've got a miracle machine up your sleeve for polishing steps?'

He laughed then, a wide smile creasing across his face. 'I'd be a millionaire by now if I could claim that distinction. But I do have something else to offer. It's called elbow grease, plain and simple.' And, before she could protest, he got down on his haunches, dropping his leaflets down by the wall and grabbing her duster. 'I used to do this for my mother every Sunday morning,' he told her as he polished briskly. 'Only our step was white and she insisted on Dad and me and me sisters stepping over it whenever we came in or went out, not on it. When we forgot we'd get a right rollicking. Now, for the final touch.' He took a handkerchief from his pocket and spat on it, then rubbed the stone very hard.

'Don't! You'll stain it!' Rose cried out in alarm.

'A few years ago that might have been true, Mrs Weaver. But not now. This handkerchief would come up like new in a washing machine.' His blue eyes were twinkling. 'In fact this has given me an idea. All those steps along there need polishing, right? And what with? Dusters, yes? Now what's the best way to clean a filthy duster?'

'To buy one of your washing machines no doubt,' Rose answered dryly.

'See your duster there, I'll take it away and clean it for you. Ten to one you won't recognize it again.'

Rose shook her head slowly. 'No thanks, I'll keep me duster and you keep your washing machine, but I give you ten out of ten for trying.'

'Oh well, some you win some you lose,' he concluded happily to himself, and she watched in amusement as he returned his concentration to her step. 'Not a bad job if I say so myself,' he nodded with a last flourish.

'You'd better not put that hanky back in your pocket. It's filthy and so are your hands.'

He waved them comically in the air. 'Oh, that'll soon come off.'

'Not without soap and water it won't.' She couldn't help laughing as he rose to his feet inspecting the bright red stains on his fingers and making a face.

'Ah well, it's nice to have a laugh,' he chuckled as he picked up his leaflets and left red finger-marks all over them. 'And you've got a lovely smile. Really smashing.'

Rose knew it was pure flattery, but she took pity on him. 'You'd better come in and wash those hands before you leave. You can't walk up the road like that. The kitchen's through there. I'm leaving this door wide open, mind.'

'To let in the breeze no doubt,' he said dumping his leaflets on the ground and entering the hall.

'No, to let you out again. So be on your best behaviour. The soap's under the sink, behind the curtain.'

'Where?'

Reluctantly she went after him. 'Behind this curtain here.'

'All right, I'll find it.'

'No you won't, you're a man.'

They looked at one another. Suddenly they were both laughing.

'Yes, that does put me at a disadvantage,' he agreed, the smile lingering on his lips as she stared into his eyes. A disturbing little flutter in her stomach caused her to breathe sharply in. They stood quietly then, in the silence of the kitchen, the bar of soap still in her hand. Rose felt a warm wave of pleasure flow over her as he looked at her, the blue of his pupils turning to slate. Then suddenly she realized she was standing there like a fool and her pleasure turned to embarrassment. 'Here,' she said abruptly, 'take it.'

He reached out and the tips of his fingers drew lightly across her skin. She snatched her hand away as if she'd been scalded.

'Don't worry, I'm harmless,' he said quickly. 'You can boot me out as soon as I'm clean.'

'Don't worry, I will.' Rose turned and folded a towel that was hanging over the back of a chair. She felt distinctly strange and kept her face averted as Bobby Morton splashed his hands vigorously under the cold water.

A minute later he was drying them on the towel she had just taken so much care to fold. 'You know, you could fit a washing machine in nicely under there.' He nodded to the draining board.

Rose rolled her eyes once more. 'I told you, I'm not interested.'

'Can I ask why are you so opposed to washing

machines?' he asked curiously, handing her back the towel. This time she kept her fingers well out of reach.

'I'm not. It's televisions I don't like.'

'Pardon me?'

'I don't like televisions,' Rose repeated, wondering why she was having so much difficulty with an ordinary sort of conversation. Was it because her instincts told her that Bobby Morton wasn't exactly an ordinary kind of visitor?

'I'm sorry to hear that,' he answered, with a perplexed look on his face. 'As I said, they're very popular now. Especially with families.'

'Not this family they're not,' she snapped. 'Now, if you're finished?' Without waiting for a reply she marched along the hall, pulling the front door open. 'Don't forget your leaflets, either.'

Still looking baffled, her visitor walked past her. He piled his leaflets into his arms, then stood erect. 'Well, thank you for being so hospitable.' His long fair lashes reminded Rose of a big, friendly puppy just waiting to be acknowledged. 'And I know what you're thinking, that all I'm after is a sale, and maybe that was true – initially. But you've been kind enough to give me your time—' He stopped and added shyly, 'and your lovely smile. To be honest, I haven't even managed to get one lead. So, well, just – thank you.'

Rose felt awful now. She had been rather rude and he looked so dejected. He was thanking her for a smile – which cost nothing except the effort. The truth was, if he'd been an old man, trying to earn a few pennies towards his retirement, she might even have offered him a cup of tea. 'All right, I believe you,' she conceded, 'though thousands wouldn't. By the way, what do you mean by a "a lead"?'

'It's where someone says they're interested in one of your appliances,' he explained eagerly. 'Then you say, would you like a demonstration? They say how much is a demonstration and I say, no cost at all. Then they say they'll ask their husbands and before they change their mind I ask what time's convenient to call again? It's all a lead-up, you see, to a sale.'

Rose laughed. 'Well, I'm afraid you're going away empty-handed from here. Despite me shining step I still don't want to buy anything. You know, you might have done better with mops and brooms.'

'Yes, possibly,' he nodded. 'But I had this dream, you see. When I was in the desert with sand right up to me eyeballs, I promised myself if I ever survived Rommel's lot, I'd do something special with me life, not fritter it away. So when I was demobbed I trained with the electricity company and Bob's your uncle, I discovered me calling.'

'You were in the desert?' she asked in astonishment.

'Yes. North Africa.'

'It was rotten out there.'

'Yeah, well, it was hot,' he joked lightly.

'My husband was in France,' Rose replied. 'He had a rotten time too. But I always knew he'd come home.'

Again, they stood in silence, but this time no words were needed to convey the emotions that these memories evoked.

'He was a lucky bloke,' Bobby Morton said at last,

looking deep into her eyes. 'Lucky to have the girl of his dreams waiting for him. Perhaps that was the reason he did make it home safely, eh?'

Rose could hear the sounds that made up her life; a horse and cart somewhere, children yelling, a boat's hooter, a distant wireless set. But as she stared into the young man's gaze, her ears were suddenly full of her own heart's heavy and excited beat.

'Well, I'd best be on my way.' He paused a few seconds longer, then turned.

Rose couldn't stop herself. 'Wait! Wait a minute, er . . . Bobby!'

He swivelled round and stood uncertainly on the pavement.

'Give me one of those things. I'll read it if I can find the time.' She held out her hand. 'But taking it doesn't mean to say I'm interested in buying anything.'

He walked towards her and handed her a leaflet. Rose grasped it almost afraid to look into his face as she took it. But she did and her tummy flipped all over again.

Bobby Morton said nothing, just smiled and it was Rose who ended the moment, hurrying indoors to close the door without looking back.

Placing the leaflet on the coat-stand, she waited, holding her hands over her burning cheeks. The temptation was irresistible. She hurried into the front room and looked out of the window. A tall, fair haired, broad-shouldered figure was standing outside the Parkers'. Would Olga answer the door? He waited, but after no reply, swivelled slowly on his heel.

Rose dodged back behind the curtain as he glanced across the road. Her heart was thumping heavily and she swallowed. A few minutes later she dared to peep again. The street, as far as she could see, was empty. Bobby Morton had gone, but Rose was still, as her mum would have remarked, 'all of a fluster'.

Chapter Eight

It was Saturday evening and Rose was in the backyard, sweeping the cracked paving stones. The girls sometimes played hopscotch on them and the chalk marks were still visible from their last game. The worn brown grass in between sprouted dandelions and thistle and a few brave daisies had unwisely reared their pretty heads.

The soft and balmy air made her think of her own childhood evenings spent playing with Em in this yard, just as Donnie and Marlene did. Only then her father had planted dahlias and snapdragons mixed with wallflowers that seemed to grow without any trouble at all under his supervision. Unlike her own children who had carte blanche when it came to the yard, Rose recalled with a smile her father's strict orders as to where they could play and where they could not.

On Sunday mornings she and Em would walk to Granny's house at Blackwall. Her grandfather smoked a clay pipe which had seemed to be an extension of his moustache and long grey beard. The living quarters of their elderly relatives had consisted of the ground floor of a small terraced house. It was here her mother had been born as the eldest of seven children though only three had survived. Here the family had lived until her mother left home to marry her father who worked in the offices of the Port of London Authority.

The memory of their visits was still clear in her mind. She could taste, even now, the distinctive carraway-seed cake that was baked especially for their visits. The ritual was always the same: elevenses taken in the kitchen, a big room dominated by a huge black cooking range. The table spread filled most of the room, its wooden top scrubbed daily with Sunlight soap by Gran dressed in her long black skirt and white pinafore. On top of the table stood the cake and best china cups and Gran would pour rich dark tea from a heavy brown teapot that seemed to contain far in excess of their needs.

Granddad would sit puffing away, his sombre gaze never leaving their faces as they ate the wedges of cake that Gran served up. Granddad rarely spoke, just puffed and watched. It had been Gran who had asked after her mother and tried to extract what little information she could obtain from her two awe-struck grandchildren.

Rose smiled to herself as she set aside the broom and leaned against the fence, once more recalling the yard in her father's time. It would have been unheard of then to threaten the safety of the flowers with any larking about. She and Em had always played, as Marlene and Donnie were doing now, in the street. Those were the carefree days of the mid-1930s when the islanders were still oblivious of the horror of war to come.

Rose wondered if her dad and mum were watching

now from some silver-lined cloud and feeling proud of their two granddaughters, even if they had wrecked the yard he had tried so hard to cultivate. Her parents had never seen her children, never held their newborn bodies in their loving arms. They would have made the perfect grandparents, but it was not meant to be. Even so, Rose had a faith that went beyond every day life and felt certain they were there, guarding and guiding her girls.

Just then a loud curse came from behind her and Rose turned to see Anita pushing her bike through the kitchen door and into the garden.

'Hello, love. I'm getting too old for this lark,' Anita muttered as she leaned her bicycle against the fence, tugging her overalls from the saddlebag and wiping her damp forehead with the back of her wrist.

'At least the rain kept off,' Rose commented looking up at the overcast sky. It had grown humid and still. 'You should catch a bus to work and give yourself a break.'

'Saving up, ain't I?' Anita bent down and squeezed the front tyre. 'Sod it, I've got a slow puncture.' She gave the wheel a token kick, then grinned at Rose. 'Did you get to market today?'

'No. Thought I'd give it a miss and do some housework.'

'When's dinner, Mum?' Alan called from the back door.

Anita glowered at her son. 'I was hoping you had it there on the table awaiting me arrival,' she yelled, hands on hips.

'I gotta go out soon,' Alan yelled back, inured to his mother's wit.

'Where?'

'Just out.'

'You're going nowhere till your father comes in.'

'Aw, but it's Saturday night!'

'I don't care if it's Christmas,' Anita bellowed back. 'You'll see him first.'

'Can we make ourselves a sandwich, then?' David hovered on the doorstep, scowling under his mop of black hair.

'No. You'll spoil your appetites. Stick the kettle on and make your mother a cup of tea. And if you're looking for something to do you can peel the spuds on the draining board.' She turned back to Rose, arching her brows. 'Boys, who'd have 'em?'

Rose smiled. 'Where's Benny today?'

'On a long haul. He left Thursday night with a lorry full of tyres to be delivered to Bristol. Then he had to load another lot and go up north.'

'Does he sleep in his lorry?'

'Yeah, he kips wherever he can, at the side of the road or in a lay-by. They ain't choice jobs. A lot of lorry drivers avoid the heavy, back breaking stuff as now there's all these mechanical lifters. But Benny always says as long as the goods aren't nailed to the ground, he'll lift 'em, whatever it takes.'

'Can't one of the boys help?'

Anita snorted. 'They can hardly lift themselves out of bed in the mornings to eat their breakfast let alone lift a lorry-load of tyres.'

Rose admired Benny for the hard work he put in with

his lorry. He worked from dawn till dusk, sometimes seven days a week, to justify a windfall his mother's uncle had left him two years ago. He'd taken a risk and bought a lorry determined to use his initiative to improve his family's standard of living. Of paramount importance to the Mendozas was their overdue holiday. They'd never had a proper holiday before, only stayed in Wales with relatives. Butlin's Holiday Camp was their dream and Rose knew every penny was saved up for it. 'You look a bit peaky girl.' Anita frowned at Rose's pale face.

Rose laughed softly. 'I had a funny five minutes in Joan's yesterday. I think it was listening to Cissy and Fanny in front of me.'

Anita nodded vigorously. 'Anyone would feel lousy listening to them.'

Rose felt a little flush creep over her cheeks as she thought about what she might say next. 'I took it out later on someone who was calling door to door,' she said hesitantly glancing sideways at her friend. 'He said he'd just opened a shop up the Parade.'

'What's he selling?'

'Televisions.'

'*Televisions!*' Anita's face was incredulous.

'Televisions and washing machines, that sort of thing. I gave him short shrift but then before I could close the door he was down on his knees polishing me step and telling me the hanky he was using would come up good as new in one of his washing machines.'

Anita's jaw fell. 'You didn't say you'd buy one?'

''Course not.'

'They try anything to get you on hire purchase.'

Rose shrugged. 'He didn't mention that.'

'I didn't get a leaflet through my door.'

'You were all out, I expect.'

Anita smirked. 'You was watching then?'

'Well, I did see him go over to Olga's. But she didn't answer.'

'She'd probably have clocked him one if he mentioned a telly,' Anita spluttered. 'It's a wonder you didn't an' all.'

'I felt, well, a bit sorry for him,' Rose replied cautiously, aware that her friend was studying her intently. 'He fought in North Africa and the thought of opening a shop when he came home was all that kept him going. I relented a little after he told me that.'

'Like a lot of them poor buggers, just trying to make a living,' Anita agreed, then quirked an eyebrow. 'What's he look like?'

Rose shrugged indifferently. 'I don't really remember.'

'You're blushing!' Anita gasped. 'I bet he chatted you up!'

Rose went scarlet and Anita threw back her head and laughed. 'Well, good luck to you, girl. No harm in a bit of attention from the opposite sex.'

'It wasn't nothing, Neet. He was just a really nice bloke.' Rose giggled. 'And yes, to answer your question truthfully, he wasn't a bad looker.'

Anita hooted. 'Well next time he calls just make sure you send him round to me.'

'Oh, he won't be calling again, I'm sure,' Rose said a little worriedly. 'I don't think Eddie would like that.'

'Talking of lover boy, you've heard nothing from him, I suppose?'

'No, nothing.' Rose had forgotten her troubles for a little while then as she thought of Eddie in prison her heart sank again.

'Well, I'm off to cook dinner for those lazy sods.'

'Yeah and I'd better finish the yard.'

A few minutes later, Rose had returned to her sweeping and was thinking about the laugh she'd had with her friend. Suddenly the girls came running from the house. 'Can we sweep too?' they shrieked.

Rose handed them the broom. 'Well now, what a good idea!'

For a while they had some fun in the evening sunshine chasing around with the broom and making a din. Rose tried to ignore the unpleasant sensation in her stomach that kept returning every now and then and catching her short. She made a note to buy a bottle of Milk of Magnesia to stop the unsettled feeling, probably a result of all the upset.

That night as she lay in bed she thought of her visit to Eddie. She had been shocked at the cramped and dismal conditions of the prison. She wanted to put her arms around him, to hold the man she loved and to hear him tell her everything would be all right. She snuggled down on her pillow and fell asleep wondering if Eddie was thinking of her. She had only flirted a little with Bobby Morton, but even so, she felt a bit guilty!

Two days later, Rose turned on the wireless to hear that John Christie was standing trial at the Old Bailey. A moment later there was a bang at the front door and she went to open it. Alan Mendoza was standing there.

'Mum said to listen to the radio,' he told her breathlessly. 'It's about that bloke who murdered all them women.'

'Yes, I heard,' Rose nodded. 'Tell Mum I'll be in soon.'

When she got back the announcer was ending with the news that John Christie was pleading insanity, a major development in his trial. A few minutes later Rose hurried round to the Mendoza's.

'What do you think of that?' Anita shouted from the kitchen. 'Poor bloody Eddie, in with a loony.'

Rose found Anita and her son bent over the radio, which was sitting on the plastic covered kitchen table. Unlike Rose's heavy old valve cabinet, Anita's radio was a small brown Bakelite model with a brass knob to tune the programmes. The kitchen was minus its usual fog since Anita's resolution to stop smoking was still taking effect. The bad news for Benny was that she had forbidden him to smoke in the house too.

Anita turned down the volume. 'Blimey, they think he gassed his victims and stashed the bodies in cupboards and under floors, anywhere in fact, there was space.'

Rose shuddered. 'How gruesome.'

'Once he was a special copper too,' Alan said straddling a chair and enjoying the macabre story. 'Must have been right off his trolley even then.'

'He knew what he was doing all right,' Anita pronounced darkly. 'He was clever enough to fool the police.'

'What do you think, Auntie Rose?'

'He still hasn't been convicted,' Rose answered thoughtfully, wondering if people had already judged Eddie as guilty. 'And if he did perpetrate such terrible crimes he can't be sane, can he?'

'So you don't reckon he should be hanged?' Alan asked aggressively.

'I don't think two wrongs make a right, Alan.'

Alan looked sceptical. 'Not even when he's murdered so many women!'

'Here, you clown,' his mother interrupted, wagging a finger in his face, 'stop pestering the girl.'

'I reckon he deserves all he gets,' her son stated fiercely.

'And I'm wondering why you're at home skiving when you should be at school.'

'You know why,' her son retorted. 'I've left.'

'Not in my book, you haven't,' Anita rounded, pink spots appearing on her cheeks. 'Not till you find yerself a job.'

'Yeah, well, I'm looking, aren't I?'

Anita lifted her hands in exasperation. 'Then why ain't you out there, elbowing the competition out the way?'

'All right, muvver. I'm going, I'm going.' Alan stood up, his broad shoulders sagging as he pushed his big hands in his pockets. 'What about bus fare?'

Anita's eyes nearly popped out of her head. 'What about it?'

'I'll need some if I go up West.'

'I go up every bloody day on me bike, don't I? And I'm geriatric compared with you,' his mother said scornfully as her son slouched out of the room. She turned to Rose with a deep sigh. 'Talk about spoon fed.'

'He's only young, Neet. Have you forgotten what it was like to be fifteen?'

'You're a soft touch you are,' Anita murmured, nodding to the chair. 'Sit down and take the weight off your feet.'

Rose did so, eager to discuss her new idea. 'Coming up the market on Saturday? I've got something special in mind.'

Anita rolled her eyes. 'What?'

'I'm going to try to find this Syd.'

Anita looked startled. 'The bloke who sold Eddie the telly?'

'Eddie said he was wearing a hat and one of them long camel overcoats. He also had knuckle-duster rings and a big watch on his wrist. And there was the van of course. A Humber or a Morris, dark in colour.'

Anita shrugged. 'Well, who knows? We might be lucky.'

Rose nodded thoughtfully. At least she would feel she was doing something towards helping her husband.

On Thursday, after school, Rose was met by two long faces.

'What's wrong with you two?' Had there been things said again? Rose wondered anxiously.

'Dinner was disgusting.' Donnie turned up her nose. 'It was all sloppy.'

Rose was relieved the trouble wasn't about Eddie. 'Sloppy food won't hurt for one day.'

Marlene dragged her heels. 'I didn't eat mine.'

'Well, you should have. You know I don't approve of waste, not when there are so many people in the world who are starving.' Rose knew full well though, that any food set in front of her daughter, even the worst of school dinners, would not be ignored.

'I think they put glue in it,' Donnie grinned mischievously at her mother. 'To keep us quiet in lessons.'

Rose raised her eyebrows. 'I bet you aren't quiet, though.'

'My mouth ain't got any glue it,' Marlene shouted and ran off. 'I can talk as loud as I like.'

'We don't need any proof of that,' Rose chuckled, knowing her daughter well.

'Can we buy some sweets?' Donnie asked as they drew close to home. 'I've got two lemonade bottles and I'll get thruppence back on each of them. Marlene and me can share it between us.'

Rose nodded. 'I don't see why not.' Then she realized what she'd said. The newsagent's was next to Bobby Morton's shop. Did she have the nerve to look in and say hello?

For once it was a lovely summer's evening and an eggshell sky stretched high above the island like a ceiling of soft blue silk. They collected the bottles from home and walked up to the Parade which comprised a post office, grocer's and newsagent's. And now, Rose thought ruefully, an electrical shop.

The girls made a beeline for their sweets. In February, the government had ended sweet rationing and although sugar itself wasn't to be de-rationed until September, the children now had their choice of a wide variety of confectionery. For over twelve years favourites such as toffee apples, nougat, liquorice, boiled sweets and chocolates had been available only on coupons. But for the last five months the newsagent at the Parade had extended his shelves of rare delights for his young patrons' benefit.

Rose paused to look in the shop next door. The window was full of washing machines and vacuum cleaners. Outside had been given a coat of paint. It looked very bright and cheerful, just like Bobby Morton himself. At that moment a van pulled up at the kerb beside her with a screech of brakes. She turned to see the driver clamber out, dragging with him two big bundles of newspaper tied with string.

'Guilty as hell,' he called to Rose as he crossed the pavement in front of her.

'Who is?' Rose asked as she followed him in and he dropped his burden at the base of the counter.

'Christie, of course,' he replied, staring at her in surprise. 'Never was any doubt though, was there?'

Rose glanced down at the headlines clearly visible under the criss-cross of thick, knotted twine. *Christie Guilty*. She swallowed. The case had been expected to last weeks, months even, but was over in four days! Rose read on. The jury had shown no mercy and decided he was not mad at all, just evil. His sentence was death by hanging.

Rose forgot all about Bobby Morton. There was just one thing on her mind now. Would Eddie's case come up sooner now that Christie's was over?

★

The following day the name Christie was on everyone's lips. Rose found it a depressing subject, but Anita said her boys and Benny had lapped up every detail.

'The police think he done a lot of other women in,' Anita was saying as they walked to market, the two girls running ahead as usual. 'But he's not owning up. He's too crafty for that.'

'But how do you commit such terrible acts of violence if you aren't insane?' Rose asked, bewildered.

'The same could be said of Hitler,' Anita pointed out as they turned into Cox Street. 'But he was as sane as you or I.'

'So you think he should hang?'

''Course I do. Though no doubt he'll appeal. He may even get away with it yet. There's always a chance right up to the last minute, apparently.'

'How do you know?'

Anita turned to stare at Rose. 'Ain't you been reading the papers, gel?'

Rose shook her head. 'No. It's too upsetting.'

'Well, your Eddie will know all the goss, I'm sure.'

Rose hoped he didn't. All she wanted to do when she next saw him was to tell him how much she loved and missed him. And try to find a way out of their problems. She felt sickened by what was printed in the papers.

Also it disturbed her that Eddie would be subject to the same powerful system of justice that could take a man's life. A jury of twelve men and women who knew nothing of Eddie's good character would hold his future

141

in their hands. Would they show clemency to a loving father and husband? Or would they accept his guilt on the evidence of the police?

'Penny for them?' Anita was staring at her as they approached the fruit and veg stall.

Rose blinked. 'I was thinking about Eddie's case.'

'Worrying won't help,' Anita reminded her gently. 'Now shouldn't we be on the lookout?'

Rose came back to the present. 'I'll go to the right and you go left, that way we'll not miss anyone.'

'Suits me,' Anita nodded. 'Meet you in half an hour at Alf's.'

But half an hour later they had walked the length and breadth of the market and no one of Syd's description had been spotted.

'No luck,' Anita sighed. 'What about you?'

'None.' Rose shrugged dispiritedly.

'Where are the girls?'

'Over at the toy stall. Come on, I'm hungry. Let's have something to eat.'

'Hello me darlings,' Alf welcomed, wiping his greasy hands over his apron. 'What can I do you for today?'

'Cheeky,' Anita grinned, batting her eyelids.

'Four sausage baps with onions and tomato sauce, two mugs of tea and two lemonades, please,' Rose ordered.

'Coming right up, me lovelies.'

The smell of frying onions filled the air as they watched the large figure of Alf do a conjuring trick with the food. Steaming sausage baps, greasy onions, sauce, scalding tea and lemonade all suddenly appeared. 'Two and eight to you girls,' he grinned, pushing a not very clean cloth over the grubby counter.

Rose dived into her purse. 'Thanks, Alf.' She glanced at Anita. 'The shoe box can stand it.'

Anita licked her lips. 'Are you sure?'

Rose nodded, then looked up at Alf once more. 'You don't happen to know anyone by the name of Syd round here?'

'Who wants to know?' Alf asked suspiciously.

'He sold my Eddie the telly that was stolen.'

Alf appeared to be turning this over in his mind before replying. 'I know half a dozen Syd's maybe more, but don't everyone?'

'That's true,' Anita conceded. 'But this Syd's got a dark coloured van and you don't see many of them round here.'

Alf tipped a basin of onions into the fat and nodded across the road. 'You could ask Dol and her old man over on the clothes. She's been here the longest. But don't hold yer breath – she ain't quite with it these days.'

Rose knew Dol. She was with it enough to demand good money for her second-hand clothes. Anita nudged Rose's arm and grinned.

But neither Dol nor her husband were very forthcoming. Either they didn't know, Anita commented, or wouldn't tell. Anita wanted to ask round, but Rose felt it would be unwise and even more risky to ask about Syd. She didn't want to raise anyone's suspicions that they were on the lookout. Market traders were very canny about giving information away since much of their business was done off the books.

'If we can't ask, we've come to a dead end,' Anita sighed, watching Donnie and Marlene gulp their lemonades.

'No sense in drawing attention,' Rose decided. 'He ain't here, that's for sure.'

'Yeah, let's go home,' Anita conceded.

Rose sighed. 'I've got to help Eddie somehow.'

'What can you do, though? There's dozens of markets.'

'I could try them all.'

Anita looked shocked. 'You're joking!'

'No, far from it.'

'But your feet'll drop off.'

'The exercise will do me good.'

Anita grabbed her arm. 'Tell you what, you can use our Alan's old bike. The crossbar's lower than average and it ain't got any brakes to speak of, but the tyres are good. And it's got a pump. You could tie a tea cosy over the saddle.'

Rose was delighted. 'Are you sure Alan won't want it?'

'He wouldn't be seen dead on it these days.'

'Well then, I can wheel it to school in the mornings and ride off from there.'

'You really are serious about this, aren't you?'

Rose nodded. 'It's better than doing nothing.'

'Well, I give you full marks for trying,' Anita shrugged lightly. 'Now, I want you and the girls to come to dinner tomorrow.'

Rose glanced at her friend. 'But it's Sunday.'

Anita rolled her expressive eyes. 'That's why I'm asking. I'll buy a nice joint from the butcher. Benny's at home for a change.'

Rose didn't want to impose as it was Benny's only day off and he was lucky to get that. 'I'd planned to write to Eddie and Em tomorrow,' she excused, aware her friend was offering to give up her valuable time and, more importantly, a rare family Sunday. 'But thanks anyway.'

'Shame,' Anita said generously. 'Another time perhaps.'

'Yes,' Rose nodded, 'when there's four of us again.'

''Course, love. And it won't be long I'm sure.'

Rose smiled wistfully at the thought of Eddie tucking in to his Sunday dinner, giving her a wink over a pile of roast spuds that vanished from his plate in the blink of an eye.

Chapter Nine

Eddie opened his eyes and tried to remember where he was and how he got there. One part of his brain didn't want to know, needed to fade back into unconsciousness again, while the other part struggled to surface from the limbo into which he had fallen.

Where had it all begun? He could remember slopping out; carbolic soap and soiled clothes still reeked in his nose together with the sight of his fellow inmates in vests and baggy prison trousers, their towels slung over their shoulders. One of these men had approached him. He remembered the smile on his face, a smile that had not reached his cold, hard eyes and was anything but friendly.

A sharpness had dug into his ribs forcing him to shuffle backwards, distancing himself and the man with the smile from the watchful screws. Finally he'd found himself in the piss-pot recess. It was then that his memory played tricks. Had he heard a voice whispering? Or was it a sixth sense that made him turn? Too late though, as his arms were pulled back and a blow indented the pit of his stomach. More blows followed and last night's corned beef and mash had flowed upward and over the wet floor.

He lay face down in the urine, briefly astonished at the violence. Wondering how a beating of such force could take place without intervention. After that came darkness.

He'd woken up in the hospital wing, a guard beside him. He'd endured an interrogation, denying fiercely that he had cut another prisoner, drawn blood from the man whose smile had been the precursor to incredible pain. After a while his folly was clear. They required no answers. The system was at work. You heard nothing, said nothing, saw nothing.

Eddie looked round the small, dark cell into which he had been transferred; Punishment Block, solitary confinement with nothing but a mattress, a jug and piss pot to keep a man company and the wait that would stretch endlessly ahead.

He was beginning to understand. He was here because others wanted him here. From the moment Syd had appeared in his life, events had been orchestrated and, no doubt, would be again. Just as for the last two years he'd been a fool, believing he could turn a loss into a win with just one sure-fire tip, getting more and more into debt as he did so. Norman Payne had offered him ready cash, made it seem possible, even *easy*, to provide for his family in the way he'd seen other men provide. Men whom he'd envied so deeply that their wealth had obsessed him.

He lifted himself with difficulty from the mattress and slung his legs on to the cold floor. His body ached unbearably but his mind was in deeper torment. He dropped his head in his hands. What had he done? How had he got mixed up with the likes of Norman Payne?

Suddenly there were voices. Feet approaching. The door of the cell banged open. Eddie stared up at them and instinctively shrank.

'Edward John Weaver?'

The voice was an outsider's, brimming with disdain. Eddie squinted up into the shaft of light let in by the open door. Silhouettes. Four of them. They moved forward, surrounding him.

'I represent the Board of Visitors.'

He blinked, trying to see which one was speaking.

'I'm here to ask if you wish to make a complaint?'

Eddie realised he wanted to laugh. Complaints? No. He was loving his own six feet of hell.

The small man, the central figure, moved forward, all upright and shoulders back. 'Come now, have you anything to say?'

Eddie stared at the other three, the guards with their silent menace transferring itself to his bowels. A response was a ticket to oblivion and he knew it. Yes, he knew the rules now and would abide by them.

'Speak up, whilst you have the opportunity.'

He closed his eyes, swallowing the bitter anger inside him. A lump of cyanide burned through his belly. He was trapped. Norman Payne wanted him here; he knew that for certain now. And in this world there was only one law. Keep shtum and take the punishment meted out. Whatever was ahead, he had to face without complaint. Fight and he was dead meat.

'Mr Weaver?'

He thought of Rose, of her beautiful brown eyes and

sweet-smelling hair and the way they made love, his arms around her slender waist as he felt the pleasure grow inside him. There was nothing in his world except the two of them.

'I take it then, you have none?'

No, he had no complaints.

'I ask you one last time, Mr Weaver. If you have anything to say, now is the time to say it.'

Eddie lowered his eyes and stared at his knees. A lifetime later, the heavy door banged and he lifted his head. He was alone. 'Rose, I'm coming home, I promise you,' he whispered, sinking back on to the mattress and closing his eyes, trying to remember what home was like.

On Wednesday morning, Alan delivered the bike, improvements made. The tyres were pumped up and an old black beret was secured around the saddle with string.

'Where are you going on Alan's bike?' Marlene queried the next day as Rose pushed the bike to school.

'To the market, pet.'

'But it ain't a lady's bike. It's got a crossbar.'

Rose, clad in trousers, demonstrated her new found skills by elegantly lifting her leg and perching on the saddle, carefully maintaining her balance with the tip of her toe.

'You look funny,' giggled Marlene, but Donnie was impressed.

'I wish we could come with you.'

'You can on Saturday.' Rose looked at her two daughters dressed in their navy blue uniforms. She was so proud of them. Donnie's hair was plaited neatly, her satchel swinging by her side. Marlene already had her top button undone and her tie was crooked. She'd forgotten her shoe bag as usual, but Rose just smiled and said quickly, 'Now off you go and I'll see you at four.'

Ten minutes later, Rose was riding Alan's bike with the soft wind blowing her brown hair over her shoulders. One trouser leg was bound by a bicycle clip and her sandwich was safely in the saddlebag.

She'd made a list of the markets she intended to visit. Petticoat Lane and Whitechapel, Columbia Road and Kingland Waste. Covent Garden was a little too far and Billingsgate was fish. But she'd earmarked Chrisp Street on the Lansbury Estate for Saturday with the girls.

Rose arrived at Mile End out of breath and overwhelmed. The crowds were thick and the stalls crowded. But she pushed her way through, looking and listening. She had never seen such a variety of traders. Fruit and vegetable stalls, flowers, plants, tailors, butchers, bakers, milliners, second-hand and new clothes stalls, antiques and books of all kinds. She finally came to a halt at a jewellery stall.

'Do you have any watches?' she asked the trader who had fingers full of rings and a wrist laden with gold bracelets.

'Along there, gel.' He pointed to a stall further down. 'Dunno why you want 'is rubbish though. Treat yerself to a nice bit of hot and cold. Look, this little piece is a cracker.' He slid a thin gold bracelet from a box and dangled it over his fingers enticingly.

But watches were what she was looking for and Rose thanked him politely and went on her way, amused by his patter as he tried to hook another punter.

'Are you Syd?' she asked the man who was selling watches illegally from a pile of boxes heaped upon one another. A makeshift cover lay over the top to display the merchandise. Rose began to get excited as part of the description fitted. The trader was in his forties and though not wearing a camel overcoat, his fingers were dripping with rings.

'I'm anything you want me to be, sweetheart,' he smiled, giving her a wink. 'Ten bob for this little darlin'. But blow me down if I don't like your face so I'm giving it away almost free. Two and six and you're its new owner.'

'Well, I'm afraid—'

'Go on then, two bob to you, Mrs. You twisted me arm till it broke.'

Rose looked at the cheap metal watch that was far too big and vulgar for her tiny wrist. 'It's very nice, but—'

''Ere, how much is this?' A young blonde in tight leopard-skin trousers tapped him on the arm. She was holding a child's watch with Sleeping Beauty painted on its face.

'That's a give-away, duck,' he told her softly. 'Breaks me heart to sell it 'cos it's the only one I've got left. Four and six to you, sweetheart. I ain't called Honest 'Arry for nothing, you know.'

Rose felt her excitement evaporate. 'You're not called Syd, then?'

The trader turned back. 'What?'

'Your name isn't Syd?'

'Who's asking?'

'Would you know of anyone else who specializes in these, um . . . watches?'

He smiled craftily. 'Why? Who wants him?'

'Only me,' Rose said with a shrug guessing she would be lucky indeed to receive a straight answer from Honest Harry.

The trader looked at her suspiciously. 'Sorry gel, can't help you. Now, as I was saying about this little cracker—'

He turned his attention elsewhere and Rose realized she was wasting her time. Finally, exhausted by her search she climbed on her bike and, ignoring the hoots and curses of the motorists on the busy main road, she rode away.

On Saturday morning Rose took the girls to Chrisp Street. Anita declined the outing as she was spring-cleaning, though Rose knew the real reason was that her friend was on another one of her Butlin's economy drives.

The market was busy and though Marlene and Donnie enjoyed the excitement of new stalls to look at and candyfloss to eat, Rose made no headway with her investigations. Syd was definitely not present in his watch-selling guise and neither was there a van remotely like the one Eddie had described. She did, however, buy a bottle of Milk of Magnesia from a chemist on the walk home and on Sunday administered herself a generous dose or two.

But on Monday morning Rose still felt queasy. She was about to take another spoonful of the unpleasant medicine when a letter dropped on the mat. She gulped the liquid down and ran along the hall. Her heart was racing as she recognized the familiar scrawl. Not a letter writer at the best of times, Eddie explained he was well and cracked a joke about the food. He promised he would send a visiting order soon and signed off with love to them all. Three big crosses concluded the letter.

Five minutes later Rose was pedalling towards Hackney High Road, ignoring the waves of sickness that flowed over her. The shops and markets were busy, people content to browse and buy under a dazzling sun. Rose looked in windows and studied each stall. One little word, she told herself, might provide the clue that changed the course of their lives.

Her tummy had finally settled and she was able to enjoy all the East End had to offer. Pearls and diamonds, sable and seal furs, expensive perfume, praying shawls and car manuals, old violins and gramophone records, toffee apples, humbugs and exotic bundles of sharks' fins. Delicate ivory bracelets, fancy cow bells, gum copal, graphite, sacks of chicory and sheets of old music. Any item that anyone could possibly want in one lifetime.

Despite Syd and his van not appearing, Rose felt more like her old self. As she pedalled towards school, she decided the Milk of Magnesia was beginning to work.

'Eddie's in the nick love, not Buckingham Palace. What do you expect him to write? That he's happy with the waitress service?' Anita observed dryly as they discussed the contents of Eddie's letter. It was Thursday morning and the July sun was shining as they stood talking outside the corner shop. 'Now tell me how you got on at the markets.'

Rose shrugged. 'Not a lot to tell. I didn't see anyone of the description Eddie gave me and no one knew who or where Syd was. So really I've come to a dead end.'

Anita frowned. 'Have you heard from Em?'

'Not a word,' Rose said resignedly. 'Arthur's death was a bit of a blow, I expect.'

'He would have left them comfortable no doubt,' Anita stated flatly.

'As far as I know.' Rose paused. 'Talking of money, I've been thinking—' She stopped in mid sentence as Kamala Patel came towards them, her red and green sari lifting softly in the breeze.

'Hello, love,' Anita smiled. 'Lovely day.'

'Yes, indeed.' Kamala replied. 'How are you both?'

'Fine, thanks, ' Rose and Anita said together.

'And the family?'

'Keeping us on our toes,' Anita replied briskly.

The Indian woman looked kindly at Rose. 'I was sorry to hear about Eddie. Your husband was very good to us when we moved in. He gave us a table and chairs, you know, when we first came to the street.'

'Did he?' Rose said in surprise. Eddie never ceased to amaze her.

'We shall not forget his kindness. If Balaji and I can help in any way . . .?'

'That's nice of you, Kamala.'

'Fancy Eddie giving them a table,' Anita said when Kamala had gone.

Rose nodded. 'He never said.'

'I 'spect he thought he'd get a rocket.'

'From me?' Rose asked in surprise. 'I don't object to him giving things to people, it's doing business on our doorstep I don't like.'

'Yes, well that makes sense,' Anita agreed, refraining from mentioning the television. 'Now what was it you were going to ask me?'

Rose hesitated as she wasn't certain if her friend would be in favour of her new idea. 'Well,' she said hesitantly, 'it's about a job. I've decided to look for one. I thought I could do cleaning in an office or something.'

Anita's eyes widened. 'Blimey, the shoe box ain't run out already has it?'

''Course not,' Rose said a little defensively. 'But it's best to be prepared.' Last night she had counted the money remaining and had given herself a shock. Eddie's five hundred pounds was now down to four hundred and thirty five. After settling their debt with Olga, paying the month's rent of ten pounds and purchasing a few groceries, sixty-five pounds had vanished in no time at all. Even buying snacks from Alf seemed extravagant now.

'But you can use a typewriter, can't you?' Anita asked after a while, her forehead crinkled in a deep frown.

Rose nodded doubtfully. 'Well yes, but that was a long time ago, just after school in fact, when I worked at Horton's.'

Anita waved her hand. 'Oh, you'd pick it up again. Bit like riding a bike!'

Rose wasn't so sure. 'I'd be all fingers and thumbs. It takes a lot of practice to type forty-five words a minute, in fact that's quite slow compared to some.'

Anita looked unimpressed. 'Yeah, well, sitting all day long at a desk never appealed to me so I wouldn't know. But what would you do with the girls in the holidays?'

'If it was a cleaning job I could take them with me and they could sit and wait. An office cleaner for instance, or in a factory when the staff aren't around.'

Anita chewed on her lip. 'You could do worse than ask Joan. She's always complaining Charlie's too slow and the bonus in that is you wouldn't be far from home.'

Rose turned and glanced at the shop. 'Yes, that's an idea.'

Anita nudged her arm. 'No time like the present. Go and ask.'

Rose took a deep breath. 'Do you think I should?'

'Yeah, no harm in asking.'

After a moment's silence Rose nodded. 'Wish me luck, then.'

Anita grinned. 'I might be buying me bread off you yet.'

Rose smiled. She really liked the idea as the shop was only a stone's throw from home.

Rose bought a piece of cheese and found the courage to ask as Joan cut a thin slice from the big yellow wedge with a long thin wire before scooping it on to greaseproof paper and firmly folding the ends. Joan shook her head, 'Sorry love, I'd like to help but trade isn't what it used to be. If you'd come to me five years ago it would have been a different story as a lot of stuff was still on ration and we had the custom. But now everyone goes to the big shops as it's cheaper and there's more variety. Eggs, cream, butter, cheese – you name it – all the food that once was on coupon, is now becoming available. The only advantage to anyone shopping at a little corner shop like this is that I'm on their doorstep. Me and Charlie are struggling on, but I can't see us lasting much longer.'

Rose hid her disappointment. 'I'm sorry to hear that, Joan.'

'And I'm sorry I can't take you on, love,' Joan said sincerely. 'But if I hear anything on the grapevine I'll be sure to let you know.'

'Any luck?' Anita was waiting eagerly outside.

'No, trade isn't brisk enough anymore,' Rose said, trying to look as if the refusal hadn't hurt her pride. 'She even hinted they might be closing.'

'Well, nothing ventured nothing gained,' Anita said, a little too cheerfully, as they began retracing their steps home. 'Are you going to market today?'

'I might.' Rose was uncertain if she felt like riding as the tummy upset had returned.

Anita laughed aloud. 'You're gonna need a new bum after all the mileage!'

Rose grinned. 'I don't know what I'd have done without Alan's bike.'

'You're welcome to keep it.'

'I couldn't do that!'

'You might as well,' Anita scoffed. 'Can you see him cocking his leg over a beret?'

Rose had to laugh. She hadn't cared what she looked like but then Alan was young and fashion-conscious as all teenagers were.

'He wants a new one,' Anita admitted as they arrived at their front doors. 'But I told him he'd have to save the same way I do. Save the pennies and the pounds will look after themselves.' Anita glanced across the road. 'Talking of which, have you seen Olga lately?'

'Not for ages.'

'I saw Brenda Weller up Stepney. She was waiting for a bus and I stopped to say hello. She said Olga's been ill.'

'Ill? What with?'

'Dunno. But she ain't been seen for weeks.'

Rose stared at the net curtains in Olga's window. 'How does Brenda know that?'

'Ron, the coalman, is her husband, remember? He delivers on his horse and cart. Well Olga could hardly get herself to the door last time he called. She said she was sick and in bed and for him not to call again.'

'She did look awful when I last saw her. How is she managing with her shopping and everything?'

'I dunno. I suppose her old man must do it, though he don't look the type. Come to think of it, I ain't seen him for weeks either.'

'Do you think we should call and ask if we can help?' Rose suggested uncertainly.

Anita looked askance. 'We ain't exactly in her good books are we?'

'Still, if she's ill . . .' Rose murmured thoughtfully.

But her friend made a swift decision. 'Can't stop now, anyway. I'm meeting Alan up Kirkwood's at East India docks. He's got an interview there. You know, the building people.'

'Building? Is that what Alan wants to do?'

Anita grinned. 'Not bloody likely. He says he's going places only he don't know where.'

Rose smiled. 'Well, he's a young man now, not a kid any more.'

Anita shook her head regretfully. 'Yeah, I can't clip him round the ear like I used to. I have to leave that to his father.'

'Well, good luck to him I say,' Rose said gently. 'Alan's got personality. I reckon he'll go far.'

Anita smiled. 'He's got personality all right. Him and that swagger he puts on, pushing out his chest and eye-balling the girls. They all think they're bloody film stars these days!'

'Times are changing,' Rose agreed, thinking of how quickly her own two girls were growing.

Anita was about to leave then stopped. 'I'll ask Mrs H if she knows anyone who needs a cleaner – if that's what you really want?'

'I'd give anything a go really.'

'See you tomorrow, then.'

''Bye, Neet.'

Rose went indoors and looked around her modest little home. It was clean and tidy, if not luxurious. Cycling everywhere lately, she'd done her housework after the girls were in bed, the advantage of which was she'd found herself too tired at the end of the day to worry about Eddie. When would she see him again? How long would they be apart? She quickly took herself off to the kitchen, made a jam sandwich and slipped it into her saddle bag. Taking the letter she had written to Em, she closed her front door and cycled off. She'd post it then try a market or two.

Rose passed a big brown car at the top of the road. It was parked beside Fred and Mabel Dixon's house on the corner. She glanced quickly inside but the driver was unknown to her and he looked the other way as she passed. Rose shuddered. It reminded her of the police car on Coronation Day. For a moment she hesitated, wondering for some reason she wasn't quite sure of, whether she should return home. But then she decided she was allowing her vivid imagination to get the better of her. For who was to say that he wasn't just waiting to visit someone in the road, or perhaps had lost his way?

It was Thursday and Rose had decided this was to be her last day searching for Syd. The sun-baked roads and pavements were more crowded than ever as she rode through the streets keeping her eyes peeled. A pretty antiques stall caught her attention. The trader had made a fan of umbrellas, along with some delicate looking china vases. Beside this was a table full of car parts, which the men swarmed round whilst the women shunned it in favour of the materials, inspecting the fabric with a critical eye. Exhaust fumes, curries and baking bread permeated the air like an invisible fog.

She stopped to watch a pair of brightly harnessed dray horses pull their heavy load from the breweries, whilst road sweepers toiled in the heat and rubbish steamed in the sun. As she pushed her bike through the narrow side streets, seeing sights that were commonplace yet were all the more interesting for being reinvented by some clever soul's bright idea, Rose thought how she loved every bit of the East End.

At lunchtime she began to feel a little tired, nothing to worry about she told herself, fighting off the niggles of nausea that refused to go away. The cycle home seemed more arduous than usual and by the time she reached Ruby Street she would have gladly collapsed into a chair. But she remembered Olga and gathered the courage to knock to ease her conscience.

'Yes?' Olga opened the door a few inches. The roots of her dyed blonde hair were black and she wore a shapeless baggy jumper that emphasized her gaunt, pale face.

'I heard you haven't been well,' Rose said a little shocked to be met with this un-upholstered Olga. 'Can I get you any shopping?'

Olga stared at her. 'You are the last person I would ask for help.'

Rose was upset. 'That's not a nice thing to say.'

'Well, it's true.'

'I'm only trying to be friendly.'

'I don't want your friendship.'

'You used to,' Rose said, unable to bite her tongue

considering her motive for calling had been to help not hinder.

'You are a troublemaker. Go away.'

Rose reached out to stop the door from shutting. 'Look, I'm sorry if you think I'm the reason for your troubles, but I never wanted Eddie to sell you the television in the first place. I don't like him conducting business in the street. But since he did and I felt responsible, I gave you back your money. Wasn't that good will enough to bury the hatchet?'

Olga scowled. 'You made a laughing stock of us. Now go away.'

'I'm sorry you feel—' The door banged in Rose's face. She felt hurt and confused. What more she could do to reach her neighbour?

I've tried my best, she thought wearily as she walked away. She decided as she crossed the road that before she met the girls from school she would have forty winks in the chair. Try to forget all about Olga and the olive branch that had been well and truly shunned.

Chapter Ten

Rose poked her hand through the letterbox and drew up the string, slotting the key in the lock. She pushed the door open with the wheel of the bike, then froze. Scattered on the lino in front of her were fragments of china, the remnants of two little boxes that Eddie had given her when they were married.

She dropped the bike against the wall and went down on her knees. What had happened in her absence? Who had done this? Then she jumped up quickly, her next thought for the front room. Her heart sank as she walked in and surveyed the full extent of the damage. The radiogram was tipped on its side, the two floorboards beneath, removed. She walked slowly towards the gaping hole. Rose stared into the empty gap. The enormity of what had happened was so overwhelming that she felt she could very easily cry. Bending down she pushed her hand into the darkness. There was nothing there.

No one knew about the floorboards, only Anita and she wouldn't tell a soul, not even Benny. Rose closed her eyes and opened them. Then slowly it came to her. When she had left this morning there had been a car at the end of the road, unusual in itself since motor traffic was scarce on the island with only the milkman and baker to clatter along the road with their laden carts. If only she hadn't cycled off and returned home instead, trusting to instinct about the car. Could the driver really have been the thief?

Rose replaced the two floorboards and looked around the room, her eyes stinging as she saw her lovely couch with its stuffing pulled out and the moquette all frayed. Whoever it was had searched very thoroughly, much more so than the police. Fighting the tears she picked up the biscuit barrel and replaced it on the mantel. What was she going to do? All Eddie's money was gone!

Suddenly there was a bang on the front door. Her heart was beating fast as she walked into the hall and stared at the bedraggled figures of her sister Emily and nephew, Will.

Her sister saw the broken china and dropped the bulging bag she was carrying. 'Oh, Rosy love, what's happened?'

'We've been burgled!' Rose gulped.

'Burgled?' Em repeated slowly as if Rose was speaking a foreign language.

'I've been out on me bike and when I came in I found all this.' She pulled her sister into the front room.

'Oh, no, your lovely couch!' Em gasped, covering her mouth with her hand. 'And Dad's gram. Is it broken?'

'I don't know. I haven't had a chance to find out. Can you help me lift it?'

'Will, give us a hand.' The three of them pushed and

pulled until the cabinet was righted and put back on its feet. Rose turned it on gingerly. A strange little whistle was followed by the reassuring sound of a cut glass voice announcing the forthcoming premiere of the film musical, *Gentlemen prefer Blondes* with Marilyn Monroe and Jane Russell.

'No damage done, I don't think,' Rose said, as she twiddled the knobs and all seemed well.

'Dad used to say it was indestructible,' Em murmured faintly. 'How did they get in?'

'With the key on the string, I suppose.' Rose turned round and stared at the gaping hole in the floor. How was she going to explain all this to Eddie?

'What's this?' her sister asked as she stepped closer to the hole.

'Eddie kept a bit of cash down there,' Rose economized as she replaced the two floorboards quickly. 'And now it's all gone.'

'But who would know it was under there?' Em was shocked.

'Only Anita next door. And she wouldn't breathe a word.'

Tears welled up in her sister's eyes. 'And here am I with all me troubles and I didn't even let you know we were coming.' She dragged a hanky from her sleeve. 'It's ridiculous. I can't stop crying.'

'No wonder. You're a widow now,' Rose offered gently.

'It isn't that, it's – oh, I can't tell you.' She looked around, sniffing loudly and Rose waited patiently whilst her sister shook her head as if fighting every syllable known to man and mumbling something inaudible instead.

'Here, dry your eyes, love.' Rose offered a clean hanky from her pocket. 'Poor Will, I haven't said hello,' she sighed as she turned to her nephew. Like his mother he looked dishevelled, a lock of blond hair hanging over his big blue eyes, an expression of complete bewilderment written in them. 'Come here and let me give you a hug.'

Eager arms went around her as she wrapped him in the biggest of bear hugs, inhaling the familiar Lifebuoy soap that Em had always favoured. Rose gave him a big kiss on his cheek. 'You're almost as tall as your mum.'

'Did they go upstairs, Rosy?' Her sister walked into the hall and looked up the staircase. 'They aren't in the house still, are they?'

'The front door's been open,' Rose shrugged. 'But I didn't hear anything.'

'I don't know how you can keep so calm.'

'I'm not,' Rose admitted. 'Inside I'm all of a shake.'

'Do you think they were watching, waiting for you to go out?'

Rose shrugged. 'I saw a car at the top of the road. It was just parked there as if the driver was . . . well, on the lookout for something or someone.' She stopped, not wanting to accuse the person or persons without proof, yet she was almost certain now that the occupants of that car had been responsible for this deed.

'Shouldn't you tell the police?'

'What could they do?' Rose asked as she walked into the hall and stepped carefully over the broken china. 'I've had enough of their big feet traipsing all over this house. As I told you in my letters, I never want to see a policeman under my roof again.' She could well do without an inquisition by the police. Five hundred pounds was a fortune in her books and no doubt in theirs. She couldn't explain where it had come from nor where it might have gone to.

'Yes, yes of course,' her sister agreed in a small voice as Rose closed the front door. 'Do you think the burglar went upstairs?'

'There's only one way to find out.' Rose pulled back her shoulders and they ascended the stairs in silence.

'Oh no!' Em's voice shrank to a whisper as they walked in the small bedroom. It took all Rose's strength not to weep at the sight of the girls' mattresses. Just like the couch, someone had ripped away with a sharp implement exposing the horsehair inside.

'These were our mattresses as kids,' Rose murmured, wondering if she possessed a needle and thread strong enough to repair the damage.

Em nodded, trailing her fingers over the rough edges. 'They survived the Blitz even. Mum and Dad carried them downstairs to put over the table before we had the shelter.'

'How could they do such things to children's beds?' Rose questioned fiercely. 'They couldn't have had hearts.'

'It's downright malicious,' Em agreed hoarsely.

'I'm beginning to get angry now.' Rose turned to lead the way to her bedroom. It was as if these people had not only stolen Eddie's savings, but intentionally violated their home, too.

'They've done the same in here,' Em said faintly as they stood on the landing staring in. 'Oh Rose, they're monsters.'

At the sight of her big double mattress all ripped and torn Rose wished she could humiliate these sick people as she felt humiliated, degrade them in a way that removed all power from their thieving, brutal hands.

Rose walked slowly in. All the drawers of her dressing table were open.

'Your underwear, Rosy! To think they've touched your knickers.'

Rose replaced her belongings, trying to hide her anger. She went down on her knees. All Eddie's socks in the bottom drawer were pushed to one side. The navy blue pair were still rolled in a ball. She pulled them apart with fingers that shook so much she could hardly control them. Lo and behold the little string of pearls slithered down on her palm.

'Mum's matching necklace to my earrings,' Em whispered as the necklace glowed softly in the daylight.

Rose nodded. 'They're safe, Em, and that's all that counts.' Rose knew in her heart that if she'd had to choose between the money and the necklace, there would have been no contest. The pearls meant more to her than any amount of money, even though they were probably worth very little.

'It's a good hiding place.' Em stroked the silky smooth surfaces that had once hung so attractively around their mother's neck. 'Aren't they beautiful?'

Rose nodded, holding back the tears. 'Just like she was.'

'Eddie would have done better to hide his money in his socks,' Em said as she sank down beside Rose.

'And I should have thought to take the key off the string,' Rose said wearily. 'But it didn't cross me mind.'

'Keys on strings are part of everyday life round here,' Em said with a shrug.

'We always did it and it's a hard habit to break,' Rose nodded as she replaced the pearls and sat back on her heels. 'I'll have to tidy up before the girls come home.'

'Why don't we put covers on the mattresses and couch for now? We can mend them later,' Em suggested.

Rose nodded slowly. 'Yes, I've got some old blankets in the cupboard which would do.'

'And Will can make use of himself and sweep up the china, can't you, love?'

The ten-year-old had been silent up till now and Rose looked up at him. 'Will, I don't want the girls to know about this,' she said gently. 'It might frighten them.'

'I won't tell them.'

'That's very grown up of you. Can it be our secret?'

The boy nodded solemnly.

His mother lifted her hand to his shoulder and sighed. 'He's good at secrets is our Will.'

Rose didn't know what her sister meant but she could guess that a great deal had gone on in their lives before leaving Eastbourne.

'Mum, I want go,' he said looking at Em under his fair lashes. 'I'm busting.'

'Do you remember where the toilet is?'

Will shook his head.

'No, well, you were very young when we last paid Auntie Rose a visit.' Em gestured to the door. 'Downstairs, in the backyard you'll find the washhouse. It's a little shed and the toilet's in it.' After he'd gone, she sighed. 'That takes me back Rosy. We didn't think anything of going outside for a wee, summer and winter alike. Sometimes our bums froze to the seat.'

Rose was thinking the same. 'I still cut up squares of newspaper to tie on the back of the door.'

Em was shaking her head as if in a daze. 'I've been living the life of Lady Muck, enjoying all that Arthur provided and forgetting my roots. This is who I am, Emily Read of forty-six Ruby Street, a two up and two downer, and I should have been proud of the fact.'

Rose was shocked to hear her sister speak in such a way. 'Em, whatever do you mean?'

'Just what I say. All these years you've been struggling, making ends meet and don't deny it, I know you have. And there's me, pretending to own a posh house and going out shopping and wearing nice new clothes as if money was no object at all. But in my heart I knew it was wrong. I knew it was a sin.'

Rose stared at her sister. 'That's ridiculous, Em. You deserved a good life, you're a good woman.'

Em turned to her as a little tear trickled down her cheek. 'You don't know the half of it.'

'Then why don't you tell me?' Rose said gently as her sister drew out a hanky again.

'I would if I could stop crying.'

Rose reached out and pulled the stiff little body against her. 'You'll stop crying all right. And when you do I'll be here for you, and just as always we'll find a way out of all our troubles, both yours and mine. Now, how about a quick tidy before I meet the girls?'

Her sister nodded and pushed herself away. 'Just like old times,' she said with a hitch in her voice.

Rose nodded. 'Just like old times.'

Rose was deep in thought as she walked to school. Every penny of Eddie's savings was gone. What was she going to do? The answer to her problems was to find a job for without any money they were certainly on the breadline. What would Eddie say when she told him? Well, she wasn't going to. At least, not yet. First things first. There was only one way to pay the rent and fill the larder. She'd have to get a job – and quickly.

The ice cream man sitting on his gaily-coloured pedaltrike whizzed by. She hoped they didn't bump into him on the way home as the girls would ask for their favourite ice cream cornets. What would she do on Sunday when Barney came round with his handcart? She always bought a bag of winkles for Sunday tea. It was more a ritual than a meal. A whole hour was taken up with the fun of piercing the little black eyes and curling the winkles on a pin. It would be those little treats that would be denied to them and she grieved their loss.

But there was no use fretting, she told herself robustly. And ten minutes later she was standing at the school gate with a smile plastered across her face. 'Auntie Em and your cousin Will have come to stay with us,' she told the girls as they rushed out, all eager beavers today.

'Are they sad about Uncle Arthur?' Donnie asked at once.

'A little. But we'll cheer them up, won't we?'

'What's Will like?' Marlene was curious as usual.

'He's a very nice boy,' Rose assured her as she gathered the pieces of paper on which they had drawn and coloured during their lessons.

'As long as he ain't bossy,' Marlene decided and skipped the rest of the way home.

There were lots of hugs and kisses in the front room on their return. 'Are you me real cousin?' Marlene sat on the newly covered couch staring intently at her bemused relative.

He nodded, adjusting to the glare of Marlene's wild brown eyes assessing him under a cloud of vivid red hair.

'You don't talk much, do you?'

'He can't get a word in edgeways that's why,' Donnie said jumping to the rescue.

Marlene scowled. 'Well you ask him something, then.'

'All right.' Donnie was all light and sweetness. 'Do you like arithmetic?'

'Yes,' he nodded. 'It's me favourite.'

'Good. You can do me homework for me then,' Marlene grinned.

'No he can't,' Donnie objected haughtily. 'That's cheating.'

'It ain't, not if I couldn't do it in the first place. Miss

won't have to write so many red crosses will she?' They all began laughing and Rose knew the children would get on like a house on fire, something of an achievement it had to be said, after the events of the day.

Supper consisted of thick wedges of bread, bloater paste, corned beef and a slice of Em's own homemade fruitcake that she had brought with her in the heavy bag. After everyone had stuffed themselves full, the girls wheeled Will out to meet their friends and Em and Rose sat drinking tea.

'They're lovely girls,' Em commented. 'You and Eddie have done yourselves proud.'

'I just wish he was here,' Rose murmured softly as she twisted the teacup between her fingers. 'Still, he isn't and I ain't gonna moan about it.' She looked up and caught her sister watching her. 'Was Arthur ill before his heart attack?'

Em's mouth twitched. 'No, it was quick,' she said offhandedly.

Rose sighed. 'How dreadful for you.'

'Dreadful? Merciful, you mean.' Her sister's voice was bitter.

'Em, what do you mean?'

'It's the truth, Rosy.' Her face went very pink and her eyes shifted this way and that. 'I couldn't have stood living with him any longer.'

Rose gasped. 'But you and Arthur were happy!'

'You don't know the half,' her sister burst out as she gripped the table and her knuckles showed white. 'No one knows what goes on in other people's lives.'

Rose had always thought that Arthur, despite his righteous ideas and his stuffiness, had provided a comfortable life for his family, a lovely home by the sea and no money worries for his wife.

Em looked down at her hands. 'If you've been wondering why you weren't asked to his funeral, it's because there wasn't one. At least, not in church.'

'But wasn't Arthur a member of St John's?' Rose asked in surprise. 'I've still got that picture you sent me of him standing next to the vicar in his black gown at his investiture as choir master.'

'You can tear it up and burn the pieces,' Em said vehemently as she hid her face behind her hands, little sobs shaking her body. For a while Rose sat there, wondering what terrible events had befallen Em to make her so unhappy. They were not tears of grief falling from her eyes, Rose understood that now, but because she was ignorant of the cause of her sister's pain she didn't know what to say.

Eventually Em sat back, her body slack against the chair. Silence enveloped them and Rose studied the ravaged face in front of her, a shadow of the pretty young girl her sister had once been.

As if coming out of a deep trance Em stared around the kitchen. 'Do you remember our strip washes at the sink?' she asked so softly Rose almost didn't hear. 'It was so cold in here we had goose bumps the size of St Paul's. I longed for Dad to drag in the old tin bath and tip in the saucepans of hot water that made all the condensation drip from the windows so that we could draw pictures on them with our fingers. That was lovely. I can still feel the warmth now, the smell of soap . . . Sunlight, wasn't it . . . that Mum used?'

Rose nodded as the pleasurable memory engulfed her. 'Yes, and afterwards when we were all dry and wrapped in our dressing gowns, you'd sit on my bed and read me a story from Grimm's. Your voice lulled me off to sleep, you know.'

Em's eyes were faraway. 'Mum let me have a go on the Singer if you went off quick enough. Well, you were only six and I was twelve. I could make a dress at that age, in fact I did, for both of us.'

Rose smiled faintly. 'You were so good at sewing.'

'Mum taught me everything I know.'

'I was like Marlene, impatient to get things done, but you took your time, even when the bobbin kept sticking and breaking the cotton, you'd just wind it all through again.'

Silence descended once more until Em shifted on her seat and said in a resigned voice, 'Oh Rosy, I'm such a coward.'

Another statement that shocked Rose. 'What on earth do you mean, Em?'

'Look at you after all that's happened. Eddie in prison, the burglary, me turning up with all me troubles and you haven't shed a tear.'

'Oh yes I have. Plenty of them.'

But Em wouldn't have it. 'I'm weak, I've always been weak.'

'Stop it, Em, you're talking daft. You've lived through

a war and survived it and whatever happened between you and Arthur, well, you survived that too.'

'I'm not sure that I have.' Em's bottom lip wobbled. 'Look at me, I'm a wreck.'

'If you say that again I'm gonna scream. Now let's talk about something nice and practical, sleeping arrangements for instance.'

Her sister smiled faintly. 'Me and Will can sleep on the floor.'

'I wouldn't dream of it,' Rose said firmly. 'We can sleep in my double and Will can have the camp bed which will fit nicely by the wall in the girls' room. Though of course, thinking about it, a boy of ten would probably need his privacy. If so, the front room will be better.'

'He'd like to be with the girls I think, at least for the first couple of nights. Sometimes . . . well, sometimes he wakes up. He has bad dreams.'

'Poor little lad,' Rose said, dreading to think what the dreams consisted of. 'Well, he won't feel alone with Marlene I can tell you that for certain. In fact, she'll probably cure him of nightmares keeping him awake all the time.'

'You know the last time I saw Marle was when she was ten months old,' Em said faintly, her eyes misting again. 'Arthur drove us down for the day, remember?' Her bottom lip quivered and Rose spoke quickly.

'Will was what? Five?'

'Yes, he'd just started school.'

'Donnie would have been nearly three. It's unbelievable, isn't it?

Em nodded slowly, then giving a deep sigh she picked up her little black bag from beside the chair. 'Now, I'll give you some housekeeping.'

'But you've only just arrived,' Rose said, embarrassed.

'And I don't expect charity,' her sister said with a big sniff. 'Here's five pounds. I can well afford it.'

Rose hesitated, embarrassed again. Five pounds would go a long way to stocking the larder, but could her sister really afford it?

Em looked into her eyes. 'I've got Arthur's pension, you know. At least they didn't stop that. Now take it.'

Once again not understanding her sister's comment, Rose reluctantly accepted the five pounds. She had to feed them and she couldn't perform miracles. Perhaps when she was working she could repay the money. 'Actually, I'm looking for a job,' she said as she tucked the money into her own purse and slipped it into her bag.

Em stared at her. 'Really?'

Rose flushed under her sister's scrutiny. 'I know what you're going to say. That Eddie never liked the thought of me working and it's true he didn't. But circumstances have changed, haven't they? And most women round here work part time at least.'

'But it's the holidays coming up. What are you going to do with the girls?'

Rose repeated her little mantra. 'If I find a cleaning job, I can take them in with me. I've seen the cleaners at school and they take their kids who wait in a classroom or playground. The same happens in offices and factories when the staff aren't there.'

Her sister sat up eagerly. 'Rosy, what if I looked after the children for you? It would be one way of repaying your kindness. And you know they'd be safe with me.'

It was dawning slowly on Rose that her sister and nephew's visit was going to be of some duration, not just a few days or even weeks. She couldn't help asking, 'But what about Eastbourne, your home and all your friends?'

Em looked at her solemnly, her big hazel brown eyes fluttering as she tried to form the words that she had resisted saying all day. 'I . . . I haven't got any friends, none at all after what's happened. And I haven't got a home, either. All we have is the clothes we stand up in and those we brought with us in the bag.'

Once again Rose couldn't believe what she was hearing. 'What happened to your lovely house by the sea?'

'My lovely house, as you put it, was never Arthur's property despite how he lied about owning it.'

'But I thought Arthur said he bought it outright?' Rose still recalled the endless hours of lecturing Arthur had given them on his house purchase before they moved to Eastbourne. The lectures that Eddie had found too much to swallow and for which he had disliked his brother-in-law.

The bitter expression returned to her sister's eyes. 'Yes, that's what he wanted everyone to think. But the truth is, after his death I found out about a lot of things. Some of them I just hadn't admitted to myself though I would have had to have been blind not to know. Other things, I was really and truly ignorant of. The day after he died the landlord came round and asked me for six months back rent that Arthur hadn't paid. I was so shocked I just stood there looking at this bloke who I didn't know from Adam. He was telling the truth, of course, and chucked us out.'

Rose shook her head wordlessly. 'Oh Em, you poor thing.'

'There's a lot I have to tell you, but I'm so ashamed.'

'It's not your shame,' Rose said in a shaky voice. 'It's Arthur's. I still can't believe it.'

Em clutched her hand. 'Could you put us up for a while till I get on me feet? Will Eddie mind?'

'He's not here to mind, is he?' Rose said without thinking, then realized her mistake. 'But if he was, it would be no different.'

Suddenly the front door burst open. Three happy children came running in. The girls had roses in their cheeks and Will had a big grin plastered on his face.

'I like it here, Mum.'

Em sniffed deeply. 'Yes, love, I knew you would.'

Rose held out her arms. 'Come here you lot, it's bedtime, but we want a cuddle first. A big family cuddle.' She intended it to be the first of many.

On Saturday morning, Rose and Anita met at the fence as usual and behind Rose there was a long line of striking white washing blowing in the breeze. 'Em scrubbed all that at the crack of dawn,' Rose said, frowning at the house and hoping her sister wasn't still working in the kitchen. 'Ever since arriving she's been on the go.'

'Is she feeling better?'

'A bit. She doesn't say much.'

Yesterday Rose, Em and Anita had spent an hour in Rose's front room catching up on all the news of Em's arrival and the burglary. Anita's recommendation had been to report it to the police and Rose had given it some thought overnight. Not that she had really done much thinking for Em had tossed and turned beside her, and although they'd covered the mattress with an old linen sheet, Rose still had unpleasant images flicking up in her mind. Neither of them had slept well and Rose had been woken at the crack of dawn with a cup of tea made by a restless Em.

'What about the coppers?' Anita asked as Rose knew she would. 'Are you going to tell them?'

'No, it's too risky.'

'They were quick enough on the doorstep when they were after Eddie. You should make them earn their keep.'

'I don't want to tell them about the shoe box.'

'Leave it out, then.' Anita shrugged, inhaling deeply on a Woodbine. She had started to smoke again and was making up for lost time.

'They might not believe me. There's only the couch and beds with rips in to show anything happened.'

'You've got Em as a witness.'

'I don't want her brought into it.'

Anita put her two lips together and blew out a cloud of smoke. 'Still, I really think you should report the facts.'

'But what good would that do?'

'Well, they'd have a record, somewhere to start, just in case it happens again.'

'Charming!' Rose looked appalled. 'You don't think it will, do you?'

'You never know.'

Rose shuddered. 'You're scaring me now.'

'I just think you should report it, that's all. I would, if it was me.'

'But you've got nothing to hide.'

Anita laughed. 'Neither have you, you silly mare.'

Rose wasn't so certain about that. There were lots of unanswered questions in her life and combined with those that she already knew the answers to, she was beginning to wonder if Eddie had always told her the truth. For instance, why had trade been so good recently when last year it had been so poor. They'd been penny-pinching before Christmas, buying second-hand toys for the girls and sacrificing their own presents to find the money for a heavy winter's electricity bill. Yet six months later they'd miraculously accumulated savings! The more Rose thought about it the more she had doubts.

From a window upstairs, a sheet came flying out under the sash to be shaken fiercely. 'I wish I could get Em to relax a bit,' Rose mused.

'What's the matter with her?'

'She says being on the go helps to stop her headaches. I said fresh air would probably be better, but she won't have it.'

'She's probably feeling rotten after Arthur.'

'Yes, probably.' Rose hadn't mentioned the Arthur

business. She didn't know the whole of it herself yet, and Anita would want to know all the gruesome details.

'Are we going to market this morning?' Anita asked, flicking her ash on to one of Benny's spare tyres, carelessly abandoned in the yard.

Rose shook her head. 'I don't think so. What about you?'

'Well, if I don't go out I won't spend.' Anita raised a discerning eyebrow. 'Talking of which how are you gonna feed another two mouths when you're brassic, girl?'

Rose was swift to her sister's defence. 'Our Em's paying her way, bless her.'

'Well, that's good to know.' Anita threw her cigarette to the ground and stuck her heel on it. 'By the way, I asked Mrs H if she knew anyone who wanted a reliable cleaner. She's asking around. But there is something else I thought might interest you . . .'

Rose was all ears now. 'What?'

'Alan went to Kirkwood's Construction for his interview.'

'Oh, I forgot to ask,' Rose apologized quickly. 'Did he get the job?'

Anita grinned. 'He starts immediately.'

'Oh, Anita, that's wonderful.'

'They've taken him on part-time till he's fifteen in October. He'll be earning three pounds fifteen and six when he's on full pay. Of course, I'll take twenty bob off him for his keep which I've informed him of immediately,' Anita said dryly. 'But listen, when Alan was up in the offices there, he spotted a board with a vacancy pinned up on it. It was for a clerk.'

Rose felt her cheeks flush. 'I couldn't do that.'

'Why not?'

'I'm not experienced.'

'You worked in a factory once. 'Course you're experienced.'

Rose was filled with apprehension. A clerk's job. A responsible position. She was just a housewife.

'I've got to get Benny's dinner early,' Anita said then. 'He's driving to Devon and needs his belly filled first so I'll have to shoot.'

'Thanks, Neet. Is there anything you want at Joan's?'

'No, ta. Say hello to Em for me. And think about that job. They don't come up all that often.'

As Rose walked back to the house, she could see Em through the kitchen window, head bent, a turban tied round it and her sleeves rolled up. She simply couldn't relax. But perhaps it was the only way she had of forgetting Arthur.

Rose lifted the empty washing basket and steadied the prop under the line. It was a good drying day with the promise of a real summer's sun. The question was, did she have the courage to apply for that job?

Chapter Eleven

Rose had almost forgotten about the trouble at school, but on Monday morning when they arrived at the gates her eldest daughter's face was all gloom.

'What's the matter, love? Don't you feel well?'

'I've got a tummy ache.'

'Fibber,' Marlene accused.

Donnie's face flushed red. 'Shut up, you.'

'Donnie,' Rose coaxed. 'What's wrong?'

'I feel sick.'

'No you don't, you're frightened of Diane Balls,' Marlene cried as she turned to stare through the railings. 'There she is now, the old cow.'

'*Marlene!*' Rose exclaimed. 'Watch your language.'

'Couldn't help it.' Marlene squirmed, pulling a face. 'It just popped out.'

'Well, don't let it pop out again.' Rose patted her bottom. 'Now off you go into the playground.'

'Is Donnie coming?'

'In a minute.'

Marlene slouched off, her red hair flaming as it always

seemed to do when she was upset. What had gone on, Rose wondered, that she was ignorant of? Had something happened last week when she'd been preoccupied with the burglary and Em's arrival?

'Now, pet, this isn't like you.' Rose noticed a girl with untidy brown hair in the playground was staring at them. 'Is that Diane Balls?'

'Don't look, Mum.'

'Why not?'

'She'll think I'm telling tales.'

'Why should you tell tales?'

Donnie looked up under her long dark lashes. 'Because she just does.'

'I don't recognize her.' Rose peered over Donnie's shoulder. 'Is she a new girl?'

'Yes.'

'Why does she frighten you?'

'Because she picks fights all the time.' Donnie pursed her lips and tightened her hand firmly around Rose's.

A fleeting memory of what it was like to be terrified out of her wits at school came back to Rose. Singled out for special attention by the class bully she could remember the humiliation of the walloping she'd suffered at St Joseph's. She'd just started senior school and was small and thin for her age, indeed a head and shoulders smaller than Maggie O'Sullivan. But her pride had sent her red-cheeked and fists flying into battle where she'd received a clobbering that had gone down in class history. After that, her pecking order rating had risen both for her black eye and the few choice blows she had successfully landed into Maggie's fat stomach. But now she searched Donnie's gentle face and saw no such inner resource.

'Did she pick a fight with you?' Rose asked, almost afraid to hear the answer.

Donnie looked down at her shoes again. 'Can I stay home?'

The whistle blew twice and the children filed into school. Rose wrestled with her conscience, wondering what she should do for the best and weakened when she looked into her daughter's soft brown eyes. Had she, Rose, kept her child too close? Cosseted her, been over-protective?

Rose squeezed the tiny hand that seemed even smaller today. 'Well, once isn't going to hurt,' she said at last, making up her mind, 'but you must go to school tomorrow.'

'Diane said my dad was a jailbird,' Donnie told her as they walked home.

'Do you know what that means?'

'It's not very nice, is it?'

'No, it's not. It's a bad expression for someone in prison. And I'm quite sure Diane has no idea what she's talking about but using bad language that she's heard somewhere.'

Donnie looked up with huge brown eyes. 'You mean it's a bit like what Michael Curtis said about Daddy's ball and chain.'

Rose hesitated. 'Yes,' she agreed. 'And you must tell Miss Keene if it happens again.'

Donnie shook her head slowly. 'That won't do any good.'

'Why won't it?'

'Because it wasn't Miss Keene who stopped Michael saying nasty things. It was Marlene.'

Rose looked puzzled. 'What do you mean?'

'She told him she would ask Daddy to come round his house one night and throw his ball and chain through the window. And when he found Michael in bed he would murder him.'

'She didn't!'

'She did.'

Rose was aghast. 'Why didn't you tell me?'

'Because Michael stopped bashing Marlene after that and now he's even frightened of her.'

Rose was shocked that her youngest daughter had told such tales, but one thing was certain, Marlene employed the law of the jungle to resolve her problems and it had worked.

'I couldn't say that about Daddy to anyone,' Donnie said haughtily.

'I know, sweetheart.'

'You're not going to be cross with Marlene?'

'No, not cross, but—'

'Because she'll know I've split on her.'

At home, Em was wearing a turban and polishing hard. She looked up when they walked in. 'Donnie, aren't you well?'

'A bit of a tummy ache,' Rose dismissed quickly. 'Where's Will?'

'In the yard, learning his tables.'

'Can I go out too?' Donnie suddenly looked brighter. 'We can test each other.'

Rose smiled. 'All right, but change into old clothes first.'

Em looked mystified as Donnie ran up the stairs and Rose put her finger to her mouth. 'I'll tell you when she's out,' she whispered as they went into the kitchen and Em discarded her duster for the kettle.

Five minutes later the tea was made and the two children were sitting outside in the sunshine, their books spread across their laps in front of them. Rose explained what had happened at school as they drank the dark brown tea that tasted so much better, Rose decided, when brewed by Em.

'Well, a day or two off won't harm,' Em said, echoing Rose's thoughts.

'No, but it's all the other days I'm worried about.'

Em nodded sympathetically, her restless fingers running over the table as though attempting to clean it. 'It happened to Will, too.'

'Bullying, you mean?' Rose asked in surprise. 'But he goes to a private school – St Barnabus – doesn't he?'

'Private schooling doesn't make any difference to bullies, in fact it's probably worse,' Em said as she plucked at her turban. 'Will's never been very strong and always painfully thin. Then last year, when – well, when the rumours began—' Em shook and sniffed and twitched all at once. 'Well, he got picked on.'

'What did you do about it?'

Em lifted her chin and said in a high voice, 'I took him

out of school. Unofficially of course. In fact, we used to stay out as much as we could because I knew with all Arthur's . . . well, *trouble*, that I was better off out of the house.'

'But where did you go?'

Em's small chin tightened. 'Everywhere. One day we'd catch the bus to Bexhill or Hastings or even Brighton. When it became too cold we would sit in the library or go to the swimming baths.'

Rose sat in shocked silence. She didn't understand, couldn't understand the problems that caused such drastic action on her sister's part, but each revelation seemed more staggering than the last. Again a silence overtook them and this time Rose didn't break it. If Em wanted to elaborate on what she now termed 'Arthur's trouble' then now was her opportunity. But she sat tight–lipped, her body taut, even the wisps of hair that escaped her turban, shivering a little.

Rose finished her tea. 'Em, are you serious when you say you'd look after the girls?'

'Course I am.'

'There's a job going at Kirkwood's.'

'The building people?'

Rose explained what Anita had told her. 'I don't suppose I'd get it though. I don't have the experience.'

But Em had already dispatched her cup to the sink. She pulled Rose from the chair. 'Of course you have. You could type fifty words a minute at Horton's in the war. Even I couldn't keep up with you. And you can take shorthand. There's no reason you couldn't do it all again with a bit of practice.'

Rose was bundled out of the kitchen. 'But I'm not dressed up and me hair needs washing,' she protested as she was pushed along the hallway. For once it was like old times, with Em taking the lead and telling her what to do. Rose went upstairs still protesting and claiming she didn't have the nerve to go after such a responsible job. But half an hour later she was walking towards the docks.

Wearing the green dress that she'd visited Eddie in and with the wind lifting her long chestnut hair and despite the trouble at school, or possibly because of it, her spirit felt revived. She loved seeing the docks in action again and hearing the cry of the gulls overhead as they mewed and swooped by the cranes that stood like sentries along the crowded waterfront. Rose noted the abundance of forklift trucks on the dockside, an American idea now part of the English scenery, just as the roll-on, roll-off system had been inspired by the wartime shipments of tank landing craft from the States. Lorries went directly on to the ships and out again at their ports of destination.

During the war Rose had watched the American influx from her window in Horton's Engineering, which overlooked the docks. After the Yanks had entered the war, incensed by the carnage of Pearl Harbour in 1941, Britain had become a changed country. She remembered how the glamorous GIs with their tailored uniforms and inexhaustible supply of cigarettes and stockings had wooed the British women, drawing resentment from the poorly clad British rookies. But Rose only had eyes for her Eddie and thinking of him now in prison saddened her as she wandered along the waterfront. They had survived the Blitz and everything else Adolf Hitler had to offer yet now he was separated from his family and all because of that bloody telly!

Rose deliberately turned her attention to the noisy, trundling and often filthy lorries that arrived to unload and collect their goods on the docks. She was determined to concentrate on her mission and, dodging several big vehicles that turned towards the wharfside building that belonged to Kirkwood's Construction, she asked herself once more if she really had the nerve to apply for this job.

But before she had decided on the answer, a booming voice stopped her dead. 'Watch where you're walking love!'

A big man in a cap and dungarees waved a clipboard at her. 'It ain't very safe around here for pedestrians,' he shouted gruffly.

'I'm looking for Kirkwood's offices,' she told him, realizing she had almost stepped in front of a lorry as she'd been thinking of Eddie.

'Up there.' He gestured to the staircase built on the outside of the warehouse. 'But watch how you go, it's steep.'

She thanked him and made her way carefully up the reinforced wooden steps, holding tightly to the wooden handrail. At the very top she paused to stare over the river and her breath was taken once more. Ships of all kinds were moored on either side of the Thames, some even laying two and three abreast, disgorging or loading their cargoes one by one. Vast new sheds had been erected to house the goods and the smell of tar and timber was as inebriating as alcohol.

Just as unique as the smell of burning oil and petrol was during the war. Despite the daily terrors of the bombing she had been happy working in the armaments factory and loved the atmosphere of them and us, the feeling of real comradeship as the nation rallied against invasion. Rose inhaled and a little shiver of pleasure trickled along her spine. No one had thought the island would ever look like this again.

'Just look at it now,' Rose breathed wonderously, amazed and delighted as she hovered on the small, windy landing feasting her eyes.

She gave a deep sigh and turned back to the small wooden door in front of her. 'Time to sort the men from the boys,' she told herself as she pushed it open and walked inside.

It was the noise that surprised her the most. Big, clattering typewriters pounded away, the heads of the women who operated them all bent as they struggled to keep the mountains of paperwork in order.

No one looked up, even when the draught she let in rattled through the office. Rose looked for the board that Alan had seen. But before she had time to search all the walls that seemed crammed with every conceivable size of notice, a young woman with short fair hair and spectacles walked towards her. 'Can I help you?'

Rose went red. 'I've come to apply for the job,' she mumbled, wishing now she had pinned her hair up and worn a nice white blouse and dark skirt just as this smart young woman had. 'A clerk's vacancy?' she added, clearing her throat.

'Oh, that one,' the girl shouted above the clack of type-writers. 'It's gone I'm afraid. Went almost immediately.'

Rose couldn't hide her disappointment. 'Oh, what a pity.'

The girl frowned, removing her spectacles to trap one end thoughtfully between her neat little teeth. 'Are you experienced, then?'

Rose had already decided on her answer for this. 'I worked as a typist at Horton's during the war.'

'Did you now? You must have seen a lot of action.'

Rose smiled. 'A bit. I need to find a job quickly, you see. I have two small children and I'm the breadwinner of the family at the moment.' She hoped she wasn't going to be asked more.

'I see.' The girl hesitated and Rose's heart leapt. It raced even more when the young woman smiled brightly and crooked a finger. 'Come with me, you can't hear a word in here.'

Maybe there's a chance, Rose thought excitedly as she followed the slim, neat figure through a door and into a smaller office furnished with two medium-sized desks. A young man wearing a striped woolly jumper sat behind one of them. He looked up and smiled in a friendly, absent sort of way then went quickly back to his writing.

'That's Ben, our bookkeeper,' the girl introduced. 'And I'm Phyllis, the general manager's secretary. You would be—?'

'Rose. Rose Weaver.'

'How do you do?' She shook Rose's hand. 'Well, Rose, it's a question of how desperate you really are.' She gave a rueful smile. 'I know our canteen supervisor is looking for a temporary replacement. But if you are a skilled typist, you won't be interested I suppose.'

'Canteen,' Rose pondered then shrugged. 'Is it full time?'

'I think so. Wait a moment, I'll find out.' Phyllis picked up a telephone. She covered the mouthpiece and gestured to a chair. 'Sit down.'

Rose did so, noting the big, wide windows that stretched the length of the room. The office was elevated and she could see the tops of the forklift trucks as they went about their business downstairs.

'Yes, I've someone here now,' Phyllis was saying. 'What shall I tell her?' The conversation ended rather abruptly and she looked at Rose. 'Mrs House is coming to speak to you.'

'Is Mrs House the supervisor?'

'Yes and she's really very nice. A heart of gold actually, so don't be daunted when you meet her.'

Rose wondered what this could mean. She suddenly felt very nervous, but Phyllis was talking again. 'So you didn't evacuate in the war?'

'No. I didn't want to be parted from my sister.'

'What about your parents?' the girl asked curiously.

'They died in the first of the raids. I was eleven when war was declared, Em was nearly seventeen.'

'Oh, you poor things.' Phyllis sighed. 'I was evacuated in the war and missed all the excitement.'

Rose smiled. 'At least you were safe.'

'I couldn't get home quick enough. I didn't like the country at all.'

'How long have you worked here?'

'Five-and-a-half years. I live in Greenwich and have to walk through the foot tunnel to get here but it's worth it. Kirkwood's are a good bunch. But we are terribly busy. The typing pool isn't big enough to cope now the docks are so lively. Post war regeneration and all that. We're thinking of expanding, actually.'

'So there might be clerical jobs in the future?' Rose asked hopefully.

'Oh yes, indeed. At least you'll be on the spot to apply for it.' The girl's bright eyes sparkled.

Rose felt much more positive now. 'Thanks ever so much.'

'Not at all. I hope we'll meet again. Must go now.' She stood up and gave a broad smile to the woman who walked into the room. 'Oh, Gwen, this is the young lady I was telling you about. Rose Weaver meet Gwen House our canteen supervisor.'

Rose stood up holding out her hand to one of the largest women she had ever seen in her life. She was taller than many men and shaped like the trunk of a tree from her head which had very little neck to balance on, down to her swollen and rather painful looking ankles. A vast white pinafore draped over her huge breasts added to the illusion of size. She had small, rather piggy eyes set in a heavy-featured face. Her hair was invisible as it was clamped to her broad skull by a thick white net.

'So you're after a job, then?' came the unnervingly loud demand and Rose nodded dumbly as the woman looked her slowly up and down with, Rose thought, a rather sceptical eye.

Em was working at the sewing machine in the bedroom. One of Marlene's dresses was under the needle, a seam in the process of repair.

'What happened?' she asked eagerly as Rose walked in.

'I had an interview.'

'You did?

'Yes. And I start on Monday.'

Em leapt to her feet, throwing her arms around Rose. 'Oh you clever, clever girl.'

Rose smiled faintly. 'Don't get too excited. I missed the clerk's vacancy.'

'Well, never mind,' her sister shrugged, taking Rose's hands and steering her to the hard-backed wooden chair. 'What did you get instead?'

Rose sank down. 'I'm going to be a canteen assistant.'

Em's face fell. 'Oh Rose!'

'A girl named Phyllis who works in the typing pool at Kirkwood's told me the job was going and asked me if I was desperate enough to take it.'

'But you're skilled, Rose. You seem to have forgotten that.'

'Beggars can't be choosers.' She realized what she'd said. 'Oh, I don't mean that literally, but clerks jobs go very quickly. The advantage of working at Kirkwood's,' she added quickly as her sister looked more and more dismayed, 'is that they're expanding. And if any jobs are advertised, I'll be able to apply immediately.'

Em nodded slowly. 'Yes, I see the sense in that.'

Em sat back on the chair. 'Well, I think you're a good sport, Rose. But then you always were.'

Rose smiled at her sister's response. 'Anyway, I've got a month's trial. If I don't like it, there's no harm done.'

'Are you given a uniform?'

'An overall,' Rose explained, shuddering even now at the thought of the one she'd seen Mrs House wearing, and that horrible thick white net across her head . . . Rose sighed inwardly but kept the smile on her face for her sister's benefit.

'Are you sure this is what you want?'

Rose nodded firmly. 'Yes, I'm sure. I'm very lucky to have you to look after the girls.'

Em gave one of her increasingly frequent little twitches, a shake of her head and a sigh combined. It was almost like a tic, Rose thought worriedly. When had it first started?

'I'd better get on,' Em said with a little flourish of her hand. 'I'm just doing a few repairs.'

Rose had already noted the three piles of clothes folded neatly on the blue eiderdown of the bed. She identified Marlene's as the highest pile, the smaller one as Donnie's and finally her own, which consisted of two skirts and a pair of trousers.

Em was squinting, licking the white cotton thread as she pulled it through the needle of the machine. 'Mine and Will's are complete. Yours won't take very long.'

'But Em, I should be doing those.'

'I want to make myself useful.'

'I know, but all the same . . .'

'Tell me if you'd rather I didn't.'

Rose knew that tone of voice, and although she felt strange having someone else doing her work, she didn't want to hurt her sister's feelings. 'Just don't tire yourself out, that's all.'

'Of course not. I like to keep busy.'

The heavy treadle began to echo round the house. 'I'll go down and see the children.'

Rose watched her sister working with intense concentration as her nimble fingers passed the material deftly under the needle. Realizing she was in another world now, Rose went downstairs to the kitchen.

A big pot of stew was on the hob. It smelled delicious. Rose marvelled at her sister's domestic dexterity. The house had never looked so clean, the food had never smelled so good or the tea tasted so sweet. Even if Eddie's shoebox had been stolen and they were poorer than they had ever been in their lives, even if the trouble at school seemed insurmountable and even if she hadn't got the job she wanted, she was grateful for all she had.

Rose looked through the window and saw Donnie and Will in the yard. They were playing ball, their books abandoned. Will's blond head caught the sunshine and Donnie's dark locks were set free from her plaits flowing like silk over her shoulders. Will, at ten, was taller than his cousin, but he was all skinny arms and legs. Donnie on the other hand looked a picture of rosy-cheeked health.

Rose thought how happy they looked. She was relieved that she wouldn't have to take Donnie and Marlene with her to a school or factory whilst she cleaned. She was quite looking forward, now, to working in the canteen.

Will had fallen asleep on the camp bed but the girls were still awake and listening attentively as Rose told them her news.

'Who will look after us when you're not here?' This from Marlene.

'Auntie Em of course.'

'Is she going to live with us?'

'For a while.'

'Can we still play in the street?'

'Yes, if Auntie Em says so.'

Marlene seemed satisfied. 'Auntie Em's stews are lovely.'

'I know,' Rose grinned.

'Do you have to work on Saturdays?' Donnie's dark eyes were anxious and Rose was already anticipating her reluctance to attend school in the morning.

'No. We can go to market as usual.'

'Alan Mendoza's got a girlfriend,' Marlene said, bursting into giggles.

Rose raised an eyebrow. 'How do you know that?'

'I saw them kissing. They was on the debris.'

'What were you doing there?'

'Nothing. I just walked by it.'

Rose found herself suspicious now of her younger daughter. There was a lot more to Marlene, she acknowledged after the Michael Curtis episode, than met the eye.

199

'Well, Alan's at work now. He's old enough to have a girlfriend.'

'How old do you have to be, then?'

'That's enough questions,' Rose decided as she pulled up their sheets and kissed their soft, sweet-smelling heads. 'Goodnight and God bless, darlings.'

She was just closing the door when she heard Marlene's noisy whisper. 'You should tell that Diane Balls our Dad's gonna knock her block off when he comes out of prison. That'll scare the daylights out of her!'

Rose lay awake in bed that night, her mind busy. She had actually got herself a job. How would she like working in a canteen? Could she do what was expected of her? She had only ever cooked for the family; would she be expected to know how to prepare intricate dishes? Mrs House had indicated that her job would include washing up. She was safe there; she could wash-up blindfolded!

Suddenly there was a scream and Em sat bolt upright in the bed beside her.

'No, no,' she shouted, waving her hands and staring at the wall in front of her.

'Em, wake up,' Rose cried, her own heart thumping.

'Leave him alone!' Em shouted again as she fought off an invisible assailant. 'You devil, leave him alone!'

'Em – you're dreaming, wake up,' Rose cried as she caught her sister's wrists, afraid she would do herself some damage. But their struggle went on until Rose shouted very loud indeed. Em sat suddenly quite still and as stiff as a poker.

'Lay down dear,' Rose coaxed softly. 'Go to sleep now.' She pushed her back and pulled the sheet up to her chin. Rose felt chilled. What had happened to make her sister dream such nightmares?

A few minutes later Rose listened to the rhythmic breathing beside her. The nightmare was over. But Em had called someone a devil. Could that be Arthur? Rose tucked under the covers too, her eyes peering around the dark room. It was full of shadows. She hoped Arthur's spirit was not in the vicinity, for if truth be told she had never been fond of him in life, let alone death.

'Sleep tight, dear,' she whispered to Em who rolled on her side with a deep, satisfied sigh.

Rose closed her eyes. Within minutes, she was asleep.

Chapter Twelve

'Bye, Mum.'

'Bye, love.' It was Tuesday morning and Rose kissed the top of Marlene's head. Her youngest daughter skipped happily into the playground.

'I feel sick,' Donnie said, not unexpectedly.

Rose drew her to one side as the other children passed by. 'Do you remember how David killed Goliath?'

Donnie nodded uncertainly. 'With his sling.'

'And a tiny little stone.'

Donnie thought about this. 'Yes, but we're not allowed to throw stones.'

'Of course not,' Rose smiled. 'The stone is just a symbol of David's courage. He took aim with his sling and his stone killed the giant, but he had to be brave and trust in God.'

'But that was a long time ago. Before Jesus was even born.'

'It doesn't make any difference. The Bible tells us these stories so we can put them to use in our lives.'

'But what shall I do if Diane wallops me?'

'Bullies will back down if you show you're not afraid.'

'Like the giant you mean?'

Rose smiled as her heart almost broke at the sight of Donnie's drooping shoulders. 'Yes, like the giant.'

'So I have to wallop her back?'

'It won't do to run away,' Rose said gently. 'And if you don't want me to come in to speak to your teacher—'

'No,' Donnie replied fiercely. 'I don't.'

'Well, then.' She gave Donnie the note. 'I've told Miss Dent that you had a tummy ache yesterday.'

Rose watched Donnie walk slowly through the school gates. The whistle was blown and the children formed lines. Two minutes later the playground was empty.

'Rose, are you ill?' Em shouted from the yard.

'I'll be out in a minute. It's just a gippy tummy.' She would have to go to the doctor and get something stronger than the Milk of Magnesia. It was no use at all, in fact the medicine seemed to make her worse. She was certain now that she was developing an ulcer, a condition her mother had suffered with after her pregnancies. Rose could remember the discomfort her mother had undergone when she'd been tempted off her diet and eaten fatty foods. Tummy ulcers had blighted her life until rationing. For the first two years of the war her mother's health had improved under the austere, enforced diet, the irony being that she was in better health than ever before when she lost her life in 1942.

Rose had examined all round her stomach and sometimes imagined she could detect a small round lump, which was ridiculous. Ulcers were embedded in the lining of the stomach but she knew enough about them to recognise her symptoms. She hadn't been eating regularly lately, at least not until Em had arrived and insisted on two square meals a day. But now the sickness refused to go away whatever she did. As healthy as Em's meals were, Rose had no real appetite for them.

A quarter of an hour later she opened the washhouse door very gingerly. The warm summer's morning was a delight to behold and Rose wished dearly she could summon up some enthusiasm for life. She hoped Em wouldn't fuss.

'You look dreadful,' Em said as Rose walked into the kitchen.

'I feel better now. Where's Will?'

'He's out in the street with Ashley Green a little boy from number forty-two. He's off school with a swollen ankle but he seems to be walking around all right.'

Rose nodded approvingly. 'Ashley is Sharon and Derek Green's eldest. He has two sisters who sometimes play with the girls.'

'Yes, they got to know each other that first day we came. He's a nice kid.'

'I'll just sit down a minute.'

'What is it, do you think?' Em's fingers were already busy with the teapot, pulling a cozy over its lid and patting its fat round sides. 'A tummy upset?'

Rose nodded. 'I expect so.'

'A nice cup of tea will soon put you right.'

'No, I don't think so, dear. Perhaps later.' She really did feel wretched.

'It's something for you to go off your cuppa.'

'I'm sure I'll feel better soon.'

Em sat down beside her. There was a smell of Sunlight creeping through the house as all the smalls were spread neatly over the clothes' horse, some of them still giving the occasional drip. Several of the girls' vests and knickers and a liberty bodice of Em's that despite being snow white looked as if it harked back to the war years, half hidden as it was by one of Will's white shirts. All hand-washed and rinsed. Poor Em. Arthur, despite his flaws, had installed a washing machine in the kitchen of the Eastbourne house.

Rose decided if she had that four hundred and thirty five pounds still sitting under the floorboards she might very well pay Bobby Morton a visit. Investing in one of his new-fangled appliances would ease her conscience considerably as far as Em was concerned. But since there was no shoebox, there would be no washing machine.

'Should you go to the doctor?' Em was staring worriedly into Rose's white face. 'Let him check you out.'

'I'm fine,' Rose protested wearily. 'I've been taking Milk of Magnesia in the hope it would settle me.'

Em looked doubtful. 'Well, I know Mum favoured it for her stomach, but it can be very constipating.'

Rose nodded, guessing what was coming next.

'You may have inherited her problem,' Em suggested as Rose knew she would. 'In which case, the sooner you discover what's wrong, the quicker you'll know how to treat it.'

They both looked at one another. Rose gave in. 'Perhaps I'll go along to surgery later.'

'That's a good girl.' Em smiled softly and Rose felt affection flow through her as she always did when Em asserted her motherly role. Being six years older, Em had always fussed like a mother hen, although Rose knew herself to be quite capable when the need arose.

Their bond had strengthened throughout the war and when marriage and babies had come their way they had still kept close, even when Arthur whisked Em off to Eastboune at the end of 1945. Their weekly letters had substituted for the physical contact they both enjoyed. That was, until now, with the biggest shock being Em's neglect to invite them to Arthur's funeral.

It was an hour later when Rose was just beginning to feel better and actually felt like drinking a cup of tea, that Anita appeared at the front door. 'Look what I've got,' she cried breathlessly. 'It's me lucky day!'

Rose stared at the shiny brown bottle clasped tightly in her hand. 'What is it?'

'Cream sherry, of course. And a bloody good one, too.'

'Where did you get it?'

'Mrs H gave it to me. It's her birthday and all her relatives descended as a surprise, like. She had so much booze in the house she made me put this in me saddlebag. I've got birthday cake too and the rest of the day off 'cos they're all celebrating and it wasn't any use cleaning. She still gave me full pay, mind.'

'That was nice of her.'

'Yeah, well she knows when she's well off, if I say it meself,' Anita remarked dryly. 'Grab this will you and I'll get the cake.'

Anita planted the bottle in her hand and hurried off. She was still wearing her cycle clip around her ankle, her brown trousers billowing out round her thighs like water wings. Soon she was back with a cake tin, the Queen's head embellished gaudily on the lid. 'Where's Em?' she wanted to know as they went into the kitchen.

'Putting out the smalls. She's been at it again.'

'Well, call her in. We're all gonna celebrate another piece of news with a glass of plonk and a slice of Swan Lake. I'm busting to tell you.'

Rose was thankful Anita hadn't called an hour earlier for even the thought of sherry or cake made her feel queasy. But she could see Anita was really excited and wanted to hear whatever it was that had put her into such a good mood. Rose went to the kitchen door and looked out. Em was carefully pegging a sheet on the line next to two pillowcases and a white tablecloth she had never seen before.

'Em, Anita's called.'

'I'll be with you in a minute.'

'She'll wash this bloody house away if she's not careful,' Anita grinned as she rubbed her red, worn hands together. 'Your line's full to busting every time I look at it.'

'Don't make me feel worse,' Rose acknowledged glumly. 'I just can't stop her. I've tried everything.'

'Not this you haven't,' Anita remarked as she leered at

the bottle then began to search the china cupboard for glasses.

'But Neet, Em doesn't drink.'

'Well she does now.' Three large, cheap glass tumblers appeared on the table.

'And I'm not all that keen to—'

Anita looked up and frowned at her. 'What's wrong? You aren't abstaining too, are you?'

'No, well, it's just that . . .' Rose stopped short. She had been careful to hide her little problem from Anita who would have wheeled her along to the doctor at a second's notice. Never one to tolerate sickness without a good cause, her friend was a firm believer in the miracle of the National Health and all its many benefits.

'Come on, just a thimbleful. It won't kill you.'

Rose gave in. Perhaps when Anita wasn't looking she could tip it down the sink, a pity because it was probably very expensive. 'Just a tiny one then.'

Em came in from the backyard, rolling down her cardigan sleeves. 'Hello, love,' she smiled at Anita. 'My goodness. What have you got there?' She stared at the three generous measures of rich amber sherry that Anita had poured.

'Sit yourself down and I'll tell you.'

Cautiously Rose and Em sat at the kitchen table.

Anita lifted her glass. 'Here's to – well – what shall we toast?'

Rose was trying hard not to inhale the strong alcohol fumes as she lifted her drink.

'I don't usually,' Em said weakly. 'Arthur was teetotal.'

'Well, good luck to him I say,' Anita replied tartly clinking their glasses with fervour and licking her lips. 'He had his reasons no doubt, but he ain't here to object, God rest his soul. I'm sure one little sip will do you a power of good.' Anita added with a serious expression, 'And provide you with enough oomph to do another three lines of washing.'

Rose was tempted to smile at the picture they made. The three of them sitting round the kitchen table at eleven o'clock in the morning about to knock back Mr H's cream sherry. Anita still wearing her trousers and bicycle clips, Em in her turban and thick woolly cardigan, and she, Rose, looking like death warmed up no doubt. 'Well, put like that,' Em caved in giving another of her little headshakes and sighs as she raised her eyebrows briefly.

'Let's be selfish,' Anita said suddenly. 'Let's drink to us, the three of us. The blokes can take a back seat for once.'

Rose nodded. 'Yes, why not?'

Em gave a little mew of assent.

'To us! Women of our times!' Anita roared and kicked back the sherry in one, gulping noisily. Rose watched in fascination as her friend closed her eyes and let the alcohol burn down her throat, an empty glass still poised at her lips. 'Blimey, I enjoyed that,' she gasped.

'Me too,' Rose said faintly, licking her lips.

'The bee's knees,' Anita sighed loudly, in a world of her own.

'It is rather nice,' came a little voice, and Rose looked across the table to see her sister sipping daintily from her glass. 'I can't say as though I've tasted anything like this before. I had a gin and lime once at one of Arthur's town hall dos. He didn't know I'd been given it — he didn't approve of me drinking.' She giggled.

'Well here's your opportunity to develop a taste for the good stuff,' Anita said as she lifted the bottle and took aim at her glass.

Em giggled again. 'It looks like cold tea.'

'Yeah,' grinned Anita glancing at Rose. 'My father-in-law has already sussed that one out.'

Suddenly all three of them were laughing. In fact they were laughing so much that Rose actually wondered if she should try a little sip, but the nausea was finally receding and she wanted to keep it that way. She also realized that Anita was merry enough not to notice how much she was drinking from her glass and was clapping Em on the back as though they'd been drinking partners for years.

Not that Em seemed to mind. In fact, her sister's glass was now empty and she made only a half-hearted protest to Anita topping it up. 'I really shouldn't.'

'Go on, treat yourself,' Anita grinned. 'What about you, Rose?'

'In a minute I will.'

Her friend smiled magnanimously. 'All right,' she nodded, raising her glass once more. 'Lift 'em up lassies.'

They all did.

'To Mrs H!'

'To Mrs H,' they all chorused.

'Right,' Anita said a minute later as she sloshed her drink

over the edge of the glass. 'Here's to . . . here's to . . .' A little frown etched itself on her forehead. 'Bugger me, I've forgotten what.'

They were all in fits again as Anita attempted to think of the reason for her celebration. Then suddenly a look of absolute bliss crossed her face. 'Ladies, raise your glasses to the Mendoza family who are leaving this bloody street for a fortnight's holiday next month. God bless you, Billy Butlin!'

'Oh Neet!' Rose cried. 'You really are going, then?'

'You bet your life we are. I used Mrs H's phone to confirm the booking this morning. We're off to Skegness in four weeks, three days time.'

'That's wonderful, dear,' Rose said breathlessly.

'Bloody wonderful, ain't it? Cheers.' She tipped the last of her drink down her throat and did a little whoop of delight.

Rose decided to put on the kettle. 'I'll make a cuppa.' When she turned round she stopped dead. Anita was staring at Em who was sitting there with tears rolling down her cheeks.

'What's the matter, gel?' Anita asked boozily as she peered into Em's face. 'Was it something I said?'

'Not really. It's just that—'

'Have another drink,' Anita fumbled with the bottle and dropped more of it on the table than in the glass. 'Bloody hell, I'm pissed.'

Rose took her hanky from her sleeve. 'Here, love, give your nose a good blow.'

Em took the hanky and gave a trumpet. 'It was the

mention of Butlin's, you see. Arthur always promised he'd take me and Will there one day.'

Anita sat back with a sigh. 'Trust me to put me foot in it.'

'I believed, foolishly I suppose, that he meant it.' To Rose's astonishment, her sister drank the remains of her sherry then said rapidly, 'Arthur and me didn't share the same bed.'

Anita hiccuped. 'You have been missing out then.'

'Yes,' Em replied vacantly.

Anita dragged one leg over the other, rolling her eyes at Rose. 'He was all there was he, in that department?'

Rose was even more astonished when Em, appearing quite unoffended, replied, 'Oh yes, but not how you mean.' She held out her glass. 'Could I have another sherry, please?'

'Em, I don't think you should,' Rose advised but Anita waved aside her objection.

'Why not? She's enjoying herself, ain't you, Em?'

Noticeably flushed Em nodded. 'I do feel a bit better, actually.'

'You was telling us about Arthur,' Anita prompted as she poured two stiff measures of the amber liquid.

'I've never told anyone this but it doesn't seem quite so awful today. I don't know why.' Em picked up her glass and gulped. Then slowly she drew a long breath. 'I thought Arthur was . . .'

A moment passed and Rose watched in breathless suspense as her sister began the usual procedure of trying to form words on the subject of her departed spouse. She had never got past this stage, a strange, silent panting that inevitably led to silence, but now Em's lips were soft and mobile and her tongue flicked out to wet them. 'I thought Arthur was having an affair,' she gasped at last.

'An affair?' both Rose and Anita echoed together.

Em nodded, her eyes very bright. 'Even if he had been with another woman, I could have forgiven him that, even tolerated it as I blame myself for not being very clever in that area.'

Rose nearly fainted. Em had never talked like this before, in fact Rose had always been rather reluctant to delve into that part of her sister's life, instinctively knowing she would be embarrassed.

'Sex is overrated if you ask me,' Anita responded, completely unfazed. 'Not sex itself, but ways of doing it, if you see what I mean. Each to his own I say. What's one man's meat is another man's poison, ain't it?'

'Do you really believe that, Anita?' Em asked in surprise.

'Yes, too bloody true I do.'

'That's very generous of you. But, dear, I never truly understood that side of things. You see, Arthur being older—'

Rose and Anita waited as once more Em sought to explain her thoughts. After what seemed an eternity she said very softly, 'Arthur had certain tastes. He couldn't . . . he wasn't . . . he was—'

Anita sighed in exasperation. 'Blimey, gel, spit it out.'

Em swallowed. 'He didn't like women. He liked men.'

Anita snorted. 'Well, bugger me.'

Em nodded. 'Yes, that too.'

Rose wondered if she'd heard properly but as she was digesting the most recent and, as yet, the most shocking of all Em's revelations, Will walked in.

'Hello, love,' Anita said, swift to regain her composure. 'We was just having a drink in celebration of something.'

Will looked at his mother. 'Ashley wants me to go round his house.'

Em stood up shakily and very carefully made her way across the kitchen. 'All right. As long as you don't go anywhere else.'

'Can I take me ball?'

'Yes. Don't break any windows though.' She gave a high-pitched giggle but her son didn't seem to notice and ran out into the yard. The next moment he appeared with his ball under his arm.

''Bye then.'

''Bye, dear.'

Em carefully negotiated her way back to the chair and sat down. She looked at Rose. 'The church was very unforgiving when it all came to light, which seems to me to be very uncharitable. Arthur put a lot of time into St John's.' Rose was still struggling to come to terms with what she had just been told as Em said softly, 'I'm so glad Will is able to mix with children again. For the last six months we've been living in a kind of bubble.'

'But you and Arthur had a baby, Em,' she blurted suddenly.

'Yes. Will's conception was the only occasion we ever made love.'

'Struth!' Anita knitted her eyebrows. 'And he's ten!'

'So all these years—?' Rose persisted.

'Yes.'

Anita leaned forward. 'How did you find out about his, you know what?'

'Someone came to the house.'

'What, from the church?' Anita gasped.

'No, from London. He was much younger than Arthur, a boy really.' She sniffed as tears welled in her eyes. 'He wasn't the first to call and I realized, after a while, the younger the better really. One of them went to the vicarage and spoke to Reverend Small. It was only his word, of course, against Arthur's, but by that time someone at the Town Hall had complained too.'

'At Arthur's office?' Rose asked incredulously.

Em nodded. 'Arthur had begun to be careless or just . . . greedy, perhaps.'

Rose and Anita sat in silence. Rose looked into her sister's face and couldn't imagine the hell she must have been through. She also couldn't imagine not making love with the man you married for ten whole years. What had possessed Em to continue the relationship if there was no love involved, which there obviously hadn't been?

Em sniffed again. 'I know what you're thinking. How was it I didn't know or suspect something earlier? Well, I simply don't know. I stuck my head in the ground, I suppose, like the proverbial ostrich. You see, Arthur was always very good to me. He gave me everything I wanted and I didn't have to work. He was so respectable. A real gentleman. And he never pestered me in that way.'

'But blimey, girl, didn't you want it?'

Em thought for a moment. 'Well, the one time it happened was rather . . . well, disappointing.'

'And you ain't ever had another bloke since?'

'Oh no,' Em said affrontedly, 'I wouldn't – *couldn't*. I was married.'

Anita and Rose looked at one another then watched Em reach across the table to lift Rose's full glass. She gave two hearty gulps of it and closed her eyes. 'It's funny but I feel very tired all of a sudden.'

Rose sprang to her feet. 'Em, dear, watch out!' Rose caught hold of her sister just as she slid from the chair. 'Anita, help me, she's passed out.'

'Crikey, the poor cow,' Anita said as she staggered to assist Rose.

'Let's get her to bed.' They pulled an arm each around their shoulders and very slowly took her through the hall.

'It'll be a miracle if I can get up them stairs,' Anita slurred as she missed her footing and Rose shouldered all Em's weight. 'Sorry, love, everything's double.'

'Perhaps we could lay her on the couch,' Rose hesitated, she didn't want Will to see his mother like this.

'No, I'll make it,' Anita muttered, steadying herself against the wall and still managing to hold on to Em.

Some while later, the stairs negotiated, they lay Em on the big double bed and Anita flopped down beside her. 'Phew, that sherry had a kick in it. Did I really hear that Arthur was as queer as a three speed walking stick?'

'Yes, I'm afraid so.'

'And she never said before?'

Rose slid off Em's shoes and drew up the cover. 'No, never.'

'Always thought he was a bit iffy,' Anita muttered, unable to disguise her contempt. 'And yet she stuck up for him. Did you hear? Respectable, I ask you. Well, it's obvious why. He needed a good front and she was it, bless her.'

'And I thought I had troubles.' Rose bent down and kissed her sister's forehead. Gently removing her turban she brushed her dull fair hair over the pillow with the tips of her fingers. 'Oh Neet, her life must have been so un-happy. She never said a thing in her letters.'

'Would you?'

Rose had to agree she probably wouldn't.

'That bloody Arthur.'

Rose nodded. 'It was like keeping her a prisoner.'

Anita made no comment except to sigh, 'She'll have a snorter when she wakes.'

Rose drew the heavy curtains. 'Come on, I'll make you a cup of tea.'

'Yeah, I'd better sober up before me old man comes home.' Anita giggled. 'We polished off the bottle, you know.'

Rose softly led the way downstairs. She needed that cup of tea now.

'I did it, Mum, I did it!' At four o'clock Donnie was bursting with news. 'I did what you said. I stood up to Diane Balls.'

Rose felt her heart thump. 'You did?'

'We was in the playground and Diane came up and poked me in the shoulder.'

'What did you do?' Marlene queried as they all gazed at Donnie.

'I poked her back as hard as she poked me.'

'Lummy,' Will gasped looking impressed. Rose had brought him with her so that Em could rest undisturbed.

'She thought I'd run away,' Donnie said with a toss of her head.

'But you didn't?' Rose asked.

'No. I just stood there. I was scared stiff really, but I remembered David and how he stood up to the giant.'

'What giant?' Marlene demanded as Rose urged the three children along the busy pavement.

'Come along, Donnie can explain on the way home.'

'Goliath of course,' Will said decisively as they went. 'He was nearly seven feet tall and really ugly.'

'And David was just an ordinary person,' Donnie continued. 'But he had a catapult and five little stones. He aimed one of them at Goliath's head and it hit him right in the centre of his forehead, killing him dead.'

'How do you know that?' Marlene frowned.

'It's in the Bible,' Will said simply.

'I don't like the Bible,' Marlene objected moodily, 'it's got too many long words I don't understand.'

'Well, you should look at the pictures then. There's lots of lovely colour ones in the Bibles at school.'

'I ain't a baby,' Marlene replied, blushing.

'Anyway, you were telling us about Diane,' Rose

interrupted in order to return to the subject of Donnie's triumph.

Donnie nodded, her face grave. 'Then she called me a bad name, a very, very bad name and everyone started to laugh.'

Rose sighed. 'Oh dear.'

Donnie went red. 'So I called her one too and said if she hit me again I was going to hit her back even harder.'

Rose stopped in the street. 'That was very brave of you.'

'Like David,' Donnie said cheerfully.

'Yes, like David.'

'Sally Piper said she ain't ever heard me speak like that before.'

'What was the name you called Diane?' Marlene asked interestedly.

'I mustn't say it again, must I, Mum?'

'No.'

Donnie's face glowed. 'I didn't run away. I just stood there and looked her in the eye and all she did was kick the railings.'

Rose was close to tears. What a world! Her poor Donnie. But she'd won the first round of a lifelong battle.

'Can we go to the sweet shop?' Donnie asked shyly.

Rose smiled. 'I think you deserve a treat.'

'Have we got any lemonade bottles at home?' Marlene asked expectantly.

Donnie nodded. 'Two.'

'We'll save the bottles,' Rose intervened quickly, since she didn't want to disturb her sister. 'I'll give you sixpence each.' The offer was very extravagant but she still had some of Em's grocery money in her purse. Instead of stopping for groceries she'd make do with sardines tonight.

'I'm gonna buy some brandy balls,' Marlene decided at once.

'I think I'll have me favourite,' Donnie said thoughtfully. 'Sherbet dabs. They melt in your mouth.'

But Will was silent until Marlene demanded his choice.

'Do they sell wine gums, Auntie Rose?' he asked cautiously.

'Yes, dear. They sell just about any sweet you could possibly think of.'

'I've changed me mind,' Marlene interrupted noisily. 'I might have two ounces of them chocolates with toffee insides. Or I might have a bag of gobstoppers.'

'They never stop your gob,' Donnie giggled and they all burst into laughter including Marlene.

Rose took the road that led to Amethyst Way, joining in their happy chatter. Her cares were temporarily forgotten and she wondered if she would see Bobby Morton in his shop. Perhaps she would look in as they passed by. Not that she had any intention of displaying any interest in a washing machine, even if she had warmed to the idea lately. It was a luxury someone like her couldn't possibly afford, not unless you had four hundred and thirty five pounds hidden under the floorboards at home!

Chapter Thirteen

Rose inhaled the aroma of frying onions permeating the small waiting room. This was once Dr Harding's parlour and was now Dr Cox's waiting room. Up until two years ago, Dr Harding's patients had squeezed on to six hard-backed wooden dining chairs lined like skittles in the draughty hall. But now Dr Howard Cox was installed and the arrangement had changed.

Rose had mourned the loss of the family doctor who delivered both of her girls at home. With the assistance of the midwife he had brought Donnie and Marlene into the world with very little fuss on his part and not very much more on Rose's. She'd had complete faith in him, instilled from childhood and the happy visits she'd made to the gentle, smiling practitioner. Dr Harding had made a joke at every one of them, tickled her under the chin and very rarely prescribed anything unpleasant to swallow. Looking back she wondered if this was because she was rarely ill or because he really was a saint of a man whom the whole neighbourhood had loved and admired.

Islanders, a generally friendly bunch, had few words to

say on the new doctor. Rose knew their silence was more a testament to their feelings than outright criticism. Dr Cox, a much younger man, guessed at being somewhere in his late thirties to early forties had brought with him a wife and four young children, all crammed into the three bedroomed house that comprised living quarters, surgery and waiting room. Sitting in the dull little waiting room and staring up at the pagoda shaped lampshade that dangled an unequal fringe around its base, she noticed the mauvish cloth covered flex adorned with a fly paper. She didn't like to think of the tiny dead insect bodies struggling there and averted her eyes to the picture rail. This had once sported Dr Harding's chosen photographs; the children he'd delivered, the women and men he had treated, his own wife and family and other portraits and landscapes of the Island community that he had served for over forty years. These were all now banished and only their outlines remained like pale ghosts clumsily masked by Dr Cox's stark white certificates confirming his medical training.

Rose also noted the rose decorated wallpaper was beginning to peel at the corners. Also, the six original wooden chairs on either side of the room had lost their patina, once so lovingly polished by Mrs Harding. Rose considered the oblong table in the centre of the room. It boasted chromium legs and a green painted top, an addition made in the hope it would revive the spirit of the room. But instead it looked dreadfully mismatched, as did last year's spring editions of *Punch* and *Life* magazines lying neatly untouched on its shiny surface.

Rose had always enjoyed browsing through Dr Harding's dog-eared copies of *Woman's Own* and *My Home*. Indeed any tattered offering from the Companion Book Club had held his patients spellbound as had the toppling piles of knitting, cooking and sewing magazines. For the children there had been *Tom Sawyer* and *Ivanhoe* or the much-loved *Anne of Green Gables*, minus its dustjacket.

It was clear to see that Dr Cox had made a clean sweep. Sacrificing his living room for his patients, he had made an attempt at modernization, but there was nothing left of the reassuring atmosphere, Rose decided with dismay.

A woman exited from the white painted door labelled afresh in large hand-written capitals, SURGERY. Rose beamed a smile as she hurried off, but her head was bent and her walk brisk.

Rose was beginning to feel a fraud, having convinced herself her trouble was not an ulcer, but an anxiety problem. Doctors had so much more to do these days with their practices extending as Dr Cox had informed them his had. Would he think she was wasting his time?

'Mrs Weaver?' Dr Cox beckoned her. She quickly assessed his appearance as being very professional. A white coat under which he wore a dark suit, light brown hair cut so short that his sideburns were almost non-existent and his skin had a very clean, washed look, as though he'd scrubbed himself thoroughly after each patient.

Rose saw that inside the consulting room there was a marked change to the decor. Steely white walls reflected the doctor's own high standard of hygiene, which, Rose thought, should in some way have bolstered her confidence. Instead it had the effect of making her more apprehensive as she sat down on the chair by the desk.

'I'm a little at twos and threes still,' Dr Cox apologized as he drew out a folder from his shoulder-high file cabinet and studied the contents. 'I don't appear to have your notes to hand.'

'I came last year with Marlene, my youngest daughter—'

'Then I should have you here.' He went back to investigating the drawer.

'I have another daughter too, Andrea, but we call her Donnie. And there's my husband, Eddie—'

'This really won't do.' Dr Cox was apparently talking to himself as he fingered a set of papers with obvious disdain.

Rose waited patiently, aware of the plastic clock positioned strategically on the desk directly in front of her. Its tick was as loud as an elephant's heartbeat and she wondered how he could possibly concentrate when the noise seemed so jarring in the otherwise silent room. Dr Harding had never seemed to possess a clock. It was always first come, first served and wait in the queue until surgery had ended. No one ever bothered about time. It took as long as it took. Now the clock seemed to be counting the minutes aloud and there was an unspoken urgency in the air.

'My wife has been acting as receptionist,' he said, not looking at Rose but still lost in his cabinet. 'And we don't seem to have you under W.'

'You could try R. Read is my maiden name and my family were with—'

'Very unsatisfactory,' he cut in, shuffling his fingers.

Rose waited again, wishing now she had abandoned the idea of this visit. She had felt better this morning and would definitely have abandoned coming if Em hadn't pushed her out of the house.

The doctor made a severe clucking sound. 'Very unsatisfactory indeed.'

'Have you found us?'

'Yes, but in quite the wrong place.' Dr Cox returned to his seat, his face disgruntled. He had a thin, severe mouth and Rose at once felt sympathetic towards the absent wife who not only cooked, fed and kept clean her large family but acted as his bookkeeper too. Rose appreciated how much effort it took to keep factory records in order and assumed it to be much the same with a doctor's practice.

'Well, what is wrong today?' he sighed at last, looking up with a frown that stretched across his previously unlined brow. His face was shining under the bright bulb above them, his cool, pale eyes fastening on her for the first time since she had taken her seat.

Rose sat forward, gripping her handbag tightly. 'It's probably nothing—'

'Shall I be the judge of that?' His intense stare and clipped voice made her start. She felt quite intimidated.

'Well,' she hesitated. 'I've had these bouts of sickness and as my mother suffered from ulcers—'

'The two conditions are not necessarily connected,' he told her sternly.

'No . . . no, I suppose not,' she agreed meekly. 'But I thought ulcers might run in the family and—'

'How long have you been feeling unwell?' he interrupted again and Rose was forced then to explain her other theory, about the anxiety problem stemming from the events of Coronation Day.

Dr Cox listened without expression and Rose tried bravely to stick to uncluttered facts, but she still couldn't make Eddie's arrest and the subsequent events sound any better.

Apparently unfazed by her revelations he then asked her several questions about her health. When these were answered to his satisfaction he stood up and gestured to a long flowery curtain attached to a rail by shiny brass rings. 'I'd like to examine you,' he told her shortly. 'Undress down to your undergarments please and lie on the examination couch.'

Rose was horrified. She hadn't expected this at all.

'But it's only a tummy upset,' she protested weakly.

'So you keep insisting,' he replied, head bent once more as he scribbled on the notes in front of him.

Rose had no answer to this and obediently went off to install herself behind the flowery curtain. She took off her dress and hung it on a hook, then lay nervously on the examination couch in her petticoat.

'Try to relax,' he told her as he pressed carefully around her tummy. As apprehensive as she was, Rose had to admit that Dr Cox was very professional in every way and examined her with the utmost care.

'You can get dressed again,' he nodded eventually and

soon she was sitting before him once more. The clock didn't seem quite so loud now and his stare failed to be quite so off-putting, in fact she was certain his lips were tilted into the beginnings of a smile.

'Congratulations, Mrs Weaver.'

Rose stared at him blankly. 'On what?'

'You are pregnant.'

Rose stared at him as if he was speaking another language. 'But that's impossible,' she heard herself mumble in confusion. 'We . . . we've not been able . . . we didn't think . . . we—'

'When was your last period?'

'I – er well, before my husband . . .' She stopped, trying to calculate. Eddie had been arrested on 2nd June. She hadn't had a period since May and she knew why. The same thing had happened after her parents had been killed. Her periods had stopped for eight months and Dr Harding had simply told her it was shock and not to worry, they would return in time, which they had.

Rose began to explain all this to Dr Cox, in a rushed, hectic sort of way, watching him write down the details in his large, neat longhand.

'I would like a sample of your urine, of course,' he said, looking up at her with raised eyebrows. 'From what you've told me my calculation is that your baby is due in February, the middle of the month rather than later.'

'February!' she repeated, feeling poleaxed. 'But . . . but I've just got a job!' was all she managed to splutter.

'Have you indeed?' He nodded slowly. 'Well, depending on your health, which as far as I can discern is good, you would be able to work for several months ahead or as long as you feel able, depending on the type of work you intend to perform. You'll need to take care of yourself, rest, eat a sensible diet . . .'

Dr Cox's words faded into the distance. Even the loud ticking clock could not penetrate Rose's consciousness. She was pregnant. She and Eddie had made a baby. Ever since Marlene they had hoped for another child to come along. Eddie wanted a son, but the years had passed and nothing had happened. Until now.

'See me again in a fortnight and we'll arrange future appointments,' Dr Cox was saying as he stood and escorted her through to the waiting room.

Rose walked out as if in a dream, leaving behind her the smell of frying onions, which from this day onward she would associate with becoming pregnant.

Rose didn't want to go home. She couldn't face Em just yet, she wanted to think about what Dr Cox had told her. She was expecting a baby! A tiny form was growing in her tummy, a vulnerable, precious presence that one day she would hold in her arms.

Thoughts of wonder raced through her mind as she wandered along the street. What would Eddie say? They had wanted a baby for so long and now their wish had come true. Perhaps everything would work out for the best now, she thought hopefully. This might be a new chapter in their lives. Hope began to spread through her like a warm, refreshing glow.

A whiff of smoke blew across her face as she turned the

corner. A group of workmen had set light to a pile of rubbish on a building site. The shell of a ruined house was being fully demolished and the area cleared. Waves of dust blew across the road and swept in her face as a forklift tractor scooped the rubble before it. Everything was in the process of change.

Just like her body. Just like their lives. Fast and furious came the changes sweeping them along, yet all her worries now seemed surmountable. Eddie would get his bail, return home and find Syd. He'd make the man admit to selling him the television and the police would revise their opinion and drop the charge of assault. With this baby, their lives would change.

Rose turned down the opposite street, her step lighter and brisker. She kept walking, not knowing where she was heading, just wanting to extend the wonderful feeling inside her. She needed to savour the miracle of her conception. Would their baby be a boy or a girl? Would it have red hair like Marlene or dark locks like Donnie? Eddie's grey eyes or her own deep brown ones?

Rose viewed all her surroundings through new eyes. The old Victorian terraces looked as though they were sprinkled with stardust and not soot. The small enclave of prefabricated homes, tiny two bedroomed bungalows that were hardly bigger than caravans, now sparkled like little pixie cottages. Life felt suddenly better and more beautiful than it ever had before.

Rose found herself in West Ferry Road and directly in front of her rose the sturdy spire of Christ Church, one of the few churches on the island to survive the Blitz.

Below it, the green branches of a very tall tree waved gently over the buildings below. Set either side of the wide, cobbled road the streetlights formed a picturesque arch. How many times had she walked up this road with her parents and Em to Sunday morning service?

Rose's heart beat fast as she thought of the future now wrapped in a golden glow in her mind like a fairy story. The sun broke the downy haze and splashed hotly on her face. She breathed in its health-giving rays and felt its power travel all the way down to her baby. She realised her happiness must have shown because passers by paused and smiled and even commented on how wonderful the summer was. The world was a beautiful, radiant place and Rose felt like singing her news aloud. But she turned then, eager to be home and to share her wonderful news with Em.

There was a stranger standing on the step of number forty-six as Rose entered Ruby Street. For a moment she held her breath for she didn't recognise the figure and she didn't want anyone or anything to spoil this wonderful day.

But as she grew closer, she exhaled with relief. The stranger was none other than Bobby Morton carrying what looked like a large cardboard box.

'Hello Mrs Weaver,' he said in rather an abashed tone as she approached. 'I've just this minute called by.'

Rose smiled, glancing at Em, who looked like a frightened rabbit about to scuttle away to its hole. Her turban was askew, a few wisps of fair hair straggling out to curl round her chin. Rose banished a swift but unfair urge of irritation as her sister peeped out from the almost closed door.

'Hello Bob – Mr Morton,' she corrected herself, glancing quickly at her sister. 'I'm . . . er, surprised to see you back in this neighbourhood again.'

'Rosy – you've been ages!' Em interrupted angrily. 'I've been so worried about you.'

Rose shrugged. 'It's such a lovely day I didn't rush home.'

Bobby Morton nodded vigorously. 'It's summer at last. Very nice indeed.'

Rose realized the young man was embarrassed, his condition worsened by her sister's unfriendly attitude. Rose smiled at him. 'Don't tell me you want to polish me step again?'

He blushed under his fair hair which was now slightly longer and rather more untidy than Rose remembered it. 'I sold a vacuum cleaner to number eighty-seven and I've just delivered it. This is the box.' He rattled whatever was left inside.

'You sold a vacuum cleaner to the Dixons?' she asked in surprise.

'Yes, they came in my shop last week.'

She was impressed. 'Well, you finally got your lead then.'

'Oh indeed. I gave them a demonstration and they bought an Imp Mark One. A very nice little cleaner that will make all the difference to their lifestyle. Mrs Dixon has a lot of difficulty bending with her arthritis, you know.'

Rose wanted to laugh, but didn't. 'Well, congratulations. But that box looks a bit heavy?'

'More awkward than anything. Next week I'm going to buy myself a small van.'

'Business must be booming,' Rose teased.

'Not really. But I must provide an efficient delivery service. However, back to the reason for my call. I must apologize. I told the Dixons that I knew you.'

Rose raised her eyebrows. 'Did you, now?'

'People are less suspicious if someone can vouch for them,' he said apologetically. 'And the only person I'd met on my travels was you. I said we had a very interesting talk on the merits of washing machines.'

Rose looked stern. 'What if I'd told them you were a rogue?'

He jumped. 'But I'm not!'

'No, you're not, you're a very nice young man,' Rose agreed truthfully, which drew a frown of reproach from her sister.

'That's all right then,' he sighed and glanced at Em. 'I'm very sorry to have disturbed you.'

Her sister's response was no more than a blink and a twitch and Rose felt another wave of irritation. Couldn't Em be a little less hostile? Rose decided she should formally introduce the two.

'Bobby Morton, this is my sister, Emily. Em, this is the young man I was telling you about who's taken over the shop in Amethyst Way.'

'Very pleased to meet you.' Bobby Morton put down the box and offered his hand but he could almost have been pointing a revolver, Rose thought in alarm, as Em gave a visible start. She gave one of her nervous little twitches and stepped back into the house. 'You must er . . . excuse me, I . . . I've got the tea on.' The tiny, turbaned figure disappeared. Rose was embarrassed as they stood there. She didn't know how to excuse her sister's rude behaviour.

'Oh dear,' he sighed as they looked at one another. 'I was in two minds whether to tap or not but I didn't want you to think I'd taken advantage of our first meeting if the Dixons spoke to you. I wish I hadn't now. I think I must have upset your sister.'

'Don't worry, it's not you,' Rose apologized as she pulled the door to so that they couldn't be overheard. 'Em's had – *we've had* – a difficult time lately. Amongst other things, we've been burgled and you're a little more cautious about who you open the door to after that.'

'Burgled!'

'Yes, I'm afraid so. My sister arrived on the day it happened. Naturally, we are still a bit jumpy.'

'Did they catch the culprits?'

Rose shook her head. 'No chance, I'm afraid.'

'Your husband must be very angry,' he said with emphasis.

Rose looked into his shocked face. 'Didn't the Dixons tell you when you mentioned me?'

He stared at her blankly. 'Tell me what?'

Rose hesitated, but she felt sure she could trust this young man. 'Well, you'll probably hear about it sooner or later. Eddie, my husband, was arrested for selling a

233

stolen television to one of our neighbours. He's innocent, of course, and somehow we intend to prove it.'

He blinked his fair lashes. 'No wonder you didn't want to know about televisions!'

She smiled. 'That's not to say I can't see the logic in all your labour-saving devices. Believe me, I was only thinking the other day that if I had the money I'd buy a washing machine. We could do with it with three kids.'

'Three? Didn't you say you had two?'

'My sister has a son of ten.' Rose added quickly, 'She's recently widowed. That's why she's staying with us for a bit.'

'Oh dear,' he commiserated, 'you have been in the wars.'

Rose smiled. 'Yes, just a bit.'

His blue eyes met hers in a rather familiar way and Rose lowered hers. She had no desire to be flattered or flirted with today. There was a very special excitement inside her that surpassed all others.

'Well,' he said, stepping back, 'please apologize to your sister for me. I really didn't intend to frighten her, or you, come to that.' He paused, then added in a rush, 'In fact, I was hoping to meet you again. I've passed your door a couple of times and never had the courage to knock.'

'Oh,' Rose said heavily, as the penny dropped. 'I see.'

He let out a long sigh and groaned. 'Oh dear, I can see by your face I've overstepped the mark.'

Rose blushed. 'Well, you see, Bobby,' she added kindly, 'I've had some wonderful news this morning. Really wonderful. Me and Eddie are . . . expecting.'

'A *baby*, you mean?'

'Yes.' She giggled a little hysterically. 'I'm just so happy, Bobby. So very happy.'

He nodded slowly, unable to hide the disappointment as it dragged down his face. 'Well, all I can say is, he's a lucky man, this Eddie of yours. He really is. So, apart from congratulations, I'm happy for you both. Truly happy.' He looked hard at her, then sighed. A second later he had lifted his box and was grinning over it. 'Well now, off you go and tell your sister the good news.'

Rose smiled. 'Good luck with that new van.'

He walked off, struggling, and Rose hurried in to the kitchen. Em, as usual, was at the sink. She turned and said quickly, 'Who was that?'

'I introduced you, didn't I? He's Bobby Morton and a genuinely nice young man.'

'If you say so.' Em gave her a huffy shrug. 'Well, what happened? What did the doctor say? I've been waiting all day to find out.'

Rose ignored the cross tone and smiled. 'Come and plonk down and I'll tell you.'

They sat at the table. 'Oh, Rosy, what is it?'

'You'll never guess. It's the best piece of news I've had in ages.'

'Is Eddie coming home?' Em gasped.

'No, I wish he was though, especially now. Em, I'm going to have a baby.'

'A baby?' Her sister's gasp was audible.

'All this sickness . . . it isn't an ulcer or worry or anything like that. I'm perfectly healthy. Em, I'm pregnant!'

Rose felt a bubble of laughter rise in her chest. Em gave a little scream then flung her arms around her neck. She had almost forgotten what it was like to be so perfectly, wholly happy, when even the air tasted like a mountain stream and the light that flowed through the kitchen window seemed like a shaft of pure silver. The whole world was alight with breathtaking beauty.

'A baby,' Em repeated in a daze. 'I can't believe it.'

'Nor can I.' Rose blinked her damp lashes. 'But Dr Cox is certain. According to me dates, the baby's due around the middle of next February.'

'Oh Rosy, didn't you guess?' Em asked incredulously.

'I missed me period but I thought it was the upset of Eddie going.'

'What about your job?'

'I don't know.'

'And what will Eddie say?'

Rose giggled. 'I hope that he's pleased. We always wanted another one, a boy if possible.'

'Well, yes . . . but—'

'You're going to say,' Rose cut in, 'that it couldn't have happened at a worse time.'

Em nodded slowly. 'Something like that.'

'I don't care,' Rose said defiantly. 'I want this baby more than anything else in the world – except us all being back together of course.'

A little smile flickered across her sister's face. 'Oh Rosy, 'course not.'

'I'll be able to work for a few months yet.'

'You mean you're still going to work on Monday?'

'Why not? Nothing's changed.' Rose pulled back her shoulders.

'You're not going to tell them you're expecting?'

'Not until I have to. What they don't know won't hurt them.'

The two women sat in silence, until Em stood up with a little switch of her head and a sigh. 'Well, this won't do. I'm behind as it is. This floor needs cleaning.'

Rose suddenly saw the funny side of things. She could have just announced an earthquake was imminent and her sister's only concern would have been that she was behind with the housework. She watched Em go to the cupboard and take out the mop and pail, her brow slightly furrowed under the turban. Rose thought of Bobby Morton and his labour saving devices. She smiled. Although Em and Bobby didn't know it, they had a lot in common.

'What would you like for tea tonight?' Em called over her shoulder and Rose saw and heard not Em, but their mother standing at the sink. Both were similar in stature and height at an inch or two over five foot. Both had narrow yet very straight shoulders and efficient little arms always appearing to be busy. Rose had always felt comforted by the sight of her parents in the kitchen. They worked as a team and her father had rarely declined the offer of a cloth if it had been thrust his way. Now there was no short and stocky masculine figure to stand like a helmsman at the wheel and no Eddie to dance around doing exactly the reverse, attempting to escape from it.

Rose sighed softly. Neither her father nor her husband were here to share in the joy of today's discovery. The two men she loved most in her life were absent. But how much worse must it be for Em?

Arthur had lived in this house for a short while after their marriage and had occupied the chair in the front room for most of that time. Eddie always observed cryptically that Arthur had glued his braces to the cushions. But Em had seemed so blissfully happy in those days. The days of innocence, Rose thought a little sadly, when Arthur's peculiar predilections had not yet surfaced to shatter their lives. Rose wanted to reach out and hug the busy little turbaned figure. She wanted to tell her sister that everything was going to be all right. She knew this because her baby was telling her so. The unbelievable miracle that had happened to Rose would spill over into Em's life, too, and light it up.

'I went up the shop and bought six sausages,' Em said as she lowered the pail to the floor and plunged in the mop. 'I know the girls like Toad in the Hole. Will does too. For afters we could have sponge and custard.'

'Lovely,' Rose said, retracing her steps backwards into the hall as the mop came swishing across the floor followed by a slim little body wielding such energy that Rose retreated quickly to the front room.

Here she sat on the couch and stared at the radiogram. No longer was she preoccupied with the past. There was too much to live for in the present. With a soft smile on her lips she drew a cushion in front of her and hugged it tightly. 'My baby,' she whispered breathlessly, 'my darling baby.'

Chapter Fourteen

'Mr Weaver, the facts relating to the robbery are not in dispute. The issue is whether you were one of those who participated in it.' Charles Herring irritably shuffled the papers in front of him and looked up with an impatient sigh.

'But I never saw the inside of that warehouse, Mr Herring,' Eddie protested once more, wondering what he had to do to convince his counsel he was innocent. Eddie was beginning to think that the brain of Mr Charles Herring, acting for Mr Lance Puckley–Smythe his defence QC, was as impenetrable as the grey November mist outside.

'But you were in the area at the time, you admit to that?' demanded the clerk again.

'Yes, I told you, I'd been up West for the day.'

The severe-faced young man with neatly oiled dark hair and pince-nez spectacles who sat on the other side of the small table, raised his shoulders in a dismissive shrug. 'The newspaper vendor identified you. As a witness for the police – a surprise witness may I add, his testimony is critical to the charge of handling stolen goods.'

Eddie wondered if he'd needed his brains tested on that early spring night in May. Fancy buying a paper when he hadn't even intended to read it? But he'd felt conspicuous walking up and down waiting for his punter. Maybe he should be relieved that his man hadn't turned up and he'd returned home empty-handed. If the newspaper seller had noted a transaction taking place, then he really would have landed in the proverbial soup. 'I just bought a newspaper,' Eddie said brightly. 'It was a coincidence I was in the area.'

'A coincidence indeed,' the young man sniffed.

'Coincidences happen all the time,' Eddie answered dismissively. 'Anyway, do you think I'd really have been daft enough to flog me neighbour a telly that I'd nicked from this Whitechapel job?'

'It's not up to me to surmise,' was the curt reply from a deadpan face. 'But the prosecution are attempting to link your presence in the area to the warehouse burglary and subsequently the sale of the television to Mr Parker. We have to account for your movements on the day of the Whitechapel burglary. This is our foremost concern.'

Eddie listened vaguely to the imperious voice ringing in his ears. He was weary of the constant use of 'our' and 'we' when it was he alone who was being accused of crimes he didn't commit. It was even more ridiculous that he couldn't tell the truth about what he was really doing on that day. Eddie was forced to smile at the irony.

But the young lawyer scowled, glancing at Eddie as though the cat had dragged him in. Eddie felt hot and uncomfortable in his shabby suit, which was suffering the creased effects of five months prison storage. It was his old demob suit, the one that had been donated to him at the end of the war, along with an overcoat, a shirt with two detachable collars, a tie, two pairs of socks, a pair of shoes and a hat. Eddie hated hats and had given it away immediately. The shirt, collars and tie had long gone, but he still wore the suit, shoes and overcoat, thanks to Rose's careful efforts to preserve every stitch of clothing she'd gathered over the last eight years. The suit was as good as new when pressed to perfection by the heavy old iron heated on the grille over the fire. To think he had felt so confident when he last wore the suit on Coronation Day as he strode into Olga Parker's front room. He'd thought himself the cat's whiskers and even the news that Olga had dropped him in it hadn't dampened his spirits. Now he knew the foolishness of his actions. Rose hadn't been far wrong when she'd begged him to avoid close contact with their neighbours.

Eddie began to wish, as he had done innumerable times whilst incarcerated, that he had listened to his wife all those years ago. If only he had bought the licence from Ted Jenkins when he'd retired from his market stall. Cheap enough then, too. Ted had no family and looked on him as a son. But shouting his lungs out behind a stall all day hadn't appealed to his inflated ego and instead he'd continued to trade on the streets and in pubs and at the racetracks. Eddie shivered at the thought of the debt he had incurred since Marlene was born. The next bet was always the big one, until he lost.

But that was water under the bridge now. When he

got out of this tangle he'd settle down and do as Rose wanted. The lesson he had learnt on remand was a bitter one. Three days ago he had climbed the steps to the dock with his heart in his mouth. Here he was, Eddie Weaver, King of the Road, on trial at the most famous criminal court in the world, the Old Bailey. He'd felt numb with shock to find himself a prisoner under the hallowed roof where the majestic figure of Justice lifted her sword and scales above the City. He'd felt physically ill at the sight of all that gleaming, polished wood, black gowns and powdery white wigs. And when Lord Justice Markbury had taken his seat, accompanied by twelve members of the jury on the bench, it was then that Eddie had known the meaning of true fear.

He'd wanted to scream out loud that he hadn't nicked a telly much less been part of a gang wielding hammers and a shotgun. Eddie shivered again. He hated firearms. He was a peaceful man and went out of his way to avoid confrontation. He deeply sympathized with the ware-houseman who had been assaulted and bundled into a cupboard whilst the villains had driven off with thousands of pounds worth of valuable gear.

Eddie believed in British justice, but today he had begun to wonder if anyone would ever believe him. Yesterday he had pleaded Not Guilty to the charges against him. But today had been a nightmare from which he seemed unable to wake. Rose had attended against his wishes. He knew his appearance in the dock would be distressing enough for her in her condition. But he hadn't reckoned on his own feelings of humiliation, which had been the most painful he'd ever experienced. Every now and then she had met his eyes with a look of confused desperation. He'd felt powerless, ashamed. All he'd been able to do was try to convey an apology in his eyes.

'The gang members wore balaclavas,' continued Charles Herring in a flat, detached voice as Eddie returned to the moment. 'Therefore identification of the thieves remains impossible. However, it has been suggested you could have been a lookout.'

Eddie rolled his eyes despairingly. 'All I was doing was walking home minding me own business. Honest.'

'Walking from where?'

'I've told you a thousand times. I'd been up West for the day – trading – and I was on me way home.' By now Eddie had convinced himself this was the truth, for there was no way he could reveal that his trade was made up entirely of punters eager to place their next illegal bet on the street. Added to which, Rose hadn't the least idea of what he had been doing for a living since their second daughter was born. Not that she had ever asked, Eddie thought a little self-righteously, even though at times he had wanted her to. His agreement to keep his business dealings as far away from their doorstep as possible had answered the problem of Rose's concerns. But it had also provided him with carte blanche to do as he liked. If ever he had a twinge of conscience about using their pact for his own ends, he'd smothered it as quickly as it appeared.

The truth was, he was a natural floater, a street runner employed by the bookmakers to extend their business.

Eddie had enjoyed collecting bets from the punters using his street cred to build up a nice little business. It was a job he'd practically fallen into when he'd handled a transaction as a favour for a bookie. The temptation of repeating his success had been overwhelming and very soon he'd become hooked.

'You won't get caught,' the other floaters assured him. 'Lookouts are posted now and watch our backs, so there's no risk. And you can have a nice little bet on the side if you fancy a flutter.'

Because he'd wanted to believe them and because he yearned to give his wife and young family the security he never had as a child, he became putty in the bookies' hands. Rose never questioned his movements and he was free to build up his career. Marlene was just a baby and Donnie only two years old. He promised himself he would give it a few years, just until he was rich.

Eddie loved the thought of wealth. He'd buy a house and a car, move to a posh area of London. He made up little stories of walking in Oxford Street, going in to the stores and buying clothes and jewellery. He spun them in his mind as he began his floating just before eleven and completed by three in the afternoon. He was in the process of concocting a holiday abroad on an island filled with palm trees and surrounded by warm blue water that Wednesday in early May. As he waited to meet his punter in Whitechapel, he was picturing himself and Rose and the girls drinking from coconuts as he waited to meet his punter in Whitechapel. He knew he shouldn't have hung about when his man didn't show, but he hung on hopefully, dreaming away. And then made the fatal mistake of buying a newspaper.

Eddie intensely disliked the patronizing tone of Charles Herring. More important, though, was justifying his reasons for floating. The bottom line was he wanted a better standard of living for his family. He wanted a future. And he'd done everything in his power to achieve one.

He wasn't like the other men in prison. He wasn't guilty of hurting anyone or stealing their property. He wouldn't dream of nicking a pint of milk from a front doorstep; he had always been respectful of other people. He had convinced himself that what he did for a living wasn't wrong. Where was the harm in laying a few quid on a nice little filly? You could bet quite legitimately at a racecourse, so why not in the streets? It was just a question of location. And since the streets of London were his backyard he saw no reason why he shouldn't earn his living from ready money betting. He was good at it. Much better than he was at flogging junk.

'So where are our witnesses, Mr Weaver?' Charles Herring was staring into his eyes and Eddie jumped.

'Witnesses?'

'The defence currently boasts a grand total of two. Mr Edward Dunkley, landlord of the public house The Lock and Key, and this . . . er . . .'

'Syd.'

'Exactly. We know nothing of this man except his first name.'

Eddie blinked. He was staring sightlessly at the face in front of him. There it was again, the royal 'we' which was beginning to irritate him even more than the mention of the mythical Syd. 'Mr Herring, I've been stuck in jug for the past five months,' Eddie said vehemently. 'Me bail was turned down, remember? How am I supposed to turn him up?'

'Your appeal was refused on fear of flight.'

Eddie laughed. 'Where would I have flown to? I'm a family man. I've got a wife and kids and a baby on the way. Can you see me doing a runner?'

The young man folded the large brown file together, returning it to his briefcase. He removed his spectacles and slid them carefully into an expensive looking leather pouch, whereupon he stared Eddie straight in the eye. 'Now, to the assault charge—'

Eddie groaned aloud. 'It's all cobblers, ain't it? Old Bill fitted me up on that one. You know it, I know it and they know it.'

'But the jury doesn't, alas.'

Eddie shrugged. 'Well then, let me explain. Put me in the box, Mr Herring. I need to defend meself. I know I can convince them. They're ordinary Londoners just like me, most with families. I'll wager they will understand when I describe how the coppers came marching in me house and steam-rollered all over the place.'

His visitor sighed resignedly, 'I hope your faith in human nature is justified, Mr Weaver.'

Eddie looked puzzled. 'Well, this is England, ain't it? We've got the best system of justice in the world. You told me yourself they have to prove you guilty beyond a shred of doubt.'

Charles Herring said nothing.

Eddie sighed. He didn't care for this man, this trumped-up clerk who clearly didn't believe a word he said. 'I need to talk to the guv'nor,' he decided, determined to corner the elusive QC who was fighting his case but rarely seemed to appear in the flesh.

The young man effected a smile and stood up. He collected his papers and signalled to the officer on duty. 'Mr Puckley-Smythe has a busy morning tomorrow, but I'll see what I can do.'

Eddie listened to the echoing sounds of metal doors swinging open and closing. In the claustrophobic confines of the small interview room he was alone but for the guard. His palms were running with sweat. What would happen tomorrow when he was in the box? His need to persuade the court of his innocence was so strong he could almost taste it. He refused to consider the possibility of going down for a stretch that would see his kids teenagers by the time he was free. The thought made his blood run cold. Instead he pictured Rose and the girls waiting for him as he was released, the jury having found him innocent. He couldn't wait to hold his family in his arms.

'Blimey Benny, mind them holes, she'll be having it on the seat if you're not careful!' Anita clung on to Rose's arm. The lorry hit yet another dip in the road and Benny swore under his breath.

'Sorry, ladies.'

Rose was squashed in between Anita and Benny in the

cab of the lorry. Surreptitiously, she tried to alter her position but her bump restricted movement. 'Don't worry about me,' Rose shrugged, although with each sharp descent her back, under the baby's weight, gave an unpleasant creak.

'Are you still sure it's a boy?' Anita nodded to Rose's cherry red coat, one she had borrowed from Jane Piper to wear for her trip to the Old Bailey. Having no coat large enough of her own, the bright red raglan sleeve had seen Jane through three pregnancies and would probably do for the fourth. Rose had felt a little conspicuous entering the court this morning in such a striking colour, especially as Anita had worn her best smart, dark suit. But tonight she didn't care what she looked like. The proceedings of the day had left her utterly confused. Rose's attention had been fixed on Eddie and sometimes she'd lost track entirely as she'd tried to look into his eyes. For a few precious moments they had seemed to join together in a world of their own until their attention had been wrenched back to the proceedings.

'Yes, I'm certain,' Rose replied as Benny swerved again and the big wheels of the lorry grazed the kerb. She gripped the seat as the jolt shook the cab.

'Benny Mendoza, look where you're going will you?' Anita leaned forward, shouting across at her husband.

'It's these bloody roads,' he muttered peering through the windscreen.

'It's your bloody driving.'

At six-and-a-half months pregnant Rose hadn't been able to attend the first day of the trial because of the long journey into the City, but Benny had offered to drive her on the second day, since he was delivering locally. Should he fail to show up at Ludgate Hill on his return from Essex, their contingency plan was to use the nearest tube at St Paul's. But Benny had promised to collect them and was, in fact, early. He had managed to park his lorry close to the designated meeting place.

'I'm really grateful for the lift,' Rose told Benny, who looked a bit downcast as he struggled to negotiate both the busy traffic and the bumps.

'Think nothing of it,' Benny grinned, crunching the gear lever. 'I'm doing a Blackheath run tomorrow, so I could do the same again if it would help.'

'That would be wonderful,' Rose smiled. She was trying not to think about the next day but knew she had to face it. Today, Tuesday, the prosecution had called a witness, a newspaper seller, to testify that Eddie had been seen in the area of the robbery. It was a surprise for everyone, including Eddie it seemed who had gone chalk white when the witness took the stand.

'You ain't going back to work are you?' Anita asked then.

'No. Gwen said I was to take the week off. The woman I've stepped in for comes back next month. The leg she broke is better now.' Rose added wistfully, 'Anyway, I don't think I could go on much longer. I'm showing a lot now and even though Gwen put me on sandwich and roll filling and all the sit down jobs, I've been feeling top heavy lately.'

'Did you get any joy from the old Assistance?' Anita

asked, knowing Rose had visited the council offices last week.

'There's a lot of paperwork involved,' Rose replied, shuddering at the memory of the harassed and patronizing young woman who interrogated her. 'But yes, I qualify for help with the baby, I hope.'

'It's your right to claim whilst Eddie's away,' Anita shouted above the sudden grind of the engine as Benny slowed in traffic.

'Did you speak to Eddie today?' Benny interrupted as they came to a standstill.

'No, there wasn't time.'

'Poor bugger,' Anita said hoarsely. 'He don't deserve all this.'

Rose swallowed hard. 'No. And even though he was seen close to the warehouse on that day, the gang all wore balaclavas and can't be identified.'

'So no one can say it was Eddie then,' Benny declared as they began to move forward once more.

'It was just bad luck,' Anita nodded, 'Eddie being close to that Whitechapel warehouse.'

'Yes, a coincidence,' Rose agreed.

After this there was silence until Anita said hesitantly, 'Don't Eddie ever say where he's been, then?'

Rose shrugged disinterestedly. 'We don't have much time to talk about anything except the kids. It's only Friday nights he's in early.'

'But does he often trade up West?' Anita persisted.

'Sometimes,' Rose nodded and looked away.

The journey seemed to take an age as Benny drove

towards Poplar. Rose didn't want to be rude but she just couldn't face one of Anita's grillings, as well intentioned as they might be. Fortunately it was the weather that put an end to the subject of Eddie's movements.

'I don't like the look of this,' Benny grumbled as he crunched into gear. The evening was drawing in as were the veils of silvery white that threaded across the bonnet of the lorry.

'Are we nearly home?' Rose shivered.

'Not too far.' Benny peered through the windscreen and flashed the headlights. 'It's gonna be treacherous later.'

'At least it's slowed you down,' Anita said grimly.

'I ain't a fast driver,' her husband protested. 'You should see how fast some of the blokes go. They sit right on your bumper if you don't get a move on.'

'I'd put two fingers up to them if it were me,' Anita said bolshily.

'You wouldn't last two minutes on the road,' her husband grinned. 'You ain't got the patience.'

'Hark at it,' Anita retorted sarcastically. 'He can't wait two minutes for his dinner without complaining it's not ready, or five minutes for the khazi. The only place he waits in silence is at The Lock and Key and that's because his tongue's stuck to the roof of his mouth with thirst.'

Rose smiled fondly as she listened to her friends familiar banter, a welcome diversion from the gruelling events of the day. The sight of the forbidding law courts had made her feel faint and to see Eddie in custody standing high in the box, had filled her with dismay. An ache had gripped her chest as she'd listened to the charges read aloud and Lord Justice Markbury, the officiating judge, possessed a deep, brusque bark that made her quake inside. The baby had moved restlessly all that morning as she'd listened to the details of the warehouse burglary, a property owned by a prestigious London store. The thieves had tied up one of the terrified employees and waved a shotgun. As it was a Wednesday half day the man had been alone and was easily overpowered. The valuable electrical goods, reproduction antique furniture and silverware due to be dispatched to the store had been loaded into a removals van and driven off by the thieves. The prosecution counsel suggested Eddie was a lookout, linking his movements on this day with the sale of the television a month later.

Rose wondered what the jury were thinking. Would they believe Eddie was part of the gang? If only she had been able to find Syd and prove that Eddie had bought the television in all honesty.

'Cheer up, it may never happen,' Anita said softly beside her as Benny crunched a gear. 'Tomorrow is a new day, love. Your old man will come out trumps, wait and see.'

Rose nodded faintly. She missed Eddie so much and had been shocked to see his face so gaunt and his big eyes full of pain. She promised herself things would be different when he came home. She would take a real interest in what he did and where he went. Show him that she cared about his work and wanted to be part of it. She knew she had become involved with the girls to such a degree her home and family took pride of place, whilst

Eddie came last. She loved him dearly but accepted she had taken him for granted. She wanted to be like Benny and Anita, flinging the insults back and forth and never taking offence, sitting down in the evening and discussing what had transpired in Benny's day. Anita knew all Benny's movements, the stops he made and the people he spoke to. She was always telling Rose of amusing little incidents, and she insisted the boys sit down to an evening meal whenever possible with their father. Their family holiday at Butlin's this year had been a resounding success, just as Anita had planned.

Rose considered her own efforts to unite the family. Were they satisfactory or had she allowed bad habits to creep in? Perhaps she would allow the girls to stay up half an hour later in the evenings to see their dad before they went to bed. Rose sighed wistfully. And after they were asleep, no matter how tired she felt, she would sit down with Eddie and discuss all he had done instead of wasting time with trivialities.

'Here we are,' Benny said then as a familiar row of post war council housing came into view. 'Fifteen minutes and we'll be home.'

But the fifteen minutes weren't up before Rose gave a gasp. She tried to muffle her indrawn breath. A pain shot across her tummy and held it in a vice-like grip.

'Are you all right, love?' Anita frowned in concern.

Rose bit her lip and nodded. Perhaps this was cramp. She couldn't relax as she waited for the pain to disappear, but her brow was beaded with sweat and Anita noticed.

'What is it, girl, tell me!'

'I don't know, Neet.' She held the sides of her tummy as panic curled into her throat. 'I can't breathe . . . me stomach is like lead.'

'Hold on, love, we'll get you to the doctor,' Anita yelled above the noise of the engine. 'Benny, take the next left for Dr Cox's.'

A clammy wave of nausea engulfed her. The pain deepened and she clutched her tummy with trembling hands. As Benny changed direction through the fog, she felt a hot little trickle between her legs. All she remembered thinking was that her coat was red too and wouldn't show the stain.

Em, Anita and Benny were all staring down at her. 'How are you feeling, love?' Anita asked with unusual concern.

'The doctor said you'll be all right as long as you keep your feet up,' Em interrupted before Rose could reply as her sister pulled the sheet tightly across her chest.

Rose tried to resist. 'I want to get up.'

'Well, you can't,' Em and Anita shouted at the same time.

'You gotta take notice of the old King's Proctor,' Benny said in a gentle tone from above the heads of the two women. 'You've been overdoing it, gel.'

'Dr Cox said bed rest from now on,' echoed her sister once more tugging on the eiderdown as if she was wrapping Rose in a straightjacket.

'But I've got to be in court tomorrow!'

Anita and Em were shaking their heads even before she'd finished her sentence and Rose stared up at them helplessly. Anita sat stiffly on the bed. She had worn a dark wool two piece suit to the Old Bailey and a little scarf pinned at the collar with a marquisette clip, matching leaf earrings adorned her earlobes and her short fair hair was, for once, neatly combed. She said very gently, 'You want this baby safe and sound don't you, love?'

'Of course I do, but—'

'There's no buts where a pregnancy is concerned. You lost a few spots today and you know what that means.'

At this Benny flushed, cleared his throat and shifted away from the bedside to disappear very quickly out of the door.

'Rosy,' Em said as she clutched her hands together, 'you know you could have miscarried, don't you? I don't want to be an alarmist, but you must think of the baby.'

Rose knew her sister was right, had known deep down in her soul as Anita and Benny had helped her into Dr Cox's surgery that the symptoms she was exhibiting were danger signals. The young doctor had confirmed her fears as he listened to the baby's disturbed heartbeat and taken her blood pressure. 'I'm sorry, Mrs Weaver,' he'd said slowly after giving her a thorough examination, 'but I must advise rest – total rest – from now on until the baby is born. Your blood pressure is raised and added to the show of blood, I urge great caution. Of course I don't want to worry you—'

Rose looked at the two women at her bedside. Her sister stood upright like a wraith, bedecked from head to foot in black but thankfully devoid of the turban, whilst

Anita sat on the bed in her smart suit, both of them with expressions of regret yet quiet determination on their faces.

'Our Benny said he'd stand in for you,' Anita said with a little smile. 'And he'll get word to Eddie that we're making you take it easy.'

'But he'll worry,' Rose protested unhappily, 'if I'm not there.'

'He'll worry more if he sees you carried out of the courtroom on a stretcher,' Em pointed out bluntly.

Rose sniffed as the tears were close to spilling. She couldn't let Eddie down. She had to be there. He would need her moral support even if she couldn't say anything to help him.

'Look, love,' Anita began reasonably, 'you're not in pain now so it's natural for you to want to continue as normal. But if you move about you'll put the babe at risk and you've got to bring that blood pressure down. You don't want another turn like today because the consequences are unthinkable. Dr Cox said you've had a warning. The question is, are you going to be sensible and listen to it?' Anita patted her knee under the eiderdown. 'Take his advice. For little 'un's sake.'

'There's no two ways about it,' Em said in an authoritative voice, which Rose thought was bordering on hysteria. 'You have to do what he says. Or . . . or—'

'Or we'll all be worrying silly,' Anita settled for, giving Rose a sly wink as Em turned away and fussed with Jane Piper's cherry red coat.

Rose screwed her hands together under the sheet then

drew her fingers over the nightgown that Em and Anita had helped her to put on, swinging her legs up on to the bed as if she was geriatric. She wanted the best for her baby, of course, but she'd planned to stay on at work until Christmas to earn a bonus and most of all, she had been preparing herself for the remainder of Eddie's trial. Now all her plans were in jeopardy, added to which the thought of staying in bed for the next two-and-a-half months was inconceivable.

Suddenly there were voices on the landing outside and a big knuckle drummed on the door. Benny's voice shouted, 'Is it all clear to come in?'

'Yes,' Anita and Em shouted together.

In came Benny carrying Marlene, who was dressed in her nightgown and looked almost asleep. 'The boy and Donnie are asleep but Marle just woke up,' he said gruffly, 'and wants a cuddle.'

'Come on pet, slip into bed with Mummy,' Rose murmured as she struggled to pull back the bedclothes.

'Here, wait a moment,' Em said as she went to Rose's aid and helped her niece snuggle under the warm bedclothes.

'You're in bed early, Mummy,' she yawned as she threaded her arm over Rose's bump.

'Yes,' Rose smiled, burying her nose in the thatch of red curls that smelt deliciously of Sunlight.

'Was you tired?'

'A little,' Rose nodded, but her daughter's eyes were already closed and her breathing smooth. In seconds she was asleep, effortlessly curling around Rose's bulky shape.

She felt a wave of pleasure flow through her body at the close physical contact and knew then that her priority was her girls and the vulnerable life growing inside her. 'I know you're all right,' she conceded as she looked up. 'You can stop worrying, Em, I won't try to escape.'

'I should hope not,' her sister sighed, visibly relaxing.

'So we won't need to post a guard, then?' Anita confirmed.

Rose smiled for the first time. 'I know when I'm beaten.'

'Could've fooled me,' Em sniffed. 'I've been trying to persuade you to give up work for the past two months.'

'Well, now I'll have to, won't I?' She looked up at Benny. 'Benny, are you certain you want to go in my place?'

He gave her a growl, looking like a big brown bear in his patched driving jacket and old trousers, and his tight dark hair growing down the back of his neck. 'Wild horses wouldn't stop me, gel. There ain't nothing I can't do next week with a bit of shifting around.'

Rose felt the baby move under Marlene's arm. Her heart did a little somersault as it always did when Number Three was up to his antics. She arched her back carefully lifting her spine as she imagined the baby stretching his limbs.

'It's definitely a boy,' she said as she looked up with shining eyes. 'He's playing football again.'

'Then he's a Stanley or a Matthew, ain't he?' Benny remarked dryly. 'There ain't no one in the world plays a better winger than Stanley Matthews.'

They all laughed, and Rose allowed herself the luxury of imagining Number Three outside in the backyard, bashing a football against the Anderson fence with Eddie running around with him, teaching him how to dribble and head the ball. And there she would be, cooking the dinner and watching them play through the kitchen window, simply bursting with pride. Rose sighed contentedly. She wasn't that keen on Stanley for a name, but Matthew would do very nicely. Even when shortened to Matt, it had a ring to it. Matthew Weaver, yes, she liked that. With a lump in her throat she wondered if Eddie would too.

Chapter Fifteen

'Ding-de-dong, ding-de-dong, ding-dong,' echoed the radio downstairs. Daphne Oxenford's clear, articulate voice drifted up from the kitchen radio to the boys' bedroom where Anita was cleaning. Today, Friday, she had given the house a once over, since Mrs H was away for a long weekend and didn't require her services until Monday.

Anita was trying not to think about the proceedings at the Old Bailey today. Eddie's evidence and the summing up would be over by now. Had the jury come to a decision? Her mind felt exhausted with different hypotheses and she was trying to fill every moment to avoid creating yet another. She didn't dare go in to Em and Rose next door. Not until Benny came home and then they'd go in together.

The boys' bedroom, an antidote to the tension, was at the top of Anita's hit list of chores. She had discovered dirty pants under the beds along with socks as stiff as walking sticks. Crumpled shirts were dropped carelessly on the floor of their wardrobe and a box of rubbish smelt to high heaven. Anita was not impressed.

Did they think she lived for their benefit alone? Stripping the sheets off the two mattresses and throwing them over the banister, a small object landed at her feet.

Anita bent down and picked it up. The dog-end had been clumsily concealed under the pillow, no doubt for revival tonight. She couldn't be certain from which bed it had fallen, but she had expressly forbidden smoking in their room. For the last twelve months, whilst she had been trying to abstain herself, she had forbidden smoking at all in the house. The fact that she was secretly puffing once more made no difference to her overall plan of action. Benny had almost set himself alight in the front room one evening when a Woodbine had dropped from his fingers to the cushion whilst snoozing. The boys had had a good laugh at Benny's expense, but Anita had implemented the rule immediately. No smoking in the house. Although they denied it flat, her boys smoked like chimneys. After a Saturday night out they had dog's breath and smelly clothes to prove it.

She would have a word with the buggers tonight, although a flat denial was all she'd receive. God help her, the sooner the little sods were taken off her hands, the better. Anita energetically scooped up the clothes that littered the small bedroom. How many years had she been tidying up after men?

Suddenly the familiar voice of Daphne Oxenford broke into her thoughts. *Listen With Mother* always evoked bittersweet memories no matter how hard she tried not to get sentimental. How her two little boys had once loved that short fifteen minutes of pure escapism!

Daphne Oxenford was Anita's own favourite reader with her cut glass accent and beautiful lilt. Catherine Edwards came a close second. Anita paused to recall Alan and David as healthy, happy four and five-year-olds, their beautiful dark eyes filling with wonder the moment they heard those tempting words, 'Are you sitting comfortably? Then I'll begin.'

Anita had always set aside time to be with her young sons even when she'd started to work part-time as a cleaner. She'd even persuaded them to sit a little longer and endure ten minutes of *Woman's Hour*. But as they'd grown older, the novelty had worn off. Anita hummed softly to herself. 'The Old Clockmaker' was the theme tune to *Jennings at School* and she loved it even now. The boys had sung along with her then, both of them with voices like foghorns even as kids.

When had it happened that *Children's Hour* faded into oblivion and *Dick Barton, Special Agent*, had stolen their affections? She couldn't remember now, but she could still hum that theme tune too.

'Da-da-dad-drrra-da-drrr-dadadahh . . .' Anita sang as she turned to the window and pressed her forehead against the cold glass. Her breath formed an opaque curtain in front of her nose and she stroked it gently with her fingertips.

Her boys had grown up so quickly. From babies in nappies to grown men almost. There had been so much more she'd wanted to do with them. Holidays for instance. She'd dreamed of taking them abroad, visiting the Eiffel Tower and the Arc de Triomphe in Paris, a city she'd always wanted to see. None of them, except Benny, had ever been abroad. And he'd only travelled in the Merchant Navy. At least they had made Skegness this year.

Anita turned away from the window, her gaze landing on the two boys' beds and all the accoutrements of youth. On the chest of drawers lay an untidy assortment of combs, brushes, Brylcreem jars and a signed photograph of a young blonde Redcoat. She had chosen Alan to dance with her in the Princes' Ballroom and although he'd gone beetroot he'd obliged very nicely. No two left feet for Alan, Anita thought proudly. Unlike David, Alan was a born dancer and lately spent his Saturday evenings jitterbugging at a local dancehall. Now he gazed at the Redcoat's photograph every day, swearing he was going back next year to dance with her again.

Anita wondered if they would all return to Butlin's as a family? The two weeks this year had been the best holiday of their lives. She was saving again. David had engineered himself a job after school at the bike shop in Poplar. And Benny, equally impressed by Butlin's, was working as many Sundays as he could find. So maybe they might make it again. Just one more time. Once before her babies left the nest . . .

The front door banged. Anita jumped. She left the boys' untidy room and hurried out on the landing.

'Benny? Is that you?'

No reply. David or Alan would have yelled out, immediately wanting something. But Alan didn't knock off from Kirkwoods until four and David was going straight to the bike shop. On the other hand, Benny would have come up directly to tell her the news.

Anita went slowly down the stairs. The light was on in the kitchen and the fire was alight in the front room flickering shadows across the bottom of the stairs. The November evening had darkened swiftly but the house felt warm and inviting.

A figure stepped towards her and Anita gave a startled cry. 'Benny! You scared the life out of me!' She stopped abruptly on the bottom step. Her husband's face was grey and lined despite his youthfully olive skin. He'd worn a dark suit especially for court this morning and when he'd left, it seemed to fit him perfectly. He was stocky and muscular and finding a second-hand navy blue suit at the market had been one of Anita's most satisfying buys. The trousers had needed an inch off the bottoms but Rose had managed the alteration for her. She'd also let down the sleeves to encompass Benny's unusually thick arms. Being one size larger than Benny's normal size, the jacket had easily accommodated his broad shoulders. But now he seemed to have shrunk inside the cloth. He'd pulled out the knot of his tie and undone the button of his white shirt. Anita felt a frisson of attraction flow through her and then, unexpectedly, a great tenderness.

'Come and sit down,' she said and he followed her into the front room. He took his usual armchair by the fire and she one of the dining chairs. Anita was shocked as she met his eyes. She knew straight away what was wrong. He had been weeping.

'I'll make a cuppa,' she blurted, confused by her

discovery. She had never seen Benny weep, once perhaps when Alan was born, but those were tears of sheer joy. Anita knew that Benny's emotions were kept tightly under lock and key. He would die rather than expose his true feelings of sensitivity, yet it was clear in his face that something had touched him to the core.

Benny shook his head and lifted a hand to stop her from leaving. 'No, don't go,' he muttered as his eyes moistened and he continued to shake his head. 'It's all over,' he whispered hoarsely, 'poor bastard.' He shivered physically. 'Neet, I never want to go through anything like that again. I'd rather die before I saw David or Alan come up before a beak.'

'Struth, Benny,' Anita breathed anxiously, 'what are you talking about? Our boys ain't criminals.'

'Nor is Eddie but that didn't make no difference today. It don't make sense, it really don't. Eddie's a family man, innocent of any of those charges and yet . . .' His voice was shaking and Anita swallowed.

'Benny, tell me what happened?'

He sank back against the cushion and exhaled. 'Eddie went down, gel.'

Anita closed her eyes. The news was not unexpected to her. No matter how much they had all hoped otherwise, she'd secretly feared the worst. 'How long for?'

'Two years.'

Anita stared at the top of her husband's head as it sunk to his chest. She had never expected Benny to lose the raven black, wiry hair that clung to his skull with such determination. But she could see clearly now the faint pink outline of his scalp that a few years ago had been masked to the eye by thick, tight curls. Her heart gave another treacherous lurch as slowly she allowed Benny's words to sink in. 'Poor bloody Rose,' she whispered brokenly.

Benny looked up, taking a huge breath that startled his wife. 'It ain't as bad as it seems, you know.'

Anita snorted, fighting back the tears. 'You could have fooled me.'

'They couldn't prove the warehouse job but they found him guilty on handling the stolen telly and obstructing the coppers. The assault charge was thrown out and the old beak gave him two years to run concurrently, not consecutively, thank Gawd.'

'You mean he might have had to do four?' Anita gulped.

'Yeah, it could have gone that way.' Benny gave a twisted smile. 'They couldn't pin the warehouse on him and that's a lot to be grateful for. And the jury must've listened to what he said about the police doing him over because they went for the obstruction instead.'

Anita shook her head sorrowfully. 'But he shouldn't be doing time at all.'

'I know that, gel. He's as clean as you or me.'

'Eddie's a good bloke,' Anita agreed heatedly, 'but I wish he was a bit more savvy. If you ask me, he's easily led up the path.'

'Yeah. But his intentions are good.'

Anita raised an eyebrow. 'Yeah, but ain't the road to hell paved with 'em?'

Benny looked at her with his sad eyes. His big, swarthy face was regaining a little of its natural colour. 'Neet, I'd rather walk down a road with Eddie than I would share a cloud with the Angel Gabriel. Eddie's me mate and when I saw him take that little lot on the jaw today, me heart nearly broke. And that's not an admission I'd make to anyone but you. It's so bloody unfair when there's devious buggers about that would steal from their own mothers if they had the chance. No, Eddie ain't no villain. And he may be easily led, but he's got a heart of gold and I love him for it.'

At her husband's words Anita was powerless to stop the tears from falling from her eyes and they slipped down her cheeks, resisting her efforts to sweep them away.

Benny rose and came towards her, lifting her gently and folding her into his arms. 'We gotta be strong for Rose, love,' he whispered against her forehead. 'Her and the kids will need all the help we can give.'

'I know, poor cow.'

'First off, we'll slip Em a few quid from the holiday fund.'

Anita looked up in surprise. 'You'd really give up our Butlin's money?'

Benny nodded slowly. ''Course I would. We had one blooming good holiday with the kids and we couldn't top that, could we?'

'Oh, Benny, you're a good man.'

He grinned, shrugging off the rare compliment. 'Don't you believe it. I got ulterior motives. I was trying to think of a way to get out of all that old time dancing stuff you kept dragging me into.'

Despite her husband's attempts to make light of his generosity, Anita felt humbled; Benny was indeed a good man but he never failed to surprise her. After eighteen years of marriage she thanked God for the precious qualities that were stored like gold nuggets in the deep layers of his soul.

He tilted her chin with his rough fingers and she leaned into him, her rock. 'I love you, Mrs M,' he murmured and kissed her, rubbing her wet cheeks with the coarse pads of his thumbs.

'And I love you, Benny Mendoza,' she sighed. 'But don't tell anyone, will you?'

They kissed again, a little longer this time, then hand in hand they went next door to see Rose.

The baby's bonnet was almost complete; all she had left to do was stitch the ribbon to the sides and add a tiny silk bow to the top. The matching bootees and mittens, both knitted in a shade of blackbird's egg blue lay on the dressing table along with the lemon matinee coat Anita had brought in and the soft white shawl embroidered with cross stitch that Em had made.

Rose let the bonnet slip from her hands on to the eiderdown as the baby moved, his elbow, foot or knee gently jerking under her stretched skin. Her fingers lay lightly on her nightdress and she held her breath at the joy of his presence within her. He was so active, more so even than Marlene, who had provoked backache and indigestion throughout the whole of the pregnancy. But this little body gave her only pleasure and for his sake, Rose intended to be brave.

Two years. Twenty-four months, of which Eddie had already served six. Just one year to endure, really. The following year, 1955, would be easier. Benny had said there would be time off for good behaviour. Rose felt herself go hot, then cold. She had prepared herself for today, accepting that only a fool would have dared to hope for a verdict of Not Guilty to all the charges.

Rose lifted the little bonnet with shaky fingers. If she had some blue ribbon left she could have finished it tonight. Beside the bed was a small wooden table and on it lay her knitting and sewing bag. This would be her lifeline until February. She would knit and sew every day, using all the skeins of silk and unpicked balls of wool that she had been given to prepare for the baby's birth. She would not think of what had happened today, but look forward to next year, to the blessing of her son.

Rose sat dry-eyed, refusing to allow outside events into the sacred world of her unborn son. She didn't care if she had to lie to herself for the next two-and-a-half months; her priorities were clear. She would tell Matthew everything there was to know about Eddie, about their lives, their history, their beginnings and their island community. She would leave nothing unsaid in the small hours when she was restless and yearning to be free from the bed and on her feet again. She would put every minute to good use, educating her child, telling him how much he was loved and how dearly he had been wanted.

Rose felt the kick again and smiled. 'Matthew,' she whispered and lifted herself slightly against the pillows. 'Matthew Weaver, how does that sound?'

Another little kick and Rose nodded as though she could hear the baby's reply. She talked softly, her hands clasped across her belly tracing the movements. She told him all that Benny had said about Stanley Matthews being the best footballer in the world, about the backyard and the street they lived in, the school he would go to and the wide and wonderful river that flowed through the City.

She was just beginning to tell him about the tall ships that had ploughed so gracefully through its waters for centuries before the Coronation of the Queen of England, when she heard a movement outside the door.

'Donnie? Is that you?' Rose asked softly.

'No, it's me.' Em appeared, the collar of her thick, grey, woolly dressing gown up to her ears where curlers dangled neatly from her head. 'I thought I heard voices.'

Rose blushed. 'I was just talking to the baby.'

Em closed the door and tiptoed in. 'Are you all right?'

''Course I am.'

Her sister stood shivering and frowning. 'Are you sure? After what happened today—'

'Em, it's not the end of the world, is it?'

For a moment a pair of hazel brown eyes looked startled. 'I don't understand. We thought you'd be—'

'Well, I'm not,' Rose cut in before her sister could make a song and dance about Eddie's two year sentence. 'I'm going to get through this, Em, for the baby's sake. And for the girls, of course. Eddie will want to return to

a family, not a house full of shivering wrecks.' Rose
threw back the eiderdown. 'Come and sit in with me. I
know it's late, but you'll freeze out there.'

Em didn't need telling twice and slipped under the
warm sheet, snuggling against Rose as she had done
before Rose was confined to bed. 'I hope you aren't in
delayed shock,' she said cautiously, pulling the eiderdown
across her chest. 'It happened to me after I found out
about Arthur. I couldn't stop shaking for a week.'

Rose slid her warm hand through the crook of her
sister's arm. 'You poor old thing. And you had no one to
share your problems with. Why didn't you write to me
and explain?'

Em gave a shuddery sigh. 'How could I put what
Arthur had done in a letter? It was hard enough to believe
meself.'

'I wish I could have helped. I should have been there
for you.'

'That's daft, Rosy,' Em said with feeling. 'Me and Will
would be on the streets if it wasn't for you.'

'No you wouldn't. I told you, this is your home and
always will be.'

'It's just till I get on me feet that's all.'

'Anyway, Eddie said he was pleased you're here,' Rose
replied as she recalled the second prison visit she had
made in August after writing to tell Eddie she was
pregnant. She had received a visiting order soon afterwards and Benny had driven her to Brixton. It had been
a visit of mixed emotions as Eddie digested all that Dr
Cox had said. He'd been convinced his appeal to be

bailed would be granted. Rose had been on the point of explaining about the money, but decided at the last minute not to. She didn't want to spoil their short time together. And if push came to shove, she would pawn the pearl necklace and every last stick of furniture in the house. But Eddie's appeal had been turned down. He'd written to say that he didn't want her to travel all the way to the prison again in her condition, even though Benny had offered to drive her.

Part of her was relieved at his decision. She recalled the pregnant mothers with their tense, unhappy faces and huge bulges lining up in the prison courtyard. But not seeing his dear face had saddened her deeply. She ached just to be close to him once more.

'He still doesn't know about the money, does he?' Em's quiet voice broke into her thoughts and Rose shook her head.

'No. I shan't see him until after the baby is born either.'

Em gave a deep sigh and they both stared out of the window, the bottom half draped with a frilly net. Rose could no longer see the full moon, a cheesy whole that earlier in the evening had hidden behind the big, racing clouds. The mists had evaporated since Benny and Anita had left and sleep was impossible at midnight, even though she had the whole of the double bed to herself. Em was sleeping on the couch downstairs in the front room and Will had returned to the girls' room after decamping twice.

'Are you sleeping all right?' Rose was concerned that Em's nightmares were continuing.

'Fine, thanks. I made those tatty old curtains stored at the back of the girls' wardrobe into a proper cover. You said you were only keeping them for rags, so I stitched them tightly around the arms and sides so that the holes in the seat are well and truly padded.'

Rose wondered if her sister had deliberately misunderstood her question but Em seemed happy enough to be sleeping downstairs so she smiled and said quietly, 'You're so talented with your fingers, Em, Mum would be proud of you.'

Surprisingly, Em giggled. 'I wonder if she's watching now and telling us it's time to put out the light? You know, like when we were kids and got in the same bed to keep warm. Your feet was always like toast, mine like ice. You always let me warm me toes on you.'

'Happy days,' Rose agreed wistfully. 'Now Donnie and Marle and Will are sleeping in our room and you and me are in Mum and Dad's. We've not gone far, have we?'

Em turned to look at her balefully. 'No, but sometimes I feel like I've lived one lifetime already and I'm on borrowed time. Sometimes it feels as if . . . as if—'

'As if what?' Rose asked anxiously.

'Nothing, nothing really,' Em whispered and looked away.

Rose stared at Em's profile, at the small nose and neatly pointed chin, the rather gaunt cheeks that seemed too fragile to support the huge hazel eyes above capped by thick brown eyebrows. Her sister had suffered and it showed. 'Em, you've never – well, never got *that* low have you? You wouldn't ever do anything silly?'

Her sister looked down and after an unsettling pause, shook her head. 'No, I wouldn't now.'

Rose swallowed. 'What do you mean – now?'

'I mean I felt so ashamed when I found out about Arthur and those boys, I thought about putting me head in the oven and just drifting off. If it hadn't been for Will, I might have.'

'But you had nothing to do with what Arthur did!' Rose exclaimed in dismay. 'You were a good wife and mother and have nothing to reproach yourself for.'

'Haven't I?'

''Course not. Arthur had everything. He wanted for nothing with you as his wife.'

'Except sex,' Em replied in a dull voice. 'We had Will and that was enough for him. I don't think he could bear to touch me afterwards.'

'But you had no control over that, dear,' Rose said gently. 'You were a young girl in love, who had never been with a man before and Arthur was a man of the world, someone who should have known better than to get married if he felt the way he did. He couldn't suddenly have developed his appetite for young men or boys. He must have known what he was like at his age. You weren't responsible for the decisions he made to ruin his life – or yours.'

But Em shook her head. 'I wish I could see it that way. I feel . . .' she stopped, her mouth twitching again, the tick that had been subdued before now flaring up as she blinked her eyes and searched for words.

'You feel what, love?'

'Ugly. Dirty,' Em replied in a small voice as her little curlers began to tremble around her head. 'I don't even like people looking at me. I hate going out. I feel as if they can see right through me. I'm really ashamed of meself.'

Rose slid her hand down into Em's cold fingers and squeezed them tight. 'Oh dearest, I had no idea you've been thinking all these morbid thoughts.'

'I wouldn't have burdened you,' Em whispered hoarsely. 'But it's like being kids again, telling each other our secrets.' She looked up slowly. 'Rosy, I know you're trying to be positive about Eddie, but it must be awful having to lie there and go over things.'

'I've told you the truth,' Rose assured her. 'I can fill every moment until February with knitting and sewing and after the baby comes along time will fly by. Judging by his antics,' she patted her bulge, 'he's going to keep us all on our toes.'

Em hitched an eyebrow. 'You're still certain it's a boy, then?'

'I know it,' Rose nodded firmly. 'Mathew.'

'Eddie will have a son to look forward to, then.'

'Tomorrow I'm going to write to him and bugger the censors,' Rose sniffed determinedly. 'I want him to know every detail about the baby even down to how he moves in me stomach. Yes,' Rose added contentedly, 'even though Eddie's not here, he's gonna be a fount of knowledge on childbirth, right up to the time Mathew pops his little head out between me legs. I always wanted Eddie to see Marlene and Donnie born. They looked like

275

little red sausages wrapped in transparent silk till Dr Harding wiped them clean. They were the two best moments of me life.'

Em was listening attentively, then gave a giggle. 'Let's hope the censors have got strong stomachs then – if Eddie don't faint first, that is!'

That set the two of them laughing and as Rose gulped in breath she felt the baby respond as though he was happy too. She would do everything in her power to keep him that way. Placing Em's hand on her swollen belly, Rose stared into her sister's eyes. 'Feel him?' she whispered and after a pause, Em nodded.

'I think I'll sew a blue pram cover and matching pillow set,' she pondered, her eyes widening as the movement increased. 'Blue and white, with a pair of football boots embroidered in the corner.'

The baby kicked wildly as if he had understood and both girls gave a cry of delight. Rose was now even more determined to make the months until February utterly productive.

Christmas Day was over. Rose had happily broken all Em's rules and survived. She had abandoned her sick bed and negotiated the stairs, very slowly, with Marlene, Donnie and Will in close attendance. If she couldn't have Eddie, she'd stated determinedly, she could have the next best thing. Christmas dinner. And she was going to eat it in the kitchen with the rest of the family.

It was the first time she had ever eaten at the kitchen table in her dressing gown and slippers. The turkey, stuffing, potatoes and mince pies were a surprise package from the Mendozas and the Weavers and Trims made short work of it. Although Rose missed Eddie, she felt blissfully happy in the bosom of her family.

'Happy Christmas, darlings!' Rose toasted with her glass of water and the kids drank lemonade.

'Happy Christmas Mummy, happy Christmas Auntie Em!'

Rose thought that Donnie, Will and Marlene looked like characters from a Dickensian scene. The room was warm from Em's cooking and condensation ran down the window. The children's faces were pink with excitement and all wore their best clothes. Rose knew they couldn't wait to unwrap their small presents in the front room. She had knitted three red and white stockings and Em had hung them up last night. Apples, oranges, pears, toffee apples and sweets were all wrapped in greaseproof paper along with little novelties from the market. This morning the children were desperate to unwrap them.

'Can we go and look?' Marlene asked as she blew out her cheeks. 'I've eaten everything on me plate, even the cabbage.'

'What about your pudding?' Rose asked.

'Can I let me dinner go down first?'

She turned to Will and Donnie. 'What about you two?'

They both looked at each other. 'Can we open our presents?' they asked.

Rose laughed. 'Go on then, and we'll have the pudding later.'

'It's not quite finished steaming either,' Em said as the children ran off and began to clear the plates away. 'I must take the scones out of the oven too.'

'When are they for?' Rose asked curiously, guessing the answer.

'Tomorrow, I suppose,' Em replied nonchalantly.

Rose watched her sister open the oven. 'What a nice treat.'

'But a nuisance,' Em complained as she placed the tray of plump scones on the hob. 'We could have listened to the wireless tomorrow afternoon if no one was coming.'

Taking the no one to be Bobby Morton, Rose smiled ruefully. 'We did that all day yesterday, that and stuffing ourselves with mince pies and playing games with the kids. It will be nice to entertain a guest for once.'

'We had Anita and Benny and the boys over,' Em sniffed as she took care to test the scones.'

'I know but they're like family.'

'Exactly. We hardly know *him.*'

'Oh Em,' Rose sighed. 'The poor man is lonely. He doesn't have any family to speak of.'

'Well he should have,' Em argued, slicing the scones energetically. 'It's not right living by himself at his age. He must be in his mid-thirties, wouldn't you say?'

'Not too old to start a family,' Rose said softly. 'And he's definitely not married. I asked when he last called. He's got a brother somewhere, but his parents died when he was young. His father in an accident and his mother from TB.'

Em turned to frown at her. 'Well, I'm sorry for him, of course, but pity doesn't blind me.'

Rose sighed. 'You sound bitter when you talk like that, Em. He's bent over backwards to be nice, calling round to see if we're both okay.'

Em waved the jam spoon in the air and sniffed. 'Yes, and what for? He just wants to get his feet under the table in my opinion.'

Rose burst into laughter and the baby kicked as if enjoying the fun.

'What's so funny?' Her sister dropped the spoon and placed her hands on her hips.

'Nothing,' Rose smothered her amusement. 'It's just that the only table we've got is this one.' She gestured to the cramped, crockery covered top that was spilling with dirty plates.

Em cast her eyes down and smiled. In seconds they were both laughing so much that tears streamed down their cheeks.

Chapter Sixteen

Rose was listening to *Woman's Hour* as she sat comfortably on the couch in the front room and gave Matthew Edward Weaver his afternoon feed. She couldn't imagine life without him now and wondered if she had really existed before his birth. A birth that had been so swift that when Dr Cox had arrived on a bitter February evening he'd only just had enough time to remove his coat before Rose delivered her baby at a scale-tipping nine pounds and two ounces. Despite Rose's slender proportions and the fact the infant was ten days premature, he had slipped like a fish into the world with a lusty cry and a mass of dark hair.

What a wonderful week that had been, Rose reflected as her thoughts drifted back six weeks to the night of 5th February, 1954.

'He looks like a coconut,' Marlene had decided as the two girls sat on either side of the big double bed. 'Like you see at the fair.'

'You looked just the same when you were born,' Donnie had argued in defence of her newly arrived brother.

Marlene stared woefully at Rose who was feeding her baby for the first time but she had soon become entranced, holding the starfish hand that boasted miniature nails. Will, however, had made a quick exit after commenting that he couldn't wait for Matthew to grow up and play out in the yard.

Anita and Benny had called at ten-thirty, an hour after Dr Cox and the midwife had left. 'I'm broody, Benny,' Anita murmured, her eyes misting over as she stood next to her husband, gazing spellbound at the baby. 'But I suppose it's too late now?'

'Too right it's too late,' Benny had agreed, but Rose had seen the longing in his eyes as he'd bent over the little boy and curled back the shawl around his tiny feet. 'He's a cracker, Rose. Look at them plates of meat. They're good solid articles they are.'

'Our Dave and Alan sent these in.' Anita lay a dog-eared album on the dressing table. 'It's their collection of football cards. They want the babe to have it. By the time he's old enough to play, he'll be able to flog the cards and buy a good set of boots.'

Rose had been overwhelmed with joy that night and despite feeling utterly exhausted had let the girls sit with her until everyone was gone. Em had settled them eventually and taken the baby downstairs in a Moses basket she'd found under the stairs on the pretext of giving Rose chance to rest. Rose knew that Em would probably stay up half the night just watching him.

Two days later she'd written to Eddie and told him every bit of news describing the baby down to the last detail. He had replied, overjoyed, from a new prison in Sussex, where offenders not classed as potential escapees were housed. For the first time his letter had sounded like the Eddie she remembered. He told her how much he loved them all and how the time would go quickly now their son had arrived. He asked her to write again soon.

Suddenly Rose came back to the present as a rather breathless female voice began to recall the events of 1953. She realized *Woman's Hour* was over and this programme was a trip down memory lane. The commentator spoke of the Queen's Coronation and then the conquering of Mount Everest by Edmund Hillary, a handsome New Zealander accompanied by his Sherpa guide, Tensing. She then went on to describe the charismatic and popular American senator, John F. Kennedy who had married his beautiful bride, Jacqueline Bouvier. Rose listened as Matthew fed contentedly. She had spent much longer today feeding him and cuddling him. He seemed to listen to all that she told him and even seemed to like the wireless noise.

A pleasant melody filled the room, the theme tune to a film called *Genevieve*, about a veteran motor car and the London to Brighton run. Although Rose hadn't seen it, the film had captured the nation's heart last year. There was also the birth of a new series on the radio called *The Goon Show*, a crazy comedy which had converted Rose and thousands of other listeners to a brand new form of humour.

Rose was hoping that all these wonderful events would register in her tiny baby's brain. She sat down at the same time each day to breastfeed him, introducing him to *Listen With Mother* and *Woman's Hour*, just as she had done with the girls. Matthew's almost black eyes stared up at her like tiny ebony beads set in his still rather red face and two little dimples appeared on his cheeks as a windy smile formed around his mouth. Rose gently lifted him on to her shoulder.

Rose was blissfully happy. Every time she sat down to feed Matthew, she felt closer to Eddie. A wonderful contentment filled her. She loved just holding him close, even in the middle of the night. *Especially* in the middle of the night, when everyone else was asleep and she had him entirely to herself.

The kitchen door banged and Matthew jumped. He gave a little cry and Rose patted his back, smiling.

'You'll have to get used to loud noises in this house, my darling,' she chuckled. 'It's like Piccadilly Circus sometimes.'

In just nine months, their lives had changed dramatically, Rose thought as she held Matthew back to her breast for the last few minutes of his feed. The family had expanded and though the rooms always seemed full of noise and chatter, Rose never minded. She had always wanted a big family and now she had it.

'Rosy? Fancy a cuppa?' Em bustled in, her cheeks red and her hazel eyes wide. She was wearing an apron and held an empty wicker laundry basket in her hands.

'That'd be nice. Look Em, he's lost that reddy colour and his skin's going quite peachy.'

Em dropped the basket and came to sit beside her.

She reached out to grasp the baby's finger. Matthew responded immediately and Em gave a gasp of delight. 'He knows me, I know he does!'

''Course he knows you. You're his Auntie Em.'

'No, I mean really knows me. He squeezed my finger.'

Rose smiled. 'Want a hold?'

'Can I?'

'He needs his wind brought up.' Rose did up her blouse with one hand and then wrapped the blue and white shawl with the football boots around his firm little shoulders.

Em let him sink into her arms as if he was marshmallow. She gave a sigh of pleasure as she rubbed his back and a pocket of wind erupted. They both laughed and Matthew looked up with beady black eyes and another windy grin.

'I've never seen a baby so alert,' Em noted proudly drawing her fingers over the ebony cap of hair. 'I do believe he knows everything you say.'

'No doubt about that,' Rose agreed as she pulled on her cardigan. 'I was certain he could hear me when he was in my tummy.' She lay her hand on her flat stomach. She had lost all the extra weight she'd put on during pregnancy.

'Better be careful then,' Em giggled. 'Keep your secrets to yourself.'

'Haven't got any,' Rose replied innocently.

Em looked deliberately suspicious. 'What about the shoebox, then!'

Rose grinned. 'I'd forgotten that.' She had too, she was surprised to discover now. Eight months ago she had thought it was the end of the world almost when someone had broken in and stolen all Eddie's savings, but Matthew's birth had changed all that. She hadn't even been upset when the *Evening Gazette* had printed a half page on Eddie's trial and sentence. Not that she'd had to endure any comments from Ruby Street as she was resting in bed at the time. It was poor Em who had been forced to leave the house since shopping had to be done. Rose smiled at the memory of her sister rising at the crack of dawn on Saturdays to arrive at market before everyone else. Even the girls, who Rose had worried about at school, had dealt successfully with playground confrontations.

Rose was still smiling as she looked at her sister. 'Anyway, I'm not the only one with secrets. Who had a washing machine for Christmas, then?'

Em went bright pink. 'Not me. It was for you – for us both!'

Rose made a little humming sound. 'Mr Bobby Morton knows my views on such luxuries, thank you very much.'

'You still said yes to having it,' Em sniffed.

'Well, it cost next to nothing,' Rose shrugged. 'I could hardly refuse.'

'Exactly,' Em said burying her face in Matthew's shawl as she lifted him against her cheek.

'You know he's keen on you, don't you?' Rose said daringly. Her sister was very touchy on the subject of Bobby Morton.

'I'm going to pretend I didn't hear that, Rose Weaver.'

'Oh Em, you know he is. And he's so *nice*.'

Em cradled Matthew in her arms and, suddenly serious, she looked up at Rose. 'Nice blokes don't exist, except your Eddie and Benny next door,' she mumbled darkly. 'Now stop pulling me leg and let me get on with cleaning the kitchen. Take your little lad and grab another ten minutes of cuddle before it's time to collect the kids.'

Rose took Matthew back in her arms and watched her sister bustle out again. The small, square, slightly battered washing machine had come as a complete surprise, when, on Christmas Eve, Bobby had driven up, not in a small van, but a newly purchased shooting brake. They all went out to examine it.

The roomy, elegant vehicle sported wooden panels down the side and two big headlights on the front placed strategically over a shining chromium bumper. The windows sparkled and the seats smelt of real leather. 'I can use it for all my deliveries,' Bobby told them, 'and take the kids out for a ride if they want.'

'It's lovely.' Rose nudged her sister in the ribs.

'Yes,' said Em distantly.

Bobby had hurried to the back doors and opened them. 'I thought this might come in handy,' he told them, pulling a battered washing machine out and lifting it down to the ground. 'It's only second-hand and minus a wringer but I've repaired the motor, although the outside looks a bit rough. A customer traded it in against a better one.'

'We don't want hand-outs, thank you very much,' said Em quickly.

'It's not coming free,' Bobby told her gently. 'You can have it for four pounds, a few shillings paid each week to clear the balance.' Rose thought he winked slightly at her as he said it.

'It would help, wouldn't it Em?' Rose urged as her sister sniffed and twitched.

'If you say so,' she'd shrugged and hurried back to the kitchen.

Rose looked at Bobby apologetically and noticed how his eyes had followed Em's retreat. It was then she'd guessed it wasn't financial profit on his mind, but another sort of interest altogether.

Rose had asked Bobby to Boxing Day tea, grateful for his offer of the washing machine. Washing by hand for a family of five, soon to be six, was proving a mammoth task for Em. In return Bobby had accepted Rose's offer and arrived to spend an enjoyable hour at 46 Ruby Street at four-thirty on 26th December.

'I'll make you that cuppa before I clean the kitchen,' Em shouted along the hall and woke Rose from her reverie. 'The larder needs sorting. Someone left the milk out and it's almost gone off.'

Rose always kept the milk fresh by standing it in a bowl of cold water and placing a cover over it. But Em had achieved higher standards of hygiene when Rose was confined to bed. When Christmas had arrived warm and windy rather than cold and frosty, the whole kitchen had been under review. Rose hadn't had the heart to protest that the smell of disinfectant was nauseating.

Em's famous words were, 'When the baby is here we'll

have to pull our socks up!' As though an infant was going to revolutionize their whole existence. And to be fair, Rose thought ruefully, Matthew had.

Rose looked down and found her son asleep. Tiny black lashes lay closed on satiny cheeks. Yes, his colour was now peaches and cream, the rosy hue vanished. He was the most beautiful child in existence, Rose decided as she gazed at the cherubic mouth and button nose.

She sighed in wonder, imagining Eddie beside her, as one day he surely would be.

A week later, Rose was pushing the deep bassinet pram towards home. She had walked to Cox Street market before ten and purchased vegetables and a nice piece of cod from the fishmonger and stowed them under the belly of the pram. Previously used for Marlene and Donnie, the pram had been stored under the stairs, acting as receptacle for innumerable items. Rose had restored it with a dab or two of paint and brushed off the cream and brown upholstery. It looked as good as new despite its antiquity.

Matthew was snuggled under Em's blue and white cover and Rose was wrapped warmly in her old winter coat, a paisley scarf tied over her hair. She was in a world of her own, thinking of Eddie, as she made her way to Ruby Street. She had just posted a letter to confirm she would be visiting him on the first Wednesday in April. He had sent her a visiting order and plans were now in motion to make the long journey from London to Hewis Prison in Sussex. Bobby had offered to drive the whole family in his shooting brake and Rose was delighted.

The weather was still chilly, but dry and Rose considered what she and the children should wear. Though Rose had no money to spend at market, Dolly had offered her a two piece for three and six. But Rose refused although the smart herringbone suit would have done very nicely. Money was short, though she had saved her wages from Kirkwood's. With Em's contribution and Anita and Benny's generous gift of ten pounds, they were managing to survive.

Rose thought about the long car journey. She would take a picnic and some sweets to keep the children happy on the three hour journey. Today there was a promise of sunshine, with a soft spring breeze. What would be appropriate to wear? Dresses, coats, trousers, jumpers – she wanted to impress Eddie, who had not seen the children in over nine months. And Matthew – well, that was easy. His wardrobe was impressive. She had been knitting continuously throughout her confinement in bed. He was the best-dressed baby this side of London Bridge.

Rose was smiling to herself as she turned the corner and walked past Fred and Mabel Dixon's. Then she stopped dead. Ten yards in front of her, parked on the other side of the road, was a big brown car.

'Em! Em!' Rose hit the front of the pram on the door-frame and woke Matthew. 'Sorry, darling – oh Em, Em!' She pushed the pram into the front room where it spent most of its life now, parked by the gram, and despite a little wail from Matthew, Rose ran back to the front door. She slammed it closed and pulled the key off the string, a key that had only recently been replaced. Rose stepped back, staring at the door, her eyes wide with fright. Her legs felt as if they were turning to sponge. She was shivering and her heart was drumming in her ears.

'Rosy, whatever's the matter?' Em hurried along from the kitchen. Her brow was creased, the tips of her brown eyebrows almost meeting over her nose.

'He's out there again! It's him!'

'Who, love? Who?' Em shook her arm, but Rose was petrified. All the old fears had flooded back and her eyes were glued to the door.

'It's the car, the brown one. It was here that day—'

Em stiffened, a look of fear also creeping over her face. 'You don't mean—'

'Yes, the one I saw on the day of the burglary. He's out there, waiting. I know it's him, I just know it.'

'But . . . but that was a long time ago,' Em said weakly, her eyes also swivelling to follow Rose's gaze. 'How can you be sure it's the same one?'

'I'll never forget it. Never.'

'But we don't know if it was him . . . if it was the person in the car even. It might just be a coincidence, or a car very like it.'

'He looked at me,' Rose breathed hoarsely. 'As I pushed the pram past. He looked me right in the eye and I knew it. Oh, Em, it was as if he wanted to me to see him, as if he was sitting there deliberately.'

Em gave a twitch and a little laugh that wasn't really laughter. 'Oh, Rosy, why would he do that?'

'To frighten me,' Rose said without hesitation as she recalled the moment she had met his gaze. Under the trilby hat she had seen a face she would never forget now. The window was down and he was smoking a cigarette. He'd puffed out the smoke as she passed and looked directly up at her. She had never felt so terrified in all her life. His big, ugly features and thick, moist lips were unforgettable. Last time she hadn't been close enough to see him. This time she had been only inches away. If he'd wanted he could have reached out and touched her.

They stood looking at the door, Rose's hand clenched to Em's arm and the key hidden in her fist as though she was frightened it would disappear.

'Are you sure you didn't imagine it, love?' Em's voice was small.

'Go and look for yourself,' Rose said, hoping that her sister would. She couldn't bring herself to look out of the window. Perhaps he had climbed out of the car and was walking across the road? Perhaps he was outside the door this very moment? Rose felt her skin crawl.

Em didn't move, until suddenly Matthew gave a loud wail, annoyed at being left in his pram. Rose started, then hurried into the front room as though Matthew himself was in danger. She pulled him out of the pram and held him to her breast. For a few seconds she took comfort from his small, warm body wrapped in the pram cover. He nuzzled contentedly against her shoulder thankfully oblivious to all that was happening around him. Rose turned slowly round. Em was at the window, her nose pressed against the net. She adjusted her position and looked the other way. Still with a frown on her forehead, she shook her head slowly. 'Rosy, there's no one there, dear. No one at all.'

'There must be.' Rose still wouldn't go to the window. 'I've looked both ways—'

'Up by the Dixons', on this side.'

Em craned her neck and adjusted the curtain. 'It's completely empty, the pavement, the road. There's no one there. Only Debbie Price walking towards Dora Lovell's.'

'The car was parked opposite, between the Dixons' and Dora's.'

'Well, if it was, it's gone now.'

Rose walked slowly towards the window. She stood behind Em and looked over her shoulder, holding Matthew firmly against her shoulder. Em was right, the street was devoid of vehicles.

'I saw it there, Em. He looked at me. He knew who I was, I swear it.'

'But how could he know? I mean, have you seen him before?'

'No.'

'Not on the day of the burglary?'

'No, the car was too far away then.'

'So how do you know he knows you, then, dear?'

Rose hugged Matthew against her as Em turned round with wide, innocent eyes. 'You don't believe me do you? You think I'm being fanciful.'

'I do believe you,' Em said hesitantly. 'I'm just trying to get things straight in my mind. Why, for instance, would a thief come back to a place he's already burgled and make himself known?'

Rose had no answer at all. She couldn't even begin to guess at what the man in the car had wanted, other than to frighten the life out of her. But how had he known she would walk by? Had he followed her? Watched her leave the house this morning? Rose quaked at the very thought. She had felt a little like this last year after the five hundred pounds was stolen. She had been suspicious of every stranger for a while, but it had never seriously worried her that she might be burgled again, even though Anita had warned her to report it to the police. Now she wished she had. At least she could have told them she had seen the car again.

'Hold Matthew will you,' she whispered, wishing she had Eddie to turn to.

'What are you going to do?'

'Look outside.' Slowly she went to the door and took hold of the latch. Would there be anyone standing on the step? What would she do if there was?

Slowly she opened it, steeling herself to close it quickly if the man was there. But no one was. The wind rippled in and touched her cheeks and the sun momentarily peeped from behind a cloud. Across the road Olga's door was shut tightly as it had been for months and the front room curtains drawn.

Rose looked up to the Dixons' then back down the road to Len Silverman's house and farther down to the

Patels'. The long, straight street was empty save for Debbie Price who was talking to Cissy Hall on the far pavement. They both turned and waved. Rose waved back.

She took one more glance to her left then went back inside. She leaned her back against the door.

'Well?' Em asked with a frown.

Rose shook her head. 'He must have driven off.'

Em sighed gently against Matthew's head. 'Perhaps it was just a coincidence after all.'

Rose was under no such illusion but what was the use of arguing. 'I'm going to keep this key on the mantelpiece. The children will have to knock when they want to come in.'

'They'll want to know why it isn't tied on the string,' Em pointed out.

'I'll tell them,' Rose said resolutely. 'Not about the burglary of course, but I'll warn them not to talk to strangers and to come and tell me if they see the brown car.'

'Won't they want to know why?'

Rose shrugged. 'I'll tell them the truth, that one has been seen parked in the road and we don't know who it is.'

'I hope that won't frighten them,' Em replied vaguely.

'I'll tell them in such a way that it won't,' Rose murmured. 'I'll tell Anita and the boys and Benny too.'

'I'm sure we're making a mountain out of a molehill,' Em said as she lay Matthew back under his cover, then lifted the shopping bag from under the pram. 'Now, enough of all this silly business, Rosy, take off your coat and scarf. I'll put the kettle on while you sit yourself down and give Matthew his feed. The poor little mite must be ravenous.' She was halfway along the hall when she called out, 'And I've a special treat for you today, I baked a cinnamon cake this morning. I'll slice you a piece with your tea.'

Silly business . . . was that what Em really thought of what had just happened? Dismayed at her sister's reaction, Rose removed her outdoor clothes and hung them on the clothes stand in the hall. She couldn't blame Em for dismissing the incident as coincidence – perhaps it was another car altogether! All the same, she would still speak to the children tonight.

Rose lifted Matthew from the pram and sat down on the couch. 'Who's hungry for their dinner?'she cooed, opening her blouse and pressing his hungry mouth against her breast. His small, angelic face looked up and his nose wrinkled as he began to suck. Soon she forgot all about the brown car and its driver, lost in a world of wonder as she stared down at her beautiful son.

Chapter Seventeen

'Are we nearly there?' Marlene stretched uncomfortably on the back seat of the Austin shooting brake. Next to her sat Rose, who held Matthew in her arms, and Donnie sat on Rose's other side. Will was curled in the rear space behind the passengers along with the shopping bags, outdoor clothes and parcels of food that Rose had brought with her.

'About another twenty minutes,' Bobby replied as he drove steadily through the leafy countryside. Beside the driver sat Em, her head bowed over a large square Automobile Association map from which she was navigating.

Rose felt Matthew stir in her arms. He had dozed for the entire three hours of the journey, ever since half past nine this morning when Bobby had arrived to collect them.

Now they were near to Hewis, their destination, and Rose was fighting off butterflies. What would Eddie think of his new son? And would he see a change in the girls? They had been excited all week, hardly able to concentrate on anything but this adventure. Rose hoped the prison wouldn't be as daunting as Brixton.

The family's first long ride in a motor car was a resounding success. The girls enjoyed sitting on the luxurious leather seats whilst Will spotted numberplates from the rear. Halfway through their journey, Bobby parked on a verge overlooking the glorious Sussex countryside. The sky was a cloudless blue rolling endlessly across green downs. Their sandwiches and hot flask of tea disappeared down hungry throats in no time and the big bag of apples and pears that Bobby provided followed the same way.

Rose stared at the back of her sister's bent head. Em seemed to be enjoying herself despite her suspicions of the young man who was now clearly courting her. Navigating from the map, she eagerly announced each town or village and the children cheered at the appearance of the big black and white nameplate that followed.

'Hewis is the next town on the map,' Em called over her shoulder. 'Perhaps it would be a good idea to give Matthew his feed, Rosy?'

Matthew was still asleep, but Rose gently woke him. She parted her coat and blouse and adjusted his head to her breast. Soon he was sucking as if he hadn't been fed for a week.

'When's he gonna eat food like us?' Marlene asked curiously, stroking Matthew's dark hair affectionately.

'When he's weaned,' Rose answered, quickly adding, 'in other words when he can eat solid food.'

'Did me and Donnie drink your milk like that?' Marlene wrinkled her nose at the very thought.

'Yes, just the same way.'

'I can't remember a thing,' Marlene disowned.

To while away the last of the journey they all sang songs. Bobby started with 'Old Macdonald's Farm' and then 'One Man Went to Mow'. They were in the middle of 'Ten Green Bottles' when Will shouted from the back, 'There's a signpost, look! To Hewis Prison.'

Rose was accustomed to the word prison now, though it still sent a chill down her spine. She closed her blouse and clasped Matthew against her. She couldn't wait for Eddie to hold him. The baby's long lashed eyes were now a light blue-grey, more grey than blue. With his thatch of dark hair, he was undoubtedly Eddie's son.

'Wow!' exclaimed Will from his space at the rear as he peered between the girls' heads. 'I've never been in a prison before.'

'Nor have we,' Donnie answered guilelessly. 'Daddy didn't want us to go to the other one because it was so horrid.'

'I'm glad I put me best dress on,' Marlene agreed, sitting forward and grabbing the back of Em's seat.

'Me too.' Donnie looked flushed, Rose noted, her cheeks rose pink framed by her abundant brown hair. Both girls wore their best dresses. A green velvet for Marlene with a creamy frill that Rose had laced around the collar. Pale blue for Donnie, a dropped waist linen dress that made her look very tall. Will was wearing his school clothes, grey short trousers and pullover with a clean white shirt and tie. Rose had settled on a grey wool dress that sheathed her slim figure. Second-hand, it was a recent purchase at the market, a snip for a few pennies.

Rose glanced at her sister who looked very smart in her dark suit and had pleated her fair hair into a chignon. Bobby wore a sports jacket and navy trousers. Rose thought they made a very handsome pair.

Rose was glad now that she had encouraged the girls to talk about Eddie being in prison. She didn't want his existence ignored and they knew their father was innocent and intended to clear his name when he was released, a promise he had reaffirmed many times in his letters.

'Here at last!' Bobby yelled as they came to a five bar gate. Clusters of bobbing daffodils bent their heads on the green verges as though waving a welcome. Unlike Brixton, Rose knew Hewis was minimum security as Eddie had explained the wartime hospital used for injured servicemen had closed its doors to patients in 1947 and opened them a year later to young male offenders. But Rose was surprised at her first glimpse, for the barrack-like quarters had no high walls and she marvelled at the wooded park in which the prison was situated, the singing of birds and fresh country air.

Bobby drove them through the gate where a man in a peaked cap told them to drive on to Reception, a long, low building that looked rather like a huge prefab, a little further up the road.

'Are you sure this is the right place?' Em asked as he parked the car outside.

'Yes,' he nodded and peered out of the window. 'Not so bad after all, is it?'

Rose agreed. The prison felt much more pleasant and

queues of visitors weren't as long or noisy as those at Brixton. But by the time they had climbed out of the car with their coats and luggage, Rose's heart was thumping. Eddie would be waiting for them just a short distance away.

They all trailed along to the Reception area, where Bobby stopped and handed Em the big shopping bag they had brought with them filled with sweets and a packet of Woodbines for Eddie.

'I'll wait here,' Bobby told them courteously.

'Why can't you come with us?' Marlene, who had taken a shine to her aunt's new admirer, asked.

'Because I have to check the engine,' he replied, glancing at Rose. 'Cars tend to overheat you know.'

Rose smiled gratefully and clasping Matthew in one arm and her daughter's hand in the other, they left him, as arranged previously, to his own devices. She hoped he would be able to amuse himself for the next two hours.

They all trooped along the hot, stuffy corridor and filed into a waiting area at the end. People were already waiting on benches and chairs, the children sitting quietly on the floor. Rose hoped it wouldn't be too long to wait before they went in. Matthew was stirring and the girls couldn't wait to see their father. Em looked tense and Will sat silently on a chair beside his mother.

At two o'clock prompt the doors opened. A uniformed officer appeared. He checked everyone's credentials and then signalled them to file through. To Rose's relief, there was not the awful smell that permeated Brixton. The big, airy visiting room was more like a cafeteria.

There was even a refreshments bar at the far end and dozens of small tables and chairs spread over the floor, thankfully not squeezed together.

Rose settled on a round table with six plastic chairs, obviously arranged for a family group. She sat down in the middle with the two girls either side. Em perched stiffly, looking with wide eyes at the assortment of visitors. Will stood at her side, leaving the remaining chair for Eddie.

'When's Daddy coming?' Donnie asked in a small voice, rearranging the skirt of her blue dress.

'Very soon.' Rose couldn't wait to see him. She wanted him to gasp at the sight of his son and little girls. She wanted to see the joy and the pride shining out of his eyes.

'Daddy!' Marlene sprang to her feet. Rose tried to catch her arm but she was gone. Donnie followed and Rose's throat contracted as she saw the tip of Eddie's dark head buried under the exuberant embraces of his daughters.

'I was sorry to hear of your loss, Em,' Eddie said sincerely as he rocked his son in his arms. He was so proud of the tiny scrap he could burst with pride. But his pride only intensified his longing for the family he hadn't seen in nearly ten months.

'Thanks, Eddie,' his sister in law replied nervously. 'Are you sure you don't mind us living at the house?'

''Course not. Our home is your home, you know that.'

'It's only till we get a place of our own.'

Eddie was too absorbed with his traumatized feelings to worry much about his sister-in-law. He hadn't wanted his family to visit him in Brixton and, if truth be told, he had only agreed to this visit because of Matthew. His newborn son was the apple of his eye and he wanted to know what he looked like before he grew older. But he felt ashamed that his two daughters had to see him here. It was the last place on earth they should be, even if Hewis was a palace compared to Brixton.

For the next ten minutes he attempted to satisfy all their questions. Where did he sleep, work and eat? Could he read books or listen to the wireless? Eddie considered each question gravely then, as usual, responded with humour.

He knew he looked shabby in his dull blue shirt and coarse grey trousers. He hated his short haircut and felt embarrassed about his appearance. As for his Rose, she looked wonderful. He wanted to reach out and touch her thick brown hair, to run his fingers through it. He loved her so much and felt ashamed that she had to see him this way. But from somewhere deep inside he dredged up a smile.

'You should see what I pile on me dinner plate,' he told Marlene with renewed enthusiasm. 'Sausages, bacon, onions, pies, you name it, I eat it.'

'Auntie Em makes even better pies,' she trilled as she climbed on his knee. She glanced at her baby brother snuggled in the crook of his arm. 'Matthew only drinks milk though, until he's wee-eened.'

Eddie laughed. 'I bet he's a right guzzler. But I can tell

you right now he'll be on eggs and bacon in no time at all.'

Donnie laughed softly as she leaned against her father's shoulder. 'Oh, Daddy, babies eat everything mashed up till they get some teeth.'

'Ain't he got no teeth, then?' Eddie stared at her innocently. 'Well, we'll send him back to fetch 'em shall we?'

All the children burst into laughter. He felt a warm glow inside him as he cracked jokes right, left and centre. The experience of being with his estranged family was as painful as it was pleasurable.

'Now what have you all been doing while I'm on me holidays?' he asked cheerfully.

Marlene giggled. 'You ain't on your holiday, Daddy, you're in prison!'

'You're only jealous,' Eddie responded with a wink. 'It costs a lot to stay here, you know.'

'Daddy!' Marlene slithered off his knee. 'That's fibbing!'

'It ain't Toots. See that bloke over there, the one with the big fireman's hose?' They all looked very slowly to where Eddie inclined his head. A few tables away a small man with a very large nose sat talking to a well-dressed older woman.

'Yes,' they all said expectantly.

'He's worth a fortune is old Solly. Made his bees and honey in the rag trade. We got a lot in common, though. They failed to get him on tax evasion so they framed him for fraud. But the beak only sent him down for six months and the fuzz are seething. His lawyers are sorting it out right now.'

'Where does he live?' Donnie asked wide-eyed.

'He's got a manor in the country and a castle in Scotland. With a moat an' all.'

Everyone gasped.

'He said we could all go up for a holiday if we want.'

'When?' both girls asked at once.

'Soon as I get me marching orders.'

'When's that?'

'Next year.'

He saw Marlene wasn't impressed. 'That's a long time off. Anyway, I bet he ain't got a castle!'

'If you don't believe me, Toots, go and ask him.'

'We don't speak to strangers,' Donnie said before her sister could reply. 'Mummy says so.'

As Matthew whimpered in his arms, Eddie turned to Rose. She raised her eyebrows and nodded. 'It's me new rule, Eddie.'

'And a fine one it is too,' he agreed vehemently. He looked back at his daughters. 'Your mother's right, Princess. No speaking to strangers, unless you know them!' He chuckled at his joke.

'Especially,' Marlene added with emphasis, 'strange men in brown cars.'

'Yes, Toots, especially strange men in—' Eddie stopped as he realized what he was saying. '*What* brown car?' he asked, puzzled.

'The one Mummy saw in the street the other day.'

Eddie turned to his wife. 'What's she talking about, love?'

'Oh nothing much,' Rose dismissed. 'It was a car that was parked outside the Dixons'.'

'Mummy's seen it there before, though,' Donnie continued. 'Haven't you, Mummy?'

Rose nodded. 'Yes, yes, I have.'

'Mummy told us not to go near it and we're to run and tell her if it parks in the street again.'

Eddie looked at his wife. 'What's all this about, Rose?'

'I . . . I didn't like the look of the driver, that's all.'

'Why not?' Eddie felt a coldness building inside him, an icy fear that he had pushed to the back of his mind ever since the beatings at Brixton.

'It's just me being fussy. You know what I'm like with the children.'

Matthew wailed loudly and Eddie looked down at his son. With a rush of protectiveness he stroked his finger across the furrowed brow now turning pink with annoyance. A tiny fist clenched, followed by a bellow that made Eddie's heart contract with love.

'He probably needs changing,' Rose said as she bent to lift the wriggling bundle into her arms. 'Em, would you take him out to the car? I've left a bag with clean nappies in and filled a bottle with water. A drop or two will settle him till the next feed.' Eddie watched in silence as his sister-in-law carefully wrapped his son against her chest, adjusting the shawl to his body. Eddie felt full of regret as he watched the activity around him. Matthew would be walking on two sturdy legs by the time he was home.

'Come along, children,' Em called.

'I don't want to go,' Marlene said sullenly. 'We only just got here.'

'Do as your Aunt says,' Eddie said gently, reaching out

to draw his two daughters into his arms. He wanted to hold his children close, to protect them, but how could he in here? 'Send me some nice pictures, girls and Will, you tell the bloke that brought you here – what's his name?'

'Bobby,' Will replied eagerly.

'Tell him to drive carefully on the way back. He's carrying a precious load.' It was all he could think of to say. He didn't know the man, but Rose had written saying he fancied Em and was a real gent. Eddie had decided that he had no option but to believe that his intentions were honourable. But as he looked up at his family, a feeling of utter powerlessness gripped him. He could do nothing to help his family in any way, shape or form. He just had to grin and bear it.

The little group departed. Eddie watched them go. His heart felt as though a dagger pierced it as the children waved. He plastered on a big smile, waving back.

When they'd gone, he gave a shuddering sigh. Slowly he reached to hold Rose's hand. She gripped his fingers tightly. 'Oh Eddie, you don't know how much we miss you,' she murmured and again his heart felt as though a knife was going through it.

As usual, he applied humour to pain. 'You'd better make the most of it. I'll soon be under your feet again.'

'You've never been under me feet as much as I wished you was, sometimes.'

He would never be able to tell her how much he regretted his absenteeism. If he was back in Ruby Street right now, he'd prove to her that his family came first and foremost. 'I'd forgotten how beautiful you are,' he said bleakly.

Rose lifted her hand to his cheek. 'It was awful watching you at the Old Bailey, up in that dock, a prisoner. It didn't seem real.'

'I didn't want you to come to court, not in your state.'

'I had to, even if it was only one day.'

'Are you all right after the baby?' he asked in concern. She nodded. 'I'm fine.'

'Benny was a good sort to come to me trial.' Eddie was emotional, close to tears. 'Matthew's a cracker, ain't he?' he said with a big effort. 'He's the spit of you.' She laughed then and it even hurt him to hear her laugh. He missed the sound so much. 'Oh God, Rose, I just want to be home and with you and the kids.'

'I know.' She sniffed, holding back the tears too.

'I'm in the workshop making baskets.' He changed the subject quickly. 'You know, them raffia things. I'll make you one, if you like.'

'That'd be nice.' She opened her shopping bag. 'I brought a packet of Woodbines.'

'We ain't allowed to take anything in with us. But I'll smoke one in a minute. Trouble is, I don't want to stop holding your hand.'

'Oh, Eddie, I don't know what to say.' She smiled into his eyes. Her smile was so innocent, so childlike, that again he was overwhelmed by how vulnerable his family was.

'So tell me about this bloke in the brown car,' he tried

to ask lightly. 'It ain't like you to worry about strangers. It's usually the neighbours that get you in a tizzy.'

'I know, I'm just being silly I expect.' She looked away from his gaze.

'What did this geezer look like?'

'Can't really remember. I'm sure I'm fussing about nothing.'

'When was it you first saw him?' Her eyes flickered at the harshness of his voice.

'I told you, ages ago, last year sometime.'

Eddie leaned closer. 'Look, love, it's important you tell me everything.'

She looked at him nervously. 'Why is it so important, Eddie?'

'Because it just is.' He waited, willing her to understand the urgency in his eyes.

'Oh, Eddie, I don't want to worry you.'

'You won't. Come on, spit it out.' His mouth was dry as a bone. He knew for certain now that he'd remember this day for the rest of his life.

'It was . . . last July I saw the car. It was parked at the top of the road near the Dixons'.'

Eddie swallowed. 'July – are you sure?'

'Yes. I was going out one morning and I noticed it because, as you know, we don't get many cars parked in our road. It was just waiting there, as if it was waiting for someone.'

'Did you get a look at the driver?'

'Not that I thought about it then, but I did remember him when I saw him again the next time. You see, this was the day when . . . well, when someone broke into the house.' He stared at her trembling lips and poor, pale face. His past life flashed before him. It was as if he had been living another life altogether, justifying his actions by telling himself he was doing it all for his family. And now that other life was coming back to haunt him.

'Eddie – did you hear what I said?'

He nodded slowly and found the courage from somewhere. 'They found the money, didn't they?' he said flatly.

Astonishment filled her eyes. 'How do you know?'

'It's what they were looking for. It's what they came after.'

She grasped his hands. 'Eddie, what's going on? Who are these people?'

'Bastards, love, that's who.'

She was frightened now. 'You know them?'

He wished with all his heart he didn't. He would trade his right arm now for a truth-sized slice of ignorance. He wished above all he was Eddie Weaver, street trader, small fry, making a pittance but enough to get by. Just as he had been five years ago when he'd been in his element flogging a few bits of cheap junk to his punters and bringing home the profit.

Those days were long gone, Eddie realized woefully. He would never have them back. Not after what he was going to tell Rose. He looked into his wife's eyes and wondered where he should begin.

Chapter Eighteen

Rose was wondering where to go next. It was the Easter holidays and she had left the children with Em and taken Matthew out in his pram. He'd been awake off and on all night, unable to settle. Rose knew it was only a matter of time before her milk dried up.

To soothe him she had pushed the pram from Ruby Street into Westferry Road, not stopping at the road works on the corner of Gavrick Street as he appeared to be dropping off. She'd wriggled the big pram wheels over the lumpy, broken pavement and emerged unscathed on the other side and for the next half hour had continued to push, trying to recall, as she had done a hundred times in the past week, what Eddie had said on their last meeting.

It hadn't helped much having to tell Anita, Benny and Em who'd all asked her enough questions to fill an encyclopaedia. She had been forced to reveal the news that Eddie was what was known in street parlance as a *floater,* someone who worked the streets on behalf of the bookies, collecting and placing illegal bets. But Eddie had instructed her to tell them immediately she got home. He had really put the wind up her as she had listened to his unbelievable tale.

Unfortunately, the tale turned out to be the truth. She was still reeling from it. Not only was Eddie in debt to a notorious loan shark but he feared the theft of the shoebox was a consequence of his debt. What was worse, he was convinced the danger wasn't over. Her blood had turned cold as she listened to him warning her to tell the Mendozas and Em and the children to always be on their guard in case of reprisals.

'Rose – Rose Weaver!'

Rose jumped, wondering who had called her. She found herself standing outside Hawkin's and Tipson's rope works. Two women stood inside the gates. One was tall and imposing, the other short and slender. Gwen House, the canteen supervisor from Kirkwood's had a big smile on her round face as she arrived breathlessly beside the pram.

'Hello Rose, love. Oh, I'm so glad I've seen you.' She clamped a red, hardworking hand on Rose's arm. 'Hold on, I'll just wave goodbye to our Suzie.' Swivelling on her heel, Gwen made the thumbs up sign. The girl smiled under her white turban, drew up the rope-cutting knife that was tied to a string around her waist and slid it in her pocket. With that she disappeared back into the ropeworks.

'I hate those bloody knives they have to carry,' Gwen said exasperatedly. 'But they're necessary I suppose. I've heard of quite horrible accidents happening when the rope kinks. Any amount of fingers and thumbs have been lost. I don't see the attraction in the place meself, but our Suzie seems to like it.'

'Is Suzie related to you?' Rose asked politely. The last thing she felt like doing was talking, but she hadn't seen Gwen since she'd left Kirkwood's last year.

'She's my sister's girl,' Gwen explained. 'It's her tea break and I just managed to catch her.' The buxom supervisor gazed under the hood. Matthew was fast asleep. 'Oh, he's a darling, Rose!'

'Yes, most of the time.' Rose was relieved Matthew had finally fallen asleep and looked like an angel snuggled under the cover. 'How are you, Gwen?'

'Fine, thanks, love. More to the point how are you? We wondered if you was all right. I always meant to pop round your house but you know how it is. I've been on overtime since Christmas. We're ever so busy.'

'That's nice to hear.'

'We miss you.'

'Do you?' Rose was surprised. She didn't think she'd made much of an impression at Kirkwood's, although she had enjoyed her brief time there. The work had been hard and she always seemed to have her hands in water up to the elbows but she'd made a friend of Gwen, a very fair supervisor.

'Yes, you were a reliable worker, Rose. I'd have you back at the drop of a hat. Did you know the girl who you stood in for has left? Without any notice too. That's why I was speaking to Suzie. I wondered if she'd like the job, but she doesn't fancy working in a hot kitchen.'

Rose glanced down at her sleeping infant. 'Well, I'm sorry you lost your girl but Matthew's only ten weeks old. I couldn't leave him yet. Not till he's on the bottle at least.'

'I expect you miss the money though?' Gwen asked hopefully.

Rose nodded. 'Yes, to be honest we do.'

'Well, you know where to come when you're ready, love.'

Rose smiled gratefully. 'I will.'

The large lady opened her bag and dived into it. She trickled some coins under the cover of the pram. 'That's for Matthew. Sorry I never sent a card or called round. Get him something nice from Kirkwood's.'

'Thanks, Gwen. I will.'

'How's your old man doing?'

Rose gave a swift shrug. 'As well as can be expected.' She hoped Gwen wouldn't ask any more questions. She didn't.

'Take care of yourself, girl.'

Rose watched her old supervisor walk off with long, purposeful strides. Despite her forbidding appearance, she was salt of the earth and Rose was flattered she'd wanted her back in the canteen. It might not be long before she accepted, considering Matthew's appetite that Rose couldn't satisfy. Em had offered to look after him, and after Eddie's revelations, Rose knew there was no way she would ever be a lady of leisure again. But a full time job at Kirkwood's would safeguard their future.

What would Eddie do when he came home? Rose

asked herself yet again. His floating days were over, she'd already made him promise her that. He wouldn't find a job so easily now he had a criminal record. And since he'd always maintained he wasn't cut out for factory life and had had enough of the docks, what else was left? She wondered if he would return to street trading as he had done before Marlene came along. Would she ever trust him to keep on the straight and narrow?

A river breeze lifted off the water as Rose pushed the pram through the gates of Island Gardens. Nutty odours of wood, tar and oil swept over from the docks, mixing with the chemicals from the factories. With your eyes closed you could identify where you stood – in the workhorse heart of a great big city.

The river seemed such a mighty force, she mused as she stood by the park railing and looked across the water to Greenwich. Sometimes wild and turgid, sometimes calm and inviting, it stretched left and right as far as the eye could see. Directly opposite, on the south bank, lay the smooth green lawns of the Naval College dwarfed by the Observatory's gleaming dome. A faint spring mist gathered lazily over the land, an innocent mist that would result in warmth and not fog.

A soft grumble of wakefulness came from Matthew. Rose pulled back the cover. Matthew smiled up at her knowingly.

'Hello, pet. Are you awake?' She knew it was probably wind, but his smile was infectious. She laughed. 'Shall we sit for a while in the sun?'

Rose sat on a bench where a few late daffodils still

survived the children's attentions. She would bring Will, Donnie, Marlene and the baby here in two days time, Good Friday. They never tired of the park and would play for hours with the other children.

Matthew blew bubbles as he lay in her arms. His little hands came up to curl around her fingers. Rose had rolled back the sleeves of his white romper suit, which had once been Donnie's and then Marlene's. His olive skin and light grey eyes were the spit of Eddie.

'So this is your baby?'

Rose looked up. It was a few seconds before she recognized the gaunt, drawn features of Olga Parker.

'Is it a boy?'

Rose nodded slowly. Olga's bleached blonde hair had vanished. Dull brown, greasy locks replaced her former smart hairstyle. Her purple wool coat was far too large, a coat that had once looked so fashionable. Rose noted that her neighbour had made an attempt at make-up though her efforts were a far cry from the elegant, carefully applied pan stick and mascara that Olga had once favoured. A red, uneven streak of lipstick clashed with the purple and her close-set eyes were absent of expression altogether.

'What is his name?'

'Matthew.' Olga was talking to her! She hadn't seen her since long before Christmas and then her hostile neighbour had hurried along Ruby Street without a glance. Rose had sent her a Christmas card but had never received one in return.

'How old is he?'

'He was born on the fifth of February.' Rose shifted

along the bench, leaving enough space for Olga to sit down. She was surprised when her neighbour did. 'Do you often come down the park?' Rose asked uncertainly.

Olga threaded her hands into the sleeves of her coat and shook her head. Her large nose and high forehead looked very prominent after the loss of so much weight. Two emaciated cheekbones carved a valley to her jaw and emphasized her long scraggy neck.

'How are you now?' Rose enquired after an uncomfortable silence. She didn't care for the strange manner in which Olga was behaving as every now and then she blinked at Matthew with her sad eyes.

'I always wanted a family,' Olga replied, as though she hadn't heard Rose's question.

'You mean you wanted children?' Rose hoped Olga wasn't going to take offence at her question and think she was prying. Their last meeting, when she had tried her best to be neighbourly, had resulted in a loudly banged door.

Olga reached out with white, bony fingers and stroked Matthew's thick cap of dark hair. 'I did have a son once, a long time ago. In fact I had a family, just like you. My husband was a doctor,' she said with a sudden rush of pride. 'And Siegfried was just three when—' She seemed to lose track of what she was saying as she ran her hand lightly over Matthew's delicate pink fingers. 'My mother Clara, was a German Jew,' she began again, 'my father a Polish Protestant. My real name is Anne Sarah Nimitz. I was born in Dortmund, Northern Germany.'

Rose had always felt that Olga's life had been tragic

and now she wasn't surprised at what she was hearing. It seemed almost inevitable that Olga should pour out her heart, even though Olga had never forgiven her for the humiliation of Coronation Day.

'I was twenty-six,' Olga continued, 'when my mother, husband and son were taken from our home by the Nazis and sent to a labour camp. I alone escaped capture as I was away at the time, visiting a sick friend. I never saw any of them again.'

Rose felt her flesh creep. 'What happened to them?'

The flickering eyes lowered. 'I learned that Siegfried died of a fever soon after he was taken. He was a frail, delicate child—' she paused, her voice devoid of all expression. 'My husband was executed for refusing to co-operate as a doctor, in other words he would not agree to participate in torture. No one was able to tell me what happened to my mother.'

Rose couldn't imagine what it must be like to lose a family in such a way. A child's death was terrible enough, but added to the loss of a husband and mother under such terrifying circumstances, was enough to send anyone insane.

'For the next year I survived in a cellar,' Olga murmured, 'until I was smuggled to Spain and provided with false papers. When the war was over, I came to England.'

Rose said hesitantly, 'Was there no one left in Germany?'

'No,' Olga replied simply. 'Only memories.'

'Why are you telling me this, Olga?' Rose asked sadly.

'Because there is no one left to tell.'

'But you've got Leslie,' Rose said encouragingly. 'After all the unhappiness, you made a new life.'

'A wasted life,' Olga said with sudden bitterness. 'Three years ago, when we met, I added a little *chutzpah* to his life, perhaps.' She smiled coldly. 'He did not question the lies I concocted about my past. But when the police arrived and discovered the stolen television they asked me many difficult questions. I was forced to produce my papers.' Olga took in a breath as her body shuddered. 'I desired only to belong to somewhere, to someone. I had lived many lies to preserve this skin. But now this skin no longer seems worth the effort.' Her thin lips twisted. 'I confessed to Leslie and, because he thought my troubles would incriminate him, he left me.'

'But, he's still your husband—'

'We never married,' Olga shrugged. 'This was also a lie.'

'Olga, I'm so sorry,' Rose said heavily, searching for words of consolation. 'I didn't know—'

'Even if you had known,' Olga broke in, 'would it have made any difference to the way you regarded me? I would never have been accepted here, no matter how hard I tried to become one of you.'

Rose couldn't deny there was an element of truth in this. East Enders were slow to welcome strangers into their midst, but this didn't mean the residents of Ruby Street wouldn't have eventually opened their homes and hearts to the Parkers. As for Rose, after the events of Coronation Day, she had truly regretted the embarrassment Olga had suffered. But would Olga believe her now if she tried to explain?

'I must go,' Olga said before Rose could speak. 'My time in Ruby Street is over.'

'You're leaving the island?' Rose asked in alarm. 'Is it because you think you'll be questioned again?'

Olga shrugged indifferently, as though she couldn't have cared less. 'Perhaps tomorrow, perhaps in a year . . . who knows?'

'But why don't you tell them the truth?' Rose asked in desperation. 'It couldn't be any worse than what you've already gone through.'

Olga looked at her calmly. 'I am not married to a British citizen, therefore I have no legal right to remain in your country. And Germany holds nothing for me but emptiness.' She let Matthew's fingers drop, her eyes glazed as she stood up. 'Goodbye, Rose.'

'Wait, I'll walk home with you.'

'No, that will not be necessary.' Hunching her narrow shoulders she smiled at Matthew. A flicker of warmth briefly filled her haggard face. 'He is beautiful,' she murmured softly. Then unsteadily, she walked away.

Rose wanted to run after her, try to persuade her to stay. Just when it was possible they might mend their differences, Olga was leaving!

Rose's wary eyes searched the length of Ruby Street. Groups of children played in the street, although she couldn't see Marlene, Donnie or Will, but she wasn't surprised. Em would have kept them in or sent them in the yard to play until Rose returned. After learning of

Eddie's warnings about reprisals, Em hadn't let them out of her sight.

Rose glanced down the length of the road. The only vehicle in sight was a horse-drawn cart. With a faint clip clop it passed Len Silverman's house. The old man was sitting in a chair outside his front door and when he saw her, lifted his hand in salute. She returned his wave then pushed the pram briskly to her own front door and slid the key in the lock.

'It's only me, Em,' she called, returning the pram to the front room and lifting Matthew into her arms before entering the kitchen.

'I was beginning to wonder where you were,' Em said reproachfully, as she lifted a big saucepan from the stove and on to the draining board. Scooping the froth from the surface with a cup, she glanced at Rose. 'Where have you been? I've been worried.'

'I went for a walk, that's all.'

'But you know what Eddie said about—' Em began but Rose shook her head irritably.

'I can't wrap meself up in cotton wool, Em,' Rose argued. The last week had seemed an eternity, always taking care to close doors and go out in twos and watch the children with an eagle eye.

'Did Matthew fall asleep?'

'Yes, but he's hungry again now.'

'Do you want me to make up a feed? And there's a nice bit of mashed potato I've made.'

'I'll give him what I have first and try the potato afterwards. Where are the kids?'

'Out in the yard. Ashley Green and his two little sisters are playing with our lot. Do you want me to call them in?'

Rose glanced out of the kitchen window. The children were playing hopscotch on the stones by the washhouse and she shook her head. 'No, I've got something to tell you first.'

Em placed the saucepan back on the stove and wiped her hands on her pinny. 'Well sit down and take the weight off your feet. You look pale—' She stiffened abruptly. 'You haven't seen the car again?'

'No. It's nothing like that.' Matthew began to cry. Rose sat down on one of the kitchen chairs and slid out of her coat. Undoing her blouse and sliding up her bra, she pressed Matthew's lips to her nipple. She didn't usually breastfeed in the kitchen but she wanted Em to listen attentively.

'I saw Olga today,' Rose said at once. 'Up Island Gardens.'

'Olga Parker?' Em repeated in surprise as she also sank down on a chair.

'Yes, she looked awful. No, not just awful, quite sick in fact. I'm really worried about her.'

'But she cut you dead just before Christmas.'

'I know, but today she wanted to talk. And what she told me explains so much. None of it would have happened if it hadn't been for that blessed television!'

'None of what would have happened?' Em asked in a guarded tone.

'Olga is leaving Ruby Street.'

'Leaving?'

'Yes, because when the police found the telly they asked her a lot of difficult questions about her past. You see, she's not really who she says she is and when Leslie left—'

'Rosy, love,' Em interrupted looking puzzled, 'you'd better start from the beginning. You've lost me already.'

Rose explained the whole story as patiently as she could. She began with Olga's true identity and how her entire family were taken away to labour camps in 1944 and how since her escape, Olga had lived in fear of being discovered. Em stared at her, asking her to repeat much of what she said. 'Was she telling you the truth do you think?' she asked eventually.

'I don't know why she'd make it up.'

'But she never talks to you – or me – or the children.'

Rose nodded slowly. 'I think she's been drinking and seemed to be in a dreadful turmoil. Although I must admit I couldn't smell alcohol on her breath, just a funny stale smell of old clothes, not at all like she used to be, so smart and done up.'

'Well, if it's true,' Em said sadly, 'she's had a tragic life.'

'The last straw was when Leslie walked out on her,' Rose continued. 'They weren't married, just living together.' Rose felt Matthew stir. She looked down and smiled at him. 'I'm sorry, my sweet, I'm not taking any notice of you, am I?'

'Rosy, that poor woman,' Em murmured on a deep sigh. 'No wonder she's lived like a hermit.'

'She looks terrible, Em. If Eddie hadn't sold them a duff

telly, this wouldn't have happened. Apparently everyone in the street turned against her after that, or at least she thought they did.'

'The trouble is,' Em said bleakly, 'we all worry about what other people think of us. If we didn't, we'd save ourselves a lot of heartache.'

Rose nodded. 'And there was me, in exactly the same boat. But at least I have a husband and family alive and kicking. She has no one.'

'What can we do to help?' Em asked sympathetically. 'Could we persuade her to stay on do you think?'

'I don't know. She thinks the police might come back.'

'How terrible to live in fear like that.'

'Perhaps we could take over some food,' Rose said suddenly. 'I'll bet she's been starving herself. She's as thin as a rake.'

'Do you think she would accept it though?' Em said doubtfully. 'She strikes me as someone who despises charity.'

'We can try.' Rose felt Matthew wriggle uncomfortably. He was sucking away but her nipples felt dry and uncomfortable. Suddenly he let out a yell of impatience. She tried him on the other breast, but it was no use. He began to whimper again.

'If you ask me,' Em frowned, 'you're drying up.'

'And he's not even three months old yet.'

'I'll make up a bottle,' Em decided firmly. 'All this talk of starvation makes me uneasy.'

Rose smiled down at the wrinkled nose and open

mouth now emitting a piercing scream. How lucky she was to have her son safe in her arms. How desperate Olga must have felt when they took away her baby.

'Why are we taking all this food to Mrs Parker?' Donnie asked as Rose packed the shopping bag with a fruit cake that Em had made yesterday, half a loaf and a little margarine wrapped in greaseproof paper. Will was carrying a small basin covered with muslin and tied with a piece of string under which two hefty dumplings were bobbing on the surface of the stew. The two girls had wrapped an orange and a banana in a brown bag from Joan's corner shop.

'Because she hasn't been very well,' Rose explained simply.

'She doesn't ever talk to us,' Marlene commented as she clutched the brown bag to her chest. 'She said Daddy stole that television and he didn't.'

'We know the truth and that's what matters.' Rose glanced at Em. 'Are you all right with Matthew?'

Em held him in her arms. He was fast asleep, full up with baby milk. 'Yes, but I'm not so sure now if this is a very good idea.'

'Well, she's more likely to ask us in with the children.' Rose wasn't entirely certain about this. But she had called once before on her own and that hadn't worked. As a united family, perhaps Olga would be more inclined to be hospitable.

They all followed Rose to the front door. She looked out cautiously. Only the local children played in the street and Cissy and Fanny were sitting on chairs by their front doors. There were no cars or strangers in sight.

Rose led the way over to Olga's. 'It ain't shut,' Marlene said as Rose was about to knock.

Em gave a little gasp. 'She never leaves her door open. She must have had too much to drink like you said Rosy.'

'I'll give it a push.' Rose gently pressed the door. It slowly swung open. They all gazed inside.

'It smells funny,' Marlene murmured.

'Like something's gone off,' Em said as they stepped inside and stood on the lino. The hall was empty and the kitchen deserted. The door to the front room was closed. Rose shouted Olga's name.

'Perhaps she's gone out,' Em said in a hopeful voice.

'Let's make sure.' They all crowded round as Rose opened the door. Another musty smell greeted them. 'The curtains are drawn,' Rose said, peering into the dark.

'Well, she never opens them, does she?'

Rose remembered how packed the room had been on Coronation Day and how tense the atmosphere was with excitement. She also recalled Olga's vain attempts at hospitality, which had ended in disaster for all concerned. The space where the television had stood was now filled by a footstool. The couch was in exactly the same place opposite the hearth and the big, upholstered fireside chair that everyone assumed was Leslie's rested against the wall. The room was cold as if it hadn't seen a fire in months, which was probably true, Rose thought as she stared at the abandoned fireplace. There were no ashes, no remnants of coke or wood in the empty scuttle. There was even a cobweb growing over the grate.

'Let's go home,' Em whispered anxiously. 'I feel like we're spying.'

'She might be resting upstairs,' Rose shrugged.

'Then why didn't she wake up when you called?'

'Mum?' Donnie clasped Rose's hand. 'I don't like it in here.'

'Nor do I,' said Will and Marlene together.

'Stay here and I'll run upstairs before we leave.' Rose gave everyone a reassuring smile. 'If Mrs Parker's asleep, we'll put the food in the kitchen.'

Rose went into the hall and climbed the stairs. She didn't know what she feared the worst: Olga suddenly appearing, looking aggrieved because they had entered her house without an invitation; or Olga much the worse for wear in one of the bedrooms. All the terraced houses in Ruby Street were built to the same specifications, two up, two down. Rose found herself wondering how much the stair carpet had cost. It was good quality with solid brass stair runners. The Parkers had lived in number thirty nine for two years. Before that, an older couple had rented the property. Mr Benson, an ex army man, died of pneumonia and his disabled wife had gone to live with one of their children. Rose knew the landlord lived in the West End. Had Olga kept up with the rent?

The small bedroom contained a single bed covered with a purple eiderdown. The colour reminded Rose of Olga's shabby purple coat. Was purple Olga's favourite colour?

Beside the bed was a modern looking chest of drawers and small wardrobe. The window that overlooked the back garden was, curiously, uncurtained, decorated only with a gauzy net. Rose closed the door quietly.

She trod carefully over the patterned runner to the front bedroom, more convinced than ever that Olga had fallen into a drink-induced sleep. When she had returned from the park she must have gone straight to bed and not noticed the front door was unlatched.

Rose gave a loud knock. 'Olga, it's me, Rose.'

There was no reply. She opened the door. This room was also in darkness, but a sour, unpleasant odour filled the air. Rose narrowed her eyes to the gloom. A figure lay on the bed, a silent, still figure that caused Rose to retreat momentarily. Quickly recovering she hurried round to the window and pulled back the heavy curtains. Two sets of brass runners jangled noisily, but Olga didn't stir. She lay on her side wearing only a thin dress. Her eyes were closed and her mouth open.

Rose approached the slumbering figure cautiously, as if she might suddenly come awake and demand to know what Rose was doing there. Timidly, she reached out and touched her. Rose jumped. Her skin was so cold!

'Olga, wake up!' Rose shook her shoulders, gently at first, then firmly. When she saw the vomit on the pillow and sheet, her heart gave a lurch. The next minute she was running down the stairs.

'What's wrong?' Em's eyes stared fearfully up at her.

'She's unconscious. Run along to Joan's and ask her to telephone Dr Cox. Tell him it's an emergency.'

'Oh, my God!' Em whispered hoarsely.

'You must hurry, all of you. Go as quickly as you can. Mrs Parker is very ill.'

With that, she packed them out of the door, only remembering afterwards that Em was still carrying Matthew. But it wasn't far to go, just to the end of the street. Rose ran back up the stairs. She didn't know what to do, but she knew she had to do something. Taking Olga's thin arms, she shook her and patted her cheeks.

'Olga! Wake up!' she cried again, but it was no use. Rose flew to the bathroom and grabbed a flannel soaked in cold water. She twisted it over Olga's forehead and let the water run down her face. She couldn't smell any alcohol. So why couldn't she rouse her? Had Olga tried something else far more dangerous to ease the pain of her existence? Rose stared down at the emaciated shadow that bore no resemblance to the woman who had looked so smart and sophisticated on Coronation Day.

'Don't give up, *Anne*,' Rose whispered, using her real name and hoping for a miracle. 'Life is still worth living, no matter what.'

But by the time Dr Cox arrived, Olga was parchment white and the flicker of pulse in her wrist was faint.

Chapter Nineteen

'What are you going to tell the doctor?' Em whispered as she stood with Rose in the evening sunlight. The ambulance carrying Olga's inert form had driven noisily away, leaving a hushed crowd waiting in the street.

'As little as possible,' Rose answered wearily. 'If Olga . . .' she corrected herself quickly, '*when* she gets better, she can tell them as much or as little as she wants. But for now her secret's safe with me.'

'Do you think she – you know – tried to do away with herself?'

'I don't know,' Rose replied honestly. 'I couldn't smell drink, although she was behaving very oddly.'

The crowd remained silent as Dr Cox emerged from Olga's house, closing the door firmly behind him. Rose, who was now carrying Matthew, walked over. She had grown to respect the young doctor despite his lack of bedside manner. He'd arrived within minutes of Joan Wright's telephone call and ushered them all from the house. Rose had been relieved to leave the oppressive, dismal atmosphere.

'How is she?' Rose asked as she approached him.

'Very poorly. Who is her next of kin?'

'Her husband, I suppose, Leslie Parker,' Rose said, giving nothing away.

'And where can he be found?'

'Somewhere up in the City, I think. He works in an office but I don't know where.'

Dr Cox regarded her thoughtfully. 'You spoke to Mrs Parker today?'

'Yes, we sat in the park for a while but she didn't seem like her usual self. So later this afternoon we paid her a visit. The door was open and we went in. It was then I found her upstairs and we called for you.' Rose hesitated. 'I thought she might have been drinking, to be honest.'

A pair of pale, but very astute eyes blinked behind unflattering round framed spectacles. He shook his head as he replied. 'No, I don't believe alcohol is responsible for her condition.' He seemed to be weighing up what else he should tell her and she guessed he came down on the side of caution as he added, 'All I can tell you is, if you hadn't taken the trouble to call this afternoon, Mrs Parker's chances of survival would be even slimmer than they are now.' He opened the door of his Morris Minor and climbed in. 'I should have some news in the morning,' he added brusquely.

When he'd driven away Rose turned back to find everyone watching her. Matthew whined and she transferred his weight to her other arm wondering what she was going to say. Half of the street had turned out, amongst them the Mendozas, Mike and Heather Price, the Greens, Cissy and Fanny, the Patels, Len Silverman, the Dixons and Dora Lovell.

'How is she?' Anita was the first to speak.

'Not so good, I'm afraid.'

'Did he say what's wrong?'

Rose shook her head. 'No. He'll know more tomorrow.'

'She ain't been seen around for weeks,' Cissy yelled, pushing her way forward. 'The word is her old man's done a bunk with a bit of skirt. Got fed up with her tantrums no doubt,' she added sourly. 'You could hear them rowing half a mile away.'

'What way is that to speak of your neighbour who is so ill?' Len Silverman demanded in an emotional tone.

Cissy tapped the side of her bulbous nose. 'I keeps me ears and eyes open, don't I?'

'Of that I have no doubt,' he muttered, his old eyes fixing disdainfully on his neighbour.

'And not only that,' Cissy continued, 'the coppers have been round. I saw 'em knock on her door only the other day. Two uniformed blokes that passed right by me door. She wouldn't answer them either. And I knew she was in. I reckon she's got plenty to hide.'

'You would,' Derek Green muttered. 'The poor soul can't defend herself.'

'Defend herself against what?' Fanny pushed her way angrily through the crowd. 'We ain't accusing her of anything.'

'Is there anything we can do?' Benny interrupted, and all heads turned toward Rose.

'I don't know,' she shrugged. 'We just have to wait and see.'

'Fancy it being you that found her,' Cissy muttered spitefully. 'She wouldn't normally give you the time of day after your old man flogged her that bent telly.'

'Well, she wasn't exactly banging your door down to be friends,' Anita pointed out. 'And it was lucky Rose did call or else the poor cow might've been lying there for weeks.'

Dora Lovell groaned. 'It doesn't bear thinking about.'

'Let's all go home now,' Benny sighed, catching his wife's arm. 'We've had enough excitement for one day.'

As the crowd dispersed, Cissy and Fanny remained at Olga's window peering in.

'Bloody peeping Toms,' Anita growled as she and Benny paused by Rose's door. 'Do you know they were the first on the scene when Dr Cox arrived? I'd just cycled up and was opening me door and there they were, racing up like athletes to the winning line.' She shook her head exasperatedly. 'Anyway, love, are you all right?'

'Yes. A bit shook up, that's all.'

'I'm hungry.' Marlene tugged Rose's elbow. Matthew stirred fretfully in her arms and Em unlatched the door and shooed all the children through.

When they had disappeared inside, Anita asked outright, 'Do you think Olga tried to take her own life?'

'Neet, let the girl be,' Benny warned, but she ignored him.

'Go in and put the kettle on. The boys'll be home soon,' she replied, waving her hand in his face.

Benny gave a resigned shrug. 'Night, Rose, love. You get some rest now.'

'Night, Benny.'

If there was a chair on the pavement, Rose thought, she might fall into it right now. The last few nights with Matthew had drained her. She felt she could fall asleep standing up. But Anita was waiting for an answer.

'I saw Olga up the Gardens today,' Rose continued. 'She actually spoke to me.'

'Blimey, put out the flags!' Anita exclaimed. 'What did she say?'

'She told me a long and very sad story and I think we'd better keep it under our hat for now.'

'What do you mean?'

'Olga's not Polish. She was born a German Jew. Her husband was a doctor and they had a little boy called Siegfried and along with her mother, the Nazis took them off to a labour camp. She never saw any of them again.'

Anita whistled through her teeth. 'Are you sure she's not going a bit funny upstairs?'

'She seemed strange, but I believed her.'

'What did she tell you for?'

Rose shrugged. 'She said because there was no one left to tell.'

'So how did she escape from the Nazis?'

'She said she was smuggled to Spain. After the war she came to England with false papers and met Leslie but she never married him. On Coronation Day, when the police took the telly they started asking her questions.

She thinks if they find out who she is, they'll deport her. You heard what Cissy said, the police have been knocking on Olga's door. No wonder she was at the end of her tether.'

For a few moments Anita was silent. 'You've had quite a day, love. P'raps we can have a good old chat on Saturday on our way to market.'

Rose nodded. But in three days a lot could happen.

Thursday morning arrived and Rose cycled to the surgery. Dr Cox telephoned the hospital whilst she waited. Olga still hadn't come round. She was in a coma.

'I'll come and tell you if there's any change,' Dr Cox unexpectedly offered.

She cycled home and told Joan at the corner shop who said she would enlighten her customers. Rose knew that once Cissy and Fanny were informed, the news would travel with the speed of light.

On Friday, Rose woke at the crack of dawn as Matthew crooned softly in his cot. He'd slept fitfully and before he disturbed Em who was asleep in the bed beside her, she lifted him from the cot and carried him downstairs.

It was impossible to let him bawl now that her sister had moved back upstairs. Em had disliked sleeping in the front room, eager to return the chaotic household to its former, organized state. Will was resigned to sleeping in the girls' room on the camp bed, although he had alternative plans for the summer. Alan and David had presented him with an outgrown one-man tent and his intention was to erect it in the yard.

By seven, Matthew was fed and changed and dozing in his pram in the yard. He'd gulped his breakfast from the bottle as though he hadn't been fed in years. Rose had added half a rusk and now he was away with the fairies.

Rose decided she would clean the front room window before everyone woke. Em insisted on performing the major household chores but the sun was climbing into a bright blue sky and Rose was wide-awake by now. The air was fresh with the scent of the river and being Good Friday, no one else in the street was up yet. She filled a bucket with water, took the broom from the cupboard and slipped the latch on the front door. With heavy frosts at night and high winds in January, everyone had wondered if there was to be a repeat of the wet weather last year, but so far there had been only a few damp days here and there. The melting frost sparkled off the pavement like miniature pearls.

Rose stood the bucket and broom by the wall. She wondered if there was time to polish the step as well. She was just deciding whether she should attempt the stone first when she happened to glance to her left.

A car was parked outside the Dixons'.

It was brown with bulky wings and a long shiny bonnet. Rose couldn't move. Her eyes were glued to its shape. She couldn't even look away or run inside and call for Em. She couldn't even swallow.

She hadn't wanted to believe Eddie. She hadn't wanted to believe anything about the crazy situation Eddie had got them into. One part of her was still in denial that he was even in prison!

Now the car had appeared again. Eddie had warned her that the threats were intended for him. But whoever it was that Eddie had upset, had no qualms in terrifying innocent parties. What would it be next? A fist on the front door, a window smashed, the house violated again? What could she do to protect her family?

Then all at once Rose suddenly felt her body coming back to life as a cold and icy calm spread over her. Slowly she lifted the broom and bucket and stepped into the road wishing she wasn't wearing her apron and carpet slippers, rather her best dress and court shoes, decorated as brightly as the troops who marched into battle with their colours flying.

Rose finally came to a halt. She saw nothing in the opaque window but the fluffy white clouds of the morning sky. The water splashed over the glass with a generous thud and ran in streamers along the crest of the bonnet. The pail followed, energetically dancing its way along the bonnet. For a heavy object, Rose thought, it seemed to be remarkably agile.

'Go away,' she shouted as she lifted the broom. 'Leave us alone and don't ever come back!'

In her trance-like state she was aware of the broom's echoing bang and thud and perhaps, if she really did try to recall, the peculiar sound of the surprised engine as the car growled towards her.

'Rose! Rose!'

Em was shouting her name. Rose blinked, at first feeling nothing. Then as she stirred, a pain travelled through her right arm and into her shoulder. Before she could take a breath, Benny and Anita's faces filled her entire vision.

'Stay still, love, you're all right. Just get your breath back.' Benny was lifting her arm and laying it gently over her chest. 'It's not broken, thank God.'

'What happened?' Rose looked up at the circle of faces. Em, Len Silverman, Cissy and Fanny and the Dixons. Fred said cheerfully, 'Blimey love, you ain't half lucky.'

'The driver aimed straight for you,' Em cried, squeezing Rose's left hand. 'But Benny pulled you out of the way.'

'I didn't know you could move so quick, Dad,' Alan said as he stood beside his father.

'I ain't over the hill yet,' Benny growled as Rose realized she was lying against Fred and Mabel's front door.

'Benny, you great lump,' Anita reproved as she patted Rose's cheeks, 'it's a wonder you didn't crush her.'

'That car would have bloody killed her,' Cissy pointed out as she peered into Rose's eyes. 'You don't know how close you came to meeting your maker, love.'

Rose began to shake with shock, just like on Coronation Day when they'd taken Eddie in the police car.

'Bloody maniacs,' Fanny cursed toothlessly.

'We'll try to move your arm again,' Benny said as he lifted her elbow gently. 'I'm going to stretch it out careful like. Tell me if it hurts.'

'I hope you know what you're doing,' Anita scowled.

'How's that?' Benny lifted gently, cupping her wrist with his big hand.

Rose managed a tight smile. 'All right.'

'What about this?'

'Ouch.'

'Sorry, love.'

'No, Benny, it's me bum, not me arm. I feel like I've been kicked by a horse.'

'That's 'cos you fell on it,' Benny grinned. 'I tried to get me weight under you, but me beer gut got in the way.'

There was a murmur of laughter from the relieved faces that hovered over her. Benny helped her to her feet. 'How does that feel, gel?'

She looked at him with gratitude. 'I owe you me life, Benny.'

'Think nothing of it,' he grinned.

'Nothing else broken is there?' Anita asked worriedly.

'No, I'm all right.'

'It's a bloody miracle if you are,' she sighed. 'What the hell was going on out here? Benny and me couldn't believe our eyes when we looked out the window. You was screaming your head off.'

'One minute I was asleep in bed,' Em gasped breathlessly, 'the next I thought all hell had broken loose. Why didn't you call me?'

'I didn't have time,' Rose replied as she tried to move her trembling legs. 'I opened the front door and there they were.'

'Who were?' Cissy asked curiously.

'No one you'd know,' Anita dismissed, winking at Rose.

'The repairs to their motor will cost a packet,' Fred

338

added as he pulled his plaid dressing gown round him and tied the belt.

'A car is of no importance,' Len murmured sympathetically. 'It is Rose who matters.'

There was a unanimous murmur of assent and Rose wondered how she was going to explain her irrational and, as it turned out, highly foolish behaviour. If Benny hadn't rugby tackled her out of the way the girls would be minus a mother. How stupid she had been! What had come over her to challenge those people? They had no scruples and were quite prepared to run her over if they'd had the chance.

'You might as well all know,' Rose said heavily, 'Eddie got mixed up with some unpleasant people before he went to prison. It was nothing to do with the telly, but with some bookies—'

At this a collective groan filled the air. 'Bookies!' Len exclaimed with a shake of his grey head. 'Parasites to the human race!'

'Apparently so,' Rose agreed quietly.

'That car's parked outside our house a few times,' Mabel added darkly. 'It just stays in one spot and no one ever gets out.'

'What do they want?' Fred asked Rose.

'To frighten us,' she said simply. 'Eddie owes them money and don't want him to forget it.'

'So they pick on defenceless women and children,' Len said shakily. 'If only I was a young man again.'

'Bastards,' Benny swore under his breath. 'But in future, Rose, don't go charging at any cars with your broom, will you? Come and knock on me door first and give me time to get dressed.'

Rose smiled. She had only just realized that she'd brought everyone out in their nightclothes. Anita was wearing a pair of striped pyjamas, Cissy and Fanny stood in blue and pink wincyette nightgowns, the Mendoza boys wore only underpants and Len Silverman sported an ancient pair of long johns. Benny hadn't managed to dress, but had pulled on a shirt, which flapped over his pyjama bottoms.

'I'm really sorry I disturbed you all,' Rose apologized.

'We'll chase 'em off if we see them again, Auntie Rose,' Alan said, puffing out his skinny chest, but Rose shook her head firmly.

'No, Alan, they're a nasty bunch. Don't go near them.'

'You're not to get involved,' Benny warned his sons. 'If there's any chasing to be done, it'll be me that's doing it, or the police.'

'Yeah, why don't we tell the coppers what happened?' Cissy asked, narrowing her eyes.

'No,' Rose said a little too quickly. The last thing she wanted was the police involved in Eddie's affairs. If they found out he had been a floater for the bookies, he'd never get out of prison. 'I'm sure it won't happen again,' she assured the worried faces. 'Not after today.'

'We will all be looking out for you,' Len assured her with a wizened smile.

'I reckon we should go back to bed for half an hour,' Em suggested, as she glanced anxiously at Rose. 'The kids are still asleep.'

'I'm all for that,' Benny nodded as he dragged his fingers through his receding black hair and scratched the dark stubble on his chin. 'You sure you're all right now, Rose?'

'Yes, nothing that a cup of tea won't put right.'

Once again the crowd in Ruby Street began to disperse. Despite feeling worse for wear, Rose wondered how Olga was. As soon as she felt more human she would call on Dr Cox and enquire.

'Come on,' Em whispered, taking hold of her good arm.

'See you tomorrow if you still feel like it,' Anita shouted as she pushed Alan and David in front of her.

Inside the house, all was silent. As Rose sat down with a sigh on the couch she noticed her slipper was torn on the toe. It must have been when Benny pushed her out of the way of the car. She lifted the hem of her apron. Her knee was grazed and bloodied but she hadn't even felt the injury until now.

'Oh God,' Em said in a terrified voice. 'What will they do next?'

Rose managed to smile. 'Just let them try.'

Em sucked in a breath. 'Don't even joke about it.'

'I wasn't joking,' Rose assured her sister. She might be feeling a little battered and bruised and for a while she might have gone a little crazy. But inside she was still the same Rose Weaver and she refused – *absolutely* refused – to be frightened any more.

Chapter Twenty

It was eleven-thirty on Easter Sunday morning when the pale blue Morris Minor arrived. Rose saw it draw up from the front room window and her heart turned over. She thought for a moment it was the brown car but as soon as Dr Cox appeared wearing his usual dark suit and tie and those round spectacles, she relaxed. Her relief was short lived, however, as he knocked on the door and she hurried to open it.

'I'm the bearer of bad news, I'm afraid,' he said quietly.

'It's Olga.' Rose didn't need to be told. It was written all over his face.

'I'm afraid so. She died in hospital, very peacefully, at three o'clock this morning.' He gave a reluctant smile. 'I'm sorry.'

Rose nodded slowly. 'So am I.'

'Would you have seen Mr Parker?'

Rose shook her head. 'No. Have you knocked?'

'I'll try now.' He stepped back. 'The police will call of course.' He looked a little uncomfortable, then turned to frown across at Olga's house. 'Mrs Parker was registered

342

with the surgery but not her husband. I hope he'll be able to enlighten us on one or two facts.'

Rose could have told him not to waste his time or energy and that Leslie Parker was probably the last person on earth who, according to Olga, wished to be connected with her death. But she refrained and as Dr Cox was about to leave, she asked impulsively, 'What happens to – Olga, now?'

'In view of the circumstances in which she died,' he replied, 'there will be an enquiry.'

'What sort of an enquiry?'

'An autopsy may be required,' he answered shortly.

'What about a funeral and everything?'

'I'm sure Mr Parker will enlighten you on the funeral arrangements,' he ended briskly.

Some hope of that, Rose thought, wondering if she really ought to inform the doctor of what she knew. But before she could speak again he was crossing the road to number thirty-nine and Rose closed the front door. Just a few minutes later she heard the car start up and, with a deep sigh, Rose wondered what she should do next. The children were at St Mark's with the Pipers and would not be home until dinner time. Em had pushed the pram out half an hour ago, venturing up to the corner shop and Amethyst Way. The Mendozas were probably at home. After going to the market with Anita yesterday, the cupboards would be full and the two boys, having a lie-in, would rise late for cooked breakfasts.

Rose went back to the window and gazed across the street.

'How can I help you, Olga, now that you're gone?' Rose whispered aloud as her mind flew back to Coronation Day and the poignant memory of Olga Parker looking smart and sophisticated, attempting to curry the street's favour with her new television. How deeply she must have desired the attention of her neighbours. And how sad that she and Eddie had managed, albeit unwittingly, to thwart Olga's unsuccessful attempt at popularity.

Rose sat down on the couch and stared at the radio-gram. 'The money wasn't mine to give you anyway. It wasn't even Eddie's.'

From somewhere in the distance a bell pealed out across the island. The clock on the mantel struck twelve. It was Easter Sunday and the church doors would now be thrown open to disgorge the worshippers. Rose was not a church-goer herself, but the children sometimes went to St Mark's chapel next to the school. They liked the hymn singing and the parables read aloud afterwards. Easter was special. They would all come home with an Easter card illustrated with a glowing Jesus balanced on a ray of sunshine. Even Len Silverman gave them a cube of chocolate instead of their usual boiled sweets.

Len Silverman! Of course, Rose thought suddenly. He was Jewish, although she had never seen him go to the synagogue, unlike Lena, his wife, who had been a regular attender. Rose hurried upstairs, removed her apron and changed into a cotton dress. It was Easter after all. When Em returned she would call and ask his advice. Then, with a little luck, she would know what to do.

★

'Come in child, come in,' Len invited when he found her on the doorstep. Rose hadn't expected such a welcome. On a beautiful sunny morning like this she had expected to find him seated outside in his chair. And since no one that she knew had ever been inside the old man's house since Lena Silverman's death, she was surprised at his offer. Did he still feel guilty, she wondered, over the television business?

'I would wish you a Happy Easter, Len,' she murmured as she entered the darkened hall, 'but you don't celebrate it, do you?'

'After the death of my wife, it's years since I celebrated even a birthday, Rose,' he said humorously. Then as he caught her eye, he added mildly, 'But now is the time of the Passover, a commemoration of freedom from our slavery in Egypt.'

'Do you do anything special, then?' Rose asked politely as she slowly followed him towards the front room. The house smelt of spices and herbs that somehow blended in with a not unpleasant odour of mustiness.

'Yes, it's called *seder*.'

'I don't know what that is,' Rose said apologetically.

'*Seder* means order,' he explained as he opened a loudly creaking door. 'We read the Passover story in a special order from the *Haggadah*. This is a reminder to us that we are a free people.' He paused, turning to her. 'The name Passover comes from the moment when the Angel of Death passed over the homes of the Jews. Some spilt lamb's blood on their doors in order to save their firstborn.'

345

Rose nodded. 'Yes, I know the story from the Bible.'

He smiled again. 'So you like your Bible stories eh, Rose?'

'Yes, although I'm not religious or anything.'

He turned his palms toward the ceiling. 'What is religion, Rose? You look into your heart to find God. And you are a good wife and mother. That is all that matters.'

Rose felt slightly embarrassed. In all the years she had known this old man, they had never done more than pass the time of day or spoken about the children, which he was always pleased to do. A childless couple, Len and Lena had doted on one another. After her death he showered his affection on the local kids, spending hours in that old chair of his watching them play. Rose recalled she had been in her early teens when Lena died. A plump, dark-eyed woman, she had been a friendly soul who attended the synagogue regularly.

'Come and sit down.' Len showed her into the sitting room. Dressed in his usual crumpled collarless shirt and a pair of baggy trousers and braces with his thick grey hair as yet uncombed, Rose thought he might have just tumbled out of bed to answer her knock. But then she realized the house was a mirror reflection, an extension of its owner. Each nook and cranny was stuffed with ornaments and books, all set at odd angles and managing extraordinary balancing acts.

There wasn't an inch of wallpaper showing as far as she could see. Hiding the surface of one wall was a magnificent walnut sideboard, the shiny brown wood just managing to peep out from the cluttered china and books that filled its surfaces. The rest of the room was covered with pictures and photographs of Jewish men wearing beards and homburgs and women dressed in austere black clothing. Some were encased in ornate gold frames others in simple wooden ones.

'Sit, won't you?' Len invited as he bent to push away the books and papers scattered the length of another unusual item of furniture. Rose had never seen a couch quite like it before.

'This is Lena's basha,' Len said proudly as Rose squeezed on to the heavily cushioned wooden bench adorned with an intricately embroidered cover.

As the basha almost filled the rest of the room, the remaining chair, that Rose realized must be Len's favourite, was squeezed tightly by the fireplace.

Rose stared at the hearth, the centrepiece of every Eastender's house. Instead of the regulation fireside set and coal scuttle, it was filled with an enormous army of china figurines all dressed in colourful regalia. Obviously the fire hadn't been alight for some time, Rose thought. The old man must freeze in winter!

'I put them away when it is cold,' he told her as if reading her mind, though somehow she was hard-pressed to believe him. There were so many. 'Lena loved her little darlings. She would dust them every day and remember her family in Turkey.'

'Your wife was from Turkey?' Rose asked in surprise.

'Lena's grandparents were Turkish, my dear. This *tzaki* went out of style long ago with their generation, but Lena liked to honour them in such a way.' He sighed as he sank down into the big fireside chair. Then, unexpectedly, he smiled, his bushy grey eyebrows lifting to show piercing dark eyes. 'After fifty years of married life to one woman, it is too late to change.'

'I don't see why you would want to,' Rose said kindly, although she was already beginning to feel a little suffocated in the thick, cloying atmosphere. 'It's a very interesting room,' she said tactfully.

'My Lena created it,' he shrugged. 'This was her universe. Unfortunately she was not impressed with my world.'

'Yes, of course, you were a jeweller,' Rose nodded.

'Indeed. And I loved my work. Always it was for others though, the big shops in the city. I was never enterprising enough to run my own business.' He smiled at her, folding his hands across his lap and knitting his fingers together. Rose saw how long and slender they still were, a young man's hands almost.

She knew he was politely waiting for her to explain her visit. 'Dr Cox just called on me,' she began. 'Olga died in the early hours of this morning.'

The elderly Jew sat very still and closed his eyes. He murmured a few strange words that Rose didn't understand and his cracked lips and lined face suddenly looked very drawn. 'My heart grieves,' he said eventually.

'I haven't told anyone. I wanted to speak to you first.'

'To me?'

'Yes. You see, I don't think Olga has anyone left to speak for her. Well, to make funeral arrangements and all that.'

Len frowned. 'Her husband is not at home?'

'I'm sure Olga won't mind me confiding in you that he wasn't her husband. They just lived together. And he left her when she told him about her past, which is really what I've come about.'

The dark eyes stared curiously at her. 'Rose, I am confused. What have I to do with our neighbour's past? The present was difficult enough, I am sad to say.'

'Yes, I know what you mean,' Rose agreed. 'Everyone knows that I fell out with Olga on Coronation Day but I've always felt bad about it, even though I tried to make friends.'

'And now she is dead and there is nothing you can do,' he added solemnly. 'Well, I'm hoping there is,' Rose said persuasively. 'In actual fact Olga wasn't Polish but German. She was also Jewish. Her family was taken away to a labour camp in Germany during the war and she never saw them again.'

'Oiy vey! Such a thing!'

'Yes, I know,' Rose continued, relieved to see the concerned expression spread over his face. 'It's a tragic story.'

Len looked genuinely surprised. 'You believed her, Rose?'

'Why would she make it up?'

He shook his head. 'I cannot think of a reason.'

'The thing that sticks out in my mind,' Rose sighed, 'is her last words to me. She only wanted to belong somewhere. That isn't much to ask for is it? Don't all of us want that? But she never belonged anywhere and now, if

Leslie doesn't take responsibility, she won't belong anywhere in death.'

He nodded slowly, gazing at the figurines in the
hearth, then his old eyes travelled slowly around the
room as if he were seeing it all for the first time. 'My Lena
would have understood. Ah yes, she would have understood perfectly.'

Rose wished Lena was here now. 'I don't know
anything about Jewish traditions, Len. I was hoping you
could help.'

'How?'

'Could she be buried in the Jewish cemetery?'

Len shrugged again. 'I will ask the Rabbi, although we
haven't spoken in some time.' He frowned. 'You had
better tell me all you know about her.'

Rose began slowly, trying to recall as accurately as she
could everything Olga had said.

The following Friday Rose was sitting in Anita's front
room wondering why she was going to all the bother of
persuading everyone that Olga should have a proper
burial. She didn't much fancy knocking on doors, but she
and Len had agreed it was the only way to persuade people
to contribute. And by the looks of Benny, who had just
got home from work and no doubt wanted his meal, Olga
Parker was probably the last person he wanted to discuss.

Rose bit her lip anxiously. Anita was making a second
pot of tea and taking her time in doing so. Em was sitting
on the edge of her seat looking as though she had been
dragged in here by force.

'Right you are!' Anita exclaimed as she at last walked back in carrying a teapot swamped by a huge, thick-knit cosy. Rose watched her neighbour pour the tea into four of her best china cups with meticulous care. 'Drink up, it's a nice brown brew.'

'Ta, Neet.' Rose took her cup, relieved that Matthew at least was silent. He'd finally fallen asleep in the pram parked in Anita's hall. The kids were amusing themselves outside in the backyard; Alan and David were showing Will how to erect the tent. She had better get on with what she had to say before one or all of them came screaming in. But before her lips touched the cup, Anita sat down and looked her straight in the eye.

'You don't plan to knock on every front door in Ruby Street, do you?' she asked without batting an eyelid.

'Yes, I do, as a matter of fact,' Rose nodded. 'Len says he can get everything arranged including a plot for twenty pounds, from someone the Rabbi knows up Golders Green who doesn't want the ground any more.'

'Cremation would be simpler, wouldn't it?' Benny queried.

'Yes, I suppose so. But Len told me Jews regard cremation as desecration to the body. They also believe that burial should take place the same day as the death, but in Olga's case there had to be an autopsy. That was how they found out she took an overdose.'

'What about a service?' Anita asked.

'Len is going to take care of that.'

'And all this for someone who wouldn't give you the time of day!'

Rose straightened her back. 'I think all that matters is she's given a decent send off, isn't it? She lived on the street for three-and-a-half years and we knew her as well as anyone did.'

'Yeah,' Anita nodded, 'precisely. You know, one thing bothers me. Why did she tell you, Rose?'

'She'd swallowed a bottle of aspirin that's why,' Benny said with a frown at his wife. 'It could have been anyone.'

'Yes,' Anita nodded, 'but she was still savvy enough to lumber Rose with her troubles knowing there wasn't a bloody thing Rose could do to help. She didn't tell me, did she? Or the Dixons, or even Len Silverman, who is Jewish just like her. Strikes me as she saw meeting Rose in the park as an opportunity to get her own back before she—'

'I'm not daft, Neet,' Rose interrupted. 'I'm well aware Olga couldn't forgive me and Eddie for the telly business. But I'm acting according to me own conscience now, not hers.'

'Well, it's up to you,' Anita sighed. 'But I won't vouch for the reaction you'll get from Ruby Street. Asking everyone to contribute towards her funeral when no one's seen the woman in a month of Sundays is a bit hopeful.'

'Anyway, why isn't her old man here to help out?' Benny asked, bewildered.

'Dr Cox told me that when the police tracked down Leslie he disowned her completely,' Rose explained. She'd gone over all this before. But everyone seemed to think Olga was someone else's responsibility not theirs.

'He insisted, apparently, that he was just a lodger and Olga was out of order when she called herself Mrs Parker.'

'The lying bugger.' Anita poured them all another cup of tea, spilling some into the saucers as her hand shook with anger. Then she quickly disappeared into the kitchen with the empty teapot.

Benny frowned up from where he sat on the fireside chair. His elbows were wedged on his knees, his shirt sleeves rolled up and his working trousers were still stuffed down his boots. 'She's on your side love,' he told Rose in a hushed voice, 'but she's angry you've got lumbered again.'

'I thought the same, Benny,' Em nodded primly, glancing at Rose. 'Olga isn't our responsibility.'

'Then whose responsibility is she?' Rose stared expectantly at her sister and then at Benny. None of them replied and there was an awkward silence until Anita returned bearing a fresh pot of tea. She lowered it to the table, then turned and pushed something into Rose's palm.

'What's this?' Rose asked in surprise as she looked down.

'Two quid to start the ball rolling,' Anita said a little grudgingly. 'You'd better remember to write every donation down and thank everyone at the wake or they'll be fighting over who gave what.'

'Wake?' Rose repeated, overwhelmed by Anita's generous offering but mostly that she'd come around to her way of thinking.

'Yeah. Well, you can't have a funeral without a wake, can you? I reckon between us we can throw a good spread, though we ain't Jews, and neither is anyone else 'cept Len, so he'll have to bring his own kosher grub with him.'

'Thanks, Neet,' Rose said gratefully. 'But I hope this isn't the Butlin's money?'

'Oh, that disappeared long ago,' she managed to laugh as she met her husband's questioning gaze. 'The lorry needed two new tyres more than we needed a holiday. And anyway, the boys have decided to go camping instead in Alan's new tent.' She threw back her head and laughed raucously, then sat down on the couch with a sigh. 'Right now, how long have we got to get the money together?'

'You're not hocking Mum's pearls, are you?' Em stared at Rose, disbelief written all over her face as they stood in the hall on Saturday afternoon. Rose had just completed her collection from the odd numbers of Ruby Street, ending up with a disappointing five pounds and nine-pence. Anita had already given her the seven pounds and sixpence she had collected from the even numbers, including a donation from Benny's parents and Alan and David. Most people complained Olga was a stranger in their midst and Rose found herself repeating Olga's story to win their support until even she felt quite sick of listening to it.

'Only temporarily.' Rose kept her hand on the open door. Unfortunately Em had heard her come in and hurry up the stairs to retrieve the pearls from Eddie's rolled up socks in the bottom drawer. She was hoping to take the necklace and do the deed without Em's knowledge. 'When I'm working again I'll get them back.'

'But Mum would be horrified!' Em protested in an angry tone that Rose hadn't heard her use before. Em avoided confrontation like the plague but now she was furious, all pink in the face and losing control.

Rose frowned at her sister. 'Do you really think so? I believe Mum would have given the clothes off her back to a beggar if the need arose.'

'These are her pearls we're talking about.' Em's soft features suddenly looked hard. Her hazel eyes narrowed. 'I'm getting fed up with Olga this and Olga that. We can hardly make ends meet as it is. Yet you're risking Mum's pearl necklace to throw away on a stranger. Even if Olga is on your conscience, she certainly isn't on mine. We've got mouths to feed and bodies to clothe. We only just had enough for the rent last week. In fact, as you well know, if it hadn't been for Joan slipping me that bacon and eggs cheap we'd have been on bread and water this weekend.'

Rose was aware this was true. In fact, Olga's demise couldn't have come at a worse time. Last night in bed, Rose had tossed and turned, questioning her motives for what she was doing, in Em's words, on a stranger's behalf. She also felt a hypocrite. There was never any love lost between Olga and herself and everyone knew it. She wondered why she hadn't agreed to Dr Cox assuming responsibility for the whole matter as he had offered to do. It would save everyone a lot of time and trouble, not to mention expense. But she hadn't been able to stomach the thought of a life going up anonymously in a puff of crematorium smoke. Fate had dogged Olga's footsteps whilst on this earth. Surely in death, she was owed some acknowledgement?

'I know,' Rose agreed patiently. 'But I'll be bringing in a wage when I'm back at work. Things will be easier all round.'

'That's all very well,' her sister complained, 'but you don't even know if you'll get a job.'

'Gwen House has offered me my old one back.'

'You never said.'

'I was going to. I've just been busy.'

'Yes, and we all know why.'

Rose tried not to take offence. 'I know Olga is a thorn in most people's sides. And most of those I called on this morning told me they have better things to do with their hard earned cash.'

'Exactly. To most of Ruby Street she was just a stranger – a foreigner! If anything, she should be taken back to where she came from.'

Rose had never heard her sister talk so unkindly. 'Em, she had nowhere to return to.'

'So we're supposed to foot the bill? I couldn't even provide my own husband with a proper funeral because no one wanted to know at St John's. All those pious, devout Christians, all happy to preach love and understanding from the pulpit but then when it came to Arthur, you'd have thought he was a leper!'

Rose understood now. 'This is why you're upset, because of Arthur.'

Em stared at her. She was shaking and twitching so much that Rose thought she was about to cry. But instead she turned and ran up the stairs. A few seconds later a loud bang shook the house. The bedroom door rattled on its hinges. Rose listened to the muffled weeping coming from above.

A few minutes later she went upstairs. 'Em?' she called outside the bedroom door.

Slowly it opened. Her sister fell into her arms. 'Oh, Rosy, I'm sorry.'

'There's nothing to be sorry about.'

'What made me say such awful things?'

'You've bottled up your feelings, that's why.'

Em sniffed noisily on her shoulder. 'I didn't know I had.'

'Come downstairs. I'll make some tea.'

Em pushed her gently away. 'Rosy, you're right. Mum would have done the same as you. She'd have looked after anyone who needed a helping hand – in life or in death. Go and do what you have to.'

'Are you sure?'

Em nodded, rubbing her puffy cheeks with the back of her hand. 'Yes, go on.'

'I'm sorry about Arthur not having a proper funeral.'

To Rose's surprise, her sister smiled. 'He's still up at Eastbourne Crem in an urn. I suppose one day I might forgive him and buy a rose tree and scatter him under it.' Her mouth twitched. 'Or I might go down the pier and chuck him off the end.'

'But Arthur was frightened of water,' Rose pointed out.

Em nodded, a twinkle in her eye. 'He couldn't swim a stroke. Serve him right, won't it?'

Solly Rosenberg had just endured an hour of his wife's company and he was exhausted. Even the tax man didn't worry him like his wife did. At least his accountant was dealing with the problems of his business, whilst there was no one, other than himself, to calm Alma's highly strung nature. Their only daughter Ruth, was staying with her husband's parents in the States and would not be back until after the summer. If his appeal was successful he would be out of this place very soon. Solly had high hopes of coming out of his present difficulties without a scratch. He was worth more to the tax man in employ than he was sewing mail bags.

Solly wasn't quite certain how he'd come to marry Alma thirty-two years ago, although, if he was honest, he suspected his motives had been swayed by Alma's sizeable dowry. If it hadn't been for his wife's parents, who had sadly departed this mortal coil, Solly thought as he raised his small, dark eyes honouringly to the sky as he strolled around the large playing field belonging to Hewis prison, then his life would have been far, far different. Less rich in material goods and vastly less worthy in character. Solly had always viewed his wife as an investment, just as he had his stock market shares. His chain of retail outlets, inexpensive clothing for both sexes, was nowhere near as lucrative as his stocks portfolio. But Alma couldn't sample, stroke or wear his portfolio. So he maintained his business at modest profits, content to allow Alma the pleasure of her frequent tours, inspecting the shops with an eagle eye.

Today Alma had been wearing a creation of black and white that dazzled Solly throughout the visit, as the stripes wove over her generous bosom and undulating girth in a kaleidoscope action that caused him to feel slightly nauseous.

So very different from the quiet grace of the young woman who had sat at the next table to them. Now, as Solly recalled the heart stopping brown eyes that had smiled occasionally at him from a truly exquisite face, he had realised he'd spent most of his time trying to overhear their conversation as Alma prattled on about the Knightsbrige shop and her intention to introduce to it a larger size of women's fashion wear.

Solly groaned softly. Larger women had dominated his life. His mother, his grandmother, his mother-in-law and now his wife. There was nothing wrong with large women, in fact he enjoyed them tremendously. And Alma was a sensual woman who had contributed not a little panache to his enjoyment of sex. But he was a small man in stature and his appetite had always got him into trouble.

'Give you a pound for each one,' said the voice beside him and Solly jumped guiltily.

'Oh, now that is a generous offer, my friend! I'll keep you to it.' Solly smiled, twisting his lips dramatically under his huge nose. It was a little affectation he'd learned in order to draw the onlooker's eye from the monopolizing feature above.

'Well, owing to lack of funds, it'll have to be a fag,' Eddie shrugged good naturedly. 'Here you are.'

'No, my boy!' Solly refused the roll up. 'I'll tell you for free. I was thinking of your wife as it happens.'

Eddie gave a hoot. 'Well, I'll take that as a compliment from you Solly.'

'You make a handsome couple.'

Eddie looked at him pensively. 'She's a cracker, my Rose. And too good for me by far.'

Solly studied his young companion's preoccupied face. On this beautiful early May evening, just as the scarlet sun was crawling down the dimpled sky, the world seemed a perfect place. But Solly was aware that his cell mate was unusually troubled and he wondered why.

'I've let her down,' Eddie continued as Solly discreetly kept silent. 'I wish with all me heart I'd never laid a quid on that bloody dog at White City after Toots was born. I mean, any sensible punter would have taken the money and run.'

'There is no such thing as a sensible punter,' Solly answered as they began their second lap of the big green field where a few inmates were strolling casually, enjoying the peaceful summer evening. Solly still couldn't believe that an innocent looking fence such as the one that encircled the exercise area was enough deterrent to keep in the prisoners. But then again, the inmates of Hewis had more to lose than gain by attempting escape. Remand prisoners and those with shorter sentences like Eddie kept their heads down and did their time. It was not an unpleasant place if you could stomach the terrible food and the boredom and the disembodied sensation you were half in one world and half in another.

'I've told you I was a floater,' Eddie added as he stuffed his hands in his trouser pockets. 'But what I haven't mentioned is that I owe a few quid to a pretty unpleasant character. He's been round to put the frighteners on Rose.'

'A few quid?' Solly's old heart squeezed sympathetically. 'How much precisely, my boy?'

An unpleasant few seconds passed before the reply. 'Six hundred and fifty smackeroonies plus interest.'

Solly tried not to let his astonishment show. His young friend seemed quite unlike the type to be so reckless. 'How did this happen?'

Eddie gave a hard laugh. 'Gawd knows, Solly. I kept thinking me luck would change but I just kept borrowing more to pay off one bookie and then the next. Then, just before the Coronation, I put ten quid on an accumulator. No one was more surprised than me when it came up. So I stuffed a monkey in me safe to pay back the debt and blew the one hundred and fifty on Star of the East, a sure-fire bet that turned round and ran the other way in the three-thirty, Newmarket.'

'Eddie, this is bad news, this obsession of yours.'

'Yeah, me and the rest of the universe. You ain't telling me you've never lost a quid on a pretty little filly, Solly!'

'Strangely enough, not the four legged variety, my

friend.' Solly stopped, a little out of puff from all the fresh air and exercise. 'But at least you had your five hundred to settle the debt?'

'I had it and lost it.'

'No!'

'Not in the way you think. I stashed it under the floorboards, see. And when I got nicked I thought to meself, well I won't clear the slate but Rose and the kids won't want for nothing while I'm away.' Eddie's voice shook slightly. 'I couldn't have been more wrong. The buggers broke in and took the lot. And now they're turning up and watching the house. If they touch a hair of her head—'

'Calm yourself,' Solly whispered, stretching out to lay a plump hand on his friend's arm.

Eddie swallowed heavily. 'Yeah, but it don't end there. Rose got the hump one day and went a bit crackers.'

'Crackers?' Solly shook his head. 'How is this?'

'She walloped their motor with a broom and made such a song and dance half the street came out to see what was happening. What scares me is, they won't leave it at that. And there ain't a bloody thing I can do about it,' he ended bitterly.

'Who is this man who gives you such aggravation?' Solly asked curiously.

'A bloke by the name of Norman Payne and a right pain in the backside he is too.'

For a moment the older man frowned, passing his hand over his bald patch and down the back of his short, thick neck. 'Your Rose has spirit, my boy.'

Solly watched Eddie's face tighten. His face had turned a dull grey as if all the life was draining out of it. 'Yeah, she has an' all. Do you know what else she did? On Easter Sunday, Olga Parker died. That's the woman whose husband I flogged the bent telly to, remember?'

Solly racked his brains hard, having forgotten what Eddie had told him regarding the events that had led up to his arrest. Solly had more important things to consider at the time, like how to explain to Alma that he was considering a little tidy up of the shops when he was released. The cash, bolstered by the stocks and drip fed by an off-shore account into the business books, was becoming more and more difficult to camouflage. Alma was entitled to her whim, of course, but not at the price of his freedom.

'Yes,' Solly nodded hesitantly. There were so many complications that comprised this young man's life, although most certainly he recognized the notorious name his young friend had almost choked on a minute or two ago. Norman Payne was a ruthless predator who swallowed his victims whole.

'It turns out Olga was German, not Polish. Her family were wiped out during the war by the Nazis. Olga only just managed to escape herself. But then she goes and tops herself and there's no one to give her a send-off as she's been dumped by the moron she lived with. So my Rose decides to have a whip round but ain't got enough to do the business, so she hocks her mother's pearls—'

'Your wife borrowed money on her jewels?' Solly

interrupted, trying to absorb this wealth of unexpected detail.

'Yeah, but the necklace ain't anything special, just sentimental value, like.'

Solly was even more confused now. 'But why would she do this for a woman she hardly knew?'

Eddie threw back his head and sighed. 'You don't know my Rose,' he said with a faraway look in his eye. 'Y'see, Rose felt really bad about the telly. And so did I of course. And it was because of the telly that Olga got found out, if you see what I mean?'

Solly wasn't sure he did, but nodded all the same.

'Anyway, as I was saying,' Eddie continued briskly, 'Rose gets Olga buried in the end, up Golders Green too, with her feet pointing towards the Promised Land as a mark of respect for her being Jewish an' all.'

Solly stared incredulously at his friend. 'Your wife is a remarkable woman, my friend. What did you say was this other lady's name?'

'Olga Parker. No, I tell a lie.' Eddie creased his brow as he tried to recall what Rose had told him a few hours previously. 'Her real name was Sarah something or other. Nem . . . no, Nimitz, I think Rose said it was. You know, my old lady is one in a million, Solly, and the trouble is, I never appreciated the fact till now.'

Solly nodded thoughtfully. He forgot all about the beauty of the summer evening as his interest was kindled in Eddie Weaver's domestic affairs. For to hear of a gentile going to such extraordinary lengths on behalf of a Jew aroused his curiosity. His own life on this earth had been tested from the moment he had drawn breath. He had risen to the top of the tree entirely by his own efforts; no one had lifted a finger to help the ugly little Jewish boy from an East End ghetto.

Solly frowned. What ulterior motive could this young woman have in burying a Jew — and at the cost of her own possessions? 'Come my friend,' he murmured, laying his hand on Eddie's shoulder as a fresh breeze stirred the air. 'Tell me more as we walk.'

'Blimey,' Eddie said with a grin, 'how long have you got?'

Solly laughed underneath the huge beacon of his nose. 'According to my solicitor, another month at the most.'

Eddie roared with laughter and Solly did too.

Chapter Twenty One

'Happy birthday, Benny, love. From Em and me and the kids.' Rose gave her friend a hug and pushed the parcel into his chest. 'I know Neet won't approve, so you'll have to find somewhere to enjoy it in peace.' They had bought him a soft leather tobacco pouch that was second-hand from the market but real leather and looked as good as new. Inside she had tucked a finger of medium Navy Cut, Benny's preferred tobacco and a packet of papers. The present was tied up in brown paper and a pink thread of Em's embroidery silk.

'I'll make meself scarce and indulge.' Benny winked. 'Thanks, Rose.'

'Happy birthday, Uncle Benny.' Marlene waved a hand-written birthday card. 'I done it meself.'

'Blimey, ain't you clever.' Benny lifted Marlene in his strong arms and gave her a peck on the head. He landed her quickly. 'Struth, are you putting on weight or am I getting weak in me old age?'

Marlene giggled, running off in search of food. Benny's fortieth birthday was being celebrated in style. Rose and

366

Em had been helping to prepare the party. Their efforts had taken them from nine in the morning to four in the afternoon. Most of the time had been used to chinwag whilst slapping filling into the bread rolls and whipping the custard. Rose wanted to talk to Benny before everyone arrived. Anita had described the event as open house. They were preparing for an onslaught.

'And this is from me and Will.' Donnie and Will stood in their best clothes holding a long, striped, woollen creation, the ends dangling over their hands. 'It's to cover your seat in the lorry. We knitted it. Marlene was supposed to help too, but she got fed up and left us to do it all. Auntie Em showed us how to stitch it together.'

Rose smiled as she met Benny's eyes. The kids had been knitting furiously for weeks and had only finished it last night. Benny looked impressed as he held it out at arm's length. 'Well, that'll keep me bum warm, won't it?'

'You've got it upside down,' Will said, scuffing back his unruly blond hair with grubby fingers.

'It doesn't really matter which way it is,' Marlene contradicted, nudging him.

'I'll have enough to wrap round me neck and all,' Benny grinned as he folded it carefully and laid it on the couch. 'Ain't I lucky to have you lot to look after me?'

'Can we play outside for a bit?' Donnie asked Rose.

'Yes, but don't get dirty. And take Marlene with you too.'

Benny and Rose watched them through the front window, admiring their new party frocks that Em had made from a yard of pink organza. They looked like little ballerinas in their clean ankle socks and white crêpe-soled sandals. The shoes were new, Rose had bought them from Dol's stall at the market, luckily the right size for Donnie but a shade large for Marlene so she'd stuffed newspaper in the toes to make them fit. Will wore a white short-sleeved shirt that Em had run up on the machine and a pair of grey school shorts. His hair had started out with a parting and a wet comb. However a morning in Marlene's company had put paid to all that and it now stuck out from his head and he had a button missing from his collar.

'How's work?' Benny adjusted his tie as he turned to look at Rose. She knew he hated getting dressed up but Anita had left orders. A fresh shirt, waistcoat and trousers, and a tie that seemed like it was about to strangle him.

'Busy, thanks, Benny.' Rose had been back at Kirkwood's for a month now. She was still washing up and making sandwiches. 'The money's good, four pounds ten a week plus overtime. How's the haulage business?'

'I got another account this week,' Benny said modestly. 'Shifting part-worn tyres from Pinner to Middlesbrough. Two trips a month and maybe more. I just found a new lock-up near East India dock at a quarter of the rent. I told the bloke I'd take his bananas up to Covent Garden no charge if we could do the deal.' He smiled shyly. 'How's me old mate doing down in Hewis then?'

'Not bad,' Rose shrugged.

'A year's up already,' Benny said with forced enthusiasm. 'He's on the home straight now.'

The first year of the new Queen's reign was over.

Twelve months ago Rose had been waiting for Eddie to join her at the Parkers'. 'I saw him last week,' she continued quietly. 'Bobby Morton drove me down on Wednesday.'

'You only had to ask,' Benny frowned, 'and I'd have taken you.'

'I know, but he offered, so I took him up on it. Gwen gave me the day off.'

Rose was well aware that Bobby was doing all he could to impress Em even though he had very little encouragement. He had suggested they all go in the shooting brake as before, but Eddie refused to have his girls step inside prison walls again. Rose had considered the coach but it would have meant a very long day.

'Eddie said to wish you a happy birthday,' Rose added quickly.

'Is that millionaire bloke still banged up?' Benny asked curiously.

'No, he was released last week. But I have me doubts as to the millionaire part, Benny.'

'What was he doing in nick, then?'

'The tax man was after him. But in the end, they couldn't prove anything. He told Eddie he had the best accountant breathing.'

'Pity the same couldn't be said about Eddie's counsel.' Benny shook his head glumly. 'That little squirt Charles Herring had no interest in Eddie's case, if you ask me. And the QC was no better. I reckon he turned a deaf ear to Eddie's version of events.'

Rose wished Benny hadn't said that. It reminded her

of things she didn't want to think about. She too had always felt Eddie's case had been handled badly, as had his appeal for bail and yet, deep down inside, a little voice warned her that much worse could have resulted from the past five years of her husband's dubious activity. And despite Eddie swearing black was blue that running for bookies was no great sin, she knew that British justice would never see it that way.

'I'd better go and help Neet,' she said brightly, not wanting to return to the depressing subject. 'We're eating in the yard. It's such a lovely day. And the clearing up will be easier.' She looked around Benny's front room, at the decorations pinned to the walls, the balloons and paper chains, the odd assortment of Union Flags that had been resurrected from Coronation Day. Only the sign painted in Red Cardinal polish with an old toothbrush announcing Benny's fortieth was new.

'I won't get under your feet,' Benny nodded as he took his chair and lifted the newspaper.

Rose knew he would be asleep in five minutes, with his head rolled on to his shoulder and the paper fallen on his chest. She closed the door and went into the kitchen. Em, wearing her green turban and Neet, in slippers and loose pinny, were laughing together at the sink. The kitchen table was extended to support a dozen plates all full of savoury snacks and, in the middle, was the birthday cake. Made entirely of sponge and covered in blue butter icing, forty white and blue candles were placed in a circle around the edge; 'Happy Birthday Benny' was written in large blue looped icing and a tiny picture of a lorry was glued to a knitting needle and stuck in the middle. Em and Anita had been decorating it all morning whilst Rose had made the sandwiches, at which she was now expert.

'Rosy, you look lovely!'

'Do I?' Rose blushed as her friend and sister turned to stare at her.

'I haven't seen that dress in ages,' Anita frowned.

'You should wear it more, it suits you.' Smiling approvingly, Em wiped her hands on the towel.

'It's me Brixton dress. I wore it the first time I saw Eddie.' The plain, dark green dress with the full skirt had been hidden at the back of the big wardrobe where it wouldn't remind her of that awful place. But, for some reason, today she had brought it out and tried it on together with the light brown court shoes that had nearly killed her as she walked from home through the foot tunnel to Greenwich and searched for a bus.

'I suppose I'd better try to do something with my hair,' Em said suddenly, touching her turban. 'Is there anything more to do, Neet?'

'No, ta, love. We've got an hour or so yet before the gannets arrive.'

'The food looks lovely,' Rose said after her sister had gone.

Anita whipped off her apron, pulled out a chair and sank down on it. 'Make a cup, love, would you? I don't half fancy a fag, you know.'

'How long is it this time?' Rose put on the kettle and set out two cups. Benny wouldn't want one, he'd be in the land of nod by now.

'Three months. And bloody killing me.'

'Have something to eat instead.'

'I have.'

'What about a drink then? Something stronger than tea.'

'That's not a bad idea. I'll pour a sherry. Take the kettle off the boil, will you? The sherry's in the cupboard by the sink.'

Rose replaced the cups in the cupboard and took out the bottle of cream sherry. The glasses were already on the draining board along with a dozen bottles of beer, a bottle of gin and a big bottle of lemonade and cream soda.

'Pour one for yourself and all.'

'It's bit early.'

'Yeah, well, it's a special treat,' Anita grinned as she took the glass and sipped, smacking her lips enthusiastically. 'Fortieth birthdays only come round once.'

'And fiftieths.'

'Yeah, and sixtieths.'

Rose giggled. 'All right then.'

For a little while Rose and Anita sat in the sunny summer atmosphere of the kitchen with the back door thrown wide open and the soft breeze drifting in. The children's voices could be heard over the rooftops and the lazy drone of a bee rumbled not far away. Rose smiled as she sipped her sweet, rich sherry. The bee must have lost its way since there were very few flowers in the neighbourhood to settle on. The Mendozas' backyard was as barren as her own despite the kudos of the Heath Robinson bathroom extension that Benny had thrown together years ago. But no one would notice this afternoon as the house admitted all and sundry to enjoy the celebration.

'Cheers,' Anita murmured, suddenly leaning forward to clink the rim of her glass with Rose's.

'Here's to Benny,' Rose nodded.

'And Eddie, bless his cotton socks.' She narrowed her eyes. 'You ain't seen that car around lately, I suppose?'

'No. But I keep me eyes peeled all the time.'

'Well, whatever you do, don't go charging at it with a broom again!'

Rose grinned. 'I wished I'd broken their windscreen.'

'They nearly broke your neck, you daft cow,' Anita said, suddenly serious. 'If Benny hadn't bowled you over first they might have succeeded.'

Rose didn't like to think of what might have happened if Benny had not taken lightning action. In fact, she'd never seen him move so fast. But she still didn't regret what she'd done. And maybe it had frightened them off, seeing as how most of the street had turned out to see what was going on.

Anita's eyes mellowed then and she raised her glass. 'Anyway, here's to Olga.'

Rose took another sip. 'Yes, to Olga.'

'I'm still trying to fathom out what happened at the funeral,' Anita sighed contentedly as she stretched her back against the chair. 'What with Len wearing that bloody great shawl and going off at a tangent. To be honest, I didn't understand a word he said.'

'It was a special prayer,' Rose explained as Len had

explained to her. 'Olga didn't have any family, so he delegated himself to say it. Apparently Olga would consider it a privilege to have it said for her.'

'Well, for sure she ain't gonna come back to thank us,' Anita commented dryly, 'and what was all that ripping up of her dress about?'

'It's a sign of mourning,' Rose answered. 'Usually a blouse or shirt is used. A parent would tear the left side to denote a deep loss, others tear the right side. Then their dead are buried in white shrouds with no pockets because everyone comes into this world with nothing and goes out with nothing.'

'Well, that makes sense,' Anita nodded. 'But there wasn't any flowers and to my mind, flowers make a funeral.'

'I know, but Jews feel that the bereaved families shouldn't have to spend more than they can afford. I think that's very sensible meself.'

'So you'd consider packing Eddie off in a cardboard box and a sheet?' Anita posed with a smirk.

Rose grinned. 'He'd kill me if I did that. Eddie's a smart dresser as well you know.'

'Yeah – and he's always got something in his pocket.'

Rose's smile faded and all traces of humour left her face. 'No doubt a betting slip or two if the truth be known.'

Anita smiled kindly. 'Don't take it to heart, love. Floating ain't the crime of the century, you know.'

Rose took a long sip of sherry. 'It isn't so much what Eddie did but that he didn't tell me.'

Anita reached out for the sherry on the draining board and poured herself another. 'I'll top you up.'

Rose watched as her glass was refilled. 'I still can't believe it,' she repeated vaguely. 'That for five years my husband was off every day running for the bookies.'

'Ah!' Anita wagged her finger. 'But you didn't want to know, did you?'

'What do you mean?'

'Eddie wasn't allowed to bring his business home, was he?'

'But that was different.' Rose was beginning to get upset. 'Street trading is legal.'

'Maybe it didn't pay.'

'Then why didn't he tell me?'

Anita shrugged. 'I dunno, love.'

'It's not as if I badgered him for more than he gave me. I thought we were happy as we were.'

'But perhaps he wanted more,' Anita suggested. 'There's a lot to your old man, girl, more than you think.'

Rose frowned. 'Such as?'

'Well, he married you for a start,' Anita leered. 'He backed a winner there.'

Unaccountably, tears pricked in Rose's eyes. 'If I'm so special, why did he get himself nicked?' Her voice was getting high and wavery. 'He wouldn't have told me all those lies neither.'

'Hang on, love.' Anita stared at her. 'That's a bit out of order. Eddie didn't go down specially to piss you off. And he never told any lies to speak of. Just left a bit out, that's all.'

375

'Yes, like what he's really been up to for the last five years.'

Anita reached across to grasp her wrist. 'Come on now, you're just upset. You've bottled everything up when it might have been healthier to scream at him or clock him one.'

'How could I? He's in prison.'

'Well, I'm willing to bet a lot of them women don't let prison stop them saying their piece.'

Rose couldn't deny that she'd often heard raised voices, especially in Brixton. But she and Eddie had always tried to be civilized and not let their emotions overwhelm them. Perhaps she had, as Anita suggested, bottled up her feelings to such an extent that it was unhealthy.

'Eddie's the man he always was,' Anita reminded her firmly. 'He loves you and the kids to distraction. You mean the world to him. He ain't perfect that's true, but no man is. Now, you gonna help me get this lot out in the yard and forget all those morbid thoughts?'

Rose sniffed and stood up. 'Sorry. It must be this dress.'

Anita laughed. 'Well, if you feel like that, go and change. Put on something nice and cheerful. And a word to the wise – let your hair down – literally, tonight, won't you, girl? To put it bluntly, you ain't had a good rough and tumble for the past twelve months and since you and your old man were as regular as clockwork on Friday nights, it ain't no wonder you're edgy.'

Rose felt her cheeks crimson.

Anita burst into laughter. 'Well, it's true. Made Benny

and me quite randy when we heard you through the wall, at it like rabbits you were.' She raised an eyebrow. ''Spect you hear us an' all?'

Rose nodded. 'Only when your window's open and the wind's in the right direction.'

The two friends looked at each other and burst out laughing. By the time Rose went home to change, the sherry was working wonders.

Rose hadn't seen Benny quite so drunk before. He was sitting in between his mum and dad, Mary and Luis Mendoza, his cheeks aflame under his dark skin, an almost identical expression of mirth on his face to his father. They were singing a Guy Mitchell number called 'She Wears Red Feathers and a Hula-Hula Skirt' and every time it came to the chorus, the two men would stand up and wriggle their wide hips, causing Mary Mendoza to shake her head in hopeless exasperation at the pair who might have been identical twins had not Luis lost almost every strand of his curly, dark hair.

The record player was being operated by David who, Rose thought, had grown very handsome in the last six months, springing up from a boy into a young man. At fifteen he was as tall as Alan and had a confident smile, all set to eclipse the charm of his brother. The two Travers sisters had been invited to the party and Iris was curled up on the floor beside David. She wore blue jeans and plimsolls and had looped her glossy dark hair in a ponytail.

Rose was sitting with Matthew on her lap on a chair brought in from her kitchen; Bobby, who was attempting to attract Em's eye as she offered round the sandwiches, sat next to her. The small space in the middle of the room had just been vacated by Alan and Heather Travers who had performed the jitterbug, young arms and legs swinging precariously. But as soon as David played Johnnie Ray's 'Faith Can Move Mountains' at a much slower but stronger tempo, they disappeared.

'A bit rich for me too,' Bobby shouted as Em squeezed her way out of the crowded room and Johnnie Ray's voice crescendoed. Bobby's eyes swung disappointedly round to Rose.

'What sort of music do you like?' She felt a little sorry for the young man who was now a regular visitor to Ruby Street. The washing machine had never lacked for an overhaul, the yard was dug over at the end and grass seed laid, though it had never dared to mature. Will's tent, her nephew's new bedroom, was inspected regularly for leaks or rips and the guy ropes adjusted. The crumbling bricks on top of the wall at the bottom of the yard that backed on to the lane had been replaced with new ones. The shooting brake was always to hand, Rose's bike frequently oiled and the chain repaired. The children accepted him without question and Rose noted, as she looked at her son, Matthew was giving him a wide, bubbly smile.

Bobby grinned back, catching the baby's hand with his finger. 'Me favourite's Doris Day. But I like Dean Martin and Nat King Cole.'

Rose nodded. '"Because You're Mine" is nice.'

'Do you and Em ever go to the pictures?'

Rose shook her head. 'No. But me and Eddie did once in a while. He likes Bogie and I like Ingrid Bergman. Our favourite was *Casablanca*, of course.'

'Have you heard about these 3D effects? You wear red and green glasses that give you a bit of a fright as if the things were right in front of your face. Me brother took his three kids to a horror film called *House of Wax*, and really rated it.'

'I didn't know you had a brother.'

'Yes, Ted. He's 38, two years older than me. They live in Norfolk. I only see them at Christmas. They're smashing kids. And I get on well with Nancy, his wife.' Bobby softened his voice as the record ended. 'I'd like it if they lived closer, really.' Matthew blew more bubbles and Bobby laughed. 'He's a lovely baby, Rose.'

'I think so,' she agreed, drawing her hand softly over the thick, dark cap of baby hair. 'Would you like a family?' she asked as she watched Bobby's eyes drink in Matthew's cherubic face.

'You bet I would.' Bobby's soft blue gaze lingered on the baby. 'Trouble is, all my time has been taken up with building the business. At the end of war, I had plenty of ambition and no responsibilities, so I gave it me all. But it does get a bit lonely at night when I finish for the day.'

'You'll have to get out more,' Rose advised. He was a good-looking young man and if her sister didn't snatch him up, someone else would.

'Yeah, but who with?' Bobby grinned, and Rose fancied she knew the answer but guessed Bobby's courage failed him when it came to asking Em for a real date.

'You know, in five years time, white goods are gonna be big business. I told you once a woman deserved as much help in the house as she could get. And I've been proved right,' he said as another record hit the turntable.

'Are you trying to sell me a vacuum cleaner now?' Rose kept a straight face as Perry Como's 'Don't Let the Stars Get in Your Eyes' drifted smoothly over the room.

Bobby looked at her startled. 'No of course not—'

Rose laughed. 'I'm only teasing. We're very grateful for the washing machine. I don't know what we'd have done without it.'

'I could sort you out a second-hand Hoover—'

'I was joking, Bobby.'

'But I want to help,' he said raising his voice above the music. 'I'd like to do more, but I don't want to make a nuisance of myself.' At that moment, Em entered the room and Rose saw Bobby's face brighten. Eagerly he followed her passage through the crowd, his conversation with Rose forgotten.

She lifted Matthew into her arms and decided it was about time her sister did something other than hand round sandwiches. She made her way to where Em was bending, offering sausage rolls to Mabel and Fred Dixon who had just parked themselves on the wooden chairs by the door.

'Em?'

Her sister turned round. 'Oh, Rosy, would you like one?'

'No. But Bobby would I'm sure.'

Her sister, looking flushed and attractive in a peach-

380

coloured, slim-fitting dress with a white belt, glanced across the room. 'I . . . I—'

'Just go over and talk to him won't you?'

'But I'm helping Neet to—'

'No, you're not. I am now. Take two sausage rolls and I'll keep the plate.'

'But you've got Matthew.'

'He's due for a sleep in his pram. I'll put him under the stairs and he'll go off.'

'Well, I—'

'Em!' Rose grabbed the plate, balancing Matthew in her other arm. 'Do as you're told, won't you?'

The two women looked at one another, then Rose began to smile, the twinkle in her eye enough of a message to send Em on her way, if rather reluctantly. Rose deposited the plate with Mabel and told her to pass it round, then trod over the legs and feet that lined the way to the space in the corner where Iris and David were squatting by the Dansette record player.

'Have you got something by Doris Day?' she asked, and David nodded.

'Yeah,' he grinned, shuffling through the pile of large plastic records. '"Secret Love". It's brand new.'

'Perfect,' Rose smiled. 'Play it next, will you, love?'

Rose danced her feet off that night. Alan taught her new steps to the jitterbug and Benny, despite falling over twice, managed a cha-cha, whilst Len Silverman waltzed her round the house and out into the yard. She stopped for a sherry only to be pulled up by David and Iris who started a conga. They made a human snake, hopping and kicking out into the road and around the houses, knocking on the doors in the twilight. The Pipers and the Prices and the Greens all came out and the kids and the dogs ran riot the length of Ruby Street. Someone brought out a harmonica and played it to perfection as the stars twinkled above. Cissy and Fanny plundered the food and drink then sat on their chairs outside Anita's in their winter coats and scarves, though it was a warm and sultry evening.

Luis Mendoza finally collapsed, though not as spectacularly as was expected. He lay full length in the yard, his head propped by a tyre, his mouth open and his fingers entwined across his chest. Benny sobered up, drowned in tea by Anita and lectured by his mother. Their two boys and the Travers girls were still dancing and smooching in the front room.

Rose accepted her third glass of sherry at eleven o'clock as Matthew slept through all the racket. The children played in Will's tent and spied on the grown-ups over the fence.

By midnight, only the youngsters were still on their feet. Rose, Anita and Benny sat in the yard, reminiscing and singing poignant songs: 'The White Cliffs of Dover', 'We'll Meet Again', 'A Nightingale Sang' and 'Lili Marlene', all accompanied by Luis Mendoza's rhythmic snoring. They talked of the war days and the people they had known and catchphrases that still stuck in their heads ten years down the line.

'Lend a Hand on the Land.'

'Keep the Flag Flying.'

'Your Country Needs You.'

'Dig for Victory.'

'Adolf in Blunderland,' shouted Luis and everyone laughed.

At midnight, they looked up into a dazzling sky and Rose inhaled the sweet air, thinking of Eddie. She'd missed him, but she'd let down her hair and forgotten her troubles for the time being. The brown car and Eddie's debt and the shoebox, even the back-breaking hours in Kirkwood's canteen were a distant memory. She had almost forgotten her sister too, until she peered over the Andersen fence and into her own kitchen window.

A dim light burned there and two figures were silhouetted in the pale light. Rose smiled; if Em was wise, she'd grab Bobby Morton whilst she had the chance. He was a good man and patient too. But he wouldn't wait forever.

Chapter Twenty Two

Rose carefully examined the saucepans and utensils returned to the cupboards at the end of the day. After which she would walk slowly past the worktops, running her fingers along their edges to check for grease.

Though she no longer sweated at the big double sink she couldn't break the habit formed over the last five months. A habit that gained her favour with Gwen House, allowing the supervisor a swift departure.

Rose loved these last few moments before she left for home. There was something special about the kitchen at the end of a busy day when all the staff had gone. After folding her overall into a locker, she would cast her eye over the clean surfaces and tiled floors for the last time and, when satisfied, exit by the back door, quietly closing it, as if leaving a sleeping child.

The bike shed was deserted when she left; saucer-sized pools of dog-ends swam in the gutters fuelled by a leaking overflow pipe from the outside wall. These were often accompanied by sweet wrappers or bus tickets and would remain there until George, the caretaker, pushed his broom along the concrete path, adding his own spent Woodbine to the soggy piles.

Tonight, at five-thirty on a cheerful Thursday, Rose thought the September evening could have been spring. The air was fruity and ripe and birds were singing from the smoke-soiled rooftops and the factory eaves. Gulls called noisily, searching for an uncovered dustbin that would provide supper. A few late sirens wailed into the mellow autumn air. Tomorrow was Friday and the weekend approached!

Rose always enjoyed her bike ride home. She took a blouse and trousers to work into which she was now changed and at the end of the day, when she could still smell the fried fish or the onions in her long hair, the breeze blew it out as if by magic. The unflattering round hats that all kitchen employees were required to wear did little to keep out the smells that clung stubbornly to skin, hair and clothes.

More often than not throughout the summer a kind, southerly breeze had almost blown her home. Her journey took less than twenty minutes, but on sunny days she cheated, cycling a longer route, past the Mudchute and up East Ferry Road, adding another glorious five minutes of fresh summer air.

'T'ra, Rose!' A group of girls from the flourmill waved as she pushed her bike on to the pavement. They passed her most evenings, their faces white but smiling and their footsteps light, eager to be home. She waved back as a lorry passed and the driver hooted. The girls shrieked with laughter and waved, disappearing noisily along the dock road.

There were kids playing out in every street as Rose cycled home. Glossy marbles were rolling in the gutters or along the straighter paths. An apple box had been converted to wickets and erected in the middle of one road where the kids played rounders. Another group of boys and girls were playing a game with cherry stones throwing them through a board with notches cut out of its edge.

She knew Donnie and Marlene would be eager to go out and play in the last hour of light. Matthew was nearly eight months old now and occupied himself in his play-pen, mostly surrounded by his toys or watching the older children through the gaily coloured wooden bars. Rose couldn't wait to cuddle him. He was a beautiful baby, with thick black hair just like Eddie's, and eyes that were as big as saucers. She'd sent Eddie a photograph of all the children, including Matthew, that Alan had taken with his box camera one day in the summer. They had all shouted cheese and collapsed into giggles, luckily after the picture was taken.

Rose was just imagining how wonderful it would be when Eddie could hold his son in his arms when she was aware of a movement beside her. She slowed her speed and steered towards the pavement in order to let the vehicle pass.

But it didn't. Instead it remained where it was. She increased her speed, turning left instead of right, taking a direction she hadn't intended. Still, she could do a complete circle and turn left again and that was what she was about to do when a horse and cart blocked her way.

She was forced to take a right turn and then, to her annoyance, the vehicle crept up slowly again beside her.

Rose glanced sideways, an annoyed expression on her face. There was plenty of room to pass. She caught a glimpse of the vehicle, a shiny brown wing. Her heart leapt into her throat; she would recognize the car anywhere.

She pedalled faster, but the car matched her pace. The low growl of its engine sounded threatening. What was she to do? Why had she come this way? There was the dock to the right of her and wasteland ahead. Heaps of debris alternated with commercial buildings, most of them in a state of disrepair.

She had taken the wrong turning. She couldn't get away from the car. It was like a shadow, matching her speed. At the end of the street, she wanted to stop to get her bearings. But she couldn't; she was too frightened. This area was deserted, just a few men walking not far away towards the docks. But she couldn't turn towards them. The car was blocking her way. Every time she slowed, it slowed. Every time she increased her pace, it went faster.

Where could she go? The men had gone now, the dismal street narrowed to a lane, where abandoned buildings leaned precariously over the road. This area of the docks had fallen into disrepair and was only used by prostitutes who plied their trade for the benefit of the foreign seamen who frequented the waterfront pubs.

She began to panic, steering the bike haphazardly as she remembered the last time she had seen this car. It had been coming straight for her. If Benny hadn't rugby tackled her she wouldn't be alive today.

Rose pedalled until the sweat ran down her back and in between her breasts. The car kept up its vigil, slowly squashing her against the wall. She was trapped; they intended to crush her!

Then with a rush of speed it swept in front of her. Too late she applied the brakes, which had never been very good since the day she first rode it. The worn rubbers hissed against metal but the bike didn't stop.

Rose only released the handlebars when the front wheel buckled against the car door. Her arm went up to cover her face and she was thrown forward. A moment later she was lying on the ground with all the wind knocked out of her.

'Where am I?' Rose couldn't see a thing. Someone had blindfolded her, their clumsy hands catching her hair as they did so. There was a strange musty smell in the air, the same smell of bricks and mortar that lingered across the debris in Ruby Street.

She didn't know where she was, only that she'd been bundled into the car and was now bound to a chair. The ropes were hurting her wrists and her arms were strained at an unnatural angle behind her back. She couldn't move her legs either, they were locked together and she guessed her ankles were tied with the same strong rope. She was shaking so much she couldn't decide whether her teeth were chattering or whether it was an external sound. But even if she knew that, the thumping of her heart was so loud it would have drowned out any other noise.

'So, we meet at last.' The high, nasal twang that sounded slightly effeminate sent shivers down her spine.

'Who are you?' Rose asked in a small voice.

'I am Norman Payne, my dear, your friend and bene-factor. Or to be more accurate, the goose that laid your family's golden egg.'

'I don't know what you're talking about.' Rose stared into the darkness, trying to sense where the voice had come from.

'Come now, I'm sure your husband has told you all about me.' She flinched as someone stroked her neck and then her arm. 'How slender and smooth these pretty fingers look, despite the hard work they've seen. It must be a great hardship, toiling long hours in a hot kitchen? Not like the old days, eh? Just you and your pretty little girls at home playing Mummies and Daddies.'

Another cold shiver went down her back as she realized this man knew all about her, even the fact that she now worked at Kirkwood's. 'L . . . let me go,' she stammered jerking her head right and left as she heard soft breathing in her ear. 'My sister will call the police,' she added bravely, wriggling again, but the ropes twisted painfully against her skin.

'The police?' His tone was amused. 'Now, what good would they do you? Eddie's already doing time for a crime he didn't commit.'

Rose gasped. 'How do you know about that?'

'I know everything,' he replied sharply.

'It was you,' Rose accused angrily, 'who framed Eddie. You who broke into our home and took all his savings!'

'*Savings*? Ha! That money was mine, my dear, every penny of it. Your husband owes me four times that amount.'

Rose gasped incredulously. 'I don't believe you. Eddie would never get into debt like that.'

'Then prepare yourself for a shock, young woman. He signed on the dotted line many times and I've the papers to prove it. Your husband has gambled away his life – and yours. Why, you could say he's sold me his soul!'

Rose felt the tears prick in the corners of her eyes. Was he telling her the truth? Had Eddie really got himself into so much trouble?

'Still, you've a lot to be grateful for,' Payne said slyly. 'Under the circumstances he's a lucky man. The police bungled even the simplest of tasks, not making the assault stick. It's no wonder that crime is on the increase if they fall over their feet in such small matters.'

'You mean that Inspector Williams was . . . *is*—'

'Corrupt, dear, as bent as a three piece walking stick.' He laughed coarsely. 'Inspector Williams has an appreciation of the finer things in life second only to your other half, I have to say. Fortunately, most people have a price, luvvie, including you.'

'You're wrong. I'd never lift a finger to help you.'

'Oh, think again, Mrs W, think again. What price do you put on the head of that beautiful child sitting in his pram at home? Nice little lad, the spit of his father. And your two girls, what about them? Little beauties they are too.'

'If you ever went near them—'

'What would you do?' Payne interrupted in his sing song voice. 'Charge at me with a broom and a bucket?'

'You wouldn't . . . you wouldn't dare—'

'Oh, but I would, my dear, I most certainly would. You see, I can do anything I like. Anything.'

Rose felt her stomach heave as his hand moved slowly down to her breast. She bit her lip to prevent herself from screaming as the hot, heavy fingers roughly pulled open her blouse.

'Don't – please don't!' Rose hated herself for being such a coward as tears welled in her eyes. 'What do you want?' she pleaded. 'Tell me what you want.'

'Listen and listen carefully.' Rose shuddered as his fingers caressed her. 'Your husband owes me and I want a result. Not just money, dear girl, but gratitude. After all, you've had a taste of the good life, you and your precious kids.'

'Leave us alone,' Rose managed to whisper. 'Eddie's not a thief. He doesn't deserve what happened to him. And if he owes you money, then you'll get it back.'

Payne cackled, his smoky breath on her face. 'How touching. A wife defending her husband to the last. I'm sorry to say though, I haven't the same confidence in your old man as you seem to have.'

Rose wanted to scream but she had to bear it. Eddie wasn't around to help. No one was. She was completely at the mercy of this abominable man. How could Eddie have ever got mixed up with the likes of him?

'Now,' the voice continued as he stroked her, 'I think we both agree your husband needs to be reminded of his duty towards me, his long-suffering friend and you, his family.'

'That's blackmail,' Rose whimpered. 'You're trying to make him to do something dreadful so that he'll never be out of your power.'

'Blackmail is an ugly word from such lovely lips,' he murmured into her hair. 'Let's just call it business, shall we?'

Rose pursed her lips. 'I'd rather he stay in prison forever than commit crimes for someone like you!'

There was a catch of sharp breath and the hand dragged away from her breast to tighten around her throat. 'Listen, you stupid girl, your husband has no choice. I own you. Your whole life is mine. That's the way it works Mrs W. And this is the message I want you to give him.' Two hands slid around her throat. She coughed as the pressure tightened. 'What was that, my dear?'

Rose coughed again trying to regain her breath. What was he going to do now? Was he going to kill her?

The blow sent her reeling and the chair that she was sitting on rocked. Another blow followed and her scream died as the pain filled every corner of her head. She tried to catch her breath, but she'd bitten her tongue and could taste the blood on it.

'It doesn't feel so good, does it, alone and in the darkness?'

Her eyes were wide with terror under the blindfold.

'No one to help you, no one. You must be very frightened, very frightened indeed.'

Rose sobbed then, her courage failing her as the tears began to trickle down her cheeks. The pain was like a helmet, crushing her face and jaw. She heard a kind of shuffling. Was he close? Were there others watching her humiliation?

She didn't have the power to scream again when he pulled her head back by a fistful of her hair. All she could do was to ask God for it to be quick, to make her brave and keep her alive at the end of it.

'Mrs Weaver, Mrs Weaver!'

Rose heard someone calling her name. They sounded very far off at first and then suddenly, as she tried to open her eyes, they could have been standing right beside her as the voice boomed in her ears like Big Ben.

'Wh . . . who is it?' Her head felt sore and heavy. She rubbed her jaw and felt the congealed blood at the corner of her mouth. It peeled off under her fingers and she winced.

'It's me. Vivien Keene.'

Rose found herself half lying and half sitting on the playground bench. Miss Keene's brow creased as she said, 'Oh, Mrs Weaver, have you had an accident?'

Rose didn't know what else to do except nod. Her jaw was throbbing and her head felt twice its size.

'Your bike is ruined. Did someone drive over it?'

Rose looked down at the remains of her bike. Both wheels were buckled and the chain was twisted around the pedals. How had she and the bike got here?

'I thought you were asleep,' Miss Keene continued

worriedly. 'But I couldn't understand why. Then it struck me you must have been knocked off your bike and come into the playground to recover. I hope you aren't suffering from concussion.'

With the help of the young woman, Rose sat up. She ached from head to toe and her wrists were stinging painfully. She looked down. There were red marks across them and suddenly everything tumbled back. She looked around the playground and back into Vivien Keene's concerned face.

'I'm all right.'

'You don't look it.'

'I . . . I'm just winded.'

'What happened?'

Rose peered into the twilight mist that was creeping across St Mary's school and covering the empty expanse of playground. How long had she been unconscious?

'My dear, you look terrible,' Miss Keene said again.

'I was just getting my breath back . . .'

'Was it a car that hit you?'

Rose nodded, her eyes going down to her blouse as she thought of those awful hands touching her so intimately, of the words Norman Payne had whispered in her ear. And those blows that had racked her body with pain!

'You must tell the police, but first I'll take you to hospital.'

'No.' Rose tried to stand up, then fell down again. She had no strength in her legs.

'You look dreadful, Mrs Weaver. You must see a doctor.'

'I must get back to the children.'

'But I really do think—'

Rose dragged herself up unsteadily. 'Really, I'm just bruised. The bike took the worst of it.'

'I can't believe someone would leave you like this! It was a good job I came back to collect some homework I'd forgotten.'

'What time is it?' Rose asked.

Miss Keene glanced at her watch. 'Nearly quarter to eight.'

'Oh no! I must get home,' Rose cried although she had no idea how she would manage to walk there.

'Well, at least I can drive you.' Miss Keene pushed her gently down on the bench. 'My car is parked at the back of the school. I'll bring it round to the gates.'

Rose held her arms around her as she waited and tried to stop shivering. It wasn't cold, but inside her there was a terrible chill, a coating of ice that prevented her from feeling. The last thing she remembered was her head being pulled back and then darkness. Had she fainted or had Norman Payne struck her again? She couldn't remember. Her head was aching terribly. She put her fingers up to cheek and yelped. Was there a mark there?

'Oh, Eddie,' she half sobbed, 'where are you when I need you?' Then she saw a small black car drive up to the playground gates and tried to pull herself together. She had to keep up the pretence that she had collided with a car. Miss Keene would only try to persuade her to go to the police if she told her the truth. And after what she'd learned about Inspector Williams, the police were the last people she wanted to visit.

'Are you sure you don't want to see a doctor?' Miss Keene queried several times on the journey home.

'No, I just want to go home.'

'I'll get the caretaker to put your bike in the boiler house tomorrow morning.'

'It's probably not worth repairing.'

'Probably not, but at least it took the impact. Did you see what make of car it was?'

'No. It happened too quickly.'

'And it just drove off?'

'Yes.'

'That was despicable,' Miss Keene said heatedly. 'There's no doubt you must tell the police.'

'I will,' Rose lied, 'after I get home and see the children.'

'Would you like me to wait for you? It's no trouble.'

Rose shook her head. 'Benny, my neighbour, will take me.'

Miss Keene looked at her doubtfully. 'I really don't feel happy to leave you like this.' She pulled on the brake of her small Austin Ruby.

'Thank you for the lift.' Rose tried to push open the door.

'Wait, I'll help you.' She dashed out and grabbed Rose's arm. The door of number forty-five opened before they could knock on it.

'Rose!' Em gasped, her mouth falling open. 'What's happened to you?'

'She's had a little accident,' Miss Keene volunteered as

the two women helped her inside the house. 'A car knocked her off her bike and I found her in the school playground. There are no bones broken but she really should see a doctor first and then the police.'

But Em wasn't listening. She was staring at Rose with shocked eyes. 'Oh, Rosy, what have you done to your hair?'

Rose lifted her shaking hands. Her fingers searched for the soft waves that hung around her shoulders. She felt none. They had cut it all off.

Chapter Twenty Three

'You didn't really get knocked off your bike, did you?' Em tipped the final saucepan of boiling water into the big, battered tin bath. Because Rose had been shaking so much Em had insisted she lie in hot water and warm up. The fire was burning in the hearth and the front room was aglow with a cosy, flickering light. Rose was sitting on the couch with a blanket round her shoulders.

'No, not really,' Rose admitted knowing this story wouldn't fool her sister for very long.

'Well, I don't know what's happened but when I saw your face and hair I knew Miss Keene was talking rubbish.'

'I'm sorry I worried you,' Rose apologized wondering what she looked like as she hadn't had the courage to look at herself in the mirror. She didn't want another shock, but she could tell by everyone's expressions that she was a sight.

'Well, in you get then.'

Rose stood up. Her legs were still feeling spongy but at least she hadn't made a complete fool of herself and blurted everything out to Miss Keene. And luckily the girls had been in bed and dozing when she'd come in and Will was still camped out in the tent oblivious to her late return. When the girls asked why she was late she'd made an excuse that she'd gone to the hairdressers and her bike had broken down afterwards, which in a way it had and that Miss Keene had been on hand to give her a lift home. Luckily they hadn't noticed the burgeoning bruise on her cheek.

'The hairdresser didn't cut it very nicely,' Donnie had commented sleepily.

'It'll be better when I've washed it,' Rose said self-consciously as she kissed them goodnight.

'You never go to the hairdressers,' Marlene observed as she struggled to keep her eyes open.

'Well, it's about time I did. Now God bless and sleep tight.'

Rose had stood outside their room on the landing, closing her eyes and leaning against the wall for support. It had taken all her energy to pretend everything was normal. She wanted a minute to compose herself before going down to Em where she would have to explain what happened. She felt a bitter wave of resentment sweep over her as she thought of her lost hair, her crowning glory. Why had Norman Payne cut it all off? As if tying her up and hitting her wasn't enough! Rose began to tremble again at the thought of Norman Payne's hands on her body. Her memory was coming back in little bursts. After she'd refused to cooperate he'd hit her again and knocked her out. It must have been then he'd cut off her hair.

'I'll just boil one more saucepan,' Em said, bringing Rose back from her troubled thoughts. When her sister had gone she removed the blanket and began to undress. When she was naked she looked in the mirror above the hearth. She clapped a hand over her mouth in shock. Big clumps of hair hung over her ears, all jagged and uneven. Her heavy brown locks were gone as if a knife had been used to tear them. Her face was like a papier-mache mask formed from paper, water and glue instead of skin, the gruesome purple bruise on her right cheek growing like a barnacle on a ship's hull. She prodded it carefully and jumped. In the morning it would be swollen and puffy. Her golden brown eyes were hidden behind bags of exhaustion and her top lip was slightly swollen.

Rose turned away. She didn't want to look at herself. But when she climbed in the bath she was forced to gaze at the faint red marks around her white ankles. Fortunately they weren't as prominent as the circles around her wrists. These still looked like red bracelets and she wondered if Miss Keene had noticed them.

Rose put her hands over her mouth again to stop herself from crying out. She didn't want to think about what had happened. When she heard Em in the kitchen she hurriedly splashed herself, then slipped down slowly, letting the hot water take effect and soothe her battered body.

'Now, mind yourself.' Em returned with a saucepan full of boiling water. 'Mum was always worried we'd be scalded,' Em reminisced as she bent over, her face hidden in clouds of steam. 'She used to make sure Dad poured the hot water from a jug, very carefully, against the side.'

'I never wanted to get out,' Rose sighed as the warmth at last penetrated her aching bones.

'No, but we had to because Mum and Dad went after us. Lord only knows what the colour of the water was like in the end.'

'The girls don't seem to care who goes first,' Rose said distantly, trying to keep her thoughts from wandering back to Norman Payne. 'Your poor Will, he's not used to Spartan conditions. You had such a lovely bathroom in Eastbourne.'

'You don't hear him complain though,' Em said, suddenly very matter of fact. 'He's never been so happy as he is now.' She squared her shoulders tightly. 'Now, enough of memory lane, Rosy. What happened today? I was so worried when you didn't come home. I just kept telling myself you had to work late. I was giving you half an hour more and then I was going to ask Benny to go and look for you.'

Rose bathed herself slowly, putting off the moment when she had to recall what had happened and she reached slowly for the soap placed on a saucer by the bath.

'Oh, love, what happened to your wrist?' Em gasped as her eyes landed on Rose's outstretched arm.

'It's a long story. But it begins with the brown car. It knocked me off my bike as I was cycling home.'

'*The* brown car?' Em asked in a shocked whisper.

'Yes. I was cycling home and it drove up beside me.

401

I panicked and went the wrong way and found meself down by the docks. No one was around, just a few men, but they disappeared and the next thing I knew I was flying through the air and on to the ground. These two men picked me up and bundled me in the car.'

'Couldn't you scream or something?' Em gulped.

'Maybe I did. I was so terrified I don't remember. I think I was dazed by the fall.'

'What happened then?'

'I was blindfolded, so I couldn't see where we went. And then they drove me somewhere and tied me to a chair.'

As she continued to tell her sister what had happened Rose thought Em was going to faint. Even in the glowing shadows of the fire, she looked pale, all the colour draining from her face. 'Oh, Rosy, I knew we should have gone to the police.'

'It wouldn't have helped. This man – Norman Payne, he told me who he was – boasted that Inspector Williams is in his pay, which explains why they charged Eddie with assault when he was only trying to protect himself.'

Em looked flabbergasted. 'But you only see that sort of thing on the films.'

'Well, this time it's happened in real life.'

'You must have been terrified.'

'I couldn't believe I'd been kidnapped in broad daylight.'

'But why are they doing this, Rosy?' Em asked faintly.

'Can't you guess? They want Eddie. They won't let go of him.'

'But he's in prison!'

'Norman Payne tried to make me persuade Eddie to work for him when he comes home. I said I'd rather Eddie stayed in prison than get mixed up with him, but that didn't go down very well and that was when he hit me. I think I must have blacked out for a while.' Rose decided not to mention the way Norman Payne had touched her.

Em knelt down by the bath. 'He's a monster, hitting a defenceless woman.'

Rose shrugged dismissively. 'I angered him by refusing to do what he wants.'

Em squeezed out the flannel. 'Hold still, I'll bathe your cheek.' She carefully dabbed the injury.

'Ouch!' Rose flinched.

'I've got some witch hazel in the cupboard, it'll bring the bruise out.'

Rose dredged up a smile. 'I don't think I want it to come out. I'd prefer it to stay where it is.'

'You'll have a black eye tomorrow.'

'Then I'll keep up the story I was knocked off me bike.'

'Oh, Rosy, this shouldn't be happening to you. It's hard enough as it is with Eddie away. I just don't know where Eddie's brains were in getting mixed up with such people. And if we can't go to the police, who can we go to?'

Rose had been wondering that herself. All policemen couldn't be bent, but how did anyone know who the straight ones were?

Em shook her head despairingly. 'Can you remember how you got to the school?'

Rose frowned as little pictures began to flash up in her mind. She flinched at the memory of Norman Payne's fist flying across her face. He'd tried hard to make her submit and might even have had some success if those children's voice hadn't disturbed them . . .

'I remember now,' she burst out as the foggy events suddenly became clear in her mind. 'There were children's voices and the sound of people moving hurriedly around me. Someone untied my ankles and then my wrists. The voices came nearer. They were shouting, calling – just like they do when they play on the debris. When the boys make camps – it was the children who saved me!' Rose stared into the fire, at the flames and concentrated, trying to hold on to her fleeting thoughts. 'I . . . I was dragged to a car and forced down on the seat with my face pushed into the leather.'

Em inhaled deeply. 'Oh, Rosy, thank God those kids disturbed them.'

'I don't know what might have happened if they hadn't. Next thing I remember is the crash of my bike beside me and Miss Keene's voice.'

'They must have had your bike in the boot of the car.'

'It was a warning, wasn't it? They can smash up me bike, watch the children at school, threaten us, do anything they want.'

'I won't let the kids out of my sight,' Em said determinedly, though Rose could see she was terrified.

Rose rubbed her sore cheek. She hadn't realised how painful the punches were until now. She was amazed that

Norman Payne hadn't broken a bone in her face or even her jaw.

Em was sitting back on her heels and staring at her. 'They didn't . . . you know . . . they didn't do anything else to you, did they?'

'I think cutting off all my hair and knocking me senseless was enough for one day.'

'I don't know how you can joke about it.'

'Well, I'm certainly not going to cry. There isn't another saucepan going is there?'

Em stood up. 'I'll put some on.' She pushed the poker into the coke and bright scarlet tongues twirled up the sooty chimney. 'That'll keep you warm whilst I boil it.'

The heat of the fire stung her face and she slipped as far down underneath the water as she could just like she did as a child. Bath nights with Mum and Dad in attendance were always warm and cosy. She felt a lump of nostalgia form in her throat and swallowed it away.

Norman Payne had done his best today to scare the living daylights out of her in order to gain control over Eddie. But his violent methods had only made her more determined to fight him. She needn't tell Eddie about what happened, need she? The bruise on her face would be gone by the time she next visited and her hair would have grown into shape at least. Rose gazed into the fire and decided, as she had done many times before, that what Eddie didn't know wouldn't hurt him. What could he do in prison but worry?

★

One week later, a visiting order arrived.

Her heart sank as she read the two words from Eddie, scrawled hastily across a single sheet. 'Come soon.'

She showed the note to Em. 'I'll go, of course. Me black eye's nearly gone.'

'Do you think he knows?'

'How can he?'

Em looked fearful. 'It sounds urgent. I'll ask Bobby to take you.'

'I can't keep pestering Bobby. This time I'll go by coach.'

'But you'll have to change at least twice.' Em looked worried. 'What will you say about your hair? Eddie always liked it long.'

'I'll say it's the fashion and I went to the hairdressers.'

Rose had decided her hair was the least of her worries. She had got used to the short style now, though it could hardly be called a style. Em had trimmed it with the scissors managing to even up the edges over her ears. Rose felt the loss of her thick brown waves but she felt lucky to have survived the encounter with Norman Payne, though the sensation still persisted that someone was watching her.

In the mornings she caught the bus to Kirkwood's with Kamala Patel's eldest, Nima, who worked at the sugar refining plant. Em called for Jane Piper and her kids for school and walked in a crowd to St Mary's. At five o'clock Rose joined the girls from the flourmill and waited at the bus stop for the number fifty-seven. There was always someone on it she knew and she was never

406

alone until she turned the corner of Ruby Street.

Bobby turned up at the weekend with a second-hand Hoover. The machine had a great shiny dome and a black cloth bag that blew out like a balloon when switched on. 'I don't want anything for it,' he assured Em. 'It's on its last legs and needs a new armature. But if you can stand the racket until it finally dies, you're welcome.'

'Does it suck up the dirt?' Em asked sceptically and, Rose thought, a little ungratefully.

'Of course. It beats as it sweeps as it cleans,' Bobby intoned and gave them a demonstration on the square of almost threadbare carpet in the front room. The boards vibrated with the noise but the cleaning was a success.

'I'll see if I like it,' Em said off-handedly, 'meanwhile, we've got better things to plan. Rose is seeing Eddie on Wednesday.'

'I'll take you,' Bobby insisted immediately.

Rose frowned at her sister who didn't hesitate it seemed, to make use of the kind young man. 'No, Bobby, not this time, thanks all the same. I'm going by coach.'

'But it's no trouble, honestly.'

Em tilted her head and walked out of the kitchen as Bobby stared after her like an abandoned puppy. 'You could do without the hassle of a long coach journey after what you've been through.'

Bobby was as sympathetic as ever thinking she'd been knocked off her bike as everyone else did. 'She's right, Rose. Let me take you.'

Rose shook her head. 'It isn't fair. Wednesday's your only day off.'

'So what else would I do with myself?'

'I'll pay for the petrol.'

'No need.' He grinned boyishly. 'But Sunday dinner would be nice.'

'You're welcome anytime,' she shrugged throwing a glance to the kitchen, 'though I don't know what reception you'll get—'

He put a finger over his mouth. 'I know what you're going to say. But I have to keep trying.'

'You don't have to win me over in the process.'

He grinned again. 'You're already spoken for, else I would.'

Rose smiled, but at the moment she felt like a bit of winning over, a bit of pampering. She was upset with her sister for not knowing how lucky she was to have such a gift in Bobby Morton. She was upset with Eddie for not being at her side with his sword and shield ready to slay all the dragons, one dragon in particular by the name of Norman Payne. And she was annoyed with herself for running down Ruby Street every day when she got off the bus for fear of that bloody brown car driving up alongside her again.

'I bought this,' Bobby whispered quickly taking something from his pocket. It was a small deep blue box and he glanced over his shoulder as he opened it.

'Oh, Bobby! It's beautiful.'

'Do you think so?'

Rose nodded silently as she stared at the delicate

looking ring with a starry cloud of tiny, sparkling white stones surrounded by a narrow fringe of gold.

'I didn't have the nerve to ask her today. The Hoover was just an excuse to turn up.'

'So are you going to ask on Sunday?'

He snapped the box closed and shuffled it back in his pocket. 'I'll have to work up the courage again.'

'Oh, Bobby, I hope she says yes.'

'If she does, I'll be the happiest man on the planet.'

'You deserve to be happy,' she told him earnestly and he blushed, his fair skin darkening right up to his hairline. He smiled in his shy way and took her hands into his and she knew he meant to thank her by squeezing them. But then he stopped and seemed uncertain of what to do next until with a look of sadness he touched the fading bruise on her cheek. Suddenly she felt his warm lips brush the grazed skin and, as if it was the most natural thing in the world, he gave her the gentlest of kisses. Then, moving back awkwardly, he gathered himself and rushed past her and out of the door.

Eddie took her in his arms and hugged her. He had spent the last week in gut wrenching agony and now he saw what they had done to her all his fears were realized. 'My poor Rose, my darling . . .' His body ached with anger and frustrated protectiveness and for the first time in his life he couldn't think of a gag. He couldn't make light of something so precious to him and he could hardly contain his emotion as he held her face between his hands.

'Sit down, Eddie, love, everyone's watching.' Her voice was calm and soft and he did sit down but only because he was in danger of punching the first screw who dared to come over in the face. The officers regarded embraces, when couples were locked together, starved of physical contact for so long, as the most appropriate time for passing or exchanging messages, drugs, sharp implements and other illicit items prohibited by Her Majesty's hotels.

Not that the screws were able to halt this forbidden traffic. They didn't have eyes in the backs of their heads and some of them, Eddie acknowledged generously, ignored what was going on under their noses in return for a peaceful life. His friend Solly, for instance, received information from his accountant disguised in the dog-ends that he slipped in his shirt pocket. Solly was not a smoker and he'd coughed his heart up frequently after a visit from his wife.

But when Eddie felt Rose's slender frame leaning against his own he didn't want to let her go. It wasn't a case of transferring illicit items, he had none to pass and Rose certainly had no intention of doing so. Just holding her was enough to make him live again, to resurrect the man inside that had disappeared since being wrenched from the bosom of his family.

The honest truth was he'd kidded himself into believing that he was going to get out of this mess, repay his debt to Norman Payne and start afresh. Yet when the new kid on the block had pressed a small, inconspicuous parcel into his hands last week and he'd opened it to discover a lock of Rose's lovely brown hair, he'd known it was all over.

'Eddie, it's all right. I'm fine. I just got me hair cut short, that's all.'

He stared into her sweet face as they sat down on the hard chairs and he gazed into her lovely, earth brown eyes that seemed to look right through him. She could never lie to him, not that she ever tried. His Rose, his good, sweet Rose, what had they done to her?

'I know you don't like it, but—'

'I *know*, Rose. I know what happened.'

She stared at him and fear clouded her eyes. Her lips trembled but she bravely put on a smile. 'I don't know what you mean, love.'

'You were never any good at telling porkies.'

She blushed deeply then and his heart went out to her for being so brave.

'Last week a new bloke in here gave me this packet. Inside it was some of your hair. I nearly did me nut. Tell me, Rose, what happened, before I bust me gut.' His voice shook and he had to push the anger down, hide his fury and demented worry. If she knew how he was feeling, what he was capable of at this very moment . . .

Her face was as pale as china, her hair unfamiliarly shorn from her brow. He couldn't bear to think of how it had happened, how they'd touched her, terrified her. And it was all because of him. Of what he'd done with his life, screwed it up, abused the gift of a wife who loved and trusted him.

'Oh, Eddie, I was trying not to worry you,' she said forlornly and the breath came out of her mouth on a long sigh. 'But you must believe I'm all right. They . . . they didn't hurt me. All they wanted to do was frighten me and they did that all right.'

His screwed his fingers together in anger and his heart seemed about to burst. 'It was him, wasn't it, Norman Payne?'

She nodded. 'The man you owe money to. Oh, Eddie, why didn't you tell me?'

'I couldn't,' he whispered pathetically. 'I wanted to, that first year after Marle was born I wanted to so much. But I knew you wouldn't like it. I knew you wouldn't go along with floating. I wanted to give you everything, to make life—'

'Eddie.' She stopped him mid-sentence a cold, distant look that he didn't recognize coming over her face. 'Please don't say you did what you did for me and the girls. Please don't say that.'

His blood felt chilled in his veins. He had lived so long now with the dream of making good in his heart, *the* dream, the dream to make them rich, to buy new clothes, to have a nice house full of expensive furniture and carpets, to run around in a posh car and clean it every day outside the front door. To take the girls to school and let the other parents see them climbing out of the motor with him in a brand new suit and Marlene and Donnie dressed like the little ladies they should be. This was his dream and now she was saying she didn't want to hear about it.

'But Rose—'

'I only ever wanted us to be happy, to have time together, to be a family,' she said softly. 'I didn't want

412

things, not material things. I wanted love. And you and the girls meant everything to me. All the love in the world I could ever dream of.'

Eddie stared into her face and wondered where his brains were. Which direction he had been going for the last six years without his wife. Oh, they'd compromised all right. He'd kept quiet about his dreams and so had she, apparently.

'I'll always love you sweetheart,' he protested, 'but I wanted more for us. I wasn't the same man in '45 as I was when we were kids. Me and millions of other blokes came back from the brink of death and wanted to live life with a capital L. Being bunged a few quid for a load of junk didn't satisfy the hunger in me. I needed to prove I was capable of giving you a good life.'

'You could always have got a job.'

Eddie stared at her, this woman whom he loved so much and who was almost a stranger to him. 'Me, as a nine to five geezer? Oh, Rose, you know that ain't my style.'

'And Norman Payne's way of life is?'

''Course not,' he said bitterly. 'I never meant to get into debt.'

'Was that five hundred pounds yours, or was it Norman Payne's?'

He felt the skin over his face tighten. 'By rights it was ours.'

'No, Eddie. It was bad money and I'm glad he took it back. I'd rather live on bread and water than take anything from him ever again. I told him so, too. I told him I'd rather see you in here than outside, working for him.'

Eddie swallowed, his world turning upside down. 'Rose – no one speaks to that bastard like that—'

'Well, I did and I meant it.'

'He could have killed you,' Eddie breathed fearfully. 'Not just cut off your hair.'

'I wouldn't be much use to him then, would I? He wants to get to you through me. He said you gambled away our lives and sold him your soul.'

Eddie had no reply to give her. His addiction had taken him deeper and deeper into debt and all the things he had dreamed of had slowly started to fade away. Yet he still went on, robbing Peter to pay Paul, trying to find a way out of the living nightmare he'd fashioned for himself.

She reached across the wooden table and covered his hand with her own. 'Eddie, I can take anything Norman Payne wants to dish out, as long as we're fighting on the same side. You don't want to work for him, do you? I mean, that isn't even a consideration, is it?'

''Course not.' His heart raced. He couldn't admit to Rose and barely to himself, that in his darkest hours he had been tempted. To agree to any crumb that Norman Payne might throw as him. In his heart of hearts, once or twice, he'd been prepared to quit the struggle and take the easy way out. Especially when that great oaf had pushed Rose's hair into his hand with a smirk across his pock-marked face that reeked special delivery.

Oh yes, he'd been tempted. What good was he going to be to Rose when he got out of here? He'd have form.

A record that would make him a no-no in civvy street. That is, if he wanted a job. But the thought of becoming a company man, yes sir, no sir, three bags full sir, filled him with horror. Even if someone took him on, he'd hate every breath he took in a factory, warehouse or dock. And that was all he was good for, manual work. With no qualifications, no special skills, he was as useless as a boat without a hull.

'Eddie, it's not too late. We can pay back the money—'

'How?'

'I'm working now. I've got a good job in the canteen but I'm going for an interview next week for a job in the office which will be more money.'

'Norman Payne ain't interested in HP,' he told her bitterly. 'And anyway, I don't want you to have to work.'

She sat up and stiffened her shoulders. 'Well, things have changed, love. You couldn't expect them to stay the same.'

'It ain't right. You should be looking after the kids. Matthew needs a—'

'A father, Eddie, that's what he needs.'

He felt his stomach contract with regret. He knew only too well he had been deprived of the pride and joy a father takes in a boy heir. But he hadn't intended for this to happen. It wasn't as if he'd deliberately got himself nicked. God, what was happening to him? He felt his world was slipping out of his grasp. He couldn't protect his family or look after them in here. It was so unfair – the whole bloody past year was unfair and he still had another to do.

'Anyway,' he said, trying to calm his emotions, 'the

most important thing right now is you. I was going barmy thinking you'd come to some harm.'

'No, they didn't hurt me.'

'Tell me what happened.'

Eddie listened as his wife explained how the car had knocked her off her bike and the men in it had tied something around her eyes and driven her to a place close by. Then Norman Payne had told her who he was and disclosed the truth about that bent copper who had stitched him up with an assault charge. Then the bugger had cut off her hair when she'd given him some lip, but thank God he'd been disturbed by some kids. Eddie had imagined worse, much worse during these last few days. But perhaps this time they'd been lucky. Maybe Norman Payne had made his point and the next little reminder would come from inside, as it had done at Brixton. Well, they could do whatever they liked to him. He wanted it that way. He'd take anything – *anything* – rather than have them touch his family.

'I don't want you going anywhere alone,' he told her. 'Or the kids.'

'They play in the yard now,' she assured him, 'and I go by bus with Kamala Patel's daughter, Nima and some others who all wait at the same stop. On the way home I walk with the girls from the mill.'

'What happened to the bike?'

'I don't know.'

Eddie chewed on his lip. Something, somewhere didn't sound right, but he didn't know what.

'Eddie, don't worry. We'll be all right.'

Eddie wished that was true, but he knew different. He wasn't a violent man but at this very moment he wanted to close his fingers around Norman Payne's worthless neck and squeeze tightly.

Chapter Twenty Four

Autumn was Rose's favourite time of the year but as the days grew shorter and the nights longer, she found even the cosy evenings spent indoors made her feel as unsettled as the damp, foggy weather.

The mild spells of warm and wet weather had given way to outbursts of gusty wind and in November the roof started to leak after a violent storm blew tiles off the roof. Rose informed the landlord, but as usual, nothing was done. She considered them lucky, though, to have escaped a series of gales that swept over west and north London, causing damage to property and even loss of life. Gunnersbury tube station was destroyed and further south the South Godwin lightship was overturned in freak weather conditions. An inch of rain fell on London, almost matching the record of the disastrously wet Coronation year.

Two weeks before Christmas Donnie came out in large red blotches that covered her entire body followed a week later by Marlene. Dr Cox diagnosed measles and very soon was proclaiming Will infected too. As none of the children were allowed to school and had to be

418

quarantined, Rose had no need to worry about Norman Payne's unwelcome attentions. She was, however, still vigilant when it came to work. She had now joined the typing pool of Kirkwood's, having left the canteen and a disappointed Gwen House in early November.

Anita had been right when she'd assured Rose that she'd soon recover her speed. Her fingers took no time at all in recalling their correct positions on the big, lusty half moon typewriters that clacked noisily in the office. Rose had been nervous on her first morning, making several unnecessary mistakes. But during her lunch hour, Phyllis Waters, the clerk she had met when first applying for a job at Kirkwood's, paid her a visit.

'Congratulations,' she told Rose enthusiastically as she perched a slim thigh on the stool by Rose's desk. 'I came to wish you good luck and fatten you up.' She unwrapped a rather greasy looking brown paper bag. 'Coconut Madeleine,' Phyllis giggled and offered one to Rose. 'By the looks of you, rushing around in the canteen has kept you as thin as a rake.'

Rose gratefully accepted the pastry. She hadn't brought any sandwiches with her. Coming up to Christmas every penny counted. She took a cautious bite and closed her eyes. 'Scrumptious,' she sighed as the jam and coconut melted on her tongue.

'It's hard work in the kitchens,' Phyllis said sympathetically as she picked at the cherry with her small white teeth. 'You'll soon put on a few pounds now Gwen doesn't give you the run around.'

'Gwen was a good supervisor,' Rose said loyally. 'In

many ways I was sorry to leave.' She didn't tell Phyllis it wasn't the canteen work that kept her thin, but keeping alert to a very nasty individual, causing her almost to live on her nerves. Rose thought Phyllis was far too young and naïve to know anything about Norman Payne's sleazy world.

'Mr Grimmond, your boss here, is a bit of an old grump,' Phyllis warned as they polished off the delicious cakes. 'But he is fair to his staff.'

Rose had met Mr Grimmond once, at her interview. He was a small, round and bespectacled man, close to retiring age. He had given her a test on one of the machines and seemed satisfied with her execution of a dictated paragraph that she completed slowly but efficiently. Sweat had been pouring down her back at the time as she hadn't used a typewriter in years.

Rose had been surprised when he gave her the job. She had been one of four women who had applied, and the others were all experienced typists. Her one advantage had been that she was already an employee of Kirkwood's and had her name down on the list. She was to have three months trial in the typing pool, her starting wage a princely four pounds seventeen and six pence. If she could refresh her shorthand too, her salary would rise to five pounds fifty.

Rose was thrilled at the prospect though when the children came down with measles, she didn't like leaving Em to cope alone. Having a serious job meant she couldn't take time off as easily as she had done in the canteen. But Em said she didn't mind and as it was almost

Christmas, the kids would be on holiday anyway. It was the perfect opportunity to make decorations.

Eddie was less enamoured with the situation. Rose hoped he would be happy to hear her news, but his letter, or rather note of just a few lines, was discouraging. 'Why can't you stay in the canteen till I come home?' he wrote. 'You can give up work altogether when we're back to normal. With luck, I'll be home in March.'

It was the first Saturday in December when his letter arrived. Rose opened it hurriedly before Em or the children were up. The house was cold, she hadn't made up a fire yet and a few bleak spots of rain splattered against the kitchen window. There was no visiting order enclosed.

'Thought I heard you up,' Em said coming up behind her in her plaid dressing gown and slippers. 'It's only seven o'clock. You should have had a lie in.'

'I heard the postman.'

'Is there a letter from Eddie?'

'Yes, but no VO. And I asked him to send one for us all. I wanted to see him before Christmas. Well, all of us really. The kids will forget what their dad looks like.'

Em put the kettle on, her hair in curlers still. 'Eddie knows what he's doing.'

'I sometimes wonder.'

'In his shoes wouldn't you want the same? Christmas in a prison must be a terrible reminder for men of the home they're missing. It would be like sprinkling salt on the wound seeing everyone so happy.'

'But what about the kids? They need reminding we're

a family. And he hasn't seen them since that time when Bobby first took us all up.'

Em turned round and rubbed her hands together. 'Why don't you just go up on your own? Eddie could handle that. Bobby will take you.'

Rose looked away. Bobby had been a bit of a stranger lately. She guessed he was embarrassed to face her. But their kiss was innocent. It had happened on the spur of the moment and wasn't intended. The moment didn't reflect on his relationship with Em or, indeed, with her.

'I know he would.' Rose didn't quite meet Em's eyes. Em wasn't engaged to Bobby or even going out with him, but Rose still felt guilty. She didn't think going alone in the car with him was a good idea.

As the whistle blew Em got up to lift the kettle. 'Do you know when Eddie's coming home?'

'In March, he thinks.'

'Well then, four months shouldn't be too long to wait.'

'No, it shouldn't,' Rose agreed, although at the moment it felt like an eternity.

Em gave a little twitch of her mouth and a tight cough and Rose realized it was the first time in weeks that she'd noticed the nervous tic. Not only that, but Rose hadn't been woken by Em's nightmares any more, and Em had even started wearing curlers to give bounce to her fine light brown hair. And wasn't that lipstick she'd worn last Sunday when Bobby had come round to mend the vacuum cleaner?

'Talking of Bobby . . .' Em turned round, the steaming teapot in her hand. 'Well, you see . . . I've been thinking.'

Rose guessed what was coming. She'd hoped Em would accept Bobby's proposal months ago, but it had never come. Had Bobby finally popped the question?

'Yes?' Rose prompted eagerly.

'Of course I'd never do anything now – not before Eddie comes home—'

'Oh, Em, spit it out!' Rose couldn't wait. The morning had started off so dismally with Eddie's letter. Now, as the grey sky outside was slowly breaking into sunshine over the backyard, she felt its warmth.

'Bobby's asked me to go to the pictures.'

Rose was silent. If she didn't laugh, she'd cry. 'Oh, Em, is that all?'

'I haven't said yes, yet.' Her sister sank down on the chair. 'Oh, Rosy, what if I can't – you know – *respond*? He's a young man. Healthy. Normal . . .'

Rose stretched out her hands and folded them over the thin, cold fingers. 'You're young, pet. And you're healthy.'

'But not normal. Not after what happened with Arthur. I feel like a freak. I don't know what Bobby sees in me, I honestly don't. That's why I've been so rude. I don't deserve a good man. And he's good, I know he is. Far too good for the likes of me.' She hung her head and sobbed softly. One of her curlers fell down on the table. Rose picked it up and replaced it, wrapping the hair gently back into place. Her sister's head came up slowly, her cheeks red and shiny.

'Em, do you love him?' It was the only question that needed to be asked.

Her sister gulped. 'I don't know what love is.'

"Course you do. It's what you didn't have with Arthur.'

Em sniffed noisily. Her voice was a whisper as she looked at Rose. 'Sometimes, when I'm with Bobby, I get this feeling inside. As if I'm flying. My tummy's all light and swirling and my arms and legs go numb, as though I've no control. And that's what frightens me, I think.'

'You've had to be in control in the past, but it's different now. You can set your emotions free.'

Em stared out from her clear, hazel brown eyes. 'Free?'

'Yes, you can trust again.'

'But what if—'

'What if you grow old without knowing what it's like to be loved? What if you never hold a man that you love in your arms and let him make love to you? What if you never experience the joy of going to sleep beside him and waking up in the morning knowing you'd shared the most precious gift in all the world?'

'Sex? You mean sex?' Em asked anxiously.

'Sex is just bodies isn't it? But lovemaking is mind and heart and soul, all rolled into one because you trust each other.'

'I never thought that could happen to me.'

'Well, you have the choice now.'

Em gave a long, shuddery sigh again. 'It sounds so simple.'

Rose had no comment to make on simplicity. She would have had plenty to say two years ago, but not now. Loving someone the way she loved Eddie was more complicated than she had ever imagined possible.

'I don't know a thing about electricity,' Em murmured

distantly, 'or cars. And Bobby goes on about them all the time.'

Rose smiled ruefully. 'You know a lot about cleaning things. You've got a lot in common in that sense. Anyway, he only talks about electricity because he can't say what he really wants to say.'

'And what's that?'

Rose raised her eyebrows and grinned. 'Emily Trim, you're fishing.'

Em blushed deeply. Rose thought how pretty she was looking these days even first thing in the morning in her curlers. Now that old turban was confined to the cupboard under the stairs, the flower was blooming.

'I might ask him to dinner next Sunday if that's all right.'

'With three kids watching your every move?' Rose frowned. 'Why don't you take him up on his offer?'

'Do you really think I should?'

'Meself I'd rather go dancing,' Rose giggled. 'A tea dance first and maybe the films after.'

'Oh, that's even worse! I wouldn't know a waltz from a quickstep.'

''Course you do. We learnt at school.'

'Yes, but that was years ago.'

'You said that to me about typing, that it was as easy as cracking eggs to pick up. Now it's your turn.'

'With my two left feet, Bobby'd be trampled!'

But Rose wasn't fooled for a moment. Her sister was blushing like a schoolgirl. Bobby Morton was finally on to a winner.

★

Bobby and Em's engagement party was held on New Year's Eve. It was to have been Christmas Eve, but since the measles rash still irritated the children, Rose decided to go along with Bobby's suggestion of a slap up do on the last day of the year.

On Boxing Day morning Rose sat in the Mendozas' front room surrounded by piles of Christmas paper and string. A bright red cardigan and new plaid slippers occupied the top of the sideboard along with packets of sweets, a box of Clarnico Assortment and a large jar of Turkish Delight. There were coats, scarves and hats thrown haphazardly over a chair and last night's ashes were still in the grate, a folded sheet of newspaper in front of them where Benny was kneeling.

'Anita ain't tidied up yet,' he told her ruefully. 'She's having an extra hour in bed this morning as her back was giving her gyp again last night. She's doing too much, but dare I tell her to ease up? It's more than me life's worth to open me cake 'ole and speak me piece.'

'She should get that back seen to,' Rose agreed worriedly.

'I just need a few more tyre contracts that I can rely on and she can chuck in scrubbing Lady Muck's toilets.'

Rose knew that Benny hated the fact his wife wore herself out cleaning other people's houses. But she also knew that Anita would refuse point blank to give up her independence. The prospect of another Butlin's holiday was what kept her going through thick and thin.

'I'll just start the fire and we can have a cuppa,' Benny

said as he buried his face in a cloud of ash and coughed up his lungs.

'I'm not staying,' Rose said, eager to be on her way. She wanted to get back home before Em and the kids were up. She intended to make everyone a cooked breakfast as a special treat. 'I just brought the treacle tart round as promised. Your boys are bringing their girls home for tea today.'

'Tell me about it. You'd think royalty was paying a visit. I ain't ever seen so many sausage rolls come out of an oven. Like bloody Lyons Corner House it was yesterday.'

'Neet likes to put on a good spread,' Rose said mildly. 'Em made the treacle tart with Tate and Lyle and it came out a treat.'

'Yeah, well thanks, love. I'll enjoy a bit tonight – if there's any left, of course.'

Rose smiled, watching the big man carefully sweep the hearth with Anita's dainty brass brush and pan set. At just gone eight o'clock the house had a peaceful, if rather chilly, atmosphere and Benny hadn't shaved, his big dark eyes still bleary from all the festivities.

'Bobby's asked Em to get engaged,' she said on a swift breath. 'And she's said yes.'

For a moment Benny turned, looking surprised. Then he let out a loud guffaw. 'Bloody hell. I'd never have laid a quid on that one.'

'He's been waiting to ask her for ages,' Rose said as she pulled her thick cardigan around her and shivered. It wasn't very Christmasy weather: damp and mild with strange flurries of wind, but the houses in Ruby Street were like morgues until the fires went on.

'So when did he pop the question?'

'He took Em out last Sunday. They were going to the pictures, but never got there. Bobby was so nervous he asked her to marry him as they stood in the queue waiting for a ticket. Em nearly fainted and he had to take her back to the car.'

Benny roared with laughter again, spilling the carefully swept ash on to the lino. 'Poor bugger. But I reckon they'll make it all right.'

'I hope so, Benny.'

He swept the last of the sooty waste into the pan, replaced the grate and turned to frown at Rose. 'When's the big day?'

'Not till Eddie's home . . .' She paused uncertainly. There had been no confirmation of his release date yet and she didn't want to tempt fate by guessing at a month. She moved on swiftly, 'Bobby's giving her the ring – officially – on New Year's Eve. We're having a party to celebrate. You'll all come won't you?'

'I'll be first in line to shake the brave man's hand,' Benny grinned. 'And I reckon that's really decent of them to wait till Eddie's back.'

Rose nodded but she didn't say that Eddie was less than enthusiastic about the idea. He had sent a card before Christmas that he'd made himself for the kids. It consisted of a large sheet of folded white paper and he'd sprinkled glitter over the carefully written words, *Happy Christmas Toots and Princess*. For Matthew he'd created a smaller card and had drawn a Christmas tree on the front. The children had loved these and they were given pride of place on the mantel. He'd written a longer than usual letter to Rose – two whole pages – but he sounded depressed instead of happy. 'I hope your sister knows what she's doing with this Bobby bloke,' he'd written glumly in answer to all her news on the forthcoming engagement. Added to which he'd still maintained that Rose's job at Kirkwood's was too demanding and she should give it up. What worried her most was that he hadn't responded to her query that if she didn't have a reliable income when he came home, what would they live on? Because he avoided answering her question she feared the worst, her suspicion growing that Norman Payne had already forged an unbreakable hold over him before he'd set one foot out of the prison. From what Eddie had hinted at, she was almost certain that Norman Payne had no intention of letting her husband, or anyone else that might prove useful to him, off the hook.

'Well, I'd better let you light that fire before everyone wakes up,' Rose said as she stood up.

Benny hauled himself to his feet. He wore only his vest, soiled now by the ashes and a pair of braces that stretched tightly across his barrel-like chest. His crumpled trousers resembled baggy balloons at the knees. 'Thanks for the treacle tart, love. Are you sure you wouldn't like a cuppa?'

'No ta, Benny. Be sure to tell Neet about Friday though, won't you?'

Benny grinned devilishly under his dark growth of

beard. 'It'd be more than me life's worth to forget.' He walked with her to the front door. She opened it and looked both ways as she stepped out. Benny read her mind. 'You ain't seen nothing of that bastard Payne have you?'

She shook her head dismissively but every time she stepped on the street she wondered if a car would come roaring round the corner towards her. It hadn't happened yet and she hoped they'd given up on her for the time being. 'I don't think they'd dare come down this road again,' she said more confidently than she felt.

'You've only got to bang on the wall and I'm out of here in a shot,' Benny told her stoutly.

'I know. But I hope I'll never have to ask that kind of favour.' She went on tiptoe and kissed his cheek. 'Happy Christmas, pet.'

'Happy Christmas, gel,' he grinned and blushed.

Rose hadn't been able to afford any real presents for the Mendozas but she'd made up a basket of fruit for the whole family and Em had baked one of her Christmas puddings and topped it with a sprig of holly from a stunted holly bush that Will had unearthed on the debris. As Benny closed the door behind her she glanced over at Olga's house. It was still unoccupied, two pieces of tatty board nailed up to the lower window, just like the house next to forty-six. She thought of Olga hovering somewhere in the vicinity still trying to find her home. Rose was the only one now who visited her grave at Golder's Green. From time to time she took flowers, just a cheap bunch from market, and silently she promised herself to take a big bunch of daffodils in spring.

Back on her own doorstep, Rose paused, listening to the uncanny silence of Ruby Street on Boxing Day morning. Even the docks were in slumber, with only a faint hooting from the river drifting in the morning air, bouncing like an invisible ball from the sooty, pointed roofs. Christmas 1954 had passed without snow. Except for the storm that had blown like a typhoon through West London, the weather gods could do nothing more than spatter a few wet pearls across the deserted street. Not that it would stay deserted for very long, she decided as she let herself in. Soon all the kids would be out, eager to play with their new toys on the pavements and in the road.

Inside the house the walls and ceilings were strung with the children's handmade paper chains and the smell of Em's freshly baked Christmas pudding lingered in the kitchen. The girls and Matthew had left their Christmas presents under the tree in the front room, a brightly coloured push-along train and two bald baby dolls both purchased second-hand and given an overhaul with Sunlight soap. They slept side by side in a blue painted crib with fairytale transfers stuck to the sides. This was also purchased second-hand but scrubbed as clean as a whistle. Will was still fast asleep on his camp bed in the corner, his soft snore coming gently from under the eiderdown. It was too cold now to sleep in the tent. Two books, *Biggles Gets His Men* and *Another Job for Biggles*, were placed safely on top of the gram, side by side. Em had managed to root out these dog-eared copies in a Poplar bookshop and the brightly coloured illustrations of Biggles wearing his flying goggles and big smile made Rose want to smile too.

She felt a glow of pride when she looked around her house, just as she always had, despite little money being available for Christmas extras. Rose's wages covered the rent and bills, Em's contribution filled the larder. On Christmas Day there had been roast chicken, stuffing, Brussels and crisp baked potatoes accompanied by a rich fruit pudding. No one had gone short. At tea time they had scoffed mince pies and condensed cream as they gathered round the gram and listened to Bing Crosby singing 'Count Your Blessings', a song newly released from the film *White Christmas*. The rest of the day had been one long party: board games, charades and hide and seek being the all time favourites.

'God bless our home,' Rose sighed contentedly as she looked around her little nest. She thought of Eddie and said a prayer for him too. 'Only a little while to go now, sweetheart,' she whispered, 'and you'll be in my arms once more.'

Chapter Twenty Five

They came in the night.

The car must have stopped outside for several minutes before Rose woke. She heard the noise vaguely in her sleep, a soft growl at first, then a rattle and finally a big cat's purr. The car engine revved and a bolt of terror woke her fully. She jumped out of bed and ran to the window. Headlights flashed along the street and sliced the cold night air like a sharp, bright knife. Em hadn't woken. Nor had the children. Rose was frozen to the spot, her hand lifting the net curtain as though she was lifting the lid on a time bomb.

'Please God, make it disappear,' she said aloud, though her voice was just a hoarse whisper. She wanted to be brave, but courage deserted her. She had thought they would never dare come down the street again. But they had. In the darkness, when no one was about to see what they did.

A loud crash echoed round the house. They were breaking in! They were going to kill them all! The children – the children! Rose jumped out of bed. Matthew hadn't stirred in his cot, amazingly. But Em sat up in bed, her eyes full of sleep.

'What's happened? What was that?'

'Hurry! Hurry!' Rose threw the bedclothes back. 'They're coming in!'

Em sat still looking dazed. 'Who?'

Another crash splintered the air. This time there were terrified cries from the girls' bedroom. Rose rushed along the landing. Someone was coming up the stairs. Her heart nearly stopped as the two girls emerged slowly from their room. They stood in their nightgowns, rubbing their eyes.

Rose pushed them back, herding them like sheep into safety. But she had nothing to defend them with, nothing! Her eyes went to Matthew's small wooden chair in the corner. She picked it up and ran back to the landing, lifting it high above her head.

A split second later she was standing at the top of the stairs, shaking like a jelly inside but prepared to kill anyone who tried to pass her.

'It's me, Auntie Rose. It's Will.'

Rose stared rigidly into the pale, frightened face. She felt her heart bubble as her brain tried to register what she saw with her eyes. In her imagination it had been the driver of the brown car coming towards her, his coarse, blunted features screwed up in a frightening grimace. She didn't know what Norman Payne looked like but if his appearance was anything like his voice, there wouldn't be much to choose between either man. She was certain both looked as evil as each other. But then as her nephew stepped cautiously up the stairs, his wide blue eyes filled

434

with fear and confusion, her whole body started to shake.

'Will . . . is it you?'

'Yes, don't throw the chair at me, will you?' He advanced cautiously, his striped pyjamas suddenly looking far too big for him as he crept towards her. 'Someone threw some bricks through the window. The car's driven away now.'

'Are you sure?'

'Yes, I looked out the window after it drove off. There's a big hole in the glass where the bricks came through.'

'So they really have gone?' Rose was still suspicious even though she knew Will was telling her the truth.

'Yes. Honestly.'

'Oh, thank God!' Her legs collapsed under her and she sank down on the stairs, the little wooden chair falling out of her hands against the banister.

'Rose, are you all right?' Em called shrilly.

'Mummy! Mummy!' The two girls rushed towards her. Suddenly they were all clinging together, arms locked, faces wet with tears of relief. She pulled them against her tightly choking back her own sobs as Em and Will crouched on the stairs and they all trembled together like one big jelly.

'Mummy, I was ever so scared.' Donnie lifted her face and Rose kissed her forehead.

'So was I,' Marlene sniffed. 'I thought it was Old Nick.'

Rose murmured in confusion, 'Old Nick?'

'Yeah,' nodded Marlene staunchly, her curly hair flowing over her shoulders like brilliant tongues of flame. 'Or sometimes in the Bible he's called Beeslebub.'

'Be-el-ze-bub,' Donnie corrected, giving a little hiccup. 'You always get it wrong.'

'It was only me anyway,' said Will, remarkably calm. 'I just heard this crash and another one, so I got under the covers.'

'Are you hurt, love?' Em smothered him in kisses and squashed his face in her hands as they sat on the stairs.

'No, I'm okay.' Embarrassed, Will shrank against the wall and the two girls' tears soon turned into giggles.

'Well, you could have been badly cut or knocked out by the bricks.' Em turned to Rose. 'What happened? I woke up in a start and the next thing I knew you were standing at the top of the stairs holding a chair above your head and shrieking like a lunatic.'

'I was going to stop whoever it was coming up the stairs.'

'It was only me, Auntie Rose.'

'I know that now, love,' Rose said shakily. 'But as you've slept in so many places in this house and in the yard, I forgot you were downstairs. I thought the men in the car had broken in.'

Suddenly there was a loud knocking at the door. The knocking turned into a pounding and then there were voices. Lots of voices.

'That's Uncle Benny and Auntie Anita,' Donnie cried. 'And David and Alan.'

'They must have heard the glass go,' Em said and they all tried to get down the stairs to open the front door.

Rose went back upstairs to Matthew. He was still fast asleep in his cot beside the double bed. He'd slept through everything. She pulled his blanket round him then tumbled down the stairs and joined everyone else. She still couldn't stop shaking. How many more times would this happen, she wondered, or something like it? And next time, would someone be hurt? It was just lucky that Will's camp bed was over by the gram. If he'd been under the window the glass and the bricks would have fallen on him.

Rose shivered as the cold air blew in. Benny stood in his vest and underpants and clutched a hammer in his hand. Anita was beside him, her short fair hair standing up in spikes on her head and an old frilly dressing gown pulled round her neck. The two boys were bare-chested. They wore only pyjama bottoms. Behind them were Sharon and Derek Green and Mike and Debbie Price all in coats hiding their nightclothes. Anita leapt forward and hugged the breath out of Rose.

'I'm all right, Neet. We're *all* all right.'

Anita held her at arms' length. 'What happened?'

'They chucked bricks through the window.'

'This can't go on, love. It can't. You'll have to tell the police.'

'It won't do any good, going to them.' Rose knew Anita was concerned for their safety, but Inspector Williams would probably laugh in her face.

'Not all the police are bent. There must be some good ones.'

'Yes, but it's finding them.'

★

Two days later, Bobby arrived at the door. It was half past eight in the morning. As it was the Christmas holiday everyone was still upstairs having an extra hour's sleep. Rose had just dressed and was about to put the kettle on. Bobby looked terrible, as though he hadn't slept all night.

'Bobby, what's wrong?' Rose asked, dreading the answer. Every time she opened the door now, she expected trouble.

'They've done me car in,' he said angrily, his blue eyes blazing. 'It's a write-off.'

'What do you mean?'

'I left it outside the shop last night and when I came down this morning I didn't recognize it.' He stepped inside as Em came down the stairs, her hair rapidly freed from curlers and dressed in her trousers and cardigan. When he saw her his eyes softened to their old, soft blue, but then as he pushed back a lock of blond hair from his face, he grew angry again. 'They drove nails in the tyres and poured paint all over it. When they'd finished ripping the insides up they bust as much of the engine as they could, then left their calling card. A couple of bricks through the windows.'

'Oh, Bobby, no!' Em wailed.

'I'd like to lay my hands on the bastards who did it.'

Rose felt her legs begin to shake again. 'Your lovely car,' she whispered. 'Do you think it was *him*?'

'Who else could it be?' Bobby's face was red now and his hands clenched into fists. 'He's a bad lot, this bloke, Rose. Eddie should never have got mixed up with him.'

'She knows that,' Em said defensively. 'They tied her up and cut off all her hair, didn't they?'

'Yes, and that's unforgivable. Someone has to do something.'

'I've tried,' Rose said helplessly. 'I just don't know what to do next.'

'There's no use blaming her—' Em began, but Bobby shook his head.

'I'm not. But I think we should go to the police.'

'What could they do?' Rose said, her voice rising uncontrollably. 'That Inspector Williams won't help. Eddie was put away because of him. How do we know who to trust?'

'We have to do something,' Bobby said urgently. 'Someone has to.'

Rose put her hands up to her face. Her head was aching and her thoughts were in turmoil. She didn't want to accept the truth, that the only person who could do something was Eddie. It was Eddie that Norman Payne wanted. This was how he blackmailed and threatened his victims until they gave in and agreed to do as he wanted. It was only Eddie who could stand up against him and refuse.

She looked at her sister and Bobby and saw the fear in their faces. She knew she would see that look again and again over the coming years if they didn't make a stand now.

'You're right, Bobby. When Eddie comes home, we'll go to the police. We'll find someone who'll listen to us and help us.'

Bobby looked at her with a little frown and nodded. 'It's got to be done, Rose.'

Just then Matthew cried out from upstairs. Her heart lurched unpleasantly. Both she and Em turned to run up together. They almost collided. Then Donnie called over the banister that they were taking Matthew in their room to play with him.

Em collapsed on the stairs. She looked up with wild, frightened eyes. 'We'd better postpone the party. I couldn't enjoy it, what with all that's happened. I'm sorry Bobby. Really I am.'

'Does that mean we're not engaged?'

Em nodded slowly and it was then that Rose knew they simply couldn't go on like this. As soon as Eddie came home, their lives had to change.

Chapter Twenty Six

He was filthy rich.

Eddie smiled at the screw as he stowed his saved wages from the workshop in his pocket. A ruckled, unpressed pocket it was true, but after almost two years stuck in brown paper, his suit didn't look that bad, not really. Four pounds fifteen and sixpence, yes, he had earned every penny in that stinking sweatshop. He was rich!

Somehow Norman Payne didn't seem to matter much any more. Like a bad dream, his spectre had almost vanished overnight as freedom beckoned, the bright March day holding more for Eddie than the promise of spring. His Rose would be waiting at the gate with Benny, and the three of them would drive back in style to Ruby Street where he would hold his daughters and son safely in his arms once more.

Just let Payne try it on now he was free, well, almost free. The swine was happy to bully women and carve up the cons in the nick. But Payne would have his work cut out if he showed his ugly mug in Ruby Street, though he had to admit his skin still crawled when he thought of the tiny package of Rose's hair pressed into his hand. Payne had really got to him then. He still wasn't certain he believed what Rose had told him, that they hadn't hurt her. Christ Almighty, they could have killed her – or worse.

'Don't forget your watch,' the screw reminded him as he turned away from the bench. 'Nice piece, that.'

'Yeah.' Eddie flung the cheap imitation leather strap across his wrist and felt even more like his old self. The watch, a bit flash because it really did look the business with its pearly face and luminous hands, had been the last of his stock from Cox Street. He'd bought it for a song from a punter who needed cash. The trophy was a reminder of his old street cred and he felt a renewed dart of pride. Once upon a time he'd been able to flog ice to an Eskimo and get away with it. But all that would have to change if he wanted to go legit. He'd big plans to get himself a licence for a market stall, settle down and be his own boss. No more street trading or floating, he was Payne's lackey no more. No, this time Rose would be proud of him.

'Your missus waiting?' the police officer enquired solicitously.

Eddie grinned. 'Too right, mate.'

'Then you're a lucky bastard.'

Eddie didn't need to be reminded how lucky he was to have Rose. Most cons suffered the inevitable fate, dumped by their girlfriends or wives. Some just faded away, others stopped writing or never showed up with their VOs. That's what got to the poor devils. No news, no communication, nothing. Just that silence that stretched on for years and a stray bit of poisonous gossip that did your head in.

Eddie had often joked with Solly Rosenberg that it was only Alma and Rose who kept the prison postal service going. Solly had read Alma's weekly letters dutifully, although most of them bored him stiff. They'd had a real laugh over some of the things she said, as Solly imitated his wife's nerve-twanging tone and read the family news aloud. He was a good bloke, old Solly. They'd shared a lot of laughs together and Eddie had missed his company. Solly had even written to wish him good luck on the outside.

The outside! Eddie's heart raced as he thought of being a free man again. He'd make all this grief up to Rose. As soon as he took possession of a kosher stall, he'd pay off his debts and provide for his family. Rose could chuck in that poxy job at Kirkwood's, look after the kids properly and life would be rosy again.

Eddie gave a confident shrug. 'Well, this is it then. I'll be taking me leave. I'm just going to call in and pay me respects to the Guv'nor, tell him how sorry I am to be leaving.'

'Yeah, you do that. Perhaps he'll extend your holiday for free.' The screw laughed coarsely and, tearing a sheet of paper from the book on the desk in front of him, he slid it across the stained, chipped surface of the desk towards Eddie. 'There you are, all the paperwork done. You're almost a free man. Like a smoke?' The screw tossed a filter tip across the desk.

'Yeah, why not?' Eddie wasn't bothered really. He could take it or leave it. But he picked up the fag and slipped it in his breast pocket along with his release forms. 'Ta. I won't hang around to enjoy it as it might spoil me breath. You ain't got a peppermint have you?'

The warder laughed raucously. 'No, but there's a bottle of Jeyes in the lav.'

Eddie turned on his heel and whistled his way to the far door. Another screw opened it and escorted him along a narrow, white painted corridor. For the last time Eddie inhaled the stink that was burned into his brain; disinfectant, boiled cabbage, human excretion, stale sweat. Glistening beads oozed from his forehead. His mouth was dry and he licked his lips. He had to keep a handle on his excitement, so he walked jauntily, as he used to, uncaring that his old suit needed more than a press to restore its dignity. He'd soon be wearing something smart, slicking back his hair with Brylcreem again, polishing his shoes until he could see his face in them. Life was six feet away from being back to normal.

Even so his gut went over when he was a few yards away from the outer door. He felt like running, charging at it, but he kept his head and paced himself, swallowing down the animal urge to flee.

Five minutes later he was in the fresh air. He sucked in the oxygen; his lungs couldn't get enough. They hurt as he gulped razor sharp breaths. The world was a beautiful place. Across the road, a sandy lane wound intriguingly through a wood. He could walk up it if he wanted to, right to the end with no one to stop him. Above him a tall oak tree swayed, its naked, twisted branches bereft of leaves. He could climb that tree if he wanted, right to the top.

Eddie blinked hard, relief and disbelief flowing through his body. In front of him was a gate, the last barrier to his freedom. A uniformed security guard was on duty, raising the red and white striped pole to visitors. Eddie looked round expectantly for Benny's lorry. Rose had said they would be here for one o'clock.

He checked his watch. Twenty past six. He smiled ruefully. A nice piece all right but it couldn't bloody keep time. He should have put it right before he left. He looked up, still smiling. A wind was getting up, a cold March wind cutting like an invisible mower through the grass in the field close by. What a beautiful sight. The outside world.

Freedom . . .

'That's right, Eddie, take a good, deep breath. Lovely ain't it? And it don't cost a penny.'

Eddie spun round. He froze. 'What the fuck are you doing here?' he groaned, his new found confidence immediately disappearing.

'That's no way to talk to an old friend.'

'You're no friend of mine.'

Norman Payne leered at him and raised his hand. He beckoned with his well manicured index finger and two men jumped out of a car parked innocuously by Reception. They, like Payne, were dressed in camel overcoats, their shoulders packed with muscle. They stared at him with cold, merciless eyes and Eddie quaked inside.

'Now, now, old son,' Payne said easily, effeminately curving his gloved hand against his thick silver hair. 'We've got a lot to catch up on.'

Eddie braced himself. Where was Benny? Where was Rose?

Payne smiled as if he was reading his thoughts. 'Ah yes. Your wife.'

Eddie sprang forward wanting to tear out the man's throat. The two heavies blocked his way. 'Where is she? What have you done with her, you ponce?'

Payne's smiled disappeared. 'Using the space between your ears never was your strong point, was it, Eddie?'

'Where is she?' Eddie demanded as the two minders pushed their chests against him.

'Now why should you think I've done anything with her?' Norman Payne raised his heavy black eyebrows. His expression was mock innocence. 'I merely passed the time of day with her – and her escort – about an hour or so ago. For some reason they seemed agitated when I enquired about the health of your fine children and sister-in-law. Sad to say they left in a bit of a hurry.' His hard, cold eyes met Eddie's in silent triumph. Payne tutted. 'Cause me any more trouble, Eddie old son, and you'll never see your pretty kids again. Now, be a good boy and get in the car.'

Trussed like a chicken, Eddie was delivered to the vehicle. Squeezed in the middle of Payne's two minders he tried to get his paralyzed brain to work. But he was having déjà vu from Coronation Day. Only this time it wasn't for himself he was shit scared. This time it was for his family.

As the driver of the car started the engine, Payne turned from the front seat to sneer at him. 'Not a word as we go out of the gate,' he muttered between gritted teeth.

Eddie wondered if it was possible to alert the guard to his plight. But the bonnet of the long, sleek limousine slipped unchallenged through the barrier. It was clear the operator had no intention of finding himself work.

Just my bloody luck, Eddie thought bitterly, but anyway, what could anyone have done to help? Payne held all the cards and he, Eddie, was what he'd always been. The joker in the pack.

'Please, please, let me see them,' begged Rose as she sat on the chair, as she had once before, with her hands tied behind her back.

She received no reply from the man who stood guard on the door, his face blank. He was a small man, but muscular with a neck the size of a bull's.

'It's no use, Rose. Save your energy.' Benny was sitting beside her on another chair, his wrists and ankles bound. They'd been easy prey for Payne's men when they returned from Hewis. Rose still didn't know if she'd made the right choice leaving Eddie to fend for himself. Payne had been lying after all, when he'd told them the children and Em were safe back in Ruby Street. She shivered as she thought of Payne's stomach-churning words to her back in the prison grounds.

'Your children are missing you, Mrs Weaver,' he had taunted her after striding over to the lorry like some sort of official. She had wound down the window and as soon as she heard his voice, recognized him. Although she'd been blindfolded the last time they met she'd know that voice anywhere.

'Wh . . . what have you done to my children?' she stammered helplessly.

'As yet, nothing. Leave now and you'll find them safe and sound.' Payne had smiled obsequiously. 'We'll give your husband a lift home.'

'Stay there and don't move,' Benny had yelled at her as he jumped out of the lorry. But as he lunged at Payne, the back-up intervened. They'd dragged Benny behind the lorry and she'd sat there, not knowing what to do wondering what would happen to Em and the children if they didn't get home in time.

When Benny climbed back in the cab, he'd aged ten years. There was a nasty graze across his cheek and his eyes were frightened. 'Oh, Benny, what did they do to you?'

He started the engine. 'It don't matter about me. It's the kids I'm worried about. We're going home and fast,' he muttered. 'We've no choice.'

'But what about Eddie?'

Benny stared at her, his expression resigned. 'There's nothing we can do. Payne told me if we're not back inside a couple of hours, we'll find the house empty.'

Rose had nearly fainted on the spot. She looked out of the window as Benny drove past the three men. Payne had a smirk on his lips, the other two were adjusting their coats. Benny had driven like a lunatic through the narrow lanes and cursed the traffic. But they arrived back in less than two hours; unfortunately, but predictably, to an empty house.

Payne's men had arrived within minutes. If Rose didn't cooperate, she would never see her family again. Now, as she sat beside Benny in the desolate building, she knew she was in the same place as before. She would never forget the musty, old brick and plaster smell that pervaded the air. Now she could see what her imagination had been forced to provide. Above, half the roof was missing, the blue sky visible through the rafters. A broken staircase hung precariously from one wall. Battered old filing cabinets lay on their sides and half a dozen old wooden office chairs held up the peeling walls. There was even an old typewriter upside down on a pile of bricks. The man with the bull neck was standing in front of a door. Were the children and Em through there?

'We shouldn't have believed him,' Rose said miserably. She was freezing cold and her teeth were chattering. They'd removed her coat and shoes. Her thin white blouse and skirt were no protection from the cold.

'We didn't have no choice.' Benny moved beside her. He was trying to wriggle his wrists from the ropes. Rose knew it was useless. The burns would only worsen. He still had his jacket and trousers on, but they'd taken his shoes and socks. 'He's scum of the earth,' Benny whispered hoarsely.

'Where are the kids and Em? Where can they be?'

'I dunno, love.'

'I can't bear to think—'

449

'Then don't. Just try to keep calm. None of us will do much good if we're out of our heads with worry.'

Rose knew he was right. But the fear and foreboding were welling up inside her. She remembered all too well what had happened here last time. She'd only been saved by those children's voices. That wasn't about to happen again.

'Just my bloody luck Anita's working late,' Benny grumbled. 'She was gonna buy some booze on the way home. Said we'd all need a drink tonight. Blimey, she was right there, an' all.'

'Oh, Benny, I'm sorry I got you into trouble.'

'You didn't. Bastards like Payne should be put down at birth.'

Footsteps echoed in the passage. Norman Payne and his two minders walked in. They dragged Eddie between them. His head hung down as they pushed him on to one of the wooden chairs.

Payne patted his shoulder. 'He's been having a bit of a kip in the car. Likes a little nod every now and then, don't you, my boy?'

Rose saw Eddie slump forward. One of the men thrust him back viciously. His head rolled back and Rose and Benny gasped. His face was so swollen she couldn't see his left eye. It was lost under a pouch of bluish purple skin. A trickle of blood ran down his neck from the corner of his mouth and stained the open collar of his shirt. His torn and filthy shirt hung over his trousers.

'Oh God, Benny, what have they done to him?'

'Oh, he'll be right as rain,' Payne assured her as he

450

walked behind her chair. 'Your old man gave me a bit of verbal I could well do without on a day like today. After all, we should be celebrating the start of his lucrative new career under my generous auspices.'

'No,' Rose said defiantly. 'He'll never work for you.'

Payne laughed softly. 'Oh, never is a long time, especially when you've got mouths to feed. Now, where's Syd?' he demanded suddenly, and the man at the door jumped forward.

'Out the back with the others, Mr Payne. Them kids keep hollering. And the silly cow took a swipe at him.'

'I don't pay him to nursemaid,' Payne growled. 'I want this bugger woken up.'

Benny threw Rose a curious glance. His face was impassive but she knew he was thinking the same. Was Payne referring to Syd – the man who had sold Eddie the stolen television? And was it Em and the kids who were out the back?

Payne lay his hands on Rose's shoulders and lifted them into her hair. 'Lovely hair, you have, dear. Pity I had to cut it all off last time. It's grown again now, hasn't it?' He bent over her. She closed her eyes.

'Be a good girl now. If you want to see your nearest and dearest all safe and sound, you'll change your tune.'

Rose kept her eyes firmly closed as his clammy fingers trickled over the nape of her neck. His touch was repulsive, but she forced herself not to scream, instead she prayed that Eddie wouldn't wake up just yet.

'I think we should make you a little more comfortable, Mrs W. I'm sure your husband won't want to see you all tied up like this.' Slowly the pressure on her wrists was released and the rope fell away. Payne grabbed her arm and jerked her to her feet.

'You bastard, let her go,' Benny yelled out, shaking the chair he was on so that it almost toppled over. Payne swivelled round and hit him across the face with the back of his hand. Benny's head bounced backwards.

Rose screamed. 'Don't! Don't hurt him, please!'

Payne pulled her against him, a satisfied smile on his face as his fingers squeezed her arms painfully. His breath smelt of cigarettes and a sour sweetness that made Rose want to vomit. 'And I haven't even started yet, my dear.'

Rose turned her head away. She didn't want him to see the fear in her eyes.

'You cut a nice little figure, love. Very nice indeed. My boys will enjoy your company that is, if we can't sort out our spot of business.'

'What do you want, boss?' a voice asked from the door. Payne released his hold a and looked up.

'What do you think, you imbecile, get some water and wake him up!'

Rose turned her head slowly. Was this the man she had cycled all over the East End to find? Her heart pounded as she recalled Eddie's description. Syd would be in his forties, about Eddie's height, wearing a long camel overcoat and lots of jewellery. Rose stared at the man. He wasn't wearing an overcoat, but a dark, rather flash suit that had seen better days. The brown trilby though, was in place. He was middle-aged, just tending to spread, and he looked terrified of Payne. He left the room and was soon back again carrying a bucket.

Cheap rings covered his stubby fingers and a vulgar watch gleamed on his wrist. Rose knew it was Syd.

The water hit Eddie hard in the face. Syd stepped back like a frightened rabbit.

'Well, what are you waiting for, Christmas?' Payne demanded. 'Bring in the little darlings.' Payne dragged Rose into the middle of the floor. 'Wake up, Eddie, look who's here. We don't want you nodding off again.'

Rose watched helplessly as Eddie slowly lifted his head. A patch of bright red spread over his skull and dripped down his jaw.

Payne held Rose's arms tightly. He forced her to stand before her husband as he gained consciousness.

'Ah, back to the land of the living, are we?' Payne nodded in satisfaction. 'Now then, let's start from the beginning again shall we? Only- this time, let's get it right.' Payne took hold of the top of Rose's blouse and ripped it from her body.

Everything happened at once.

Rose watched in horror as Eddie staggered upwards and leapt on Payne. She hardly recognized her placid, phlegmatic, husband whom she had rarely seen lose his temper in all the years of their marriage. His face, already disfigured, was a mask of hatred, his mouth twisted at an unnatural angle and the cry that came from his bloody lips sounded more like a wounded animal than a human being.

453

Rose realized that Payne must have been surprised, too, at Eddie's sudden recovery. Payne was taller than Eddie and well built under his camel coat, but he went down like a skittle as Eddie threw himself on to the man who had just terrified and humiliated his wife.

At the same time, the guard on the door sprang forward and the three bodies merged into one on the filthy floor. Eddie's fists flew in every direction but mostly into Payne's shocked face. Rose saw blood spurt from Payne's mouth and what looked like a tooth. He wriggled to be free as his minder pulled Eddie's head back and twisted a muscled arm around his neck. Eddie was choking to death. His face flushed from red to purple, but he refused to let go of Payne who was squirming on the floor.

Rose flung herself on Eddie's attacker. She pounded her fists on any available inch of space, but with one blow of his huge hand she went reeling. Her head met the floor with a crack.

'Untie me, Rose, untie me!' Benny was wobbling his chair from side to side. 'Quickly, gel, quickly!'

Rose tried to crawl across the floor. Little black spots appeared in front of her eyes, then bursts of light. She was shaking so much she hardly noticed the sharp little splinters from the floorboards digging into her skin. She pulled herself up on Benny's chair.

'Me wrists first, love, and I'll do me feet.'

The rope was too tight. Her fingers trembled as Benny let out a groan of frustration. The last knot untangled and Benny burst out of his bonds. Rose saw that Payne had broken free of Eddie whose neck was bent at an unnatural angle by the man on top of him. But he seemed to gain strength, rearing up from the stranglehold.

Benny kicked away the ropes round his ankles. He rushed to Eddie's aid. But two of Payne's minders ran into the room. The thud of the wooden clubs they were holding was the last thing Rose heard as she began to pass out.

'Mummy! Mummy! Wake up!'

Rose opened her eyes. They felt as if they had heavy lead weights attached to them. Her thick black lashes fluttered as she heard Donnie's voice.

'I thought you were dead, Mum.'

Rose touched her daughter's cheek. The dark brown plaits that she had woven so carefully this morning before leaving for Hewis were undone. Donnie's hair stuck out in tufts, one white ribbon trailed over her school mac. There was dust and dirt over the navy blue lapels. Rose hugged Donnie to her.

'No, pet, I just got a bump on the head.'

'Them men have got Auntie Em and Marlene and the boys too.'

Rose gazed across the room. Em came into focus. She was holding Matthew in her arms and Marlene and Will cowered beside her. They all had looks of terror on their faces.

Eddie lay on the floor. Benny was beside him. They'd both taken a beating and her heart went out to them.

Payne dusted himself down and smoothed back his

silver hair. With vicious intent, he booted Eddie in his ribs.

Rose screamed and Donnie whimpered.

'You haven't seen anything yet.' Payne lifted the club. 'I've wasted a lot of time on you, Eddie old son. You and your fucking family. Now you either cough up what you owe me, or you're officially on the payroll.'

'You know we don't have any money,' Rose cried as Donnie clung to her, pressing her head into Rose's white silk slip. The remains of her blouse lay on the floor, embedded in the dirt.

''Course I know that. But that's not my problem, is it?'

'We'll pay back every penny,' Rose pleaded. 'Just give us time.'

'I'm a businessman Mrs Weaver, not the Sally Army. You're up to your armpits in debt and if I can't have what's owed, I'll take the man himself, his family, the clothes you stand up in and the air you breathe.'

He walked over and grabbed her hair. 'So, what's it to be?' he demanded of Eddie. 'Yes or no?'

'You win.' Eddie nodded. 'I'll do whatever you want.'

Payne smiled, a mean little smile that barely showed his teeth. 'Let's have it a little louder, shall we, so we can all hear the good news?'

'I'll do whatever you want, just let them go.'

Rose closed her eyes. Payne had finally won.

Chapter Twenty Seven

'**O**h no, Eddie, no!'
'Take your hands off her, you bastard,' Eddie screamed. 'You've got what you wanted. Now leave her alone.'

Payne laughed as he looked down at Donnie. 'Lovely girl you got here.' He stuck the end of the club under Donnie's chin. Rose knew now that Payne was mad. She held Donnie tightly against her.

'Stop frightening her. She's just a kid.'

'But not for long. Pretty little girls grow up fast. Your family is going to develop talents you never knew they had, Eddie old son. They'll be raking it in as they grow older and Norman Payne'll be there, the best bloody guardian angel they could ever have.'

'I've told you I'll do what you want,' Eddie yelled again, trying to move before he got a boot in his stomach.

Rose closed her eyes. When she opened them, Payne was standing over him with the club raised. He brought it down on Eddie's left knee. He writhed in agony. Payne raised the club once more.

'Only a coward or a fool would hit a man when he's down,' a voice suddenly said.

Everyone looked into the shadows behind her, including Rose. 'Who the hell are you?' Payne demanded in total shock.

'A friend of Eddie's.'

Rose felt her heart miss a beat. She tried to think where she had seen this man before. *Had* she seen him before? As she clutched Donnie against her, the child's soft sobbing was the loudest sound in the room.

Payne turned to his cronies. 'How did he get in?'

They all shrugged. 'Through the door behind me,' the man said stepping into the light. Rose knew every eye in the room was on him in sheer disbelief. Despite being small he seemed to generate some kind of power. Dressed in a dark blue overcoat, he was entirely bald and protruding from his face was an enormous nose.

Payne snarled. 'Who was supposed to be out there?'

No one answered.

'Let him go. Let them all go,' the stranger said quietly.

Payne grinned. 'You're not for real, are you?'

'Oh yes, I'm real.'

'You're not the filth?'

'No.'

Payne narrowed his eyes. 'So who are you?'

'I told you. A friend of this man. A friend who will settle the debt.'

Payne laughed out loud. 'Now you're going to tell me you're his fairy godmother and you've got two grand stashed under that coat of yours?'

'Two thousand pounds?' The little man walked slowly towards Rose, drew out his wallet and opened it. He smiled down at her. 'Quite a sum from the initial loan.' He counted out the large crisp notes. To everyone's astonishment he offered them to Payne.

The silver-haired man, forgetting himself, dropped the club and grabbed them. 'Two grand,' he nodded as he counted. He looked up suspiciously. 'Is this a wind-up?'

'No, a business transaction.'

Payne's eyes narrowed. 'So what is Uncle Norman going to do with the goose?' he asked himself out loud. 'After all the aggro I've had with this piece of shit—' he glanced at Eddie, 'I'll accept this as a down payment for the protection of, let's see, the future welfare of his family's life and limb.'

'Then greed will be your downfall.'

'Come again?' Rose watched Payne thinking hard. His forehead was creased in a frown, assessing just how much more he could capitalize on Eddie's misfortune.

'The account is settled.'

'Bollocks. You're not walking out of here the way you walked in. You're on *my* turf now.'

The stranger walked arrogantly up to Payne. 'Are you such a fool as to believe I did not ensure my safety?'

Payne stiffened. 'What's that supposed to mean?'

'If there is one piece of advice I would give you, it is this. Be afraid of me, Mr Payne, be *very* afraid.'

A nervous laugh jangled in Payne's throat. 'And why should I be afraid of you?'

The soft voice hardened. 'I restrain myself from having

459

you arrested only because it would not be in this family's interest to drag them through hell once more. But should you ever again attempt to communicate with them, I will hand over to the authorities the evidence my investigators have gathered on your nefarious activities. I have left no stone unturned in my searches. My lawyers have accumulated sufficient material to put you and your . . . friends . . . away for a very long time.'

Payne was silent, his face totally shocked. His Adam's apple bobbed up and down in his neck like a terrified Christmas turkey. Rose knew that everyone else in the room was equally shocked. They were all weighing up who this man was and whether or not he was telling the truth; whether the statement he'd just made was worth taking seriously.

'Are you prepared to challenge me, Mr Payne?'

'Who are you?' Payne murmured hoarsely.

'I am an extremely wealthy man with a personal army at my disposal. I come well prepared, I assure you. This building is watched, your departure is awaited. Delay any longer and you will soon understand the full meaning of my words.'

Payne looked round him at the frightened faces of his heavies and the sheer terror that was slowly registering in their eyes. The small man's gaze bore into him with hatred. He shrivelled under his coat and stepped backwards towards the door.

'I'm sick of the sight of you, anyway,' he threw at Eddie viciously. 'You'll never make it straight, with or without this bastard's help. Two years down the road and you'll be flogging your own grandmother for a couple of quid.'

Rose saw Payne hesitate, still uncertain as to what he should do. But he had lost respect in front of his minions and was a beaten man. The back of his silver head was the last thing she saw as he and his men made a hasty exit. She closed her eyes as if rubbing out the sight forever.

Gentle hands supported her. 'They've gone, my dear. You are safe.'

Rose heard the cries of the children coming towards her. She looked up at the smooth round face with the monstrous nose. 'You were with Eddie in Hewis, weren't you?'

'And you are the young Christian woman who buried a Jew.'

They looked into each other's eyes. She didn't know what he meant, not really. But it didn't matter for now. Eddie was back in the land of the living. They were *all* back in the land of the living. Thanks to this man.

Epilogue

Friday 14th December 1956

Eddie watched his wife in the arms of another man and fell in love with her all over again. Except that now his feelings were deeper and more complex than they had ever been before. His life had changed after Hewis. Not that he'd expected to return to the world he'd left; he wasn't that much of a fool. He was an ex-con now. He had form. But he hadn't been prepared for just how much change there had been.

He watched her with Bobby, dancing slowly under the revolving glass ball of Kirkwood's Social Club. She was laughing and her hair tumbled over her shoulders. Every now and then a glint of pearls sparkled from her neck. Thank God he'd redeemed them in time, the first thing he'd done when he started his new job.

She looked stunning tonight in the red dress newly acquired from Solly and Alma's Knightsbridge shop, of which he was now manager. He desperately wanted to be where Bobby was. Holding her close, looking into her eyes, those huge brown eyes that never failed to entrance

462

him. He didn't want another man to touch her. Not even Bobby, his brother-in-law of one day.

Eddie shifted uncomfortably on the hard wooden chair. He tried to shrug off the dark mood. After all, the Weavers and Mortons were off to Scotland tomorrow, thanks to Solly and Alma's wedding present to the newlyweds. Four poster beds, not to mention a banqueting hall and moat.

'Come on, get up and dance, you lazy git.' A powerful hand grabbed his arm. 'You can manage a shuffle even if you do have two left feet.'

Eddie smiled at his old friend. Anita looked the bees' knees in a black two piece with a garland of Christmas tinsel strung round her neck. Her make-up had disappeared and she was swaying slightly.

'Who says I've got two left feet?' Eddie pulled her down on the chair beside him. 'They won't leave this room breathing.'

She chuckled. 'It's true you ain't no Fred Astaire, darlin', but after all the Pimms I've sunk tonight I'm capable of dragging you round the floor bodily.'

'Not with your bad back you won't,' he teased.

She clouted him over the head. 'Don't you worry about me back tonight mate. I'm one hundred per cent anaesthetized. Anyway, you can't talk with your wonky knee.'

Eddie rubbed it unconsciously. The bone had mended, but he would limp for the rest of his life. He counted himself lucky. It was only his knee that Payne had demolished, not his brain.

'I think I'll just have a fag.' Anita shook out a Player's

from the pack on the table. She put it between her lips and coughed. The next minute it was back in the pack again. 'I'm finished with those bloody things. Where's me drink?'

Eddie pushed her glass towards her. 'Yeah, and I'll just finish me beer. Get the old oil going round.'

'You don't need any oilin' darlin' You're sexy enough.'

Eddie knew she was three sheets to the wind and wasn't likely to carry out her threat. He laughed again and drank slowly. At ten o'clock he was well and truly knackered. It had been a long day. First, Bobby and Em's civil marriage ceremony at Poplar registry office, then back to the house for the nosh. The Street had all been given an invite to the club tonight. Now everyone, including a few dozen gatecrashers, were enjoying the proverbial knees up.

Eddie peered through the fug of smoke. The bar was surrounded. Most of the Christmas decorations were well and truly massacred in the free for all to obtain booze. Four young men standing on the dais were dressed in cheap mohair suits and wearing DAs. They were oblivious to the crush and sweating over their instruments; guitar, bass, drums and sax. The tiny dance floor was jam packed, rocking to the new sensation from the States, Elvis the Pelvis.

The kids would have appreciated the music. A little alarmingly, Eddie found himself missing their company. They'd had a ball today, running around like lunatics and stuffing themselves silly. David Mendoza and Iris were babysitting. Eddie wished he was home with them, his feet up on the pouffe, watching telly. Blimey, was he or was he not a reformed character? Christ, he'd even be cooking the grub next!

Anita sighed heavily. 'Don't she look beautiful tonight?'

Indisputably, Rose was the most beautiful woman in the room. Under the flickering silver light she swayed in Bobby's arms. In fact, they looked the perfect couple. His brother-in-law was not only a looker, but a mover too. Dancing was a skill Eddie had never mastered himself.

'Well, they tied the knot then,' Anita said dryly. 'Never thought it would happen meself.'

'Just goes to show.'

'You'll have the house all to yourselves now.'

'Yeah, but I'll miss 'em.' Em and Will were like part of the furniture now. He was indebted to his sister-in-law and he would not forget his debt. He owed her one and that was the truth. She'd looked after the kids whilst Rose was at work and contributed to the rent. The bills wouldn't have got paid otherwise whilst he was away. Not that he had revised his opinion of Rose as a working woman, but it was as plain as a pimple on a pig's arse that there was no way they'd have managed if Em hadn't chipped in. Eddie chewed agitatedly on his lip. He still lived in hope Rose would chuck in being old Grimmond's personal secretary. Trouble was, Rose was too bloody good at her job. And he had the unsettling suspicion she actually liked it. He didn't go along with women working, never had. They should be with their family, sort out the domestics. His Princess was ten now and

Toots eight; they needed a sharp eye. At almost three, Matthew was into everything. Eddie's chest swelled with pride as he thought of his son and heir. He adored his girls, but a son was special.

'It wasn't a bad ceremony this morning,' Anita sighed dreamily. 'Em looked smashing in that biscuit suit and floppy hat. It was next best to a proper dress, though to me, a register office ain't quite the same as walking down the aisle.'

Eddie passed no comment. He was just relieved it was all over. He took a long, slow gulp of his beer.

'Still, you can understand Em being dubious about churches,' Anita continued. 'Arthur turned out to be a right perv.'

On that Eddie was in full agreement. He'd never got on with Arthur and didn't mind who knew it.

'Just look at her, dancing with my Benny. No more queer jerks anymore and she finally chucked away that bloody turban. Bobby's brought out the best in her, God love him.'

Eddie considered the two figures crushed together on the dance floor. His sister-in-law and best mate were happily making exhibitions of themselves. Em had really come out of her shell. Yeah, she was a different person to the girl who'd lived with Arthur. Eddie admitted that a bout of green-eye had clouded his opinion of Bobby. Being a con in the nick as opposed to Golden Boy on the outside was no contest. But he conceded now that Bobby was all right, even if he was like Ali Baba's bloody genie. The house was bulging with electrical gear. They even had a telly, an article Eddie never expected to see appear under his roof after Coronation Day.

But Bobby was a decent bloke. He had a nice flat to offer Em and Will. True it was stuck over the shop, but Will, poor little sod, was over the moon with ten square feet of personal territory. He wouldn't have to sleep in a tent or in the front room any more. Eddie had never heard the kid complain whilst living in the sardine can conditions of number forty-six. He was fond of his nephew, more than he let on.

'Your old man is gonna have a corker when he wakes up.' Eddie chuckled as he watched his old friend attempting, and failing, to twirl Em under his arm.

'So will a few dozen others,' Anita grinned.

Eddie smiled as he wondered if Mr Grimmond would regret offering the social club amenities for the knees-up. The bar had been drunk dry, there wasn't a packet of crisps left in the place and even Balaji Patel had downed a Bloody Mary assuming it was tomato juice. Cissy and Fanny had wiped out the buffet table between them. Len Silverman had provided some kosher grub, all gone in half an hour, kosher subscribers or not. Solly would have approved of that, Eddie thought gratefully.

He warmed inside as he thought of his good friend, Solly Rosenberg. Back in that Godforsaken dump by the wharf, with his head lying in Rose's lap, his skull more battered than last Friday's cod, Solly's words had said it all.

And you are the young Christian woman who buried a Jew.

Eddie shook his head in wonder and slipped deeper into thought, replaying in his mind the events that had led to freedom for him and his family. If Rose had never found the shoebox, if she'd never given back the money, if she'd never buried Olga, if he'd never been sent to Hewis, he'd never have met Solly. And what a friend Solly had proved to be in taking the Weavers under his wing. Payne had not been the only one waiting for Eddie's release. Solly, too, had been waiting and watching, formulating a plan to help his old friend.

A sudden burst of clapping startled him. The boys in the band were enjoying an ovation. Anita was whistling through her teeth and clapping.

'So why ain't your mate here, then?' she shouted above the racket. 'You sent him an invite, didn't you?'

'What, Solly? Yeah, well he's gonna meet us off the coach, ain't he?' Eddie could hardly believe that tomorrow they were all leaving for Bonnie Scotland and two weeks in a genuine bricks and mortar castle. 'I wish you and Benny was coming. You know you had the invite, don't you?'

'Yeah, I know,' Anita nodded. 'But we already booked Butlin's. Brighton this time. All six of us. Me and Benny. Alan and Heather and David and Iris. Otherwise we'd have jumped at the chance of a nice piece of haggis.'

'I ain't so keen on the haggis,' Eddie admitted.

The boys started up again, another Presley number, 'Blue Suede Shoes'. Everyone was going wild.

'Who would ever have thought you'd have fallen on your feet like this,' Anita yelled a little drunkenly. 'What with Solly bunging you one of his posh shops an' all. Better than a bloody market stall, ain't it, love?'

'Yeah, I'm a lucky bastard, Neet.' He didn't mind admitting he'd had more than his fair share of luck since the nick. He surreptitiously glanced down at his fine grey suit, at the hand stitched silk lining of the jacket and the perfect fit of the trousers. No more market clobber now, no more pressing his suits under the mattress. This little whistle and flute would go straight to the dry cleaners.

Eddie still had to pinch himself in the mornings when he found himself in the shop. In *his* office. With a chair and desk and even a typewriter. When Solly had given him a chance with one of Alma's babies, he'd jumped at it. The punters, both men and women, were upmarket and trendy. He could kit out a bloke in less than half an hour and turn him out on the town like a prince – if the price was right. And up West, the price was always was right. The shop was showing a good profit. And Solly, with his wife well satisfied, was chuffed.

'Not that you don't deserve your luck,' Anita added quickly. 'You always was a smart dresser. I don't mind telling you, Eddie Weaver, a bit of good cloth is what you were made for.'

Eddie laughed softly. 'Ta, girl.'

'You'll do all right, you will.'

'You're not doing so bad yourself.'

'Yeah, well, helping Benny with the business is a lot better than sticking me head down other people's lavs.'

'Come on, you're a natural with them account books.'

Anita giggled. 'Yeah, like a bloody magician.' She pulled at the tinsel round her neck. 'Funny how life works out, ain't it?'

Eddie answered with feeling. 'You know, as good as it all is now, I'd give me right arm to put back the clock. I wished I'd never set eyes on Payne. I put everyone through grief, including Benny, and it's hard to live with meself sometimes.' He didn't talk much about Payne now. Tried not to think of him. With Payne on a lifer for a south London murder, there was no chance of their paths crossing. But he still caught himself looking over his shoulder sometimes.

'My Benny's big enough and ugly enough to take care of himself,' Anita replied generously. 'And all that matters for you now is Rose and the kids.' Anita blinked hard at him. 'You and Rose – that's what's important.'

Her gaze was sober now. He looked into her shrewd blue eyes. What had been discussed between his wife and her best mate? Anita was a bright monkey, he had to acknowledge it, and she probably knew more about Rose than he did. He himself could never tell what Rose was really thinking. If she still had respect for him as she used to . . . before – well, before that bloody telly.

He toyed with risking Anita a question or two. But then he realized it would be folly. Women were as thick as thieves and so they should be. Blokes didn't want to know the gory details. Not really. If Anita knew anything, she was keeping it to herself.

She smiled, as if approving his move. 'We all change, love. People expect others to stay the same and that's the mistake. The trick is, loving someone for the change, not knocking them for it.'

Eddie had no answer to that. He was no philosopher, but he had learned lessons. He'd never sit in judgement on anyone. Because you never really knew the score. He himself was innocent of the crime he'd gone down for but he'd flown close enough to the candle to burn his wings.

Yeah, it was funny the way things worked out.

A crescendo of guitar strumming brought the floor to a standstill. Everyone clapped and the group, sweating over their instruments, took a bow. The guitarist stepped forward.

'By popular request we'll play the last waltz. Bing Crosby and Grace Kelly's recent hit, "True Love".'

Rose, all breathless and glowing, gazed up at Bobby. Eddie watched them, the air suddenly trapped in his lungs. Every light dimmed except the revolving glass globe above. The stars flickered over the figures like a twinkling universe. Arms crept round necks. Lovers entwined.

For a moment his wife was lost to him. Eddie peered through the smoke. He didn't want to see what his eyes were searching for. A beautiful, brown haired woman dressed in red, enfolded in the arms of a tall, handsome man. But he couldn't tear his eyes away from the crowded floor. He couldn't stop looking for pain. Then, just as he thought his heart would stop, he saw her. She was walking towards him, weaving her way through the empty tables and chairs.

Eddie swallowed hard. Did she still love him? Did she love him as much as he loved her? Perhaps he'd never know. Perhaps he'd live all his life and never know her true feelings. Could he handle that? He looked into her eyes and searched for the answer.

It wasn't long before he had it. The message was coming across loud and clear. He nodded, as if acknowledging the light that had suddenly come on in his brain. How could he ever have doubted that Rose and he shared a deep and eternal, true love? He was going to believe those two words for the rest of his life. *Really* believe them.

Rose held out her hand. And he took it.